The Scheme

Carol Treacy

THE SCHEME
Copyright © 2015 by Carol Treacy

ISBN: 978-0-9964474-0-9
ISBN-13:978-0-9964474-0-9

The characters and events in this book are fictitious. Any similarity to real persons, living or dead, is coincidental and not intended by the author.

Published by Carol Treacy

Cover design by Sue Slutzky

The question is not, 'Can they reason?' nor, 'Can they talk?' but, 'Can they suffer?'

Jeremy Bentham

1

It was nothing like she'd expected. No dark wood paneling or plush leather sofas. The framed paintings were modern, not one depicted a hunting scene or resembled a nineteenth century portrait. There was a recliner next to a plaid-covered couch and she opted for it. She was the first one to arrive so why shouldn't she nab the most comfortable seat in the house? Jessica Olshansky, first-term senator from Montana, pulled the chair's lever and was suddenly looking up at the ceiling. Nice trim, she thought. White on olive green walls with an olive green ceiling. She'd never do it in her apartment, but it worked here in this colonial estate. That's why she expected to see the typical colonial style study, replete with a floor to ceiling bookcase and old leather bound books gracing the shelves. Perhaps Anita and her husband Larry don't read. Unlikely, but there was no bookcase. Just a small table in the corner with a few books scattered on it. Perhaps it was in the family room or living room. A sterling silver tray sat on the coffee table. On it was a plate filled with cookies, Pepperidge Farm Milanos, and a Wedgewood teapot with matching cups and saucers. Jessica poured herself a cup: English Breakfast. Nice. She wondered when Anita would appear. Was it her intent to keep the junior senator waiting? Was it a show of authority, seniority? No matter. It wouldn't take long for Jessica to assert herself and become a top player in politics. After all, her father had been a Montana senator for thirty-five years. By the time she was twelve, Jessica knew more about the political machine and how to play the game better than most seasoned senators. She learned from the best, even though daddy could be harsh. Jessica looked down at her feet. They were encased in orthopedic shoes. Ugly, but highly functional and comfortable.

Her heft put a lot of pressure on her legs and feet. Despite her attempts at losing weight, Jessica loved all things food. Her discipline was non-existent and despite constant harassment from her father, she loved devouring sweets and carbs. He would even go so far as calling Jessica "my Big Sky daughter." He thought it would force her to diet. It only made her eat more.

Jessica took another sip of tea and grabbed a cookie. She popped it into her mouth, barely chewing before she swallowed. She was about to grab another when the door opened. She retracted her hand so quickly, Anita Minefeld didn't notice. Jessica slowly rose, lifting her large frame out of the chair.

"Please, don't get up," Anita said as she strode purposefully toward Jessica.

"Too late." Jessica extended her hand and Anita shook it. Senator Minefeld's grasp was strong...A little too strong even for a Montanan. Again, Jessica felt like she was being put in her place. "Thanks for inviting me to your...what is this again?"

Anita sat down on the sofa. She poured herself a cup of tea. Her tall, thin frame was in direct opposition to Jessica's short, wide body. They looked like a female version of Laurel and Hardy. Anita thought so anyway.

"How's your father doing? I heard the heart attack wasn't a big one. Still, it's cause for alarm."

"He's much better. Thanks for asking."

"I'll have to send him a card and, I don't know, a fruit basket. Does he like fruit?"

"Sure. Apples, pears, oranges. He's an equal opportunity fruit lover. Oh, except kiwi. He's convinced they're aliens. Crazy old daddy."

Anita laughed. "Yes, but what a great senator he was and now you're filling his shoes and I hear you're doing an amazing job. And you're only what, forty?"

A small flash of anger raced across Jessica's face. "I'm thirty-seven."

"That's right. So sorry." Anita took a sip of her tea and delicately bit into a cookie. The doorbell rang just as Anita was going to divulge the reason for the meeting. "Excuse me. I believe one of the other guests has arrived."

Anita lightly set her teacup on the coffee table and practically sprinted out the door. Watching her leave, Jessica mumbled, "Isn't that what you have a maid for?"

Despite there only being six cookies left on the tray, Jessica stuffed one into her mouth and, once again, barely chewed before swallowing. Moments later, Anita emerged with two more guests: senators Bertram Kathala from California and Olivia Sundstrom from North Carolina. Jessica's eyes lit up when she saw Bertram. Despite the Midwestern-sounding name, he was the quintessential California 'boy,' even though he was in his fifties. His natural suntan accentuated the ice blue eyes and high cheekbones. Olivia, also in her early fifties, had bleached blonde hair worn in a bob. Her petite frame and pretty face made Jessica feel like an ogre.

The four senators had one thing in common: they were all Republicans, conservative Republicans who shared the sentiment that too many Americans were living off the government. They consistently cast their votes for cuts in food stamps, social security and financial aid. Despite her relatively short time in D.C., Jessica felt comfortable with her fellow politicians. She was hoping that soon she'd discover why they were all sitting in the olive green study with no bookshelf.

"Jessica, you know Olivia and Bert, right?"

Jessica stood up and went over to the twosome. "Of course I do. So nice to see you both. Anita didn't tell me who was coming or what this was about, so I feel a little out of the loop."

Anita feigned dismay. "I do apologize, Jessica. I thought I told you about our little group." Jessica shook her head. "Please, everyone have a seat, get comfy and I'll explain everything." She turned to her two new guests. "Would you like some tea? Cookies?" They nodded and Bert helped himself to a cookie. Anita poured them tea. There was a knock at the door.

"Come in."

The maid appeared. "Is there anything else you need, ma'am?"

"We're fine. Thank you, Rita." Anita turned to Jessica. "You probably know that your dad and I were good friends. He was my mentor when I first came to D.C. I certainly wasn't naïve, but I also didn't know the ropes and he was so willing to guide me."

He sure was, thought Olivia. If only Jessica knew how close Anita and her daddy really were, she'd hightail it out of the house, cross the senator from her list of friends and never look back. When Theodore Olshansky was in their group, he ruled it. After all, he was the senior senator, which gave him all the rights he felt he deserved.

Without his dictating every move, all three were pleased to welcome his daughter into the fold. She was his flesh and blood and may very well become a Theodore Junior, but for now she was malleable. Or so they hoped.

Olivia had been a member for nearly seven years and enjoyed the prestige and excitement of their assignments. Unlike Congress, they actually got things done. They didn't have to adhere to any rules or public sentiment. There wasn't a president to veto their ideas or stop their plans from going into action. It was one of the reasons Olivia remained a senator. Her real job was a pain in the ass. She hated public forums where she was forced to meet her constituents and sit through town hall meetings where all they did was complain. 'Where's the rec center for the underprivileged children? It was supposed to be built last year.' 'Our roads have more holes than a block of Swiss cheese. When are they going to be fixed?' Whine, whine, whine. She was sick of it. Her respite came from this group.

Olivia glanced over at Jessica and smirked. Physically, she's was a female version of Teddy. Poor thing. She inherited the man's bulky, squat frame along with his wide nose and thin lips. And that hair. She made a promise to herself to help the poor woman get a better cut. She would take her to All About Eve Hair Salon. Maybe they could give her a bit of a face makeover, too. Lord knows she needed it. Olivia was lost in thought when she noticed that the room was quiet and all eyes were on her. She automatically put her hand to her face.

"Is there something on my face?"

Anita said, "No Livie, I just asked you if you could tell Jessica a little bit about yourself before we get down to business."

Relieved, Olivia turned to Jessica. "First of all, welcome to Team America. Your father will be missed, but I think you'll fit in just fine. I'm originally from Durham, a southern woman to the core. Divorced, no children, thank God, just a Persian cat named Blythe. I recently won my third term, so I'll be on the Hill for six more glorious years. If you need any advice, just give me a call or pop into my office. Is there anything else I should tell our junior senator?"

Bertram shook his head. "That was sufficient." He turned and looked straight into Jessica's muddy brown eyes. She squirmed. His stare was intense and incredibly sexy. "We've met a few times before on the Hill. Please call me Bert. I've represented California in Congress and now in the Senate. I think Dianne Feinstein beats me in the political longevity arena by a couple of years. I've called D.C. my home away from home for almost twenty years. I love politics. Every goddamn thing about it from the grappling to the begging to the glory. It's a great job. I'm proud to be an American."

Bert reached into his pocket and Jessica swore he was going to pull out a mini-American flag and wave it. She was patriotic but didn't go around espousing her love of country.

Anita said, "Your turn. Tell us a little bit about yourself."

"I have a feeling anything I tell you, you already know. Being the daughter of Theodore Olshansky isn't an easy thing to bear, but I think I not only survived but excelled. I won the senate seat by a large margin thanks to Daddy and the slew of Republicans who dominate the great state of Montana. My curiosity is eating a hole in my stomach as to why I'm here."

Anita got up to refill her teacup. Her long, slender arms reached for the teapot, delicate hands gripping it as she poured the tea. She was deliberate in her actions as if she wanted Jessica to stay in the dark a little bit longer.

"Around ten years ago, I was ready to give up on being a politician. Between the lobbyists, the Democrats and my constituents, I felt like my arms and legs were tied to four different horses being pulled in every direction. My opinion never seemed to count and getting anything done was nearly impossible. I remember going into your father's office, plopping myself down on his sofa and crying. He let me bitch about how ineffective I felt. It seems like I went on for hours. When I was spent, he came over and sat next to me, patted me on the leg and said, 'I think I know how to get things done. Ready to take a walk on the wild side?' And that's how our little group got started. We began coloring outside the lines, eliminating the red tape, the committees, the bills, the vetoes. Gone, gone and gone! Our first line of business was buying up land in Montana for a cattle rancher who the government claimed was poaching on their property. The Bureau of Land Management had already seized his cattle. He came to your dad for help, pleading with him to get his cattle back. We appealed to some of our supporters who shelled out the money to pay off the BLM and put the land in the rancher's name. His cattle were released, some government officials became a little wealthier and our supporters have the best cuts of steak for the rest of their lives. Win-win for everyone. Any questions so far or shall I continue?"

"Please continue," Jessica said. Without thinking, she grabbed another cookie.

"After a few more victories, my attitude had undergone a major adjustment. I was excited and eager to come to work. My enthusiasm must have been obvious, because Miss Olivia stopped me outside my office one day and asked if I was on Prozac! She then proceeded to tell me about a bill she introduced in Congress that was languishing in the Committee on Agriculture, Nutrition and Forestry. She knew it would die there and was going on and on about how important it was to her. The environmentalists and animal rights fanatics were all over it, doing everything in their power to defeat it. After consulting with your dad and doing a background check on Olivia – the usual stuff: finding out if she was comfortable playing outside the Congressional playground, she became part of the group. The bill died, but we circumvented the laws and accomplished what the bill set out to do. Shortly thereafter, Mr. Kathala came onboard."

Bert gave Jessica a big, California smile: perfect teeth, very white. He reminded her of a Republican Robert Redford. Standing up to stretch her legs, she said, "What you've just disclosed is an admission of illegal behavior and what many would consider despicable. I assume you'd like me to replace the great Theodore Olshansky and carry on his work with the group." Without waiting for an answer, she said, "I'd be honored. I had a feeling Dad was up to something; just couldn't get him to admit it. I had a few, shall we say, indiscretions in law school. He made them disappear. Are you working on anything at the moment?"

Anita was ecstatic. If Jessica was anything like her father in intellect, determination and the ease with which he skirted the law, she would be a very welcome addition to their group. "First things first. Welcome! We are all so happy to have you." She went over and shook Jessica's hand. Bert was next. Olivia gave her a warm, North Carolina hug.

"We're not working on any one thing right now. We actually wanted to give you the opportunity to offer suggestions."

It took Jessica all of fifteen seconds to air her grievance. "Growing up in Montana, I was witness to some of the most amazing natural wonders in America...No, in the world. They don't call it Big Sky for nothing. I could ride my horse for hours without seeing another human being. It was glorious. Don't get me wrong. I love people. I just don't like so damn many! The U.S. population is at 317 million. America is busting out at the seams. There's still plenty of open space, but nobody wants to live there. As a result cities, towns, and suburbs are all growing at alarming rates. The U.S. Census predicts that by 2060, our population will be 360 million. Humans are gobbling up the land and choking off our natural resources. Most of our rivers and streams are polluted, smog is ubiquitous. They've even recorded poor air quality in Alaska. Wars are fought over oil and we know it's not a renewable resource. So here's what I was thinking: is there some way to weed out the weakest links? The impoverished, the drug addicts, alcoholics, the scum of society? Can we accomplish this in such a way that no one would even have an inkling that it was planned?"

The room was very quiet. Eerily so. Jessica wondered if she had gone too far. She was talking about genocide of the poor and destitute. Maybe this group wasn't prepared for her idea of bringing America back to the land of the beautiful and bountiful. Bert was the first to speak. He addressed Anita and Olivia. "Senators, if we tried, I don't think we could have come up with a better candidate. Jessica, you're beyond our expectations. I don't even think your dad had the balls to suggest what you're proposing. I say bring it on. If we could wipe Compton and East L.A. off the map, I'd be happier than a hooker at a Democratic convention."

Olivia added, "We've been kicking this idea around for a while. We just weren't quite sure how to go about it. It sounds like you've been chewing on it for longer than we have. Am I right?"

Jessica gave them all a Cheshire grin. "I have. A friend of mine works for the National Institute of Biomedical Imaging and Bioengineering. Last week, she came across a study she found intriguing. A scientist by the name of Lenore Fitzwater created a drug designed to attach itself to illness inside the human body and eliminate it. Rats in various stages of heart disease, cancer and diabetes were used and the drug showed promise. Then she went to Fillmore Federal Prison and recruited volunteers from the esteemed residents. She took a sampling of afflictions: diabetes, heart disease, cancer, stroke survivors. Within a month of the participants being dosed on a daily basis, a bizarre thing happened. All but two of the inmates died. Instead of the illnesses disappearing, they advanced at an alarming rate. Of course, the study was halted and Dr. Fitzwater was crushed. I started thinking, what if I could get my hands on that drug; get it into the worst pockets of America's inner cities? Within months, we could eliminate a good number of people that bog down our social services. The money saved on food stamps, methadone programs and emergency room procedures would be significant."

Anita rubbed her hands together with glee. "What we need is a carrier for the drug and I have just the ticket." She got up and went over to the door. She opened it and looked around. Satisfied that no one was listening in or within earshot, she continued. "One of my dear friends and top campaign contributors is the CEO of Hinton Industries. Are you familiar with the company?"

Bert said, "Everyone knows Hinton. They're the top beef and chicken processor in the country. If I'm not mistaken, they supply almost fifty percent of all the meat to the biggest fast food chains."

"Bingo. Now, if I can get Gerald Hinton on board, we have ourselves a plan. I'm excited! Are you all excited?"

Olivia held up her hand and Anita nodded. "That's all well and good, but you can't go around poisoning every fast food restaurant in the country. A lot of middle class Americans eat at those places, too. And then there are the children. I don't want their deaths on my hands. I mean, that's…"

Anita interrupted, "Let's think this through. If Hinton controls most of the burgers and chicken, why couldn't they specifically send the drugged meat only to the inner city restaurants? The majority of children who eat there are living at poverty level. What kind of future awaits them? A life of dealing drugs or getting pregnant at fourteen? In a way, aren't we doing them a favor? We're sparing them from pain, misery and disappointment."

Olivia said, "That's a valid point."

Bert shifted uncomfortably in his seat. "No offense, but can I get something a little stronger than tea, like say, scotch?"

"Where are my manners? I'm so sorry, Bert. Of course you can have a drink. Anyone else?" Both women also opted for alcohol, Jessica citing that the conversation at hand warranted it. Anita opened up the liquor cabinet displaying bottles of Jamieson Scotch, Grey Goose vodka, Sandeman Port and a variety of other spirits. She poured each guest a generous portion of their preferred beverage. After a few well-deserved sips Jessica, normally a teetotaler said, "The positive impact this kind of mass cleansing could create is incalculable. Think about it. It's like cleaning the hull of a ship encrusted with barnacles and algae. Once those impediments are eliminated, the ship can sail smoothly and effortlessly. My dad alluded to the extermination of the weak links in our species. That's why I felt comfortable bringing it up."

Bert, feeling the effects of the alcohol, was more at ease. Talking about this subject made him dizzy. If they could pull this off, they'd be heroes. Silent heroes, of course. "No one can know about this. Ever. Understood?"

Anita said, "Except Gerald."

"Of course."

"I'll feel him out first before divulging the plan." She turned to Jessica. "Obtaining the drug is critical, so why don't you find out how we can get hold of it. Have you thought about that?"

Jessica nodded. "If we don't want anyone else involved, we could set up a cover lab – a decoy lab – and I'll request permission from my friend at the institute to obtain the drug for research. I'll tell her we already have funding and the researcher. I'll make someone up. How hard can it be? They give research grants to vivisectionists studying erections in rhesus monkeys."

Olivia said, "And you know about this because…?"

"I like reading research papers. I was seriously considering being a geneticist. What stopped me was the thought of spending hours and hours in a lab surrounded by beakers and caged animals. Very depressing."

Bert added, "But necessary."

"Definitely."

"North Carolina has more than its share of dregs. Why, in Raleigh alone, we've got the market cornered on meth users. I'm sure a lot of these tweekers pop into Delaney's Fried Chicken for a meal after days of barely having a bite. I'd love to see them keel over. Boom, right on their little tweekin' heads. The heroin users, alcoholics, gang bangers. Bye-bye boys and girls. This is gonna be fun." Olivia raised her crystal tumbler of single malt Glen Fiddich scotch. "Here's to a better America. Land of the clean and home of the decent folk."

The group heartily toasted and drained their glasses.

Anita added, "And thank you to Jessica, the latest member of our most elite group. You'll fit in just fine."

Big smiles all around. The biggest was on Jessica's round face. She fit in with her peers. Daddy would be proud.

2

Most of the employees in the marketing department at Hinton Industries averted their eyes when Bonnie walked by. They didn't like her. She wasn't a likable person. And she didn't give a shit. Bonnie wasn't there to make friends. As she walked confidently down the long corridor to her office, her three-inch Manolo Blahnik shoes softly tapped on the floor. She smiled at her fellow employees whether they made eye contact or not. When it came to playing the game, she was a master. She didn't make assistant marketing director by hanging out with the underlings.

Bonnie's office exuded a mixture of femininity, strength and determination. One wall was lined with university diplomas and awards she received from various projects she worked on in and out of the office. There was always a vase full of fresh-cut flowers. Freesias when they were in bloom and pink tulips whenever they were available. Her desk was in perfect order. Not a pen, pad or stapler was out of place. Bonnie needed order. She liked to be in charge and most of the time that was possible. More out of nostalgia than anything else, she had a plaque on the wall opposite her desk. It was a gift from her first boss who handed it to her as he gave her a pat on the ass. The cheap wooden frame surrounded a bad illustration of a turtle. The caption read, *'The turtle doesn't get anywhere without sticking its neck out.'* Bonnie's mantra.

The phone rang and Bonnie answered it on speaker. "This is Bonnie. How can I help you?"

"Gerald would like to see you in his office right away," said Tina, Mr. Hinton's secretary.

"Be right there." Bonnie knew why the CEO wanted her in his office and it didn't bother her one little bit. It was all part of the job, the game, the pursuit of happiness. She grabbed her purse, found her lipstick and applied it with precision, then brushed her shoulder-length blonde hair. A final look-over in her full-length mirror and she was ready to see the boss.

Tina gave Bonnie the biggest fake smile she could muster. "Go right in, Bonnie."

"Thanks."

Gerald was on his computer, fully concentrating on the task at hand. His beefy fingers punched the keys. Bonnie stood by the door of the enormous office. She thought he was one of the homeliest people she'd ever met, aside from her geology professor at Stanford, who shared an uncanny resemblance to Don Knotts. Gerald looked like a cross between Alfred Hitchcock and Hitler. No moustache, but those intense, critical eyes. They bore through her, so she made every effort to please him. What little hair he had left was plastered to the sides of his head, leaving the top shiny and liver-spotted. He was no George Clooney but he was the head of a Fortune 500 corporation. In Bonnie's inner eyes, he was gorgeous.

Looking up from the computer screen, Gerald smiled. His hands automatically went from the keyboard to his crotch. "So good to see you, Bonnie. And just in time. I dropped something under my desk. Would you mind picking it up for me?"

"Not at all, sir," Bonnie said as she walked toward the antique, executive-sized desk. As she got closer, she could smell his breath. His halitosis was so bad, it could be detected at least ten feet from his mouth.

"I love it when you call me sir."

She heard him unzip his trousers. Dutifully, she got onto her knees and, without hesitation, gave Gerald Hinton the best blow job he ever had, to date. The last one was only three days ago. While Bonnie performed, she imagined being the CEO of Hinton Industries. She had to stop herself from smiling, lest her 'co-conspirator' escape from her mouth. She reveled in the way it was so easy to control men through their dick. With very little effort and a scuffed knee or two, she could track her ascent to the top of the company. She didn't have to prove her abilities with lengthy reports or all-nighters, working on a project. An expertly maneuvered blow job and Bonnie continued to rise to the top.

It didn't take long before she heard muffled panting, then grunting, and she was done. Bonnie got to her feet and while waiting for Gerald's breathing to return to normal, she opened the top left drawer of his desk, grabbed a tissue and lip gloss, wiped her mouth and applied the cherry red gloss. Running her fingers through her hair, she said, "So, how was your weekend? Didn't you go to your daughter's gallery opening in Berkeley?"

A few more seconds and Gerald was back to his old self. His large chest no longer heaving. He wiped the sweat from his face with his monogrammed handkerchief.

"Nancy's showing was a success. Of course, I made sure there was a full house and that many of the paintings sold."

"I would have liked to have been there."

"Maybe so, but I'm not about to expose you to Miriam."

"Of course not." Bonnie glanced over at the large oil painting on the wall of Gerald, Miriam, Nancy and Greg. The perfect family.

"That reminds me. Miriam will be out of town next weekend. She's visiting her sister in the Hamptons. We could have the house to ourselves. Are you available?"

"The whole weekend?"

Gerald nodded.

Bonnie had a dinner date with a college friend who was in San Francisco for the weekend. She made a mental note to call her and cancel. "Sure. I look forward to it."

"Don't forget to bring your bathing suit. On second thought, don't bother. It's more fun without." Gerald instinctively put his hand on his crotch. He then went back to the computer and without looking up said, "I'll see you at the 9:30 meeting."

One final fluff of her hair and Bonnie opened the door. She wasn't sure if Tina knew that she spent most of her time under Gerald's desk but she didn't care. She pulled a mint out of her pants pocket and popped it in her mouth. When she got to her office, she closed the door and let out a little squeal. She couldn't believe Gerald invited her to his home, his mansion on Pacific Avenue. So what if she'd be swimming in the buff with a man who looked more like a whale than a human? She'd be in an Olympic-sized pool, sleeping in a luxurious bed next to one of the most powerful men in the industry. Hinton was the number one provider of beef and chicken to the nation's fast food restaurants. He was worth millions. She was feeling heady. Her ascent to the top of the corporation was going at breakneck speed.

She looked at herself in the mirror and noticed the part in her hair was askew. She quickly fixed it, re-applied her lipstick, then sat down at her desk and attended to the work at hand.

3

Spencer glanced at the clock again. Ten more minutes until closing time. A few stragglers were still there. Some were sitting on small benches reading. Others perused the books on the shelves. All seemingly unaware that Warden Bookstore would be closing soon for the night. Except Spencer Rydover, Warden's newest employee, trying to make good in his sixth job since high school graduation. At twenty-four, he had had more jobs than his parents and sister combined. He liked working at Warden's and he figured he could stay there as long as he kept his mouth shut. So far, he had only offended one other employee, but his apology was immediate and accepted. He worked very hard at making sure it didn't happen again.

Five minutes before closing time, Spencer jiggled the lights. A couple of customers came up to the front desk to purchase their books. An elderly gentleman was the first to arrive. He placed a bestselling novel and magazine on the counter.

"Will this be all?" Spencer asked.

"Yup."

Spencer scanned the book, John Vernick's latest, *Carry Me Home*. He picked up the magazine, *Field & Stream*, to scan it and paused, staring at the cover: A hunter was posing with his fresh kill, a nine-point buck. It took every ounce of willpower for Spencer to scan the magazine without saying a disparaging word.

Even with the radio blasting, it was hard for Spencer to erase the image of the dead buck from his mind. He could see the smiling hunter, holding his rifle in one hand and steadying the animal's head with the other.

"Asshole! Sadistic idiot!" he screamed as he banged his hands against the steering wheel, his voice mixing with the heavy metal music. "I'd like to blow a hole through his disgusting body. Insensitive jerk!" Spencer forced himself to calm down. It wasn't easy. He couldn't understand why a person would murder such a majestic animal.

He got onto Highway 580, drove a few miles then exited at Shattuck Avenue. A left at Drew Drive, left again on Cutting Court, and Spencer was home. He parked next to his landlady's vintage Corvette, careful not to park too close, then walked through the backyard to his cottage. He looked over at the main house and saw Perry in the kitchen window. She waved and gave him a big smile. Spencer waved back without a smile, then let himself into the cottage. He was grateful it was furnished when he moved in; otherwise he'd be sleeping on a cot and eating cross-legged on the floor. His parents were so happy when he finally moved out, they offered him some of their furniture, circa 1970s. It had been stashed in the garage under old blankets. Everything reeked of mildew, from the blankets to the couch, coffee table, kitchen table and even the two end tables. When he found the cottage, he convinced them to donate the furniture to Goodwill.

Perry had a distinct flair for design. He suspected that all the items in his place used to be in her home or in one smaller than her current residence because everything went together perfectly. It was cozy and comfortable and not too feminine. The grey and light blue floral sofa suited Spencer's taste along with a grey and white striped chair. He placed his keys on the pine coffee table and fell back onto the couch, resting his head against the cushion. A few more deep breaths and his heartbeat was back to normal. Looking around the cottage, Spencer was grateful that he was living on his own. He moved in a little over three weeks ago and it still felt magnificent. He loved his parents, but having to live in a house where meat, dairy and eggs were consumed was uncomfortable. Every day Spencer mourned the loss of animals' lives. It was unconscionable that humans could be so cruel, so heartless. He told his parents about factory farming; how the animals were raised and how horrendously they died. They shook their heads and said it was indeed horrible, yet they couldn't imagine living without their morning eggs and bacon. What's dinner when it doesn't include a chicken leg or a pork chop or a T-bone steak? They respected their son's lifestyle. They simply were not compelled to follow it. Old habits die hard, they would say. And besides, we're not as strong as you. Strength has nothing to do with it, Spencer would counter. It's not wanting your lifestyle to destroy another's life.

Spencer's reflections were interrupted by a knock at his door. He yelled from the couch, "Who is it?"

"Perry."

He didn't want any visitors but he couldn't refuse his landlady, so Spencer went to the door and opened it. Perry Seidel was a slender woman in her late forties. She wore her long chestnut brown hair back in a ponytail, accentuating her golden-green eyes. He plastered a smile on his face.

"Hey Perry. Is everything okay? I didn't park too close to your car, did I?"

Perry laughed. "Chill out, Spencer. You're fine. I wanted to make sure everything was working and you were comfortable."

Spencer's stance softened. His shoulders relaxed and he moved to the side. "Please, come in."

Perry walked into the cottage, taking note of how clean it was. Renting to a young man, she half-expected to see piles of clothes dotting the floor and dirty dishes lining the kitchen counter. Instead, she was pleased to learn that her new tenant was neat. A little too neat for a twenty-something male, but she knew that Spencer was different when he came to look at the rental unit. The first thing she noticed about him was his intensity. It took her back and her inclination was to eliminate him from the list of candidates. But as she spoke to him, she saw an empathy so powerful and pure that she felt sorry for this man who wore all his emotions on his sleeve. Both sleeves. He attempted to keep them in check, but he was doing a lousy job. Perry innately knew that Spencer had few, if any, friends because most people couldn't deal with his passion for animal rights. He reminded her of herself about twenty years earlier, and that's why she ultimately chose him as her tenant. It certainly wasn't because of his background check or job history.

"Would you like something to drink?" Spencer asked, trying to be a good host.

"No, but thanks. You just got home, so enjoy the evening. I simply wanted to know if the cottage was working for you."

"The shower head is pretty weak. I don't know if it's the water pressure or…"

"Shit. I meant to get a new one. My last tenant complained about it, too, but she said she'd replace it and bill me. Never did. I'll get right on that."

"No hurry. Actually, I work close to a hardware store. Why don't I pick one up?"

"You're a doll. That works for me. Deduct it from next month's rent. Thanks Spencer."

Spencer watched Perry walk across the expansive back yard to her place. She was old enough to be his mother, but unlike Heddy Rydover, she had an athletic build and looked a good fifteen years younger than her age. Before his thoughts lingered, Spencer closed the door and went to the kitchen to fix dinner.

Perry wasn't sure what to think of Spencer. He was an interesting one, to say the least. As a fanatic, she thought he'd have crazy eyes. The ones you see staring back at you from a Wanted poster. Instead, Spencer's eyes exuded a naïvete and helplessness, like a deer seeing the hunter a split second before the bullet shatters its heart. He looked vulnerable and completely out of his element talking to her. She knew she was taking a chance on him but she didn't care. Worst case scenario, he can't pay the rent and she'd have to kick him out. Or would she? Perry didn't really need the money. Her father left her everything when he died unexpectedly a few years ago, affording her the luxury of retiring early from her job as a technical writer at Xenial Technologies. She loved the people at Xenial but the writing was so dry and mechanical. When she left, she was finally able to paint full-time. She turned one of the bedrooms into a studio, purchased a professional easel, paints and an array of paintbrushes, and dedicated her days to creating art.

Her mind drifted back to Spencer. She thought he was a cute kid. A twenty-something kid. His wavy dark brown hair fell across his forehead into his light brown eyes. His eyebrows reminded her of George Harrison's: dark and thick and a millimeter shy of becoming a unibrow. When he brushed his hair away, she took note of his long, tapered fingers. She looked down at her own. They were short and slightly crooked. She called them her potato-picking peasant hands, a nod to her Polish heritage.

Spencer was definitely a basket case. She suspected he took on all the ills of the world. The animal world. Soon that assumption would be validated.

4

Bonnie must have been staring at the Saks Fifth Avenue window for a while because she didn't notice the man standing next to her, so enraptured was she by the necklace the mannequin was wearing. It was dripping with diamonds, emeralds, rubies, and sapphires.

"Are you going to buy it or what?"

Bonnie looked to her left. Standing there was a man who reminded her of a young James Garner. He had well-coifed black hair, a strong jaw line and sensuous lips. Before she could answer, he held out his hand. "I'm Chris and you are?"

"Bonnie." She matched his strong handshake. "I won't be wearing that beauty any time soon, but someday…"

Chris sized up Bonnie quickly. She was mid-twenties, attractive and if the handshake was any indication, confident and self-assured.

"Can I buy you a drink?"

Bonnie's initial reaction was to accept, then her thoughts quickly switched to Gerald. What if he saw her with this guy? The chances were slim, but they were there and she didn't want anything or anybody getting in the way of her aspirations. It took willpower to decline his offer and his subsequent query for her number. She watched as he walked down the street, past the Levi store and around the corner. She turned back to the store window, took out her cell and snapped a photo of the necklace.

It was a little past eight when Bonnie got home. Her apartment was small, but the building was in a coveted location. North Beach had all the charm of San Francisco and then some: Sidewalk cafes, four-star restaurants, gourmet food stores and the inimitable Mario's Bohemian Cigar Store Cafe, a San Francisco institution since the 1950s. The corner restaurant and bar was in every travel guide and for good reason. Once you walked through the narrow, faded red door, you entered another country, another culture. Twenty-five patrons could sit comfortably. Add a few more and it was cramped. The air was thick with cigar smoke. Even though smoking in city establishments was illegal, the non-smoking customers expected it and didn't complain. Those lucky enough to get a seat could sip their double espresso and nibble on biscotti while watching the foot traffic walk past the tiny bar. Silvio, the imposing owner and bartender, always had a story to tell to those who would listen. The regulars enjoyed Silvio's animated tales. They added to the bar's unique flavor and ambience.

Bonnie tossed her purse onto the kitchen table and went straight to the bedroom where she happily took off her heels and traded them for slippers. Back in the kitchen, she grabbed a frozen dinner, popped it into the microwave and, while it cooked, she finished taking off her work clothes and put on sweats. With three more minutes to go before her meal was sufficiently cooked, Bonnie connected her cell to the laptop, downloaded the photo contents, transferred the necklace photo to the file labeled 'My Future' and hit save. The timer went off and Bonnie transferred the Lean Cuisine Eggplant Parmigianino onto a plate. As she dined at the glass and chrome kitchen table, she got on the internet and checked Hinton's stock. Satisfied that it was doing well, she logged onto her Victoria's Secret account and began to browse the teddies for next weekend's tryst.

5

This is what made the blood in Jessica's veins sing and rush through her body, giving her the equivalent of a climax. Men...She would like to have one, but if she had to choose between devising a plot to change the course of history or having a partner, there was no contest. Even Ryan Gosling would get the boot.

She walked into the Russell Senate Office Building, the oldest of the senate buildings, built in the early 1900s. She never tired of looking up at the skylight in the rotunda's coffered dome. It spilled the morning light onto the white marble floors and illuminated the few senators who had arrived earlier than normal, making them look ethereal.

Jessica hadn't slept well last night. The meeting at Anita's was so stimulating that when she finally fell asleep, she woke up three hours later, planning and re-planning in her head until, exhausted, she fell back to sleep.

Sitting at her office desk, she flipped through her rolodex and stopped it on Dr. Cary Deschel, director of the National Institute of Biomedical Imaging and Bioengineering. She picked up her phone to call, then realized it was only 6:30 in the morning. She didn't want to leave a message. No trail. Her assistants, Pauline and Talbert, would be in at eight, so she decided to put off the call for an hour. It gave her plenty of time to speak to Dr. Deschel in private.

Junior senators, by nature, don't get the prime offices with the stellar view, but Jessica was able to secure her father's former suite. It was one of the largest and every bit as imposing as he was. The wood paneling was a deep walnut and covered all four walls. She had replaced the liquor in the mahogany credenza with books and graced the top with her collection of rodeo trophies. Her specialty had been calf roping. She loved the challenge of riding her horse at top speed, lassoing the calf and tying it down. Her best time, a record at the Montana State Rodeo, was 6.1 seconds. Her determination was so fierce that, while roping a two-month old calf, she yanked the lasso too hard and the animal flew in the air and broke its neck. Jessica wasn't aware of the fatality until she tied its legs. Trophy in hand, she joked that they should change the barbeque from steaks to veal. The quip received big laughs and a round of applause.

At her insistence, the twenty-year-old faded carpet was replaced with a rich tan Berber. She kept the antique wall sconces, overhead chandelier, the two leather wing back chairs, mahogany coffee table and two end tables. It didn't hurt being Theodore Olshansky's daughter.

Almost an hour later, Jessica dialed Cary's number.

"This is Dr. Deschel."

"Picking up your own phone? Did they lay off your secretary?"

"Jessica. How are you?"

"Great. No, better than great. And you?"

"Good. Good. And to answer your question, my assistant doesn't come into work until 8:30."

Jessica stood up and walked around her office. She stopped at the window and looked out at the expansive view of Jefferson Park. It was overcast and cold, but there were always people, probably tourists, milling around, taking photos, sitting on the park benches, enjoying the grandeur of D.C.

"Remember the research paper you were telling me about the other day? Lenore Fitzwater's experiment gone wrong at the prison?"

"Of course I do. Her grant is up for renewal. That's why I was reviewing it." Cary rifled through the pile of papers on her desk, trying to find the study. "Why do you ask?"

"Are you going to renew her grant?" Jessica said, hoping Cary would tell her what she wanted to hear.

"We're still discussing it. I told you almost all the inmates died, didn't I? It could conceivably take years before she refines the drug."

"True, but even if it does take a while, can you imagine the impact it would have on all the major diseases? This drug could cure cancer, diabetes, heart disease, and more."

"I realize that. Fortunately for Lenore Fitzwater, my colleagues share your optimism. I'm sure her grant will be renewed."

"Is it possible to meet with Dr. Fitzwater? You know I've always been fascinated by biomedical research."

Cary sat back in her chair, rocking it back and forth. "I don't see why not."

"Great! Dr. Fitzwater is working in D.C., right?"

"She's at the main campus in Bethesda."

"Close enough. Thanks Cary. I'll be in touch with her soon."

Jessica hung up and practically danced around the room. She was that much closer to playing God and she loved it. Adrenaline coursed through her veins. She felt like she could run a marathon. Instead, she called Anita.

"Not over the phone," Anita said. "Meet me at the cafeteria on the second floor."

Anita put on her jacket and headed out the door. She was amazed at how efficient their newest member was. She hadn't even called her contact yet, but she was confident that Gerald would be honored to be part of their project.

Senator Minefeld spotted Jessica sitting alone at the far end of the cafeteria drinking a soda. She swore she could feel the woman's excitement from fifty feet away. Anita caught her eye and then motioned to her that she was going to get a coffee. After standing in a short line, Anita came over and sat across from Jessica with a cappuccino. "What do you have for me?"

Before answering, Jessica made sure no one was within earshot. Satisfied they were sitting far enough away, she began.

"The NIH is hopefully renewing the researcher's grant. Instead of creating a dummy lab, which could take too much time, I thought I would visit Lenore Fitzwater's lab under the guise of congratulating her on her efforts to eradicate humanity's deadliest diseases. While I'm there, I'll distract her and grab a vial of the drug."

Anita cut in. "And you're comfortable with this?"

"Absolutely. How hard could it be?"

"I guess you'll find out, won't you? I haven't spoken to Gerald yet. I'll do that this weekend. I forgot to mention that he used to be a chemist. Before he took over Hinton, he worked at Cinder Labs. We'll give him the drug and, hopefully, he can duplicate it and mass produce it. This may be easier than I thought."

Anita took a sip of her cappuccino. The building cafeteria wasn't Starbuck's, but they did a decent job. "Let's run it by Bert and Olivia. In the meantime, try not to look so excited."

"Couldn't my brimming enthusiasm be attributed to my senate seat? I'm new and young and full of promise." Jessica leaned forward, almost knocking over Anita's coffee. "One more thing. I was thinking that one surefire way to get the drug into the bodies of the homeless is if the four of us personally visited homeless shelters in our states and passed out burgers and chicken sandwiches. We look like we're empathetic to the plight of the downtrodden and then," Jessica closed her eyes, stuck out her tongue and dropped her head forward.

Anita laughed. "I knew the daughter of Theodore Olshansky would be a chip off the old block. We had been knocking this idea around for a while, but couldn't figure out how to execute it. And then along comes Jessica. How long have you been contemplating the death of the poor and beleaguered?"

Jessica sat back and thought about the question. As long as she could remember, her father complained bitterly about the lower class taking from the rest of the population. "It must have been when I was in graduate school. I was taking a course in environmental studies. The professor said that if the population continued to grow at the current rate and we continued to consume products and natural resources at that same rate, we were looking at major resource depletion in twenty to twenty-five years. That was fourteen years ago. The clock is ticking and, truthfully, most people don't give a shit. Sure, there is a growing concern for the environment, but when push comes to shove, don't even try to take away a family's SUV or their computers or laptops or Olympic size pools. We're Americans and we'll use and abuse until we're no longer able. Knocking off the underbelly of society is a lot more palatable than murdering the middle and upper class. At least they have promise. Where's the future for a homeless person or a drug addict stuck in tenement housing? If we can clean up the inner cities, we could stave off or even eliminate scarcity."

"I couldn't agree more. After I talk to Gerald, I'll set up another meeting and we can move forward." Anita glanced at her watch. "I have a conference in fifteen minutes so I'll talk to you next week." She finished her coffee and they both got up to leave.

The senators continued to chat as they walked to the bank of elevators. To the untrained eye, they looked like two hard-working, dedicated politicians.

6

eddy and Roger Rydover weren't sure where they went wrong. They raised two children in the same house, same schools, obviously the same parents, but one was an overachiever and the other a raging animal rights fanatic. They loved Spencer, but worried that the world would eat him alive. With him finally out on his own, they enjoyed their privacy, but Heddy doubted that he could manage to keep a job, pay bills and perform the ordinary tasks that, for most people, were effortless. It wasn't that she thought her son was ignorant or incapable of being independent. Quite the opposite. Spencer excelled in school, garnering a solid 3.5 grade point average. Heddy's apprehension was born out of Spencer's inability to keep quiet when someone or something upset him. She was hoping that, without the parental safety net, he would curtail his outbursts.

Heddy handed her husband the casserole and he dutifully placed it on the cow-shaped trivet in the middle of the table. Roger stared at the three place settings, wishing there were four. After a huge fight between the siblings at the last family dinner, Spencer declared he wouldn't eat at the same table with his older sister. She shared his sentiment.

Spencer knocked, then let himself in. Heddy bounded out of the kitchen to greet him. She was of average height and weight. She looked very much the suburban mom despite living in Berkeley, a mecca for the environmentally-minded, Birkenstock-wearing, Prius-driving crowd. At forty-seven, Heddy was starting to get a little on the dumpy side. Her only form of exercise was walking and occasionally bike riding with Roger on the weekends. She wanted to join Club One. It was the latest health club to emerge in the fitness-conscious city. It also charged sixty dollars a month, a tidy fee for the household budget. As soon as Heddy built up the courage to ask her husband, she was going to sign up.

Heddy hugged her only son and kissed him on the cheek. "Hi sweetie. How was work?"

"Still there," said Spencer as he took off his jacket and placed it on the back of the couch.

"I thought you liked it, Spence. Don't you like the people you work with?"

Spencer plopped down on the couch, the weight of his body causing him to sink into it further than he should have, a result of the deterioration of the goose down cushions.

"I think it's time for a new couch, Mom. Get one that's cruelty-free, not full of feathers from geese that had been violently plucked."

It wasn't the first time she'd received a 'lecture' about the inhumane couch. She nodded and then asked Spencer about his fellow employees again.

"The people are okay. It's just boring. I'm standing most of the day, and unless I'm asked a question or have to help someone find a book, I'm behind the counter. It's not the most stimulating job I've ever had."

Roger walked into the living room and said, "No, but it's the longest you've had to date."

Spencer glared at his father. Before he could say anything, Heddy jumped in. "Dinner's ready. Come, let's sit down. I made your favorite casserole, Spence. Zucchini and potato."

"Are you expecting anyone else?" Spencer asked.

"Don't worry. Your sister wasn't invited."

In addition to the casserole, Heddy fixed a salad and garlic bread. She was careful not to use butter but a non-hydrogenated, vegan spread. Sitting next to the salad was a bottle of Frey Vineyards Merlot, also vegan and organic.

"So, how's your new place? Is it comfortable?" Heddy said as she served her son a generous helping of salad.

"I like it. It's so quiet out there. Hard to believe it's in Berkeley. I'll have you guys over for dinner soon. Promise."

"That would be wonderful. Isn't your landlady around my age?"

"Yeah, I think so. I could invite her, too, if you'd like to meet her."

Roger said, "Are you dating anyone?"

"Nope."

"It's because you're too picky." Roger knew he was getting into rough territory. He didn't care. Between a son who verged on anti-social behavior and a workaholic daughter, he didn't know if he'd ever have grandchildren. He grabbed the wine bottle and filled their glasses.

Spencer nodded. "I am picky and I'm also not in any hurry. What's it to you?" He took a big sip of wine. His mother followed suit.

"I'd like to be a grandfather before I'm too old."

Spencer laughed. "Dad, you're forty-nine. That's young."

Heddy looked at her husband imploringly. "Roger."

"What?" After an awkward pause he said, "I'm pre-diabetic. I found out a few days ago."

Spencer didn't say it, but he wasn't surprised. His dad never deprived himself of sweets and growing up there was dessert after every dinner. Over the years, Roger developed the ever-present middle-aged gut. It was just large enough to hang over his belt. The rest of his body was in fair shape despite his lack of consistent exercise.

"If you switch to a plant-based diet, you can avoid diabetes altogether. It's even reversed diabetes in people who have had it for years," said Spencer

Roger shot back, "I'm not becoming a vegan. You know I love eating meat and there's no way on this planet that I'm giving up ice cream and cheese and milk. My doctor put me on medication. I'll be just fine. Thanks."

Spencer went over to his jacket and pulled out his iPhone. "You just said you were worried you wouldn't live long enough to have grandkids. I'll tell you right now, it's going to be a long time before I settle down and have children. What are you taking, Dad?"

"I don't remember."

Heddy said, "Metformin."

Spencer typed it into his phone.

"Sit down, son. Can we please just eat dinner? Look, I'm having a vegan meal right now."

Spencer ignored him. "Trouble breathing, swelling of the face, lips, tongue or throat. Hives, loss of appetite, increased abdominal gas. You'll appreciate that one, Mom."

Roger raised his voice. "I said sit down!"

Spencer returned to his chair, but continued to look at his phone. "Those are only a few of the side effects. Come on, Dad. Is it worth it?"

"Yes, it is. Now shut up and eat."

Spencer shot up, pushing the table away. The bottle of wine fell over, spilling its deep red contents onto the table and floor. "You have a chance to stop a disease from killing you and to stop promoting the torture and murder of innocent animals, but you'd rather not. Why? Because it tastes good. What a fucking joke."

Grabbing his jacket, Spencer raced out the door, slamming it behind him. Heddy wasn't sure if she should tend to the spilled wine or chase after her son. She decided to clean up the wine. It was a lot easier than trying to lure Spencer back to the dinner table. She wasn't successful before, so why would tonight be any different?

Roger continued to eat as if nothing happened. He was also used to Spencer's short fuse. "If he thinks he can bully me into eating his way, he's nuts."

Heddy mopped up the wine with a sponge. "He was just trying to tell you that…"

"Don't you start defending him. He's a fanatic and I won't stand for it in my house."

Heddy walked to the kitchen sink and wrung out the sponge. Under her breath she muttered, "Our house, Roger. Our house."

Spencer's anger spilled into the car, onto the highway and rolled out of the door like lava when he got home. He stomped across the expansive lawn to his cottage, not even seeing Perry wave at him from her deck. Slamming the door he went to the refrigerator and grabbed a beer. As he drank it, he paced back and forth in his small living room. "It doesn't make sense to me. The man is going to get diabetes and he'd rather take poison than change his diet. It's so twisted."

About an hour and four beers later, Spencer returned to a calmer state of mind. He opened up his laptop and checked his messages. Bay Area Animal Rights was having a protest next Wednesday at noon in front of Kentucky Fried Chicken at 2101 Lombard Street in San Francisco. He RSVP'd and started working on his sign, but not before he turned on his stereo and blasted The Smith's CD, *Meat is Murder*.

7

Jessica was glad the day was over. It had been packed with committee meetings, lunch with a lobbyist from Monsanto, and then she hosted a meeting with a group of Montanans who opposed immigration reform. Her appointment with Lenore was a welcome respite.

She drove up to the security gate and rolled down her window. "I have an appointment with Dr. Fitzwater in Building 50, Louis Stokes Laboratories. Jessica Olshansky." The guard found her name on his clipboard, then gave her directions to the designated guest parking spots. After winding her way between the myriad of buildings, she found a parking space in the visitors' section. Jessica glanced at her watch. She had five minutes to meet the researcher. Not known for her speed, Jessica did her best to hustle through the parking lot and made it to the information desk with a minute to spare.

Ten minutes later, the elevator opened and a tall, gangly middle-aged woman wearing a lab coat over her knee-length dress walked over to Jessica and shook her hand. "I'm so glad to meet you, Senator Olshansky. It's such an honor."

"The pleasure is all mine. I think your research is highly valuable. I'm sure the NIH will decide to renew your grant."

Lenore said, "Thank you. Would you like to see the lab?"

"I'd love to."

They made small talk in the elevator. When the doors opened to the fifth floor, Jessica could have sworn that it had just been scrubbed. The walls were bright white and the floor tiles gleamed. It reminded her of being in Montana during a snow storm, but here the temperature was artificially controlled and the air was devoid of character. It was odorless.

Not so with Dr. Fitzwater's research space. The small laboratory reeked of disinfectant. It was hard to believe that a person could spend their working days surrounded by so much sterility. One wall was filled with cages, some empty, others housing white rats, two to a cage. Jessica's first inclination was to hold her nose. The smell reminded her of visiting her grandmother in the hospital. It had always been Mattie Olshansky's wish to end her life at home on the ranch. The heart attack put an end to her desire. Instead of breathing in the clean, Montana air, infused with sagebrush and the pale pink vanilla-scented flowers of the clematis, her last breath was of the plastic tubing, rubbing alcohol and metal instruments in her hospital room. The smell of death was pervasive. Jessica would never forget the sadness in her grandmother's eyes. The memories came flooding back in Lenore's lab.

Spreading her arms wide, Lenore said, "This is it. It's not much, but hopefully, when my grant is renewed, I'll have a chance to continue my research on dioxythoxoda. I call it d.o.a. for short."

Jessica almost laughed. She wondered if Lenore realized that d.o.a. stood for dead on arrival. How fitting. A small refrigerator sat on one of the stainless steel tables, its glass door revealing twenty to thirty bottles of clear liquid. Her heart began to pound, knowing she was so close to securing the precious drug. Lenore followed Jessica's stare. She went over to the cold storage unit and took out one of the bottles, holding it as if it were the Holy Grail. "This is it. The potential to cure the worst illnesses plaguing man and womankind. I know that I can make it work. Did I tell you how I discovered the main component of d.o.a.?"

"You did not and I'd love to hear it, but I'm also terribly thirsty. Is there a soda machine nearby?"

"I'm so sorry. What a horrible hostess I am! Is Pepsi okay?"

"Perfect."

"I'll be right back."

Before she did anything, Jessica checked the room for cameras. It seemed as if they were everywhere nowadays. None in the corners and nothing overhead, except a bank of florescent lights.

She quickly went over to the refrigerator and grabbed a vial, then rearranged the others to fill the empty space.

"Here you go." Lenore handed her a Pepsi Light. Normally, Jessica would have been offended. Not today. She could have handed her a Slim Fast and Jessica would have still wanted to kiss her.

"Pepsi Light. My favorite."

"I had a feeling it was." Lenore walked over to one of the cages housing two large, white albino rats. She took one out and held it in her hands, alternately petting it and nuzzling it. "Let me tell you how I discovered the main ingredient in d.o.a." Lenore put the rat on the lab table. It scurried around, walking from one edge to the other. It would peer over the side, opt against jumping and walk back to the other end of the table. Jessica, never one to enjoy the company of a rat or any rodent for that matter, stayed a good four feet from the table.

Lenore began. "About two years ago, I was sitting on my back deck with Penicillin, my cat. I think he was fifteen at the time and had been diagnosed with stomach cancer. He was sitting on my lap when, all of a sudden, he jumped off and went after this beetle walking across the deck. I'd seen them in the back yard from time to time. I found out they're called, Neopyrochroa femoralis, the fire-colored beetle. Penicillin ended up eating it. As a precaution, I called the vet. He said the bug was likely harmless, but offered to check Penicillin out. Not only was the beetle nontoxic, but when the vet tested Peni's blood, the cancer was gone. Crazy, right?"

"Amazing," Jessica said. "Continue."

"I spent a year isolating the cancer-killing component in the beetle. I was able to create a synthetic version and the research group," she pointed to the cages, "responded very well. It was in the human trials that d.o.a. performed so poorly. I have some theories as to why the drug created the opposite effect in the human body and will be exploring those theories and adjusting the drug accordingly."

Lenore picked up the rat and put it back into its cage. It clearly didn't enjoy being imprisoned again and protested by sticking its tiny front paws out of the bars and clawing at the air as if it could squeeze through.

Jessica finished the soda and dropped it in the wastebasket. "I am confident that you'll be successful. And now, I must go before it gets too late. It was a pleasure meeting you, Dr. Fitzwater."

Lenore extended her hand. "Please, call me Lenore." The women shook hands and then Jessica was escorted to the lobby. As she walked outside, she took a deep breath of fresh air and blew out the stale lab air. As soon as she got in the car, she called Anita. It was picked up on the first ring.

"How did it go?"

"Very well. Need I say more?"

Anita said, "No. The less the better. Our next meeting is a week from today. Same time. Does that work for you?"

"I believe so, but I'll check my calendar in the office and call you to confirm. I'm so excited that this is coming…"

Anita cut her off. "The less said the better. I'll see you next week." The line went dead. Jessica removed the Bluetooth from her ear and put it into her purse. Her hand touched the vial of d.o.a. It was still cool. She felt light-headed and powerful and knew that this little vial would change the American landscape for the better. Jessica reached behind her seat and grabbed a small cooler on the floor. She opened the cooler and placed the vial inside between two cold packs, then covered it with the lid. After returning the cooler to its original spot, Jessica inserted her favorite CD into the player and began singing along with *Dancing Queen* by Abba.

8

By 11:45 a.m., thirty-five protesters had assembled in front of the Kentucky Fried Chicken on Lombard Street. It was a windy, chilly day, but they were prepared. All wore thick jackets and most had scarves or hats to protect them from the biting wind. Their homemade signs displayed everything from chickens being slaughtered to the male birds crammed into warehouses, restricting their movement. Spencer's sign read 'Kentucky Fu*ked Chicken' and it had a photo of a dead chicken being decapitated by an assembly line worker. It was still a little early for the lunch crowd, so they talked amongst themselves, commenting on each other's signs and sharing stories of KFC horrors, not just for the animals but for unsuspecting customers. Spencer was standing alone. He listened peripherally to conversations and chose not to join in, even though he knew a few of the protesters. There was one man who stood out from the others. He was around Spencer's age. He looked more refined, less radical. He was tall with an athletic build, short blonde hair and clear blue eyes. There was a calmness to him as if everything was going according to plan, just the opposite of how Spencer viewed life. He was grateful when he could get through another day unscathed. Intrigued by the man's demeanor, Spencer walked over and introduced himself.

"You must be new to the group. I'm Spencer Rydover."

"Kanen Weston. This is my first stint with Bay Area Animal Rights." Kanen turned his sign around to reveal a KFC bucket dripping with blood, holding dead chickens, their necks hanging over the bucket rim. Under the bucket it said, 'Serving Misery for over 50 years.' The sign looked professionally done. Spencer was impressed.

"Nice sign. Are you from around here?"

Kanen replied, "Mill Valley. You?"

"Berkeley."

Their conversation was interrupted by people walking up to the restaurant. Two teenage boys walked by the crowd. One of them shouted, "Why don't you do something useful and die?" His friend continued, "We just want to eat, assholes."

One of the protesters shouted back, "You're eating tortured chickens!"

The first teenager replied, "Yummy!" and they walked through the crowd into the restaurant.

More people breached the picket line in silence. Others read the signs, shook their heads and walked away, preferring to eat without discord. It wasn't until Spencer saw a woman get out of a taxicab and head in his direction that he became animated. He walked up to the woman and practically shoved his sign in her face. "Still eating Kentucky fucked chicken? Why am I not surprised?"

She pushed the sign out of her way and glared at Spencer. "Jesus Christ. Why aren't you working like the rest of us? Get off the streets and grow up, you dreg."

Spencer followed her. "I do have a job and it's not working for a company that promotes torture and death. You disgust me."

She gave him the finger and continued walking toward the restaurant.

Kanen was taken aback. His first impression of Spencer was that of a soft-spoken, non-confrontational person. He could have sworn that the guy was going to spit on the woman. He turned to Spencer who was still riled up. "That was harsh."

"She's my sister. Sibling rivalry doesn't begin to describe our relationship. I despise her."

"Yeah, I got that loud and clear. Was it always like that?"

Kanen detected a very slight wince from his fellow protester.

"No, not always."

A few minutes later, Bonnie exited the restaurant with a red and white paper bag. As she walked by Spencer and Kanen, she took a deep breath. "Ah, the smell of cooked flesh. Delicious." Bonnie flashed a big smile to Kanen. He wasn't sure if it was genuine or sarcastic. Whatever the intent, he clearly found her intriguing. It bothered him that he even entertained the thought of wanting to know a woman who was clearly in opposition to his beliefs.

As Bonnie walked down the street to flag a cab, Spencer yelled, "Satan's got nothing on you, bitch!"

Kanen put his hand on Spencer's shoulder. "Calm down. Can't you see she's provoking you?" Spencer knocked Kanen's hand off his shoulder and walked away, dropping his sign. He was practically hyperventilating. As soon as he was a safe distance from the group, he sat down and put his head between his legs.

Undeterred, Kanen walked over to Spencer and knelt down beside him. "Are you okay?"

Without looking up, Spencer said, "I'll be fine." But he wasn't. Kanen could feel the pain and anguish emanating from his fellow activist. He wanted to help Spencer but didn't know how. It reminded him of when he first learned about factory farming. Kanen was only five years old when his parents told him and his two brothers about the mass production of animals. How chickens, pigs, cows, sheep, goats, and turkeys were treated brutally and with complete disregard. By that time, their vegan food business was just taking off. They felt it was important that their children knew why they eschewed all animal products, including leather, silk, wool and down. Kanen's first reaction was to run to his room and cry. He couldn't understand how people could be so cruel. But his mom didn't want him to be alone. She sat on the bed and cradled her little boy until his sobs subsided. Kanen's older brothers, Grant and Dillon, reacted with anger, devising various ways to hurt the abusers. Michelle and Bill Weston told them that violence begets violence and the best way to end factory farming was for people to stop eating animals.

Eighteen years later, Weston Foods was one of the top vegan food companies in America. Kanen joined the company out of college, eventually becoming the director of marketing. Dillon and Grant remained vegan, but decided on different career paths. Dillon worked as a systems analyst and Grant opened up a surf shop in Santa Cruz.

"Let me buy you a cup of coffee. There's a Peet's right up the street."

Reluctantly, Spencer stood up. He wiped his eyes. Still hurting from the exchange with Bonnie, he agreed to join Kanen. They relinquished their signs to fellow protesters.

The men walked in silence, neither one sure what to say. After a few minutes, Kanen broke the ice.

"Where do you work?"

"Warden's in Berkeley."

"Isn't it on Shattuck?"

Spencer nodded.

Kanen said, "Nice bookstore. Do you like it?"

"It's a job. That's all. How about you?"

"I work for my parents' company, Weston Foods."

For the first time, Spencer smiled. "I eat Weston Raw Energy bars all the time. I love them."

"Which bar is your favorite?"

"Almond Cacao. It's amazing."

"Thanks. That's one of my favorites, too. Ah, here we are." Relieved that Spencer had snapped out of his funk, if only momentarily, Kanen opened the door to Peet's. They waited in a short line, gave the barista their order and easily found a window seat. Kanen wanted to know more about Spencer's adversarial relationship with his sister, but he erred on the side of caution and kept the conversation light, lest he broach a subject that could set him off again. As Kanen listened to Spencer talk about where he lived, he studied the young man's face. Even though he had calmed down, he looked anxious and tormented. His eyes carried a sadness, as if it was his responsibility for stopping the cruelty perpetrated on all non-human animals.

"Is everyone at Weston Foods vegan?" Spencer asked as he took a sip of his soy latté.

"In the corporate office. Not the manufacturing facility."

"I'd love to work for a company where everyone was vegan. It sure would make my life easier."

Kanen said, "What do you mean?"

"How do I put this? It's hard for me not to say anything when I see or hear about animal abuse. I was fired from my last job when I suggested that another employee not eat fish at their desk because it stunk of rotting flesh. He might as well have killed it and gutted it at the office. Before that, I got into an argument with a customer. His t-shirt said, '*Save the Whales. Eat a Possum*' and there was a photo of a dead opossum. Fired. You get the picture. I'm a walking PETA ad. I can't help it. It infuriates me to see such blatant indifference to other beings. Don't they know that non-human animals feel just like we do?"

Kanen patted his new friend on the shoulder. "They know. They just don't care. Let's face it, we will never change the minds of everyone, but we can make a huge difference changing the minds of many. It's going to take time and patience and, dare I say it, respect for these Neanderthals who believe that might makes right and that the human species is the only species that matters. You and I know that we're all connected and spiritually intertwined. You have to realize that no one likes being hit over the head with another's philosophy."

"Then why were you protesting today?"

"I believe that people need to be informed and protesting, silent protesting, is one way. I don't mind making KFC customers uncomfortable, but I'm not going to yell at them and berate them. Hell, some will be so pissed off that they'll continue to go back just to spite us."

"Humans are assholes."

"A lot are, but there are a lot of people who aren't aware of how food animals are raised. We have to find those humans who are open to learning about the suffering of other species."

"And in the meantime, billions of animals are murdered."

"Yeah, it sucks and it's not changing any time soon. I know how you feel. I avoid the meat department in grocery stores. I change the channel when commercials are hawking food, like burgers or ribs. I also know that we can't let the misery consume us." Kanen got up and threw his empty coffee cup in the recycle bin. Spencer did the same. They walked out of the coffee shop and back toward the protest.

Spencer said, "Thanks."

"For what?"

"Talking me down. I'd probably still be curled up in a ball. I'm a mess."

Kanen pulled a business card out of his wallet and handed it to Spencer. "Call me anytime. I'm serious. You're a good person Spencer, but you got to lighten up or you'll get eaten up by the anger and the hatred that pervades this planet."

"I'll work on it. Promise."

9

By the time Spencer pulled into the driveway, it was dark. He followed the lighted path to his cottage. Halfway there, he heard "Son of a bitch!" coming from Perry's house. It was loud enough and emphatic enough that he thought she was hurt. He ran up to the back door and knocked loudly. "Perry! Perry! Are you okay?"

Seconds later, the door opened and there stood Perry, tweezers in her left hand. She looked more than embarrassed.

"Hi. I'm fine. Just fine."

"I heard you yell. I thought something happened."

Perry paused. She wasn't sure if she should explain her outburst, but if she didn't, he might think she had Tourette's syndrome. "I was just about to have a glass of wine. Would you like to join me?"

Spencer looked confused. "Did something happen to the bottle?" Perry shook her head. "Come on in, have a glass of wine and I'll explain."

Reluctantly, Spencer walked in, surveying the area, expecting to find something out of place or broken. He was mentally exhausted from the day and the ensuing drama, so a glass of wine sounded nice.

It was his first time in the main house. All their transactions had been done in the cottage: filling out the renter's application, signing the lease and handing over the keys to his first home away from his parents. Spencer felt like he walked into Mardi Gras. The entry way was a deep ochre with turquoise wall sconces in the shape of calla lilies. A bright yellow and turquoise vase sat near the door with curly willows flowing out of it. Even the floor made a statement with its checkerboard pattern of black and yellow tiles.

"Wow."

"Wait until you see the rest of the house," Perry replied. He followed her as they walked through the living room with walls painted Egyptian blue. A bright floral couch with matching chairs sat in the center of the room separated by an antique oak coffee table. In the corner by the window was a black baby grand piano. Perry motioned to the couch. "Please, sit down. I'll go get the wine." Despite the contrasting colors, they all worked together creating an inviting and uplifting ambience.

Perry walked back into the living room with a bottle of red wine, two glasses and a bag of popcorn. She handed him the bag.

"What's wine without popcorn, right?"

"I guess," said Spencer and he pulled the bag open and placed it on the table. He was clearly bemused by his landlord. She was nothing like he would have expected a woman her age to be. But then, he was comparing her to his mother, a woman whose idea of excitement was watching *Gone with the Wind* on a big screen. The pop of the wine cork jolted Spencer's thoughts back to the living room.

"I hope you like merlot," Perry said as she showed him the bottle. "This is a wonderful winery. It's called Greenfield Springs. Have you heard of it?"

Spencer shook his head. "I'm not much of a wine guy. I do like it but I'm far from a connoisseur."

Perry poured the ruby red libation into the glasses and handed one to her tenant. "To life."

"To life." He took a sip and savored the full-bodied flavor. "Are you going to tell me what happened?"

Perry put her glass down and sat in the chair facing Spencer. She put her feet up on the coffee table. "Promise me you won't judge, okay?"

He put his hand up. "Scout's honor."

"Here goes. I was in the bathroom washing my face when I felt something on my chin. I dried off and looked in the mirror and there it was. A chin hair. A black stubble. On a guy, no biggie. On a woman. Holy shit. You're thinking, big deal. Get a grip, lady. Pluck it and it's gone. Right? Nope. That sucker is going to come back, so I'm going to have to keep an eye on it. That's fine for now. My eyesight is great, but what happens when I can't see that well? I have one hair now, but there could be more. A lot more. I could be one of those old ladies with a goatee! That's why you heard me yell. Aren't you glad you asked?"

Another large sip of wine and Spencer was ready to answer. "I'm glad it wasn't something bad."

"Speak for yourself. It is bad."

"Why don't you get the hair removed? Don't they have lasers that do that?"

"I'm sure they do. But what if it hurts?"

"It's only one hair."

"Spencer, there could be more."

Sitting back on the couch, he closed his eyes and spoke slowly. "Perry, right now there are billions of animals in more pain and agony than you'll, hopefully, ever know. We're talking about hairs on your chin. Do you see the irony?"

Perry tucked her feet up under her and cradled the wine glass. "When I first got involved in the animal rights movement, I was a whirling dervish. I volunteered at In Defense of Animals answering phones, I leafleted at the circus and SeaWorld. I even went to the Petaluma Auction Yard, protesting as the ranchers hauled their unwanted animals into the dirt parking lot. One day I got a call from PETA, asking if I'd like to participate in an anti-meat protest in front of the Safeway market in San Francisco. They were going to use us to simulate the conditions of factory farm animals by setting up a 'chicken cage' and two iron maidens. Six protesters were stuffed into the cage and I volunteered to be squeezed into the iron maiden. I never had claustrophobia until then. I lay sideways in the steel contraption as a sow would. They even Velcroed seven fake piglets onto the length of my body. I was reassured that after an hour, I would be replaced. I took slow, even breaths and kept my anxiety level in check.

"The protest was going really well. Reporters from the local stations showed up and we had a lot of curious customers asking questions. After an hour, one of the volunteers came over to release me from the iron maiden and not a moment too soon. I wasn't able to turn around, sit up or even stretch. He put the key in the lock and twisted it too hard. It broke off in the lock. I almost lost it. I began to hyperventilate and then it hit me: sows spend two years in these gestation crates. I was freaking out after the possibility of spending more than an hour. I knew I'd eventually be freed but for hundreds of millions of pigs, their freedom meant slaughter. A sense of calm came over me and I closed my eyes and lay in that cold, metal box until a locksmith arrived forty-five minutes later and released me."

Perry stood up and walked over to the picture window. "I know how amazingly fortunate I am. Every day I'm grateful that I can choose my destiny. If I bitch and moan about some rogue hairs on my face, it's simply my human vanity blasting through. It doesn't happen too often, so please allow me the extravagance. Come here."

Spencer got up and his legs felt rubbery. The wine was having an effect on his motor senses, even though he only had one glass, but he also hadn't eaten all day. He stood next to Perry as she pointed into the darkness. "Over there, about three miles away, lives a man who owns a large plot of land. He lives alone with his two dogs. Beagles. I'm friends with one of his neighbors. She said she's seen him abusing the dogs. He'll scream at them and kick them. Once, he threw the smaller one against the side of the house. It's after dark when he does it, so she can't record it. She has called the police and animal services, but when they've gone to investigate, there's no proof of abuse."

Spencer shifted uneasily. "And you're telling me this because…"

"Help me rescue them. They'll be two less animals suffering. What do you say?"

"What if we're caught?"

"Unlikely. My friend knows his schedule. He's gone for hours at a time and the other neighbors are far from his place. The houses are on two to three-acre lots. There's a spot in the corner of his property hidden by trees. We cut the fence, grab the dogs and split. Are you in?"

"Yes." As soon as he said it, he felt a surge of adrenaline. It wasn't a major heist, but it still felt exciting.

"That's fantastic! You're putting your money where your mouth is. I'll talk to my friend and find out the best day and then we can coordinate with your schedule. Thanks, Spencer."

They sat back down on the couch. Grabbing a handful of popcorn, Spencer said, "If you don't mind me asking, what do you do for a living?"

"My dad passed away a few years ago and left me his inheritance. I was writing advertising copy, but after I received the money, I began painting full time." She looked over at the far wall. It was flush with framed artwork.

Spencer pointed to a painting of a young woman.

"That's a portrait I did of my daughter, Callie, when she was twenty-six. She's twenty-nine now and lives in Taos."

Spencer got up to get a better view. It was almost whimsical, the way the colors danced and blended together. Her hair was streaked with blue, violet, rose and brown. Callie's eyebrows were colored forest green and her lips were lilac, eyes turquoise blue. Her features resembled Perry's with a strong jawline and high cheekbones. Her nose was small and straight. She reminded him of Jennifer Lawrence. "It's really beautiful. You're very talented."

Perry joined him in front of the portrait. "Thanks. Someday I'd like to have a gallery showing of my work." She noticed Spencer's wine glass was empty. "Would you like more wine?"

"I would, but I have to get going. I haven't been home all day and have stuff to do. Thanks for the wine and popcorn." He placed his glass next to the wine bottle. As he walked out the back door, Perry said, "I'll let you know about Operation Beagle."

"Great. I'm there!"

As she watched Spencer cross the yard, she smiled. She knew the kid had it in him. First the beagles, then a more complicated rescue. If he passed, he'd be ready for the big one.

10

Everywhere she looked, there was opulence and wealth. Gerald's home, his mansion, surpassed her wildest imagination. Bonnie's only point of reference was her high school friend's new home in Piedmont, but it was no comparison to Gerald's Pacific Heights' estate. Where Cynthia's entryway had a tile floor, this home had marble with gold inlay. The chandelier towered over them like a shimmering cloud of gold and glass. When Gerald turned it on, it looked like a hundred candles surrounded by crystals. The golden oak and wrought iron banister wound around the stairs leading to the second floor. Embedded in the oak were small, 24 karat gold fleurs-de-lis.

Bonnie started going up the stairs when she heard something fall in another room. She froze. "Is someone else here?"

Gerald said, "It's the cook. She'll be leaving as soon as she's done making dinner. For us, of course. Come on. Let me show you the bedroom." He grabbed her ass and then moved ahead of her. Bonnie barely noticed.

As they ascended the stairs, Bonnie lovingly stroked the banister. The affluence turned her on despite the thick, ogre-like body she followed up the stairs. No one would ever accuse him of being graceful, but walking behind him all Bonnie could see was her future and it looked very appealing.

When they reached the top, he paused. She could have sworn Gerald was winded. He turned to his left and walked to the end of the hallway. "May I present the bedroom suite."

Bonnie gasped. The size alone was awe-inspiring. Her parents' house could fit neatly into the space. The king-sized bed was adorned with a gold and pink satin comforter with matching pillows. Two high boy dressers faced the bed. An alcove in the far right corner resembled something out of a British tea room: a small, round table covered in a pink lace tablecloth with two high-back chairs. On the credenza sat a Victorian repousse sterling silver tea set.

"I feel like I'm in a royal palace."

Gerald put his meaty arms around Bonnie's waist. "Let's see how fast the king can get his scullery maid out of her clothes." Before she could respond, her dress was hoisted over her head, bra snapped off and panties pulled down to her feet. She kicked off her shoes and ran to the bed, jumping on top of the pillows. Gerald joined her, taking off only his shoes. Aside from pulling down his pants, he didn't even bother with the rest of his clothes. As he clumsily had his way with her, Bonnie almost burst out laughing, imagining herself as a princess and Gerald as a toad.

After dinner, they sat in the home theater and watched *Gladiator* on the large screen. It was Gerald's favorite movie and, even though she had already seen it, she didn't object when he announced his selection.

It was close to 10:00 p.m. when the movie was over. Gerald wanted to smoke a cigar before bed and told Bonnie to wait for him in the bedroom. He walked into his study and locked the door. Running up the stairs, Bonnie made a beeline for the bedroom. The first door she opened turned out to be Gerald's closet. Very boring. She opened the second door and walked into what resembled a store on Rodeo Drive in Beverly Hills. It was all she could do not to scream in delight. She turned on the light, closed the door behind her and walked over to Miriam Hinton's dresses, which numbered in the hundreds. They were color-coded, beginning with a snow white silk Oscar de la Renta cocktail dress and ending with a jet black Ralph Lauren floor-length ball gown. Halfway down the rack, Bonnie spied a peacock blue satin dress. She took it off the hanger and pressed it against her body. She caught a whiff of perfume. It smelled expensive. Without thinking, Bonnie quickly took off her clothes and tried on the dress. She knew Gerald would return soon, but she was on sensory overload and her will power was non-existent.

Staring back at her from the full-length mirror was the woman she wanted to be. Bonnie swore she had never looked better. She turned left and then right, and watched the fabric swirl poetically around her. "I was meant to wear haute couture."

She was about to take the dress off when she saw a glass door in the far right corner of the room. As she glided toward the mystery door, she walked past hundreds of shoes, boots and slippers on the left and racks of shirts and pants on the right.

On the other side of the glass door were furs in a climate controlled vault. Bonnie felt dizzy. She'd wanted a fur coat for as long as she could remember. She had tried on mink stoles and rabbit fur jackets, but never had the courage to visit a fur salon inside a high-end store. Without hesitation, she opened the door. Cool, dry air swept past her. There must have been at least ten furs. Some were full-length, others waist-length, like the snow-white ermine, its tiny paws draped around the sleeves.

She must have left the vault door open, because she heard Gerald calling for her. Panicked, Bonnie took off the fox stole and softly closed the door. Quietly, she went to the front of the closet and hid behind one of the dressers. She prayed he would leave the bedroom long enough for her to exit the closet undetected.

"Bonnie! Are you in here?" Gerald yelled. When he didn't get a reply, he said to the person on the other end of the phone, "I think she's checking out the rest of the house. These young girls are so impressed with wealth. So, what did you want to ask me?"

Anita had rehearsed the conversation at least half a dozen times. She wanted to make sure she said it tactfully and that there was no room for misinterpretation.

"Are you sure you're alone?"

"Yes, Anita. What did you want to ask me?" Gerald hit 'speaker' on his cell and then set it down on his dresser while he changed into his pajamas.

Taking a deep breath and composing herself, Anita said, "I have a proposition for you. Remember the last time we got together, you said it would be a godsend if there was a way we could rid America of the lower class, the drug addicts, drug dealers and homeless? I think you said something like, let's wipe the dirt and grime off America's feet."

"Sure. It was only a few weeks ago."

"I know how to get it done."

Gerald stopped unbuttoning his shirt. "You're not serious?"

"I am."

"Continue."

"I discovered a drug being tested by an NIH researcher that has the ability to speed up the effects of fatal illnesses. If a person has heart disease and ingests this drug, their demise is hastened, considerably."

"What's considerably?"

"Five times faster."

"How do you want me to help?"

Anita licked her lips. She took a drink of water and continued. "Hinton supplies beef and chicken to a number of fast food chains, right? Is there a way you can put the drug into the meat that goes to the inner city restaurants?"

Gerald finished putting on his pajamas. He grabbed the phone as he made his way to his closet. When Bonnie heard him walking toward the closet, she made herself even smaller against the inside of the door. Her heart was pounding and she felt light-headed. When she heard the other closet door being opened, she let out a soft breath. She couldn't believe what she was hearing. Poisoning fast food in the nation's slums? Murdering thousands, maybe hundreds of thousands of people?

"Yes. I was a chemist before I took over Hinton. Breaking down the drug should be very easy. Could you hold on a second?" Gerald covered the cell and yelled, "Bonnie! Where are you?"

As much as she would have liked to hear the rest of the conversation, Bonnie realized she better materialize soon. She quickly changed out of Miriam's silk dress, slipped her own back on and quietly walked to the other end of the closet, where there was another exit. She wasn't sure where it led, but it certainly was better than leaving the way she came in.

Gerald returned to the phone call. "Why don't we meet for lunch next week? I have to be in D.C. for a meeting. Set up the date with my secretary. This could be the answer to a lot of America's financial and health care problems. It amazes me that people like to blame the one percent. Hell, without us the economy would crumble."

Bonnie walked into the bedroom, trying to look as innocent as possible. Gerald immediately turned off 'speaker' mode and concluded the conversation. "Great. Talk to you next week. Yes, you have a nice evening, too." He turned to Bonnie. "Where the hell have you been?"

"I'm so sorry! I was exploring this amazing house. I didn't hear you." She walked up to Gerald and put her arms around his neck. "Nice pajamas, but why'd you even bother putting them on when you knew I'd just rip them off that sexy body of yours?"

Within minutes, they were under the covers. She went into auto-pilot, but it wasn't as easy to concentrate. She knew the man had questionable ethics, but she couldn't understand why he would willingly and joyfully poison so many people. Innocent people. Bonnie needed to tell somebody, but no one came to mind. She had no friends. She never took the time to make friends. It was a moment in her life when she felt very alone.

11

Once again, Jessica arrived before the others. Anita was already seated in the den and stood to shake her hand.

"I am so honored to have brought you into the group. You have exceeded my expectations!"

Jessica was thrilled. She hoped the others would be as enthusiastic, especially when she showed them the vial of d.o.a. She was about to say thank you when the door opened and the maid escorted Bert and Olivia into the room.

Anita waited until the maid left, then she went over to her liquor cabinet and pulled out a bottle of Kristal champagne from the mini refrigerator. The champagne flutes were already on the coffee table.

"Before I tell you about my conversation with Gerald Hinton, I'd like to make a toast. Bert, will you do the honors? Opening champagne bottles scare me." She handed the bottle to Senator Kathala who, like a pro, popped the cork in record time. Once everyone had a full glass, Anita said, "We are about to make history. We won't get any accolades, but we will reap the benefits of our actions for years to come."

"I'll second that," said Olivia, holding her glass high then taking a delicious sip. "Talk to us, Anita."

"Our junior senator here pulled off a major coup. She obtained a vial of the drug. What's it called again?"

"Dioxythoxoda or d.o.a. for short."

Bert laughed. "d.o.a.? How appropriate is that?"

Jessica said, "I know. I'm not sure the researcher even gets it."

Anita added, "I spoke to Gerald over the weekend and he's excited. He loved the idea, but wants to know more. We're meeting tomorrow for lunch. I'll give him the vial with a list of the known elements. He said he could go to a friend's lab to determine the unknown components. We didn't discuss the timeline and I'm completely ignorant to how long it will take to mass produce the drug, inject it into the meat and distribute it. I hope to have those answers tomorrow."

Bert said, "I am truly astounded by the accuracy with which we can distribute the tainted meat geographically. Gerald didn't mention any difficulties with our request?"

Anita answered, "He didn't object on the phone. I'll find out more when I meet with him."

Olivia dug into her purse and pulled out a newspaper clipping. She unfolded it and handed it to Bert. She said, "Read."

"A Rash of Crimes Drives Durham's Homicides. Reports of aggravated assaults in Durham were up 50 percent in the first half of the year, to 587 from 391 last year. Police said a series of retaliation shootings between rival gangs played a role in the jump in assaults. 'We're finding the same people, the same names, the same cars. It seems to be a back-and-forth, retaliatory type of thing,' Deputy Police Chief Larry Smith said. 'These types of crimes are hard to solve. You've got shell casings, but if people in the house don't cooperate, you're at a disadvantage'." Bert handed the article back to Olivia.

Olivia said, "Every major city in the country deals with this crap. Goddamn gang bangers. Let's hope they all have compromised immune systems. It seems highly likely due to their consumption of drugs and alcohol. If our plan succeeds, we're not only going to eliminate a lot of society's undesirables, but social services will have a lot less cases to deal with, the number of violent crimes will decrease and I'll bet you dollars to donuts that with riff raff dying by the thousands, stock in the casket manufacturing sector is going to rise. It's a win-win any way you look at it."

Jessica agreed. "I guess I should start buying stock in casket companies. The ones that make cheap caskets." She stood. "I hate to cut the meeting short, but I have an engagement at eight o'clock."

Anita leaned forward. "Do you have a date?"

"I wish. I'm having drinks with Lenore."

"The researcher?" Anita said.

"That very one. Turns out she doesn't have any friends, what with spending so much time in the lab. She probably wants to tell me more about d.o.a. I'm going to take notes. I can drop them off at your office tomorrow before your lunch with Gerald. Would that work?"

"Definitely. Any information for Gerald would be fantastic."

Bert drained his glass and put on his jacket. "I believe we're done here. Anita, shall we have another meeting tomorrow night after your lunch? I'd love to know what Gerald has to say."

Olivia and Jessica nodded.

"Let's say seven o'clock?" Anita said.

All agreed and with that the meeting of the four senators was adjourned.

12

Since he was in the neighborhood, Kanen decided to pick up a few items he needed for dinner at Whole Foods in North Beach. He was perusing the heirloom tomatoes when someone said, "You're not here to picket the meat department, are you?"

Kanen looked up and standing beside him was Bonnie Rydover. She looked radiant.

"Hell no. I was picking out tomatoes to throw at the butchers. You want to help me select some big, juicy ones?" Kanen lifted a particularly large tomato and tried to gauge its heft.

"Very funny. Please tell me you don't live around here. This neighborhood doesn't need any more bleeding hearts."

"Don't you worry your pretty little meat head. I'm just a visitor in these parts. I live in Mill Valley."

"Good. In case you hadn't noticed, my brother is a nut case. I'd stay clear of him, if I were you."

"Funny. He said that about you. Bonnie, right?"

She nodded. "And you are…?"

"Kanen Weston."

In spite of herself, Bonnie found him attractive. He looked younger than her, probably around her brother's age. He was so confident and self-assured, plus he had undeniable charm and sex appeal. Everything she stood for was most likely the opposite of Kanen's belief system, but at that moment Bonnie was drawn to him. She was as surprised as he was when she gave him her business card and said, "Call me." Before he could answer, Bonnie turned around and walked away.

Kanen watched her leave, her snake skin high heels clicking across the concrete floor. He read her card. *Bonnie Rydover, Assistant Marketing Director, Hinton Industries, 909 California Street, San Francisco, CA 94102.*

An executive for one of the largest meat processing companies in the country was interested in a man who had never tasted animal flesh. The whole idea of pursing a relationship with Bonnie was absurd, yet Kanen was intrigued. He loved challenges and, at the moment, he couldn't think of a better one. He put the card in his back pocket and continued to hunt for the perfect tomato.

Groceries in hand, Bonnie walked another couple of blocks to her apartment. She was appalled at how she handled herself in front of Kanen. "What the hell was I thinking?" she said aloud. "He's an animal rights activist!"

Bonnie pushed the elevator button. "A hot, sexy animal rights activist," she said to no one as her mind conjured up a series of scenarios: kissing Kanen, in bed with Kanen, arguing with Kanen, wanting to scream because of what Kanen was saying. Then Gerald's face appeared in her mind and she started to freak out. No man, no matter how attracted she was to him, was going to interfere with her rise to the top. She had made the decision to forget about the plot to poison fast food, no matter how atrocious or diabolical it was. Besides, she reasoned, living at poverty level would suck. Death would be a welcome respite from a miserable existence. Bonnie had a purpose in life. It was to be the best. Not the best human being, but the best executive. She'd leave empathy and a kind heart to her brother.

Traffic was always a problem mid-afternoon on Lombard Street, heading west to the Golden Gate Bridge. Kanen didn't mind. He was used to it. He had the radio tuned to NPR, the public radio station out of Berkeley. The liberal bent fit nicely into his political leanings. He was listening to an interview with Gene Baur, founder of Farm Sanctuary in Watkins Glen, New York, when his cell rang. He glanced at the number. It was Spencer. He felt a pang of guilt. All he did was talk to Bonnie, but he wanted to call her, creating deceit before their friendship had even begun.

He put the phone on car speaker.

"Hi, Spencer."

"Hi. I wanted to thank you again for helping me out the other day. I really appreciate it. Bonnie and I have a long history of fighting and every time I think I'll stay calm, she manages to bring out the worst in me."

"Siblings can do that." Kanen detected a tremor in Spencer's voice. He felt sorry for him, but he also admired his dedication to animal rights. Against his better judgment, he said, "You feel like getting together for a drink later tonight? I could meet you at Triple Rock Brewery in Berkeley."

"Sure. That sounds great. Is 9:00 good?"

"Yeah. I'll see you then."

"Bye." Spencer hung up the phone and smiled. He couldn't remember the last time he socialized with a peer outside the confines of Bay Area Animal Rights' meetings and protests.

Spencer's next phone call was tougher. He speed dialed the number and took a deep breath. "Hi Mom. I'm sorry about the other night…I love you, too. Can I talk to Dad?"

13

As instructed, Spencer met Perry at her Prius in front of the house at 8:00 p.m. He was wearing all black, including his gloves and tennis shoes. Perry was waiting for him in the car. Her hair was pulled back in a ponytail and she wore a black baseball cap, dark grey tee and blue jeans. He slid into the passenger seat. In the back seat were two medium-sized dog crates.

"I was hoping I'd get to ride in the Corvette. It's a '58 Roadster, right?"

Perry said, "Yes it is. I think men are born knowing about cars. It's uncanny. Taking the Prius is a lot more discreet than the Vette." She looked him over. From head to toe, he was dressed in black.

"You look so goth," said Perry.

"This is my ninja look."

"Love it." She handed him a camcorder. "If you don't mind, I'd like you to take a video of the dogs and their environment before we liberate them. When you start recording, we have to dummy up. Not a peep out of either of us. I'll be sending the video to local television stations and newspapers as well as the animal shelter."

Spencer took the camera from her and checked it out. He opened the viewer and played around with it so he was familiar with its operation. "So, what's the plan?"

Perry pulled out of the driveway and headed north. "My friend said that every Tuesday, Rick leaves the house around 7:30 and doesn't return until after 11:00. She called me after he left tonight, so we have a solid two hours to grab the dogs. I brought some doggie treats just in case we need them, as well as collars and leashes. Are you nervous?"

Spencer lied. "I'm fine. You?"

"Nope. I'm excited, knowing that we're going to rescue two dogs from an abusive creep."

Five minutes later, Perry parked the car on the side of Rick's property, close to a copse of trees next to the chain link fence. The dogs started barking. "I believe those are our doggies in distress. We can't see the driveway from here, so my friend said she'd be our lookout in case Rick comes home early." She dialed her friend's number and told her they'd arrived.

Perry opened the trunk and extracted a pair of four-foot bolt cutters. Spencer eyes widened. "Isn't that overkill for a chain link fence?"

"Yes, but I'm also using them to cut the chains around the dogs' necks that are bolted into the ground. Are you ready?"

"As I'll ever be."

As the dogs continued to bark at the strangers, Perry deftly cut an opening large enough for them to slip through. The dogs were about twenty feet away in a dirt enclosure. Aside from the dog houses and an old tennis ball, the area was desolate. A bowl with less than half an inch of water sat by itself, just within the dogs' reach. The beagles were dirty and underweight. When they saw Perry and Spencer, they barked even louder.

"Start filming," Perry said, then she dipped into her coat pocket and took out two doggie bones. She tossed them to the dogs who gobbled them up immediately. They looked at Perry expectantly. She complied, giving them each two more. As they ate, Spencer turned off the camera. He and Perry pet them, speaking softly. Bolt cutters weren't necessary as they unclasped the chains and gently picked up the dogs without a fight. The rescuers could feel the dogs' ribs and their hip bones protruded from their skin.

Once they got the dogs into their respective crates, Perry called her friend and thanked her again for her help, then they took off. Spencer turned around to look at the newly freed prisoners. One of them was lying down, but the other sat up at attention, looking at Spencer with his head cocked to the side. "Don't worry you guys. Everything will be just fine. You're safe now." Spencer rolled down the window. "They really stink. I bet the asshole never bathed them."

"I'm sure they weren't allowed in the house. I don't understand why someone has pets when they don't interact with them at all. There's no love, no respect. I'm guessing the beagles were there for security purposes."

"He had them chained to their dog houses."

Perry said, "Their barking probably deterred any would-be burglars."

As they approached the house, Perry pulled up next to the Corvette. "Let's get these guys cleaned up and ready for their new home."

They carried the crates down to the basement, then opened the cage doors. The emaciated dogs walked cautiously around the room, sniffing at everything, occasionally lifting their legs to urinate. Perry was prepared. She had a cloth and a spray bottle of Nature's Miracle, stain and odor remover. Spencer sat down on the floor and one of the dogs wandered over to him. As he pet the pooch, he noticed a gash on his left leg. He also had a rip in his left ear. Dried blood partially covered the wound.

Spencer said, "I should take close up video of the dogs. The light is a lot better than outside. I can get much more detail of their injuries."

"Great idea."

One at a time, Spencer circled his subjects. He made sure he included every wound. When he was done, each dog was placed in the large cast iron sink that sat next to the washer and dryer. They were gently washed, dried and brushed. Perry then called Dale, the dogs' new guardian. He lived north of Sacramento, making the likelihood of Rick finding them highly unlikely.

It was almost 9:00 when Dale left with his new pets. He was ecstatic and the rescuers were exhausted. Spencer wanted to go home and shower but Perry convinced him to celebrate their first victory with a libation. They sat out on the patio overlooking the garden. Their only source of light came from a three-wick pillar candle in the middle of the table. It cast a warm glow over the area, creating a perfect atmosphere for their celebratory drink. Spencer took a sip. It was sweet and fruity.

"This is good. What is it?"

"St. Germain elderberry liquor. I only take it out on special occasions."

"Aren't I special?"

Perry sat up and looked into Spencer's eyes. They were red from exhaustion. "Yes, you're very special. You just saved two dogs from being further abused. You deserve a medal, but you'll have to settle for some elderberry liquor and this." She pulled a joint out of her coat pocket.

"I thought I saw a couple of plants in the far corner of the yard."

"It's a strain I developed called Bazooka Berkeley. Would you like to partake?"

Spencer nodded. "Love the name."

Perry lit the joint, inhaled, and then handed it over to her renter, who proceeded to take a very big hit. He slowly blew it out and watched the smoke mix with the candle flames. For the first time in a very long time, Spencer felt relaxed. He was pleased with himself. Protests were instrumental in changing some people's perceptions of animals and because of that he would continue picketing fast food restaurants, circuses using animals and other events where there was animal exploitation. But he had never before experienced as much exhilaration as when he rescued the beagles. It was immediate gratification.

The pot was strong and he progressed into an altered state almost immediately. He took another sip of the liquor and looked over at Perry, a quizzical expression on his face. She caught him staring.

"What?" she said.

"I've never met anyone like you. You're so cool."

"Thanks. I think we make a great rescue team. As long as you're willing and able, so am I."

"So when's our next mission, boss?"

Perry was thrilled. She had a feeling Spencer was cut out for this type of work. "We're working on one right now, as a matter of fact. It's in the surveillance stage. I'm thinking it will be ready for deployment in a couple of weeks. In the meantime, I was wondering if you'd like to volunteer at the Berkeley Animal Shelter. They always need people to help in any capacity."

Spencer started to feel uneasy. He could hear the barking and howling of desperate dogs, see cats in small cages huddled in the corner with barely enough room to turn around. He could smell the fear and then he could feel his anxiety level rising. He took another hit of Bazooka Berkeley, hoping it would calm his nerves.

"I don't know," he said. "Seeing all those animals in cages, confused and scared. I might freak out. Let me think about it, okay?"

"Of course. No pressure at all." Perry looked up at the sky. It was filled with billions of stars and suddenly she felt like a speck of dust; so incidental. So infinitesimally small. "Can I ask you a question?"

"I guess."

"Did something happen to you, like an incident, that made you so sensitive to animal suffering? I've met a lot of animal rights people and many seem to have experienced a defining moment in their lives, some occurrence that permanently opened a door to the pain of others."

Spencer's mind flew back to when he was eight years old. He felt the terror, the helplessness, the rage and the extreme disappointment. All those years ago and it still hit him like a cyclone. "I don't want to discuss it. Maybe at another time. Maybe in another life."

Perry felt horrible. "I'm so sorry. I didn't mean to pry. I can feel your hurt and thought talking about it might help."

They continued to sit in silence, both feeling the remnants of the rescue high intermingled with the artificial high. Their reverie was broken by a rustling sound in the back yard. They watched as a mother raccoon tentatively walked out from a bush. Behind her trailed four babies. They sauntered across the lawn to what appeared to be a pile of leaves. Once they reached their destination, they began pawing at the pile.

Perry whispered, "That's Matilda and her brood. I leave fruit and peanuts out, hoping to stop them from going to other yards and disrupting my neighbor's pets. One of them has a pond with koi and frogs and the other has rabbit hutches."

After watching the raccoons eat their late night meal and walk back into the shadows of the camellia bushes, Perry picked up her cell and looked at the face. "It's late. Time for bed. Thanks again for helping tonight, Spencer. You're really a great kid."

"Kid? I'm twenty-four!"

Perry laughed. "I'm over twice your age. You're a kid, now get some rest."

It was after midnight when Spencer got home. His body felt heavy and his mouth was very dry. He jumped in the shower, then brushed his teeth. After drinking a tall glass of water, he slipped under the covers and fell into a deep, satisfying sleep.

14

Everything was coming together beautifully, without a hitch. Jessica wanted to believe that what she and her cohorts were doing was right. It seemed like every time she read the *Washington Post*, there was an article on a stabbing or an exposé on the deterioration of the lower class. There were smatterings of bright spots. An inner city school achieved close to a hundred percent graduating class, but they were few and far between. Besides, even if every student graduated, most would end up working blue collar jobs. She couldn't imagine how anyone could achieve job satisfaction working a menial position. She chuckled to herself. Some of those kids will be flipping d.o.a. burgers and frying d.o.a. chicken nuggets. A knock on her office door brought her out of her reverie. "Come in."

Tall and gangly with a crop of sandy blonde hair and pockmarked skin, Jessica's aide Talbert Roy popped his head in to announce a visitor, her father. Barely twenty-one, Talbert was her most enthusiastic assistant.

"Show him in, please."

A few seconds later, the great Theodore Olshansky, eight-term Senator up until recently, strode into the office, embracing his daughter in a fierce, bone-crushing hug. Jessica never got used to it, but accepted it as her father's way of showing his affection and power over his only child.

"You didn't tell me you were in town, Daddy."

Theodore sat his large, bulky body into the leather chair facing Jessica's desk. Despite her distaste for cigars, he lit one up, took a puff and coughed. She pointed to the offending stogie and said,

"You know you can't do that here. Besides, didn't your doctor tell you to stop smoking?"

His voice was loud and phlegmy. "Since when do I listen to rules and doctors?" He took another puff, blowing the smoke away from his daughter. "How are they treating you on the Hill?"

"Everything's great. I love it."

"I don't have to rattle any cages or knock some heads together?"

"No, Daddy. I can hold my own."

Theodore flicked the ash on Jessica's desk. "Well that's a first, isn't it?"

Jessica was tempted to tell her father about the fast food scheme, but stopped herself. As much as she wanted to prove to him that she was worthy of his respect, divulging the potentially explosive information would be a bad idea. Instead, she acted as she always did in the face of his derogatory remarks, with a big smile. "Is Mom with you?"

"You've got to be kidding. After enduring so many years living here, she swears she's allergic to the place. I left her at home, happy as a clam. She sends her love."

"Can I take you out to lunch?"

"Don't bother, dear. I'm going to Browning's Corner with Jeb McDaughtry. I haven't seen the bastard since my retirement dinner. We have a lot of catching up to do."

Theodore pushed his corpulent body off the chair like it was dead weight. He knew he had to lose at least fifty pounds, but at seventy-eight, the last thing he wanted to do was deprive himself of any pleasures and food was one of them. He handed Jessica his cold cigar. "Keep this for me, will you?"

"Sure, Daddy."

Jessica handled the Cuban import like an old friend she couldn't stand. They looked like dog shit and they smelled as bad, but she never knew her father when he didn't have one in his mouth or coat pocket.

Another bone-crushing hug and the ex-senator was off, leaving Jessica shaking her head at the man she admired, feared and sometimes, despised.

15

It had been a week since she ran into him at the market and he hadn't called. She was disappointed and mad, but Bonnie also realized that a vegan and carnivore match up was as improbable as a Mormon and Hasidic Jew. The only thing they had in common was her brother and that wasn't saying much. She wondered if Spencer told Kanen why they were estranged. She certainly wasn't going to tell him or anyone, for that matter. Even their parents were unaware of the reason for the rift sixteen years ago. She tried not to think about it, though she was sure that the memory was seared into her brother's delicate psyche.

Maybe she should call him. How difficult could it be to find someone named Kanen Weston? Bonnie opened up her laptop and typed in his name. The screen came alive with results. LinkedIn listed him as the marketing director of Weston Foods.

"What a trip. We're in the same field and I bet Mr. Weston is loaded."

She scrolled down, found his Facebook link and clicked on it. It was private, so she wasn't able to check out friends, photos, videos, or nearly anything else. Next, she typed in Weston Foods on the Google. The company was family-owned. Its net worth twenty-six million. In her eyes, Kanen Weston just got a lot more attractive.

Bonnie was ready to type Kanen's name into a white pages directory. In exchange for a nominal fee, the online service provided a person's basic information: date of birth, address and telephone number. She filled out the form, but stopped short of entering her credit card number.

"This is nuts. I'm cyber-stalking this guy and he's a goddamn animal rights activist. Very wealthy, but an activist, nonetheless."

She closed the laptop and walked into the kitchen, grabbed a beer from the fridge and sat back down on the couch. She picked up the book she had been reading for the last two weeks, *A Place to Wander*, the latest novel by Caroline Kerr.

The cell phone rang, breaking her concentration. Bonnie looked at the number but didn't recognize it.

"Hello?" Bonnie said.

"Hi. It's Kanen Weston. From Whole…"

"I know who it is. I didn't think you'd call."

Kanen was lying on the couch in his living room. The floor-to-ceiling windows afforded him a view of his back yard and, at the moment, a group of wild turkeys perused his garden. In the background, the radio played *Radioactive* by Imagine Dragons.

"I wasn't sure if I should call. We're not exactly a match made in heaven."

"We share the same profession. That's good for something, isn't it?"

"I market vegan energy bars and you hawk animal flesh, so I'd say that's a big no."

"Yet here I am talking to you. Am I that irresistible, Kanen Weston?" Bonnie stood up and went over to the window. She loved her view of the city, especially at night. The lights from the cars and homes pulsated and twinkled.

Kanen shook his head. What the hell was he doing? What possessed him to call Bonnie? She stood for everything he wanted to defeat and abolish. They say forbidden fruit tastes sweeter.

He said, "That must be it."

"Is that Radioactive I hear? I love that song. Hey, I just discovered another thing we have in common."

"That's two. We're on a roll now."

Bonnie loved the sound of his voice. It reminded her of Ashton Kutcher's: friendly, not too deep and self-confident. She wondered if he was going to ask her out. He was wondering the same thing.

"What were you doing when I called?"

She wanted to say, 'Looking you up online' but instead said, "Reading Caroline Kerr's latest novel, *A Place to Wander*. Have you heard of it?"

"Nope."

"It's about the British Isles during the Dark Ages. Very…um, dark."

Kanen blurted out, "Would you like to go out sometime?"

"Sure." Finally, she thought. "When?"

"How about next Saturday?"

Bonnie checked her calendar. She was free. "Sounds good. Are you going to take me to some vegan joint and make me eat plants and seeds?"

"Yes. And you're going to love it. Now give me your address and I'll pick you up at 7:30."

"664 Chestnut Street, apartment number 9. I bet you have a Prius."

"Good thing for you we didn't bet. Enjoy the rest of your evening. I'll see you Saturday."

"Bye." Bonnie was excited, even though she was breaking her own rule of only seeing Gerald. She didn't want anything or anybody to interfere with her goal, but right now Kanen was on the top of her mind. Maybe she just had to scratch the itch and then she would be satisfied. One date with someone around her age, not an overweight narcissist, and she could continue to pursue her rise to the top of Hinton Industries. Her thoughts switched to Gerald's conversation with Anita even though she didn't want to think about it. She had to convince herself, once again, that inner city slums were inhabited by people who lead tragic, dead-end lives. Killing them quickly would actually be doing them a favor. She bounded into her bedroom, opened up the closet and inspected her clothes, trying to decide what she was going to wear on Saturday.

It felt surreal. Talking to Bonnie Rydover, executive at one of the country's largest meat processors, verbally jousting with her and then asking her out. With his looks, financial status and being the heir to a highly successful business, Kanen was frequently pursued by women. Even Bonnie made the first move in the supermarket. He had no problem refusing a woman's advances, which made his attraction to Bonnie all the more perplexing.

He lay back down on the couch and picked the book up off the coffee table. "Unreal," he said as he removed the bookmark and started reading, *A Place to Wander* by Caroline Kerr.

The theme from *Rocky* woke her from a deep sleep. Without opening her eyes, she grabbed her cell phone. "Yes?"

"Do you miss me?"

"Gerald? Is something wrong?"

"I asked if you missed me. Do you?"

Bonnie sat up in bed, now fully awake. She looked at the clock. It was 1:20 in the morning. "Why do you ask?"

"I'm outside your apartment and would love to have you blow me."

Bonnie looked up at the ceiling. She mouthed, 'why me?' but she knew very well why she was in this position. She also knew she couldn't refuse him. The repercussions were not acceptable.

"I'll buzz you in," Bonnie said. While she was waiting, she brushed her teeth and splashed some water on her face.

Gerald barreled into her apartment. "I don't have a lot of time. Miriam thinks I'm out getting ice cream." Without another word, he made a beeline for the bedroom. Dutifully, Bonnie followed, detecting the smell of alcohol on his breath. She unbuckled his belt, unzipped his pants and squeezed her eyes tightly shut, all the while imagining the person opposite her was Kanen. It definitely made the task at hand more tolerable.

Five minutes later, Gerald zipped up his pants, gave her a pat on the ass and left. She went straight to the bathroom, brushed her teeth and gargled for a full minute. As she returned to the bedroom, she turned off the light and was walking to her bed when she stepped on something hard. She picked it up and turned on the light. It was Gerald's cell phone. She figured he'd be back soon, so she turned on the television to pass the time. It didn't take long before curiosity got the better of her. She was dying to know who Anita was and if the plan she overheard was gaining ground. Feeling light-headed, Bonnie stared at the phone for a while before she went to Gerald's texts. She scrolled down until she saw 'Anita,' then clicked on the text string.

She was reading it when Gerald buzzed for the second time that night.

"I'll buzz you in," she said into the intercom. Moments later, Gerald knocked on the door and Bonnie was there, phone in hand. He grabbed it, thanked her and left. As she walked back to her bedroom, she said, "No, thank you, Mr. Hinton."

16

He was working on the latest ad campaign when his secretary told him that his 3:00 appointment had arrived. Kanen finished up, then went to the reception room to introduce himself.

Ashley Knight was all smiles when Kanen walked in the room. The attractive brunette was a reporter for *San Francisco* Magazine and had been trying to get approval from the editor to interview the marketing director from Weston Foods for nearly a year. With the increasing popularity of veganism, especially in the Bay Area, she felt an article on one of San Francisco's more successful businesses would be well-received.

Kanen was dressed comfortably in jeans and a t-shirt that read, 'Apathy Kills.'

"I'm Kanen Weston. You must be Ashley."

She had seen photos of Kanen and knew he was handsome but in person, his self-confidence enhanced his looks and gave him an electric presence.

"Guilty as charged," she said with a giggle. "Thank you so much for seeing me."

She followed him back to his office, a decent-size room, tastefully decorated with original artwork that resembled Klee and Picasso. Kanen directed her to the sofa.

"Would you be more comfortable sitting here?"

"Yes. Thank you." Ashley set up the tape recorder as Kanen got comfortable on the couch next to her. His secretary, Jean, set two glasses of water down on the coffee table and left.

Ashley took a sip of water, then pushed the record button. "Tell me about growing up in a vegan household."

"I'm sure many of your readers would cringe at the thought of growing up in a meatless and dairy-free household. Raising three boys without steak, roasted chicken, or grilled fish sounds downright abusive. Not to mention the lack of cow's milk, ice cream sundaes and cheese. It's surprising the USDA didn't come and take us into protective custody. We also didn't wear or have anything made of leather, wool, silk, fur or down. Far from being deprived, we had the most amazing meals. My mom and dad both loved to cook, and over twenty years ago, the variety of vegan food wasn't what it is today."

"I understand why you wouldn't wear leather, but why not wool?"

"Good question. I'm sure there are ranches where the sheep are treated and sheared humanely, but almost a quarter of all wool comes from Australia, and unfortunately, the shearers are paid by the volume not the hour. I won't get into details but I've read that the shearing sheds are one of the worst places for cruelty to animals. Besides, almost all sheep raised for their wool are also raised for their flesh."

Ashley said, "Silk?"

"In order for the cocoon to be unraveled as one continuous thread, the worms are killed by either piercing them with a needle or dipping them in boiling water. I know, it's just a worm, but to me it's a life, and that's no way to treat another being simply because we want what they have, be it their skin or their flesh. This may sound esoteric, but ending the pupae's life cycle in this stage deprives it of entering its second stage of life as a moth. Can anyone prove that the silkmoth doesn't have a meaningful life once it breaks out of its cocoon? Who are we to rob a creature of its life be it a moth, dog, cow or whale?"

"I never thought about it," Ashley said uneasily.

"Most people don't. Humans take what they want regardless of the consequences."

"Is it difficult as a man to be vegan? Our society still equates masculinity with eating meat."

Kanen was hoping she would ask him that. He went over to his desk, picked up *Plant-Based Planet* magazine and handed it to her.

On the cover was Beyonce and Jay-Z. The headline read, '*30-Day Vegans!*'

Ashley said, "Is that your answer?"

"That's just the appetizer. Here's the main course: growing up vegan was pretty radical twenty-four years ago. A lot of vegetarians back then ate dairy and eggs, but eschewing all animal products brought me my fair share of ridicule, almost all from my male peers. I was called a wimp and was accused of being gay. That's how being different, especially when it comes to food, can be difficult for those who choose not to follow the accepted belief system. Now, here's the dessert: today, the vegan community is full of men that most people would consider extremely macho like Mike Tyson, Woody Harrelson, Alec Baldwin, triathlete Brendan Brazier and Jared Leto. I think the image of the wimpy vegan and vegetarian has been replaced by dynamic and successful men, don't you?"

"Definitely. I have to ask, though, aren't you the least bit curious to try prime rib or fresh lobster or even short ribs smothered in barbeque sauce?"

Kanen smiled. "Have you ever tried roasted duck legs?"

"You mean like the ones they serve in Chinatown? Sure."

Kanen shook his head. "I'm talking about the delicacy where the duck is placed live in a slightly hot frying pan. It's still alive as its legs are cooked and then the chef chops off its legs when they're perfectly roasted. The remainder of the duck is wrapped up and frozen for later use."

Ashley stared at Kanen. "You're kidding, right?"

"Absolutely not. When it comes to the human palate, our species knows no bounds. Live monkey brains, chickens plucked and stuffed while alive, then hung on hooks to dry. Do I miss not ever tasting animal flesh? Not for one second."

"You can't compare those atrocities to the way we raise and slaughter animals. The USDA has humane guidelines that are enforced."

Kanen leaned forward until he was inches from Ashley's face. "I wish you were right. The truth is that the living conditions and subsequent murder that befalls America's billions of factory farmed animals are horrific, and riddled with abuse and cruelty. Check out any animal welfare website, like PETA or Vegan Outreach. You'll see how the humane guidelines do absolutely nothing. Hidden cameras have caught every single food animal being flagrantly mistreated." Kanen leaned back onto the couch. "Shall we talk about something more upbeat?"

Ashley tried to laugh. Instead, it came out as a grunt. "Definitely." She went on to ask Kanen about growing up in the Bay Area and future plans for Weston Foods. Her last question, she felt, was the most important. "Our female readers would love to know if you're available and, if so, if you only date vegans."

Bonnie's image immediately popped into Kanen's head and he laughed. "I'm not dating anyone currently and as much as I would prefer to be with a fellow vegan, it's not a requirement. However, when I eventually get married, my wife will be vegan. I know couples who can pull off the plant-based/omnivore relationship but honestly, I want to be with a woman who has compassion and empathy for all beings and that's not going to happen with someone who eats meat and wears leather, etcetera."

Ashley turned off the tape recorder. "You've definitely opened my eyes to a world I tried to ignore. Thank you so much for the interview." She extended her hand and Kanen shook it.

"My pleasure. Before you go, I'd like to give you a Weston Foods goody bag." Kanen picked up a canvas bag filled with nutrition bars, a Weston Foods t-shirt and coupons, and handed it to Ashley. She looked inside the bag.

"This is so nice. Thanks!"

"My pleasure."

After Ashley left, Kanen checked his e-mails. He scrolled through a few dozen; most were work-related. As he was replying to them, his dad walked in.

In another twenty or so years, Kanen knew exactly what he was going to look like, if he stayed in shape. At forty-five years young, Bill Weston was in the best shape of his life. He jogged, used the company gym on a daily basis, practiced Pilates and took yoga classes in their home town of Sonoma. His wife, Michelle, joined him most days but her preferred mode of exercise was Zumba.

"How'd the interview go?"

"Except for the fact that I grossed the poor woman out by describing some of the many ways animals are tortured and eaten, it went very well. What have you got there?"

Bill put the plate down on the desk. On it was a very odd-looking wedge of fruit. Its orange and white pulp resembled 60s op-art and the skin was a prickly greenish brown.

"Jackfruit. You've got to try it. It's amazing." Bill cut off a piece of the orange flesh and handed it to his son.

"Wow. It's delicious."

"Here's an interesting factoid. Jackfruit was the original taste base for Juicyfruit gum." Kanen gave his father a quizzical look. "It was a popular gum when your mom and I were growing up. I thought the fruit could be one of the main ingredients in a new bar. What do you think?"

Kanen said, "I think it's a great idea. Do you have a minute?"

Bill sat across from his son. "Sure. What's on your mind?"

"If you weren't with Mom, would you consider going out with a woman who wasn't a vegan?"

Without hesitation, Bill said, "Not a chance. I don't want to waste my time with someone who doesn't share my belief system. I'd be spending my energy trying to convert them to veganism and, at this point in my life, I'm not willing to expend the energy on that kind of undertaking. When I met your mother, we were both vegetarians and didn't have a clue how cruel the dairy industry was. When we found out, we cut out dairy. It was instantaneous. Two peas in a pod. That's me and your mom." Bill leaned his elbows on the desk. "So, who's the girl or, should I say, the carnivore?"

"It's nobody."

"Liar, liar pants on fire. Tell me or I won't leave your office."

"Dad..." Kanen protested.

"Hey, you're the one who started it. Uh-oh. She must be a consummate meat eater. Does she work for McDonald's? Is she a butcher? Come on. Spill the beans."

Kanen regretted asking his father. No matter how he answered, it wasn't going to sound good. "Let's just say she eats meat, okay?"

"Are you seeing her?"

"Not yet. We're going out this Saturday."

Bill got up and put his hands on Kanen's shoulders. He could feel the tension in his son's muscles and realized how difficult this dilemma must be for him. He wondered if this girl was worth it.

"Do what feels right for you, son. It's your life and, so far, you've made great decisions. Just do me a favor and trust your gut, not your libido."

"Thanks, Dad."

Bill started to leave the office. Kanen said, "Don't forget the jackfruit."

"You want to finish it? I have more in the fridge."

"Sure."

Kanen went back to checking his e-mails, feeling more relaxed than before. His father never judged him. He always treated him with respect.

He took a bite of the jackfruit, savoring the sweet fruit. "Juicyfruit. Must have been good gum."

17

For the first time since Jessica joined the group, everyone arrived at the same time on time. She assumed, like herself, they were anxious to hear Anita's update after her conversation with Hinton's CEO. As soon as everyone was seated, Anita began.

"I'm happy to report that Gerald has broken down d.o.a. into its prime components. The synthetic beetle juice gave him some trouble, so he used a company out of Minneapolis to identify it. It could take another month or so to mass produce the drug. While he's working on that, he'll figure out the logistics for distributing the d.o.a. meat to the desired geographic areas."

"That sounds great," Olivia said as she straightened her silk skirt. She had come to the meeting from work and didn't have a chance to change. Her high heels were killing her, but she was too much of a stickler for protocol to take them off. It wasn't appropriate. She continued.

"I was watching Dateline last night. It was about a town in New Mexico where prostitutes were disappearing. Turns out, some guy, who they never found, was killing them and burying them in the desert."

Bert said, "And you're telling us this because…?"

"Well, I started thinking, why don't we set up a bogus charity that distributes our d.o.a. sandwiches and burgers to the ladies of the night. A good will gesture. Before you know it, we'll be cleaning up the streets."

Jessica joined in. "Many of these women have to have pre-existing conditions, you know. I'm sure a lot of them are drug addicts, but that doesn't predispose them to cancer, heart disease and diabetes."

"If d.o.a. preys on illness in the body, couldn't it also attack weakened immune systems?" Bert added.

"Good question. I'll have to look at the research paper again. I didn't read it in its entirety."

Anita said, "If it's not part of the findings, you may have to have another drink with your friend. She's not too boring, is she?"

Jessica grimaced. "The woman spends most of her life in a lab surrounded by rats and drugs. The last movie she saw was *Men in Black*. The first one."

"We appreciate you taking one for the team. You'll get an extra star."

"Is that code for something?" she asked.

Anita replied, "No. It's just a figurative star. We're not a glitzy group. We don't give presents or throw lavish parties. But we make things happen in a big way for the good of the greater whole. And even though you won't be able to tell anyone, you'll be able to glow in the satisfaction of knowing you were part of a plan that revolutionized American cities, cleaning them from the ground up."

It was a slow day at the bookstore, which made the hours behind the cash register slog by, despite making small talk with Melanie, the other employee. She was a few years younger than Spencer, a student at UC Berkeley, majoring in English literature. When Spencer left, it was only 7:00 p.m., but he was tired from sitting around for eight hours. He thought about going for a run when he got home.

He was about to put the key in the front door lock when he noticed a note pinned to the door. He took it off and as he read it, he felt a rage surge inside him. He couldn't focus. He dropped his backpack and ran to Perry's house, banging on the back door.

"Hold on. I'm coming!" Perry yelled. When she saw Spencer through the curtain, she said, "Hi there," but her tune changed when she opened the door and saw the anger on Spencer's face. It was as if he was surrounded by a black cloud. He was erratically waving the note.

"How dare you! How could you be so insensitive?" Spencer screamed at her. "Did Bonnie tell you?"

Perry was stunned. "What are you talking about?"

"You know!"

"Spencer, you're scaring me. Calm down NOW!"

Instead, Spencer thrust the note in her face. She grabbed it and looked at it again. It was a photo of an orange and white kitten. She had drawn a text bubble over the kitten and it was saying, 'Help Me!' She signed her name at the bottom. She turned the note over, thinking that maybe someone added something nasty or crude, but it was blank.

"I don't understand. What's the matter with it?"

Suddenly, Spencer realized that Perry had no idea what she had done. He muttered, "I'm sorry," and started to leave, but Perry grabbed his arm.

"Uh-uh. You're not bailing, buddy. You've got some explaining to do."

"I'll tell you later."

"No. You'll tell me now. You can't carry on like that, completely out of control, screaming in my face and then walk away. Sit."

Spencer sat down at the patio table. He looked deflated, like someone stuck him with a pin and released the pent up air. Perry put the note on the table and Spencer pointed to it. "Why did you put this on my door?"

"It's for another rescue. I thought it would be a cute idea to have a kitten asking for help. Boy, was I wrong! What happened, Spencer? What was so horrible that caused you to go ballistic? And by the way, if you ever do that again, you'll have thirty days to vacate the cottage. I will not put up with that kind of behavior. Do you understand?"

Spencer nodded and then put his head down on his arms and broke down, sobbing. His body heaved, like it wanted to exorcise a memory. Perry wondered what could have been so traumatic to have caused this reaction. She patted his back, then rubbed it.

"It's okay. Let it out."

After a few minutes, his tears subsided. He wiped his eyes and nose with his shirt sleeve.

"Who's Bonnie?" Perry said softly. She didn't want to get him riled up again but she suspected he was too emotionally exhausted to fight back.

"My sister."

"What happened?"

Spencer's eyes were red from crying. His upper lip trembled as he started to speak. "I…I don't want to talk about it. Please. Not now."

As badly as she wanted to know what caused Spencer's anguish, she knew this wasn't the time to push it.

"Okay," she said. "Why don't you go home and, when you're feeling better, we can talk about the rescue. That is, if you want to continue doing it. It's totally up to you."

Spencer got up to leave. "I want to do it and I'm really sorry…"

"Stop apologizing, dear. Go home and rest. Let me know when you're ready to talk." Perry gave him a big hug. He felt so vulnerable, his body like balsa wood. If she hugged him too hard, he'd break.

Spencer gently closed the door to his cottage. He didn't have the strength to slam it, but he wanted to. He wanted to scream and dislodge the years of pent-up rage. His parents begged him to go to therapy. He refused. He didn't want to tell anybody what happened. Bonnie threatened to do something awful if he did. He didn't trust the doctor/patient confidentiality agreement, so he kept the secret to himself and assumed that Bonnie did the same.

He lay on his bed, no longer interested in exercise. His appetite was gone, too, even though his last meal was around noon. He just wanted to sleep, but when he closed his eyes, he revisited the incident in Technicolor. Every muscle in his body tensed. As much as he tried to block it, it refused to fade. Spencer got up, turned on the television and started flipping through the channels. He ended up watching a rerun of *Modern Family*. Within five minutes, he was fast asleep.

It was the day before her date with Kanen. As Saturday got closer, Bonnie became more excited, anticipating the evening. She wondered where he would take her for dinner. Probably a vegan restaurant. She was fine with that, especially because she knew there'd be no chance of running into Gerald. He assumed she was only seeing him. Typical, she thought. A married man expecting his mistress to be loyal. And Bonnie was until she met Kanen. That's why being summoned into Gerald's office a few minutes earlier for the purpose of pleasing him was no longer desirable. But she complied, otherwise she could kiss the brass ring good-bye.

Gerald was fixing himself a drink when Bonnie arrived. She locked the door behind her.

"Scotch and soda?" Gerald asked her as he poured a healthy dose of single malt scotch into the crystal tumbler. Bonnie shook her head as she walked around the desk in anticipation of her chore.

Gerald pointed to the couch. "Sit." She complied and he sat next to her. "I have some great news. Miriam is visiting our daughter in Austin for the next four days. Come by tonight after you pack a bag and I'll have the cook whip up your favorite: Chateaubriand with new potatoes. Tomorrow night, we can do whatever you want."

Bonnie felt ill. She had never refused Gerald anything. Whatever he wanted, whenever he wanted it, she would obey. She looked down at her hands, hoping she would know what to say, but her mind was blank.

"I…I made plans for Saturday night, but I can come over tonight around seven?"

"Break your plans. I want you to be with me."

"I want to be with you, too, it's just that my friend is only going to be in town tomorrow."

Gerald stared at Bonnie as he took a long sip of his scotch. "I see. Unfortunately, it's a package deal. Friday and Saturday and Sunday and your job. So, where are you going with your friend?"

She willed herself to stay calm. She knew exactly what she had gotten into when she began an affair and she was committed to staying on course.

"I'll let my friend know that I forgot all about a previous engagement." Bonnie got up and started walking to the door when Gerald said, "Where are you going?"

"To call my friend."

He grabbed his crotch. "It can wait. This can't."

Ten minutes later, Bonnie walked back to her office. She grabbed her bottle of mouthwash, shoved it in her purse and walked to the restroom. She didn't bother to acknowledge Dell Turner, the Director of Marketing, as they passed in the hallway. Instead of making eye contact, she looked into her purse, as if she was trying to find something.

"I can't tell you how awesome it is to meet you after work for drinks." Lenore was positively glowing, a phenomenon considering her pale, dull complexion wasn't used to color. She flagged down the cocktail waitress, one of many hustling in one of Georgetown's most popular watering holes. Fortunately, it wasn't a favorite of politicians, which was why Jessica chose it. The clientele preferred organic booze and vegan appetizers.

The attractive, perky waitress came over and gave the women a big smile. "What can I get you two ladies?"

Jessica said, "Bloody Mary, please."

"What's your most awesome drink?"

"That would definitely be the carburetor. It's Tirade's organic licorice vodka with Kombucha and a splash of fresh pomegranate juice."

"Awesome. I'll have that." She turned to Jessica and yelled above the noise. "I love this place. Do you come here often?"

Jessica laughed to herself. Lenore was so deprived of stimulation outside the lab, she didn't even realize that the two of them looked like aliens compared to the other patrons. Lenore's attire, complete with grey polyester pants, a chiffon shirt with a bow and penny loafers, screamed conservative. Jessica's outfit was more stylish, but still conservative.

"No, it's my first time. It came highly recommended from my aide." That wasn't true. Jessica went online and looked up 'alternative bars' and this one came up. Crackerjack Charlie's was only five months old, but it was a hit with the Paleo Diet and Vegan crowd. Two very different diets. Amazingly, it worked.

Jessica wasn't great at chit-chat, but thought she should engage Lenore in idle conversation before asking her the question that brought her here.

"So, Lenore, did you grow up in D.C.?"

"Oh, no. I'm a mid-westerner. Born and raised in Canton, Ohio. I did go to the University of Maryland. I loved the area so much, I decided to stay. How about you?"

Jessica thought it was a strange question, considering she was a Senator from Montana, but she indulged the researcher.

"Born in Bozeman, Montana."

"Of course. What a dork I am!"

The waitress returned with their drinks. Lenore took a big sip and licked her lips. "Wow. This is awesome. Want to try it?"

Jessica declined. She took the straw out of her Bloody Mary and almost drank half. She would have preferred to be home, relaxing in front of the TV. Instead, she was having drinks with a woman who was socially awkward and decidedly boring.

For the next half hour, the two continued to jabber on about nothing. After their second drink, Jessica said, "Do you mind if we talk a little about d.o.a.?"

"Not at all," Lenore said. She took off her glasses and cleaned them with the cocktail napkin. Before she put them back on, Jessica noticed her eyes were slightly glazed over. Perfect timing.

"When you tested the drug on prisoners, did d.o.a. have a deleterious effect on subjects with weakened immune systems and diseases like cirrhosis of the liver or just on those with cancer, heart disease, and diabetes?"

"Why do you want to know?" Lenore's eyes narrowed and she almost looked menacing. Before Jessica could answer, she laughed. "Just kidding. You should have seen the look on your face! It was awesome! The test group all had life-threatening illnesses. The control group consisted of what I thought were healthy subjects. Of course, this is taking place in a prison. A lot of the inmates had been drug addicts and alcoholics, not to mention many had compromised immune systems due to stress, etcetera. I believe some of the control group had autoimmune disorder. I didn't test for it before conducting the trial, but almost half of the control subjects died as quickly as the test group subjects. Autopsies revealed enlarged livers, spleen damage, aneurysms – it was a mess. The warden at Fillmore asked me in no uncertain terms to vacate the premises immediately. I thought I had developed a miracle drug. Instead, they dubbed me Mrs. Kevorkian. Believe me, it was NOT awesome."

Jessica was almost giddy. She tried to contain her enthusiasm by knocking back the remainder of her cocktail so Lenore wouldn't detect the joy in her demeanor.

"That must have been devastating for you. I mean, you thought you'd discovered the magic bullet. Why do you think your cat and lab rats were cured while it had the opposite effect on humans?"

Lenore had been staring at a man on the other side of Jessica. He was clearly out of her league but her inhibitions had been stripped about two drinks ago. She barely caught the question.

"Lenore?"

"He's so cute."

Jessica agreed, then repeated the question.

"That's easy. There are too many anatomical and physiological differences between animals and humans. Did you know that ninety-two out of every hundred drugs that pass animal tests fail in humans?"

"Then why test on animals?"

"Animal research is an institution. Businesses depend on it, from animal breeders to lab equipment to animal feed. It's a multi-billion dollar economy. The FDA knows it, so they require animal testing, regardless of its inefficiency. I want to buy that handsome devil a drink." Her speech was slightly slurred.

"I think it's the other way around. The man is supposed to buy the woman a drink."

"Yeah, like that's going to happen." Lenore leaned over Jessica and tapped the man on the shoulder. He turned and faced her.

"I'd like to buy you a drink because you're so awesome."

The man smiled, clearly bemused by the offer. "That's kind of you, but how about if I buy you ladies another round?"

"I accept. Do you accept, Jessica?"

Jessica nodded. She had taken a cab to the bar, so she didn't have to worry about driving home. "Thank you."

Lenore leaned over and thrust her hand across the table, nearly knocking over Jessica's drink.

"I'm Lenore and this is Jessica. Oh, sorry. Senator Olshansky. And who might you be?"

"John Barber. Nice to meet you both."

Armed with the information she needed, Jessica could relax and enjoy the conversation, even though she swore to herself that if Lenore used the word 'awesome' one more time, she was going to scream. The myopic researcher was drunk and probably enjoying herself for the first time in a long time. Still, one more 'awesome' and Lenore was going to be d.o.a.

18

It was Saturday morning and despite certain trepidations, Kanen was looking forward to his date with Bonnie. He sat at the bistro table on his balcony off the master bedroom, dining on a chocolate chip lemon scone and French roast coffee. There was a slight chill in the air. The sun shone brilliantly on the adjacent hillside where a doe and her fawn were also enjoying their breakfast of shrubs and berries. It was going to be another beautiful day in Mill Valley, but even if the weather was inclement, it couldn't dampen the splendor and charm of this Marin County city.

A rooster crowed. Its cock-a-doodle-do bounced off the trees. Up until a few years ago, raising chickens in his neighborhood was non-existent, but backyard coops began popping up like food trucks. Kanen wasn't opposed to people having chickens for the eggs except when they butchered the hens after they stopped producing. His thoughts were interrupted by his cell phone ringing. He looked at the number. It was Bonnie.

"Good morning."

"Good morning. What are you doing?" Bonnie said. She was hoping he didn't notice the anxiety in her voice. She told Gerald that she forgot something at home so she could call Kanen without arousing suspicion.

"Having my scone and coffee. You?"

"Actually, I'm calling to cancel our date. Unfortunately, I have to work tonight. I'm so sorry. I was really looking forward to seeing you."

"Well, that sucks. I had a whole night of wining and dining planned. Are you sure you can't put off work until tomorrow?"

Bonnie inwardly groaned, knowing that work involved pleasing an overweight, foul-smelling dictator. If Kanen ever found out that this was part of her job description, she was positive he would never speak to her again.

"I'm sure. I'd love a rain check though."

"I'll call you. Don't work too hard."

She laughed. "I'll try not to. Have a nice weekend. Bye."

"Bye."

Kanen was disappointed. He detected the stress in her voice and wasn't sure he believed her. Then again, maybe it was for the better. As far as he could tell, there was no future with a woman who lived, worked and breathed meat. She was proud of what she did at Hinton Industries and it wasn't in his nature to expend energy trying to convert a meat eater into a vegan.

He popped the last bite of scone into his mouth and followed it with the remaining coffee. He watched the doe and fawn walk back into the woods. A hawk began circling an area dense with trees and low shrubs, intently staring below. It called out, then dove into the thicket, returning seconds later with something in its talons. Kanen picked up his cell and called Spencer.

Bonnie did her best to put on a happy face. It was no easy task. Instead of spending the evening with an attractive man and possibly having sex with said man, she was holed up in a mansion with a bully. Until she met Kanen, Gerald's attitude didn't bother her at all. It was expected and she saw him as her golden ticket to success. But now, his demands were unreasonable, his attitude barely tolerable and the sex, downright disgusting and demeaning.

After changing into her bikini, she walked out to a back yard that reminded Bonnie of a Hawaiian resort. Palm trees dotted the tropical landscape. Plumeria, hibiscus and birds of paradise hugged the slate patio. It was a typical San Francisco day; cool and breezy; but the swimming pool was heated to a glorious ninety degrees.

Lights behind the pool's waterfall changed the water from red to blue to green and back to red. Bonnie took out her iPhone and snapped some photos, intentionally leaving Gerald out of them. Later, she would add them to her computer file under 'my future.'

Dressed in sweat pants and a long-sleeved t-shirt, Gerald lay on the chaise lounge in a cabana cantilevered over the pool. He was reading the latest Clive Cussler novel. The pea green-colored shirt nearly covered his large belly, exposing a hairy bellybutton. Bonnie placed her towel on the lounge chair next to his, then jumped into the water hoping it would wash away the shame she was beginning to feel. She swam under the waterfall and watched the water change colors in front of her. She lost herself in the light show and the sound of the water crashing in front of her. For a few moments, she forgot who was on the other side of the waterfall.

A long, hot shower felt glorious and Bonnie took full advantage of the fineries she was being offered. The shower had three adjustable heads, massaging her neck, lower back and legs simultaneously. She turned the water off and then pressed the 'steam' button. A glass ceiling emerged from the wall, enclosing the shower and turning it into a sauna. Bonnie sat on the tile bench and leaned back against the shower wall. She inhaled deeply, savoring the moment.

"What's taking you so long? Get in here. Now!"

Gerald's command pulled her out of the sweet trance. She pressed the button again and exited the shower, followed by billows of steam. It slowly dissipated. Bonnie wished she could do the same. She put on her bathrobe and walked over to the bed where Gerald was laying naked. He put the copy of *Forbes* Magazine on the nightstand. "What were you doing in there?"

"Taking a shower, then a steam."

He sat up and straddled Bonnie's legs. She glanced up at the clock on the wall. It was 8:30. By this time, she and Kanen would be having dinner at a nice restaurant. She'd be sitting across from a beautiful man instead of the one now tightening his inner thighs around hers. Gerald's shiny, bald head had a few liver spots. They never bothered her before. Now he reminded her of a human toad, warts and all. She cursed herself again for being weak enough to lose her focus and desire another man. She would have plenty of time to pursue men afterwards. She closed her eyes and forced herself to visualize sitting behind an expansive desk in a large office. Next to the gold Cross pen was a placard facing all those who entered her domain. It read, 'Bonnie Rydover, CEO.'

Gerald tightened his grip on her, then untied her bathrobe, pushing it off her shoulders. He buried his head between her breasts as he thrust himself into her.

"Yes. Yes." A couple of grunts and it was over. He rested his head on her chest. Bonnie smiled to herself. That was one advantage of being with an old fart. They had no stamina. She just prayed he wouldn't have a heart attack or stroke while she was with him.

"My turn to take a shower. And steam. We'll eat after."

Gerald ambled off to the bathroom. When Bonnie heard the shower door close, she raced over to his cell phone and checked his texts. There were a few from his daughter, a couple from Miriam and then she struck pay dirt. Anita wanted to know when d.o.a. would be ready for launch. Gerald replied that he needed a few more weeks, then he'd conduct a test market. He asked her to pick a city. Bonnie heard the water shut off, then the sound of steam rushing into the glass shower. She had more time, but she had read all the texts. Feeling safe, Bonnie listened to his saved voice messages. Nothing from Anita, but there was one from Jim at Chriton Chemists, letting Gerald know that the analysis was ready. The message must have preceded Gerald's text.

Bonnie put the phone back where she found it and started to get dressed in her silk nightgown. The last line in the text ran like a loop through her mind: 'pick a city.' Bonnie's experience with the disadvantaged and downtrodden was minimal. On her way to work, it was nearly impossible to avoid the homeless. They seemed to be sitting on every block. Dirty, with unfocused eyes. Their hands out, asking for her hard earned money. She didn't dare make eye contact. Instead, she walked swiftly by, looked straight ahead. These people disgusted her and she honestly didn't care if they disappeared off the face of the earth forever. But families went to fast food restaurants. Is it fair to assume that their lives were meaningless and pointless because they were poor? 'Pick a city.'

Bonnie heard the steam shut off and within minutes, Gerald walked into the bedroom with a towel around his large waist.

"Hungry?" he said as he slipped on his pajama bottoms.

"Yeah."

"I'll let Freida know we're ready to eat."

Route 66 was a dive bar in Mill Valley. It was established in the late 50s and had every cliché bar accessory proudly displayed on its walls, from the neon beer signs to old gasoline logos, like Flying A and Texaco. Long ago shunned by the upper class Marinites as too tacky, it had become the favorite hang-out of the twenty-somethings.

After eating a plate of pasta primavera for dinner, Kanen walked to the bar. It was only a mile from his house. The atmosphere was lively with a reggae band playing and people dancing on the small, parquet-covered dance floor. Kanen walked up to the bar and quickly grabbed a seat as a young man left. The bartender spotted him.

"Kanen, my man. What can I get you?"

"Whiskey sour."

"Coming up."

Kanen swiveled around to check out the crowd. Weaning his thoughts off Bonnie proved more difficult than he thought, but he was determined to do just that. As if reading his mind, the woman on the stool next to his tapped him on the shoulder. Kanen turned, and facing him was an attractive redhead with a spray of freckles, bright green eyes and a mischievous smile.

"Looking for somebody?" she said.

"Not anymore," Kanen replied.

"I'm Lisa," she said.

"Kanen."

"Ooh. Love the name. Does it mean anything?"

The bartender brought Kanen's drink. He thanked him then said to Lisa, "Yes. It means that my parents were high when they named me. My father was suggesting that they name me Kane and Abel, Abel being my middle name, but my mom heard 'Kane and' but not the Abel part. I think they were on 'shrooms. And that, my dear Lisa, is how I got the name Kanen."

"Cool. Is your middle name Abel?"

"How'd you guess?"

She smiled. "I'm the smartest one in my family. Want to dance?"

Kanen downed his drink. "I thought you'd never ask."

He was never late, but this Monday morning, Kanen wasn't sure if he could make it to the office in time for the 9:00 marketing meeting.

"Are you almost done in there?" Kanen shouted through the closed bathroom door. He looked at his watch again: 8:05. He already missed the Sausalito Ferry and the bus would arrive at the Mill Valley station in ten minutes. If he left now he could make it. That seemed doubtful.

"Almost. Just got to get gussied up," Lisa shouted back. "If you hadn't kept me up so late, you naughty boy, I would have been able to get up earlier."

"What? You were the one keeping me up with your incredible body and energy that doesn't quit. I'm going to be in the kitchen. Can I get you more coffee?"

"Yes! A bucketful, please!" Lisa opened the bathroom door and held out her cup. He grabbed it and walked to the large Italian-inspired kitchen. DeSimone tiles were interspersed with the white-tiled countertops. They complemented the copen blue antique cupboard that was converted into an island. A copper ceiling pot rack hung above it, holding Calphalon pots and pans.

Kanen emptied the remaining coffee into their mugs, then rinsed out the coffee pot and set it to dry in the dish rack. Practically running back to the bedroom, he put Lisa's coffee on the bathroom vanity. She gathered up her cosmetics, then stuffed them into her bag. Her hair was tied back in a ponytail, exposing emerald drop earrings. She grabbed Kanen around the waist, almost spilling his coffee.

"I could go another couple of rounds with you Kane and Abel. Grrrrrrrr!"

"Hey there. We have to go. I have a marketing meeting at 9:00. Save that inner tiger for later, okay?"

Lisa loosened her grip. "Fine. Are you sure you don't mind dropping me off at work?"

"Not at all," he replied. "It's on the way."

Lisa suspiciously eyed his outfit. He was wearing a pullover sweater, jeans and tennis shoes. "I thought you said you had a meeting this morning."

"I do."

"You're wearing that?"

"Ours is a very casual office. Think Facebook casual with a vegan twist. That's Weston Foods."

"Got it." Lisa picked up her overnight bag and slung her purse over her shoulder.

It was 8:40 when Kanen pulled up to the curb at 101 California, a 48-story cylindrical glass building that many San Franciscans dubbed the soda can. Lisa leaned over and gave him a kiss.

"Thanks Kane and Abel. I had a blast. When can I ride you again?"

Kanen almost rolled his eyes, but stopped. Lisa was a force to be reckoned with and he wasn't sure he wanted to continue the reckoning. "I'll call you."

As soon as Lisa shut the door, he stepped on the gas, turning on Battery Street, crossing Market Street and then turned right on Folsom Blvd. Five hundred more feet and Kanen turned into the parking lot.

At 8:57, he practically bolted into the conference room. Most of the employees didn't notice. They were too busy talking.

Kanen loved marketing meetings. When the company was founded, his parents made a decision to include every employee in the meeting. Even Maureen Consuelo, the cleaning lady, was asked to join Michelle, Bill, secretaries, the graphic designer, everyone who wanted to participate. Employees weren't required to be vegans, but it certainly helped and it made pot lucks so easy.

Today, over thirty people were gathered in the large room, its walls covered with oversized photos of sheep, cows, goats, pigs, horses and chickens. In addition to paper tablets and pens, the conference table was filled with competitors' energy bars, muffins and scones. The participants had their choice of beverage, including coconut water and the latest drinks on the market. All in glass bottles, no plastic allowed. They wanted to introduce as many unique flavors to the group as possible. From those experiences came ideas. Some of them brilliant. Their most successful ad campaign was the brainchild of Clive, the CFO.

Kanen called the meeting to order. He grabbed a bottle of coconut water and twisted off the top. Inside the cap, it said, 'Celebrate Life!'

Bill was sitting at the other end of the table. "What does it say?"

Kanen turned the cap around, facing his father.

"It says *Celebrate Life!*"

Kanen's secretary, Jean, twisted off the cap on her coconut water and read the inside. "*You Are Precious.* I like that. Too bad it's not bigger. I'd like to put it up on our bulletin board."

Kanen said, "What if we designed our energy bar wrapper to come off easily and on the other side is a saying, an adage that people could put up at work or at home on their fridge? But instead of any old adage, we have it relate to animals or spirituality."

Maureen raised her hand. "I won't put it up on my corkboard unless there's a cute animal on it. Can we do that?"

Bill said, "I second the motion. Everyone loves to see cute animals. They can't be too cute, though, or men won't save the wrapper."

"I don't think every quote should include an animal. Let's make some of the quotes the entire wrapper, and others can have images. I think it would be really cool to have a white background with deep red text that said, *Apathy Kills.*" Kanen saw heads nodding in agreement. He turned to the graphic artist, Jeremy. "Can you provide us with some mock-ups for the next Monday meeting? In the meantime, everyone send Jeremy your ideas for quotes."

Jeremy said, "Not a problem. This will be fun."

"*Strong people stand up for themselves. Stronger people stand up for others.* I just read that one on Facebook. I'll e-mail it to you Jeremy," Michelle Weston said.

"Nice one, Mom. Let's move on." Kanen looked down at his notes. "Last week, we were discussing the possibility of having a booth at the Green Festival this November. Since our new tropical energy bars will be out by then, I think we should do it. Clif Bar and Lara Bar are always there, so we should be, too."

"Have you seen the sugar content in Clif bars? It's crazy. I don't know why they haven't switched to stevia, like us," said Clive. When the CFO started working at Weston Foods, he was overweight and pre-diabetic. Six months later and a vegan, Clive lost forty pounds and brought his insulin levels back to normal. He and Bill ran daily, usually before work.

Kanen said, "I know and stevia isn't cost prohibitive, so I don't get it. I had a Veganana Super bar. Twenty-three grams of sugar. It was delicious, but it will also be the last time I eat one."

Maureen raised her hand and said, "I think we should come up with an advertising campaign for the Hispanic community. You're missing a huge market."

"I agree," said Bill. He unscrewed the cap on the bottle and looked inside. He smiled and turned it to face the group. "It says *Howdy.*" He set the cap down. "Getting back to your suggestion, Maureen, I'd love to capture that demographic, but I'm not sure if Mexican Americans are that concerned with nutrition. Kanen, why don't you try and find studies related to the percentage of Mexican Americans who are health-conscious."

Kanen said, "I'll look into it."

Maureen smiled. "Thanks, Bill."

An hour later, the meeting was over and the group disbanded. When Kanen got to his office, he listened to his voice messages. There were thirty. One of them was from Bonnie. It was short, asking him to give her a call. Another was from Spencer. He wanted to get together that evening for dinner. As he thought about the situation he had put himself into, Kanen started to feel a tightening in his chest. He had resolved to end his brief relationship with Bonnie. It wasn't going to end well. He didn't see a need to call her back. After all, she was the one who cancelled their date. Spencer was another matter. Despite the guy's neuroses, he liked him. Kanen knew there was a good man underneath the bundle of frayed nerves and emotional instability. He picked up the phone. Spencer answered on the first ring.

"Hey Spencer. I got your message. Dinner sounds great."

"Cool. Have you been to Rawkies, the new raw vegan restaurant in Berkeley? It's really good."

"I've been meaning to go there. What time?"

"I get off work at 7:00, so how about 7:30?"

"Works for me. See you there."

"Okay. Bye"

"Bye."

Kanen spent the next hour listening to the rest of his messages. He returned some of the calls, most of them advertising-related, but he didn't mind at all. He actually enjoyed talking to sales reps. He couldn't keep track of all the media outlets, especially since the internet offered so many more choices, and the reps knew their medium, whether it was an online vegan magazine or a podcast or a web-TV program.

"Knock knock," Michelle said as she walked into her son's office. "Got a minute?"

"Sure."

She sat down on the couch. "Your dad told me that you had a date last Saturday with, dare I say, a meat-eater? How'd it go?"

Kanen went over and sat next to his mother. "It didn't. She cancelled on me. She said she had to work." Michelle looked him sideways. He continued, "I know. At first, I didn't believe her, but she called today and left a message asking me to call her back."

"Are you?"

"No. It would have been our first date, so I don't feel I owe her a follow-up call, even though I said I'd call her to re-schedule."

Michelle gave her son a steely-eyed glare. "Hold on there, buckwheat. You're telling me that you're going to shine her on, even though she's an omnivore, and go back on your word? I didn't raise my boys to be assholes. At least let her know how you feel."

Kanen leaned his head against the back of the couch. "It's more complicated than that, Mom. I'm friends with her brother and they're mortal enemies. I feel really guilty because her brother doesn't know about me and Bonnie. Listen, she works for Hinton Industries and…"

"Are you kidding me? The devil's company? Never mind. She doesn't deserve a call back. I'm glad we had this little chat." Michelle got up and gave Kanen a kiss on the forehead, then left his office. She popped her head back into the room, "Seriously, she works for Hinton? What are you trying to do, give me a heart attack?"

Kanen smiled and said, "Gotta love a rabid vegan."

Bonnie hated eating so late. By the time she finished her Stouffer's Beef Stroganoff, it was past 9:00 p.m. As she cleaned off the plate and put it in the drying rack, she started to fume. She couldn't believe that Kanen didn't call her back. He was the one who asked her out. Typical man. No, he wasn't a typical man. He was kind and considerate and he genuinely seemed to want to go out with her. She wondered if he knew she was lying. Maybe he thought she went out with someone else instead. She dried off her hands and picked up her cell. She started to dial his number then stopped. Perhaps it's for the best. He had her mind so distracted that she was not only losing her focus, but she was resenting Gerald and she couldn't have that. For a split second, she thought she could use the newly discovered food poisoning plot as leverage against him, but she wasn't conniving enough to outsmart him. She'd witnessed Gerald devour his opposition with unscrupulous precision. He was born devious. It was in the Hinton genes. He was proud of it and he enjoyed the challenge of defeating others. Bonnie was deft at playing the game, but he was a pro.

Bonnie sat on her couch and picked up the remote control. The TV came to life and Mark Harmon's face filled the screen. Satisfied with the TV's selection, she covered herself in a throw, sat back and enjoyed the temporary diversion from her normal mind patter.

Dinner with Kanen was great. Their conversation was lively and Spencer actually enjoyed himself. He was driving home from Rawkies, listening to the radio. *Happy* by Pharrell Williams came on and he started singing along. Thirty seconds into it, Spencer began to feel guilty for feeling good. Visions of slaughterhouses, fur farms, even monkeys in labs filled his head. They'll never know happiness, he thought, yet I'm feeling no pain at all. He turned the volume up and sang louder. It wasn't enough. Again, he increased the volume and sang at the top of his lungs to exorcise the visions. A split second after he noticed cars slowing down and pulling off to the side of the road, a fire truck, its siren whining and horn blaring, barreled in front of him at the intersection of University and Ashby. Spencer missed being obliterated by a 50,000 pound truck by a few seconds. His heart was beating so fast, he thought he was going to faint. He crossed the intersection, immediately pulled off the side of the road and turned off the radio. It was eerily quiet. He closed his eyes tight. He felt nauseous. "Get it together! Get it fucking together!" he yelled.

Spencer must have sat in his car for a full five minutes before he felt comfortable enough to drive. Once he parked, he made a beeline for Perry's. Fortunately, the patio door was open and the kitchen light was on. They hadn't spoken since that night he found the note with the kitten on it, but his need to see her preempted any awkwardness he felt.

Before he could say anything, Perry came out to the patio.

"You look like you've seen a ghost. What happened, or should I ask?" she said as she wiped her hands on a kitchen towel. Her hair was pulled back and she wasn't wearing any make-up. Spencer told her about his near collision and then asked if she had any pot.

"Come on in."

They walked into the house and Perry directed him to the family room with its turquoise walls and terra cotta tiled floor. He noticed a ceramic lizard clinging to the wall. Its multi-colored body shimmered in the lamp light.

"Is the lizard new?"

"Yeah. I picked it up at the flea market last weekend. Cool huh?"

"Very cool."

Perry disappeared into the hallway and Spencer heard her opening up a drawer and rustling around in it. She reappeared moments later with a bag of weed and a glass water pipe.

"What would I do without you, Perry?"

Perry began packing the pipe. "I'd say you'd be more of a wreck than you are, but I don't think that's possible. We have to find a way to keep that raw emotional fire of yours in check and save it for helping the animals, otherwise it's going to eat you alive, mister."

She handed Spencer the pipe and a lighter. He lit it up and took a big hit and held it in longer than he should have. When he exhaled, he had a coughing fit. He handed Perry the pipe.

"Let me get you some water." She put the pipe on the coffee table and went to the kitchen. When she returned with two glasses of water, Spencer had stopped coughing. He was completely baked.

"Berkeley Bazooka?" he said lifting the pipe.

"Yes sir."

"I totally approve."

"What a shocker. So, are you ready to discuss our next mission or shall I wait until you're in a better frame of mind. I have a feeling after what you just went through, you'll need more time to decompress."

Spencer stared at her with heavy-lidded eyes. He had a goofy smile on his face.

"What?" Perry said.

"You're pretty."

"Thank you."

"I mean, really beautiful."

Perry hadn't taken a hit and she was glad. She needed her wits about her without the influence of a plant that made her uninhibited and horny. Not that she would pounce on a man half her age, but she did find Spencer very good-looking, despite his flaws. Under normal circumstances, his eyes were penetrating. Stoned, they were quite harmless. They say the eyes are the window to the soul. Looking into Spencer's eyes, she saw a tender and delicate spirit.

"Let's not go there, shall we?" she said.

"I'm just saying that…"

"I know, but it's making me uncomfortable. Hey, you want to play cards?"

"I guess. Gin rummy?"

Perry laughed. "Who taught you to play gin rummy?"

"My mom."

Perry went to get the cards while Spencer closed his eyes and sat back in the chair. He was in a complete state of relaxation. His shoulders felt pliable, not tight like they were only a few minutes ago. He opened his eyes when Perry started shuffling the cards. She said, "Shall we keep score."

"Of course. How else are we going to tell when I win?"

"I'm sorry. Did you say you're going to win? I don't think so."

"Let's level the playing field. Take a hit."

"Fine." Perry lit the pipe and took a smaller hit than she normally would. She knew it would barely affect her. She dealt the cards feeling confident that she wouldn't succumb to any possible advances. She looked at Spencer sitting across from her, red eyes checking out his hand. He looked so sweet and disarming, but she knew better. She saw Spencer's unbridled rage and it was scary. She was also convinced that if she could find out what incident caused so much grief and turmoil, she could help him overcome it.

"Gin."

Perry laughed. "What are you talking about? We haven't even started yet."

"Are you sure?"

"Oh boy. This is going to be a long night."

19

"Ladies and gentlemen, can I have your attention please?" Sabrina spoke into the microphone, addressing the growing crowd assembled at the YMCA on Turk Street in San Francisco. She was a small, plump woman in her early sixties with bleached white hair, black-framed glasses and a perpetually positive attitude, despite the fact that she volunteered at the one of the Y's more dangerous locations. The Tenderloin, a tiny triangular neighborhood of roughly sixty blocks, but home to over 30,000 people, many of who live below the poverty level, had the dubious reputation of housing a majority of the city's homeless, prostitutes, mentally ill, drug addicts and drug dealers. It's the destination for buying drugs, any drug. Crack is for sale on Turk and Taylor Streets. Prescription drugs can be found at Turk and Leavenworth Streets. Coke, meth, heroin, weed. The Tenderloin offers every type of contraband to alter, twist and abandon a person's present state of mind.

There are a number of theories floating around as to the origin of the neighborhood's name. Some believe that a long time ago, when cops patrolled the rough-and-tumble area, they received premium pay for their efforts. In turn, they were able to afford prime cuts of meat. Others think that the police who worked in the neighborhood were paid to look the other way. Those well-paid officers could then afford to buy the best cut of meat, the tenderloin. And still another story of origin claims that the name came from the shape of the district. With Van Ness Avenue, Market Street, Geary Street and one block of Grant Avenue as its borders, it resembles a tenderloin.

During the day, the neighborhood can be relatively quiet. The streets are littered with trash and many doorways smell like urine. An occasional crazy person could be spouting bible verses or epithets, but most of the residents went about their day. Evening was an entirely different atmosphere. Under the shadow of the moon and faint stars, the nefarious characters came out to play. The night crawlers seeped into the fabric of the Tenderloin, thoroughly saturating the squalid area. They were the sellers and the buyers. They were the broken and lost. Many had nothing to lose or they had already lost it.

Senator Bertram Kathala felt it was the ideal place to launch Team America's new program, Feeding the Hungry. He figured it would be a good idea to begin the campaign with fast food that wasn't laced with d.o.a. Big & Juicy Burgers agreed to donate food for the launch. They had a location on the corner of Leavenworth and Eddy Streets, smack dab in the center of the infamous neighborhood.

Standing next to Sabrina, Bertram surveyed the crowd as he waited to be introduced. In front of the stage, a hollow-eyed man with matted black hair and dirty clothes stood with his mouth slightly open, as if he was about to speak. Next to him, a Latino girl, no older than seventeen, cradled a baby in her arms with another child, around three, holding onto her dress. It was Bertram's target audience. When he thought about the state and federal funds poured into the Tenderloin and other depressed areas, it made him sick. There were a tiny percentage of survivors, exceptional people who were able to crawl out from the poverty and utter despair of their living environment. They left behind the vast majority who would remain in the lower strata of society. Even if ten percent made it out, Senator Kathala didn't feel they were worth saving.

Before meeting Sabrina at the YMCA, Bertram visited the Social Services Department on Ellis Street. As he walked up to the entrance, the first thing that hit him was the smell of urine, feces and bad hygiene. He almost gagged as he stepped over a woman passed out on the stoop. Inside, the office was full of people, all waiting for their hand-out. The small reception area's pockmarked walls were a sickly yellow, the color hidden by an occasional piece of paper. State and federal laws were displayed, stuck to the wall with whatever was handy: tape, pushpin, thumbtack, even gum. The linoleum floor used to be a sky blue. It had long since succumbed to the grime and filth the welfare recipients tracked in on their bare feet or well-worn shoes.

He walked through the crowd, trying his best not to make physical contact while plastering a smile on his face. He almost made it to the counter unscathed, but a woman holding her belly and softly moaning lost the contents of her stomach on his shoe. His $435 Bruno Magli light brown loafers. He looked down at his foot in horror. He started to feel queasy.

"Senator Kathala!" yelled Sondra Levy. She motioned for him to come around the counter and told her associate to take over the front desk. Bertram reluctantly walked over to where she was standing, passing a young man, eyes cast downward, hands jerking, mumbling something incoherent. Sondra grabbed the senator's hand and brought him through the back to the bathroom. She wet a washcloth and started to clean his shoe. At first he objected, but when she insisted, he let the social worker continue. She was probably used to it. He looked down at Sondra's head. Her part was crooked and her mostly gray hair looked like it needed washing. She was dressed in jeans and a short-sleeved shirt. They were worn but clean.

"I'm so sorry, senator. We're used to this, but I bet it's not something that happens where you work."

Bert said, "My fellow senators and I wouldn't dare throw up on each other, but we think about doing it all the time."

They both laughed and she continued to clean off the last remnants of undigested food. Little did she know that, no matter how stellar of a job she did, Senator Kathala would throw away his Bruno Maglis as soon as he returned to the hotel.

Sondra showed the senator into an office. The only difference between it and the reception area was the smell. It reeked of air freshener. Otherwise, the walls and floor were practically identical. Sondra explained that there were way too many welfare recipients and not enough employees and money to service them all. The Tenderloin or the Loin, as it's sometimes called, had more indigents than any other section of the city. And it wasn't getter better.

"I really appreciate your food program, Senator. It will help a lot. What would help even more is a program to get these people back on their feet."

Bert surveyed the crowd from the office window, then said, "I don't mean to be disrespectful, Ms. Levy, but were these people ever on their feet?"

Sondra looked at the senator with tired eyes. She sighed. "Yesterday, a family of four came through those doors. The father had been laid off over six months ago, but he was determined to get another job. His wife is also looking for work. They're living at The Woodlands, one of the Loin's seediest apartments. It's the best they can do right now. The best I can do is find them employment. So to answer your question, some of these people were on their feet, but got knocked down." Sondra looked at Bert's shoes, his tailored suit and silk tie. She was tempted to ask him why the Republican Party was determined to eliminate federal programs that helped those in need. Instead she said, "We're living in a very hard period. I'm sure you've heard it countless times, but the rich are getting even richer and the poor are getting a helluva lot poorer. I started working in social services ten years ago. The number of people walking, crawling and shuffling through these doors has more than doubled."

Bert thought about the introduction of d.o.a.-laced food to the Tenderloin population. He was completely sincere when he said, "Sondra, I promise you that I will do everything in my power to reduce the number of welfare recipients, not only in this area but across our great nation. I can almost guarantee you that you'll see those numbers drop." He glanced at his watch. "It was a pleasure meeting you, but I'm expected at the YMCA to begin our free food program. You're more than welcome to join us."

As he stood, he looked down at his shoe and inwardly cringed at the recollection of its demise.

"I appreciate the offer Senator, but I have a lot of work to do. Enjoy the rest of your visit to San Francisco. I hope you're going to frequent some of our more elegant areas."

He wanted to say, 'You bet your ass I am,' but instead replied, "Most definitely. My hometown of San Diego is number one. San

Francisco is number two. I won't leave until I have a meal at Fisherman's Wharf."

Sondra walked him out, trying to avoid another disaster. It wasn't uncommon for some of her clients to spit on anyone wearing a suit and tie.

Back at the auditorium, Sabrina introduced Senator Bertram Kathala. There was scattered applause. He thanked Sabrina and went on to read his prepared speech, lauding the great city by the bay and the greater people who lived here. Blah, blah, blah. He knew they didn't come to meet the California senator who represented them in Washington D.C. They were interested in getting a free meal. Bert directed the three hundred plus crowd to line up at the front of the tables on either side of the room. There, they would be given a bag containing a hamburger, French fries, a chocolate chip cookie and discount coupons for future Big & Juicy Burgers purchases.

Surprisingly, everything at first was orderly and calm. About ten minutes into the giveaway, what sounded like a fight erupted in front of a table at the south end of the room. Sabrina rushed over, followed closely by Bert, who was getting ready to leave and take a long, hot shower in his hotel room. When she reached the middle of the line, she knew exactly who the problem was: Cody Brant. It wasn't his real name. That's what everyone called him because he could sing every single song the famous country singer had recorded. He stood well over six feet tall with dreadlocks that landed near the middle of his back. No one had ever seen Cody without his signature black and tan cowboy boots, well-worn Levi's and one of three long-sleeved plaid button-down shirts. His dark skin was weathered and worn, belying his age. He claimed he was forty, but looked ten to fifteen years older.

Pointing his long, bony finger at the volunteer, he said, "I told you. The extra meals aren't for me. They're for my friends who couldn't make it."

"Cody, the rules are one bag per person. Tell your friends to get over here."

Sabrina shook her head. "What are you trying to pull now, Cody?"

He turned his attention to Sabrina and Bert. "All I'm asking for are three more meals. My friends couldn't make it. C'mon Sabrina, you want them to go hungry another night?"

People in the line started complaining about the hold-up. Some were telling the volunteers to give Cody the extra meals. Others told them to kick him out without any meal at all. Finally, Sabrina asked the volunteer for four bags, then she turned to Cody and said, "I'll give you these if you sing us a song. You know, sing for your supper, Cody Brant."

He smiled and said, "Any requests?"

"*We Shall Dance*," Bert said. "It's my favorite Cody Brant song. You can use the mic on stage."

"I'd rather sing, *Keep the Beer Coming.*"

"Not your choice, Cody."

"*We Shall Dance* it is, Mr. Senator Man."

With his size thirteen boots clicking across the wood floor, Cody walked up the steps to the stage and faced the crowd. He cleared his throat, then began singing in a voice eerily close to the real country crooner.

"I can see you, standing next to him, looking like a rainbow beside a beige sky. I can hear you, talking to him, asking him shall we dance? But he can't see your beauty. He can't see your style, so when he turns away, I ask you, shall we dance? Yes, we shall dance."

As he continued to sing, Bert was dumbfounded. He couldn't believe this beautiful voice was emanating from a giant black man. Most of the people left as soon as they got their bag of food. Some stayed to listen as Cody sang the melodic ballad. No one was close enough to see the tears streaming down his face.

After the crowd talked him into singing one more song, Cody strode out of the YMCA. Grease from the French fries seeped through the four bags, staining the Big & Juicy logo, turning it a darker yellow. He walked with purpose down Leavenworth. When he reached Ellis he turned left, then right on Hyde, stepping over a broken bottle of Coors beer. As he approached the corner of Hyde and O'Farrell, he could hear the dogs barking.

Cody went to the far end of Jake's Auto Repair and Salvage garage. The chain link fence surrounding the business was bolted shut. Razor wire sat menacingly on top. Two emaciated pit bulls, chained to stakes, came as close to the fence as their restraints would allow, barking over each other, greeting Cody. They knew him well.

"San! Fran! How are you? I brought you something. What's that? Yes, it's in the bags. Want to see?" He scanned the lot until he found their water bowl. It was empty. Just as he expected. He removed a collapsible bowl from his pocket and shoved it through one of the holes in the fence. Then he grabbed his water bottle and filled it to the brim. The dogs drank greedily. When they were done, he retrieved the bowl.

As he sang *I Won't Ever Forget You*, he pulled a hamburger out of one of the bags, along with the fries. He broke the burger apart in two pieces and slipped them through the fence to each dog. The French fries were next. As San and Fran gobbled up the food at record speed, he proceeded to the next bag.

Satisfied that the dogs had enough to eat and drink, Cody continued down the street. His pace slowed as he approached an empty lot. Two ramshackle homes stood on either side, their shingles barely clinging to the plywood siding. He walked to the far end of the lot and peered over the fence. Surrounded by dirt, errant tufts of brown grass, rocks and trash, a small mutt named Carmen lay on the ground, seemingly lifeless. Her fur was matted and sores covered her torso. When she saw Cody's face peer over the fence, she slowly pulled herself off the ground.

"Carmen, my love, look how pretty you are!"

As Cody pulled the hamburger out of its wrapping and broke it into bite-sized pieces, Carmen became more animated. She got up on her hind legs and started barking. He threw the pieces over the fence and Carmen ate them up. He decided not to give her the French fries because he knew from past experience that she didn't respond well to fried foods. He did break off a tiny piece of the cookie, making sure it was devoid of chocolate chips, and threw it to the diminutive mutt. It was eaten in seconds.

"I'll see you later, pretty girl. You be good."

Carmen started to jump against the fence, trying desperately to reach her friend on the other side. Cody stretched his hand as far as he could and was barely able to touch Carmen's head. Exhausted, the little dog gave up and went back to her spot, a depression in the dirt, and lay back down. Months ago, Cody called animal control, claiming the dog wasn't being given sufficient shelter and care. A humane officer stopped by the home and found that they provided Carmen with the necessities. She had food and water, even a lean-to for shelter. They promised the officer that they would take her to the vet for her skin condition. They never did. And the humane officer didn't follow up. Cody visited her when he could, bringing her food and companionship, albeit limited. If his apartment allowed pets, he would have stolen her long ago. Instead, he had to settle for occasional social calls.

With two bags remaining, Cody crossed the street to the park and sat down at one of the picnic tables, finally feasting on his hamburger and fries. He drank what was left of his water. When he got up to leave, a sharp, burning pain seared through his left leg, nearly immobilizing him. He let out a low groan and sat back down, vigorously rubbing the affected area, hoping it would ease the discomfort. After a few minutes, the pain subsided and Cody was able to slowly walk to his last destination.

Twenty minutes later, Cody came up to a cardboard box, otherwise known as home to Della Foster, one of the first people he met when he came to the Loin seven years ago. Since then, Della had deteriorated, her mental state more fragile than when he first laid eyes on the small, frail woman. Cody guessed that she suffered from bi-polar disorder. He was familiar with the symptoms.

"Della. It's Cody." He knew she was in there. He could see her foot sticking out. Still, he patiently waited for her to answer. After a few minutes, the box began to move and Della emerged from her living quarters. She smiled, exposing more gum than teeth. "My friend."

"Hey Della. I brought you some food." He handed her the last bag. She peered inside and her eyes lit up.

"Such precious cargo," she said, picking up the hamburger and examining it as though it were a gourmet meal. She gently unwrapped it and ate it slowly, not because she was savoring it, but because the few teeth she had were loose.

Cody leaned against the wall. He absently rubbed his left leg, trying to dissolve the remnants of the ache. He started to sing,

"Every life is a journey and that journey is a gift. I look up at the sky at night and see the sun shining bright. In my heart. It's in my heart…"

Della loved it when Cody serenaded her. She thought he made up the melody and lyrics as he sang. She didn't have a clue who the real Cody Brant was. Most of the time, she didn't have a clue as to her own identity.

20

"I think this should be our last meeting for a while. The less we're seen together the better, even if it is within the confines of my home." Anita was standing next to the liquor cabinet, refilling her glass with scotch.

"I totally agree," Jessica said. The others nodded.

Anita continued. "I also think it was a great idea to do a pre-launch of the Feeding the Hungry program. It gave me the opportunity to see just how many people responded to the giveaway. I got Big & Juicy Burgers and Delaney's Fried Chicken to reduce their prices by twenty percent in the most impoverished areas of Virginia. It was a valuable marketing ploy for them, as well."

Olivia chimed in. "This whole experience was quite an eye-opener for me. I always avoided downtown Charlotte around Tryon Street, but that's where we set up the giveaway and, my oh my, I've never seen so many live people who looked like zombies. Honestly, I think we're doing these folks a favor. Can you imagine living with heart disease or cancer? I can't. If I did suffer from a debilitating illness and I couldn't afford health care or didn't take care of myself, ending the suffering would be a blessing. Big & Juicy Burgers donated the food and Victory's already signed up for next month's giveaway. The beauty of the program is that other senators are interested in creating a Feeding the Hungry program in their states. They're unknowingly helping us. I love it! How'd you do, Jessica?"

Jessica was half-listening. She was reliving her Saturday afternoon in Billings. She decided not to tell the group everything that happened.

"It was quite an experience. My dad joined me. He's such a media whore, I mean hound. He doesn't miss an opportunity to get in front of the camera. He nearly upstaged me. Nearly. Anyway, I won't get into family politics. Before I went to Billings, I asked my aide to get me statistics on the homeless." She took out a piece of paper. "Over 2,000 homeless individuals and families live in Billings during the course of one year. Almost one-third are employed. Others are on welfare, which means most of them likely frequent fast food restaurants, the most popular being Victory's. Based on that info, I got them to donate the food with coupons for the event. The number one drug in Montana is…anybody?"

Bert said, "Hay?"

"Very funny. I wish. It's meth. What I wouldn't give to wipe out the meth addicts. Oh wait, I may have my chance! We had well over three hundred people show up. For the most part, it was a civil crowd. We did have a kid who tried to knock over one of the volunteers and grab a whole box of burgers. He was restrained and taken away by the cops. I heard some people call him a tweeker. He was rail thin, had horrible acne and his teeth looked rotted to the bone. It wasn't a pretty sight. The drug should be in the food supply by our next giveaway, correct?"

All eyes turned to Anita. "Absolutely. I was assured that it would be surreptitiously injected into the burgers, chicken fillets and nuggets by early next month. That gives us time to set up the giveaways by the third week in June. Gerald wanted to do a preliminary test in one city, but I talked him out of it. I don't think it's necessary and it would only delay the grand launch." She turned to Bert. "You haven't told us about your burger party. Care to fill us in?"

There was no doubt in Bert's mind that their plan was the most efficient way to preserve the country's integrity and natural resources, yet his thoughts drifted to Cody. His rendition of *We Shall Dance* touched him. The man was unlike the others. He emanated a genuine empathy for those less fortunate than himself, a rare trait, not only among the inner city group, but anywhere. Aside from being mentally unbalanced – who memorizes every Cody Brant song? – Bert assured himself that the African American, dreadlocked Cody was physically healthy. He had nonchalantly asked Sabrina about the man's well-being and, as far as she knew, Cody wasn't an alcoholic or drug user. She said he came from a mental facility somewhere in Kansas, but wasn't sure why he had been there.

Bert began to recount his Tenderloin trip to the group, including the incident at the social services office as well as his introduction to Cody.

Jessica said, "I bet he took those extra bags of food for himself. You said he was a big guy, right? You can't trust those people."

Bert was about to question her blanket generalization, then thought better of it. Instead, he took a big sip of his scotch and let it dull his memory of the Tenderloin.

Anita said, "I know we don't need to be reminded, but I'm going to say it anyway. Please don't leave a paper or text or electronic trail. If there was the slightest supposition that we were plotting to poison American citizens, I can't even imagine the consequences. The only other person outside of this group who knows is Gerald Hinton and I can assure you he's discreet." She glanced at the clock. It was almost 9:00 p.m. "Shall we call it a night?"

"Fine with me," said Jessica. She was looking forward to going home, unwinding and watching her favorite show, *Nashville*.

Olivia and Bert nodded. They exchanged good-byes and agreed to meet at the end of June.

Bonnie's self-confidence was upended. She was positive Kanen would ask her out again, but after more than a week and no phone call, she began to doubt the power she thought she had over men. She tried to hide her wavering self-esteem. It wasn't working. The last time she was summoned to Gerald's office to perform her obligatory duty, he must have detected an attitude because he grabbed her hair, pulled her head away from his crotch and pushed her to the ground. It startled Bonnie and left her feeling even dirtier and more shameful than normal. Without saying a word, he excused her with a brush of his hand.

She had opened the desk drawer, pulled out a tissue and wiped her mouth, then applied the cherry red lip gloss. As she was leaving, he said, "Did Dell tell you that he's unable to attend the Delacross Marketing Convention? You'll be going in his place."

Momentarily caught off guard, Bonnie said, "When is it?"

"Thursday, Friday and Saturday at the Marriott in San Diego."

"As in the day after tomorrow?"

"Yes."

"We don't normally attend that convention. Why was Dell even going?"

"Not that I have to explain, but Grant Delacross is an associate and he asked me if we could send our marketing director this year. I agreed and Dell was set to go. Some last minute emergency came up and he had to bow out. Is there a problem with going?"

"No. Not at all."

"Good. You can get the specifics from Dell. Reservations at the Marriott have already been made. You can even take his flight. I believe it's on American." Before Bonnie could ask another question, Gerald picked up the phone. She got the hint and left.

By the time she got back to her office, she was fuming. She knew Dell didn't have an emergency. He set her up and she couldn't do anything about it. Bonnie dialed Dell's extension. He picked up. "Yes?"

"Dell. It's Bonnie. When you have a chance, I'd like to come and pick up the info on the marketing convention."

"It's on my secretary's desk. Any time is fine."

"Thanks."

"My pleasure." He hung up. Bonnie felt like slamming down the phone. "I'm sure it is, asshole."

Bonnie arrived at the Marriott in San Diego on Wednesday evening and by 9:00 p.m. she had changed into jeans, a pullover sweater and tennis shoes and was sitting poolside, drinking a piña colada. She could tell by the number of people lounging in the area that many of the convention participants had arrived. She slouched low in her chair, hoping to deflect any unwanted attention. Bonnie knew she should be more sociable. After all, she was representing Hinton Industries. At the moment, she wasn't in the mood to represent anything but a disappointed human being. Gerald was becoming more of a tyrant, his sexual demands frequent and perverted. She could abide handcuffs, but when he gagged her and bound her feet in wire, she had an internal fit, silently screaming and cursing him. The incident didn't last too long, but the bruises on her legs from the lamp wire lingered for days. She had given up on Kanen calling her. The one bright spot in her life was extinguished before given a chance to shine. If she hadn't had to cancel their first date, who knows what could have been.

She took a big, long sip of her very sweet alcoholic beverage, sucking on the straw long and slow, thinking about how she would like to be almost anywhere but here. She glanced over at the pool, watching the turquoise water barely moving, almost glassy. The meditation was disrupted by a teenage boy cannonballing off the diving board. Water sprayed Bonnie and some of the other guests. She shot up from the chair and the piña colada fell off the table and smashed to the ground. Normally, she would have been upset. Not tonight. Instead of complaining, she decided to call it a night and prepare for the conference. After breakfast, she was going to attend the 10:30 workshop entitled, *Creating a Mix: Using Online Advertising to Effectively Support Your Social Media Strategy*. It was being given by Oscar Rodriguez, Marketing Strategist at Victory's, one of Hinton's biggest clients.

As Bonnie waited for the elevator, she finger-combed her damp hair, trying to get it to dry a little faster. She looked down at her clothes which were also spotted with water.

"Were you swimming with your clothes on?"

Bonnie turned around and came face to face with Kanen Weston, looking every bit as desirable as when she first saw him protesting in front of KFC. He was toting a suitcase and garment bag. Her surprise at seeing him turned to anger.

"Is this your alternative to calling, tracking me down and following me to San Diego? You vegans sure are a strange bunch."

"Didn't you know, the element of surprise is essential to our survival? Can I buy you a drink and explain what happened?"

The elevator doors opened and Kanen followed her in, along with three other people. Bonnie looked him straight in the eyes.

"I would love an explanation. Shall I meet you at the bar in, say, fifteen minutes?"

"Works for me."

"Good."

They stood in silence as the elevator stopped twice, eliminating the three other guests. The thirty-third floor button was the only one lit. "Same floor," Kanen said.

"Aren't you the observant one?"

"Here's another stellar observation for you. I bet you're here for the marketing convention."

"That would be a given since we're both in marketing." Despite her anger, she could almost see the sexual tension in the small, enclosed space. She wanted to hate Kanen, but her libido was dead set against it.

Finally, they reached their floor. Kanen let Bonnie leave first and when she turned right, he followed.

"What's your room number?" Kanen asked.

"3302. Yours?"

"3304. Coincidence or fate?"

"Coincidence." Bonnie slid the key card in the slot. "Why don't we just meet right here in fifteen minutes, okay?"

Kanen nodded. "See you soon."

As soon as Bonnie closed the door, she peeled off her damp clothes. In the bathroom, she found the hotel hair dryer and plugged it in. As she dried her hair, she assessed the damage to her make-up from the cannonballer. Except for a slight run in her mascara, her face looked fine.

Fifteen minutes later, Bonnie walked out of her room looking and feeling immeasurably better than when she walked in. She traded her jeans for black slacks, the pullover for a light pink button down cotton shirt and gained three inches in height with a pair of strappy Jimmy Choo sandals. She decided to wear her new diamond drop earrings tonight instead of at the Friday evening keynote speaker dinner.

Bonnie was the last person Kanen expected to see. His normal calm demeanor was shaken, especially since he never returned her call. He felt like a heel. It wasn't how he usually conducted himself when it came to women, but up until now, he wasn't attracted to someone who worked for the meat industry, let alone any industry that exploited animals. Once he walked out the hotel room door, he was almost positive he knew how the night would end. His nerves turned into excitement. After all, Kanen Weston may be a hardcore animal rights activist but he was also a sexual being and, at the moment, he didn't care if Bonnie Rydover slept in a teddy made of steak tartare.

As Bonnie glanced at her watch, Kanen opened the hotel room door. He was wearing the same clothes, but she could tell he washed his face and combed his hair.

Trying not to gawk, Kanen said, "You clean up very nicely. You look beautiful."

Despite her lingering anger, she blushed. "Thanks."

They preferred to sit, but the bar was packed. As luck would have it, they were standing behind occupied barstools ordering drinks when a very drunk couple almost fell off the stools and left. Undoubtedly, they were going up to one of their rooms. Bonnie and Kanen quickly filled the void.

Shouting over the crowd, Bonnie said, "You have the floor, Mr. Weston. Please tell me all about why you shined me on."

Kanen lifted his gin and tonic to Bonnie, took a long gulp, and then said, "You know I find you extremely attractive. That's why I asked you out and I was looking forward to it, then you cancelled our date. Did you really have to work that night?"

"Don't try changing the subject."

"Yes, ma'am." He cleared his throat. "Where was I? Oh yes, back to the day you cancelled on me. When I said I would call you to re-schedule, I had every intention of doing so, but then the more I thought about it, the more I realized that we are so diametrically opposed to each other's values and lifestyles, that it didn't make sense to, you know, get together."

"Why didn't you call me back when I left a message on your work phone? Were you not man enough to give me an explanation? Did you think that because I work for a meat supplier, that makes me cold-hearted and uncaring?"

Suddenly, Kanen felt remorseful. "I'm sorry. I have no excuse for not returning your call. Please forgive me."

"No."

"No?"

"Uh-uh. I won't forgive you until you spend the night with me." Bonnie leaned over and kissed Kanen. It was forceful and intense and he loved it. He kissed her back just as hard.

They couldn't pay and leave the bar fast enough. Bonnie practically had to run to keep up with Kanen's long stride. Once they were in her room, they fell on the bed. But instead of ripping each other's clothes off, Kanen slowed down and gently unbuttoned Bonnie shirt, stopping to kiss her tenderly. Even when she tried to unzip his pants, he stopped her and continued to undress her unhurriedly. She finally got the hint and lay back, relishing his touch.

After they made love, Bonnie lay in Kanen's arms. She had been treated like an object for so long that she had forgotten what it was like having a man give himself to her and wanting to give in return. When he started to get up, she said, "Where are you going?"

"To get some water. Would you like some, too?"

She nodded.

Kanen returned and handed her a glass of ice cold water. He took a drink from his own glass, then grabbed a coaster, put it on top of his glass and turned it upside down. Bonnie instinctively moved away. She didn't want to get drenched for the second time. The coaster didn't budge.

"You want to know why it didn't spill?"

"It's magic?" She said.

"Nope. When the…"

"Please don't tell me." Bonnie placed her glass on the night stand and put Kanen's arm around her as she snuggled against him.

"Why?" he said.

"I don't want to know how everything works. It's nice to believe in magic, especially when I don't have any in my life right now. I haven't since…it's been a long time."

Kanen was about to say something, then stopped himself. He stroked Bonnie's hair and wondered what was going on in this complicated woman's mind. Maybe she and her brother weren't that different. She seemed so vulnerable.

"I wish we didn't have to leave this room at all. Can we forget about the convention and have sex all weekend?" Bonnie looked up at Kanen, hoping he'd agree.

"I can't. I have too many appointments and I bet you do, too. But we can meet back at the room when we're both free. As a matter of fact, I have some time right now."

Kanen turned to face her and once again, she was transported into a place that she never wanted to leave.

21

onnie practically sleepwalked through the convention. She knew that she could learn more about using social media in Hinton's marketing strategies, but it was hard to concentrate on the seminars and speakers when every part of her being was thinking about Kanen. He was the first man she'd slept with without having an ulterior motive. He couldn't give her a better test score, a free upgrade on a car or a fancier job title. It was scary and exhilarating at the same time. Her heart became part of the relationship for once. She never even came close to giving it away and now she wore it on her sleeve.

Fifteen more minutes until lunch. Kanen wanted to order room service, but Bonnie had to wine and dine the marketing director from Victory's. She promised Kanen that she would meet him for dinner. They decided to order in.

Taking copious notes on his laptop, Kanen was amazed at how he could listen to the speaker wax poetic about Digital Media Tools of the Trade and still relive the night with Bonnie. She was delicious. She was eager and responsive to his every touch. He almost laughed out loud, thinking about his parents' reaction to his latest dalliance. He didn't care what anyone thought about Bonnie, even Spencer. He also wasn't sure if this was a fling or something that could actually evolve into a full-blown romance. At the moment, he was thinking about dinner and dessert.

The customer came up to the register and gave Spencer her purchases. He smiled and took the books from her.

"How are you today?" he said to the attractive brunette. She returned his smile. "Great. How about you?"

"Fine thanks."

Spencer scanned the first book, then the second. When he saw the title of the third book, he felt sick to his stomach: *300 Recipes Using Bacon.* His instinct was to say something to the woman, but he knew that he could get fired and he needed this job, so he scanned the loathed cookbook, told the woman her total and helped the next customer in line. Thankfully, she was buying a knitting magazine.

It was after 8:00 p.m. when Spencer finally got off work. Driving home, he thought about what his perfect job would be. He knew he didn't want to work for any company involved with animal exploitation. That included stores that prepared or sold meat and dairy, and restaurants that did the same. He figured that working in a bookstore would be benign, but he was wrong. He acknowledged that his reaction to books or magazines involving animals being hunted or cooked or mistreated was extreme, yet he didn't know how to change it. Maybe Perry could help him find an ideal job. She had a lot more experience than he did. Plus, he enjoyed her company. She was one of the few people he felt at ease around. She didn't judge him or admonish him for his beliefs.

Pulling into the driveway, he was surprised to see three other cars parked along the street. Usually, the space in front of Perry's house was vacant. As Spencer approached the gate to the yard, he heard laughter and women's voices. He looked up and saw Perry sitting on her deck with four other women. He immediately felt self-conscious and tried to quickly walk to his cottage. Perry spotted him.

"Hey Spencer, get over here. I want you to meet my friends."

"I just got off work and I'm starving. Maybe another time."

He continued toward the cottage, but Perry was insistent. "I have food here. C'mon, Spence. Can I call you Spence? Who knows when these gals will grace me with their presence again?"

"I won't," said one of them.

"Hell, me neither," replied another.

"See?" Perry said. "So get on up here, mister."

Spencer knew he was outnumbered and the thought of having dinner served immediately was appealing, so he sauntered over and walked up the flight of stairs to the deck.

The table was covered with the remnants of their dinner: dirty plates, empty and half-consumed beer bottles, wine glasses and two opened bottles of wine. There remained a third of the lasagna and a healthy serving of salad in a large bowl.

Perry said, "Sit down. I'll get you a plate and silverware."

Spencer sat between Alica Ward and Lana Yarlson. Both women were in their late forties.

"We've heard a lot about you," said Alica. Her long, black hair was pulled back in a ponytail. In the evening light, she looked like she was in her thirties. "Would you like a glass of wine?"

"Actually, I'd rather have a beer. Is that okay?"

Lana grabbed an ice cold beer from the cooler behind her chair and handed it to Spencer. "Here ya go, kid. I'm Lana, by the way."

"Thanks Lana," he said as he twisted off the cap and drank. He looked at the label and laughed. "Brass Castle Brewery, Bad Kitty. How appropriate. It must be vegan, right?"

"Of course. We're all vegans here."

"Damn right we are," said Perry as she reappeared with a plate and fork. She handed them to Spencer. "Help yourself, kiddo."

"I made the lasagna. I hope you like it," said Gretchen. She was the oldest in the group at sixty-two. Her silver grey hair was cut short above the ears and her light blue eyes sparkled when she smiled.

"And I made the salad. I'm Jeannine. Glad you could join us."

She held out her hand and Spencer shook it. He began eating and as he did, the women continued their conversation from before his arrival.

Lana waved her hands in the air. "Let me talk! I can barely get a word in with you gals. Geez! All I wanted to say was that, even though I enjoyed the movie, I agree with Jeannine. Cate Blanchett was incredible, but it was tough watching her drink and pop pills to her ultimate demise. And I hated the ending."

"That's because you love happy endings and this was anything but," Perry said as she poured herself more merlot.

"It wasn't just that. It felt like a cop-out to me. There was no resolution. Like Woody Allen got tired of writing."

"I totally disagree with you, Ms. Sunshine." Gretchen pointed her finger at Lana. "The whole idea was to show how Jasmine was incapable of changing. It was easier for her to self-medicate than take responsibility for her life. She was a stuck-up bitch. And she wore fur, so I really hated her character."

Perry said, "It's just a movie. Who cares what happens at the end?"

"I care!" said Jeannine. "Why else watch it?"

"For entertainment purposes only," Perry replied. "The acting was great. It was fun seeing San Francisco and I always like watching Alec Baldwin, even though he was a womanizing jerk."

Gretchen turned to Spencer who was taking a second helping of lasagna. She said, "If you were thinking of seeing the movie, we just totally blew it for you."

Lana said, "Something tells me that *Blue Jasmine* isn't the type of movie you would watch. Am I right?"

Spencer finished chewing his food, took a swig of beer and said, "I already saw it and I agree with Lana and Jeannine. The ending sucked. I know we're supposed to believe that she was mentally deranged, one step away from the loony bin. But it would have been nice to see her redeem herself and get help."

Gretchen shook her head, causing her large, dangling earrings to make a soft, tinkling sound. "Meet Mr. Sunshine. You guys, life doesn't always have a happy ending. Most people don't have happy endings. It's a slice of life and it was realistic."

Spencer said, "I'm not saying it wasn't realistic, I just prefer to watch a movie where I'm smiling at the end. There's too much grief in the real world. I don't need to see it on the big screen, too."

"Come on, guys. It's just a movie," Perry said. "So, Spencer, how was work today?"

"It was okay until someone bought a cookbook on bacon. I wanted to say something, but I stopped myself because I need this job."

The women grimaced. Gretchen said, "It amazes me how popular bacon is, especially considering it's so bad for your health."

Perry chimed in. "You know what you should do? Surreptitiously stick *Vegan Outreach* pamphlets in the omnivore cookbooks. Hopefully, the customers will discover the brochure when they get home. If they complain to the bookstore and you're asked about it, you can deny any involvement. Anyone can go into a store and plant literature. Berkeley's full of vegetarians and vegans. It could easily happen, right?"

Lana said, "What are you trying to do, get the kid fired? That's too risky." She turned to Spencer. "Don't do it kid."

Spencer said, "First of all, even though I'm tempted, I need the job, so I wouldn't do it. Second of all, stop calling me a kid. I'm twenty-four."

"Sorry Spencer, but all of us are old enough to be your mother and that one over there could be your grandmother." She pointed to Gretchen who promptly gave her the finger.

Lana laughed. "What? You *are* a grandmother!"

Gretchen replied, "I know. I just felt like giving you the finger. It's been so long since I've used my middle digit for that purpose. It felt good." She turned to Spencer. "By the way, I wanted to thank you for rescuing those two beagles from my horrid neighbor. You and Perry did a great deed."

"So it was you who initiated the special ops. I'm glad I did it. Unfortunately, it's a drop in the bucket compared to what I'd like to do. Billions of animals suffer every minute of every day and I feel so helpless." Spencer looked like he was about to cry.

Alica said, "Listen to me Spencer. You have to realize that there's only so much we can do. There will always be human and non-human animals in bad situations. The enormity of global suffering is immense, but when you took those dogs out of an abusive environment, you made two beagles very happy. What you feel, we all feel. We're just a helluva lot older than you and have come to the realization that whatever we do to help the animals, it's better than doing nothing. Did you know that when you feel sad, you send out sad vibrations? It's like a ripple on a lake. We're all connected, so start sending out happy vibes. Speaking of happy vibes, where's dessert?"

"Well said, Miss Alica." Jeannine turned to Spencer. "It's true, you know. We really do want dessert."

"Can't you gals be serious for longer than five minutes?" Perry said as she got up. "Dessert will be served very soon so let me see smiles on everyone's face, especially yours Mr. Rydover." As she disappeared into the house, Spencer plastered a big smile on his face.

"How's this?" he said.

"Oh honey, you are so damn handsome when you smile, even if it is exaggerated. Keep it up. Now if you'll excuse me, I have to take a jet to the john." Lana got up and went in the house. Moments later, Perry returned with six white porcelain cups, each filled with chocolate and whipped cream on top. The women oohed and aahed.

"Is it pudding?" Gretchen asked.

"Nope," said Perry as she placed a cup in front of each guest. "This, ladies and gentleman, is vegan pot de crème. The whipped cream is whipped coconut milk and I added a little vanilla-flavored stevia to it. I hope you all like it."

Lana returned just in time to dig her spoon into the rich dessert along with everyone else.

"Stop the presses. This is unbelievable!" Lana took another big scoop.

Spencer agreed. "Wow. This *is* amazing and I'm not a big chocolate fan."

Gretchen, Jeannine and Alica all waxed poetic over Perry's gourmet treat.

"I'm so glad you all like it. I forgot to ask if anyone wanted tea or coffee. Anybody?"

There were no takers, so Perry continued eating, happy to stay seated. She loved being a hostess. She enjoyed being a guest more. The women took turns hosting their monthly dinner. She thought about cleaning the dishes and inwardly groaned.

It was close to 10:00 when the party broke up. After the women left, Spencer insisted on helping Perry with clean-up. She finally relented and had him clear the table while she started loading the dishwasher.

He brought in the last of the dishes, put the empty beer and wine bottles in the recycle bin, and composted the leftovers in the large round composter on the other side of the deck.

"Your friends are really nice."

Perry took the plates from Spencer and put them in the sink. "Yeah, they're pretty special. I met them all years ago when I volunteered at Animals In Need. Gretchen was the office manager. What a whirling dervish she was, coordinating events, protests, even doing the marketing until I showed up and helped her out."

"How long did you volunteer for?"

"Almost six years. It was Animals In Need that got Berkeley to ban circuses in town. I was part of that campaign, knocking on doors, collecting signatures. It was a lot of work, but well worth it. Baby steps, Spencer. We have a long way to go to convince people that animals are not ours to exploit. You have to start somewhere." Perry dried her hands on the dish towel. "It's late so we don't have to do it now, but when you have the time, I'd like to talk to you about the next rescue."

"It's not that late. I'm willing if you are."

"Good. Let me finish up here. You can wait for me in the living room, okay?"

Spencer nodded and walked into the brightly colored room. He imagined what it would be like to live in a place where it was normal to have turquoise walls and bright red furniture. He wondered if Perry would let him paint the cottage walls. He'd ask her later, when he'd lived there for at least a couple of more months.

22

It was the last night of the marketing conference. For two glorious nights and one lunch, Bonnie and Kanen were intertwined. They couldn't get enough of each other. They took turns using each other's rooms for their trysts. Kanen would playfully tease Bonnie for bringing books, like *Trump: Think Like a Billionaire* and *How to Become CEO: The Rules for Rising to the Top of Any Organization*. She would rile him for having copious amounts of energy bars, vegan jerky and bags of trail mix strewn all over his room. It wasn't a match made in heaven, but it sure felt like it when they were together.

Saturday night found Bonnie and Kanen at the gala event on opposite sides of the room. They didn't want to arouse any suspicion, especially for Bonnie's clients. It wouldn't look kosher if she was fraternizing with the marketing director of one of the largest vegan food companies in the country. The guest performance was by an up-and-coming comedienne named Dylanne Claire-Benz. Her specialty was poking fun at corporations. Over 5,000 attendees laughed as she lampooned many of the businesses in the room.

As much as she enjoyed the entertainment, Bonnie started thinking about returning to the Bay Area, back into the arms and mottled legs of Gerald Hinton. She was completely spoiled by being with Kanen. She knew this would happen and almost regretted her time with him. She had one more night with a young, vibrant, sexy man and she intended on making it the best night to date. She glanced at her watch. It was 9:45 p.m. They agreed to meet right after the show.

At 10:00, Dylanne took her last bow to thunderous applause. As Bonnie stood to leave, she was grabbed by the arm. She turned around and came face-to-face with Gerald. She must have looked like she just saw a ghost because Gerald's big smile turned to a grimace. "Well, nice to see you, too."

"Gerald, I…what are you doing here?"

"I haven't been to San Diego in ages, so I thought we'd spend Sunday tooling around the city, maybe going to the beach. I'd love to see you in a bikini again." He surreptitiously touched her crotch. "Come on. Let's go up to your room. We've got some catching up to do."

Bonnie's heart dropped so fast, she was afraid the whole room heard it hit the ground. She was also praying that Kanen was nowhere near her right now. Unfortunately, he saw the whole thing.

Kanen wasn't sure what to think. They didn't talk about work and Bonnie didn't make any inferences to being with another man. Of course, if the man was her married boss and over twice her age, why would she tell him? As the room started to clear, Kanen found a seat at an empty table and sat down. He pushed away an unfinished meal of salmon and grilled asparagus. The smell of the fish repulsed him. As he sat there, he watched as Gerald escorted a clearly unreceptive Bonnie out of the ballroom. Only moments earlier, he couldn't wait to undress her and make love to her one more time. He was going to ask her if she would continue seeing him when they returned to San Francisco. The question was now off the table. He wasn't going to share her with another man, especially her boss.

Slowly, Kanen rose and walked outside. The hotel was across the street from the ocean and the smell of the sea air was soothing. He took off his tie and put it in his pocket. Then he walked across the street, past the sidewalk, the expansive grassy area, the boardwalk, and onto the sand. He took off his shoes and socks and walked to the edge of the shore. The water was cold, but not as frigid as its Northern California counterpart. He closed his eyes and took some deep breaths. The ocean air helped quiet his mind.

After walking along the shore for a while, Kanen sat on the beach and stared at the waves. His phone vibrated but he ignored it. He knew it was Bonnie. After her third attempt, Kanen read the text: 'Can't see you tonight. Unexpected guest. So sorry. Call me Monday?' Kanen just shook his head.

He went back to the hotel and walked up to the reception desk. He could hear his fellow marketing executives partying in the bar. The dance music was loud and pulsing. Normally, he'd be right alongside them, drinking and dancing.

"Can I help you, sir?" the reception clerk asked.

"Yes. I'd like to check out, please."

"Your name?"

"Kanen Weston."

"One moment, sir."

Ten minutes later, Kanen walked into his room. He immediately turned the radio on, loud enough to drown out any extraneous noise from the neighboring room. In record time, he was packed and downstairs hailing a cab. As luck would have it, he was able to book the last flight to San Francisco at 11:35.

Bonnie's last night in San Diego was supposed to be glorious. Instead, she endured hours of pleasing Gerald Hinton, feeding his enormous ego with praise while submitting to his growing fascination with bondage. It took all her willpower to endure every touch, slap, grab and pinch she felt from his greedy, cruel hands. She kept Kanen's image in her mind and closed her eyes tight so it wouldn't leave. She prayed that Kanen couldn't hear them, especially when Gerald growled commands at her. At one point, she asked him to please keep his voice down, but he slapped her and yelled louder.

The next morning, as Gerald showered, Bonnie checked her cell phone for messages. She had a few. None from Kanen. Gerald's phone was sitting on the nightstand next to his hotel key. Bonnie picked it up, eager to find more incriminating evidence, if she ever needed to use it. As she read the latest text exchange, her jaw almost hit the floor. There it was, in pretty blue and pink text bubbles. 'd.o.a. meat launches in three weeks, right?' 'That's right, Senator. Let the games begin.' Executing mass genocide of the lower class with a senator. Our government dollars at work. She made a mental note to find out which state Anita represented.

Bonnie took out her camera and snapped a picture of the text exchange. Then she snuck out of the room and knocked on

Kanen's door. When he didn't answer, she knocked louder. She was about to knock a third time when a couple walking down the hall stopped in front of the room.

"I think it's empty," said the man.

"It better be!" the woman replied.

They opened the door and, to Bonnie's surprise, the room was made up. She suddenly felt very heavy and tired. She rubbed her arms and flinched. A bruise the size of a quarter graced her right forearm. She returned to her room and waited for Gerald to get out of the bathroom. She was prepared to tell him that she'd had enough. She wanted to excel, but the cost was too high. Her rise to the top may not be with Hinton, but she knew that eventually she would embrace the title of CEO.

Gerald walked out of the bathroom wearing swimming trunks and holding two hotel towels. Before Bonnie could say anything, he said, "Get your bathing suit on. I'd like to lie on the beach with the new director of marketing."

23

"I thought we decided that we were going to test the tainted meat at our second Feeding the Hungry event, which is two weeks from this Saturday. Do you have a problem with that, Bert?" Anita sounded testy. She had a tough day on the Hill, battling with another senator over an immigration bill. She was in no mood for any further disagreements.

Olivia and Jessica looked expectantly at Bert, the lone male in their group.

"I didn't have a problem with it at first, but think about it. If we pass out harmless meals for a second and maybe even third time, we avoid any chance of suspicion when d.o.a. meat hits the restaurants."

Bert's concern was genuine. He was also thinking about Cody. Accepting free food and living in one of the most depressed areas in the city was a clue that he may not be an ideal human specimen.

Jessica interrupted his thoughts. "You have an excellent point, Bert. Why give anybody room for suspicion? Of course, we have no idea how the human body outside of a maximum security prison will react to d.o.a. Children weren't given the drug and women weren't either. It could take weeks or months to see results, which would actually be the best case scenario, creating a wider gap between the Feed the Hungry program and the effects of the drug."

Anita said, "Fine, I'll get in touch with Gerald and tell him to wait a couple of weeks after our second giveaway. Do you agree, Olivia?"

"As much as I'd like to get this thing off the ground, I think waiting is smart. Politicians are blamed for everything anyway. This is one project where I don't want to arouse any suspicion." She turned to Jessica. "So tell me, have you socialized with our researcher again?"

Jessica rolled her eyes. "Not since we went to the bar and the woman got drunk on a healthy alcoholic drink. I think it was called something like an Engine or a…"

Bert broke in. "A Carburetor. They're actually quite good."

"It figures that you knew what it was, being from California, the land of juicing and organic everything. Anyway, every other word from her naïve little mouth was 'awesome.' I almost clocked her with my purse. Luckily, she started flirting with a man at a nearby table and I was soon forgotten. I wished her luck and headed out. I believe, I hope, that was my last excursion with the awesome Lenore."

Olivia said, "I don't see why you would need to communicate with her again. We got what we wanted. Let's hope her progress with d.o.a. is slow and unproductive."

Anita's eyes just about popped out of her head. "Do you realize what you're saying, Olivia? You hope she doesn't come up with a cure for fatal illnesses? Are you nuts?"

Olivia offered Anita a condescending smile. "Honey, did you know that the chances of developing cancer, heart disease and diabetes are a lot less likely on a plant-based diet? For example, a vegan is half as likely to develop diabetes and vegan women have 34 percent lower rates of female-specific cancers. If you want to avoid all the nasty diseases, start eating vegan."

Anita was dumbfounded. Bert and Jessica were equally stunned. They all had no idea that in their midst was a vegan.

"A vegan senator from North Carolina, the hog capital of the country?" Anita said.

"Ten million hogs to be exact. Almost all in factory farms. The conditions are horrendous. But if I oppose the pork industry, I might as well kiss my senate seat good-bye. Besides, no one is making people eat pigs. If they want to suffer the health consequences, that's their damn problem."

Bert cleared his throat. "So, Olivia, how long have you been a vegan?"

"Going on five years and I prefer to say that I eat a plant-based diet. My daddy died of a heart attack when he was fifty-nine. Mama succumbed to breast cancer. She was my age, fifty-four. I vowed not to follow in their footsteps and the best way to do that was to stop eating meat and dairy. It's not popular in my state and I've kept it a secret for obvious reasons so no telling, got it?"

They all swore themselves to secrecy. Anita scanned the group. "Any other revelations? Surprises? Jaw-dropping admissions?"

Everyone shook their heads. Bert said, "How about you, Anita. Got any skeletons in that walk-in closet of yours?"

"How do you know I have a walk-in closet?"

Bert raised his right arm and swept it across the room. "If you don't have a closet the size of a small apartment in a house this size, you've been robbed."

Anita said, "It's not that big."

"The house or the closet," Bert asked.

"The closet."

Jessica snorted. "I bet. Come by my townhouse and you'll see a typical closet. Let's get back to those skeletons. Do you have any, Anita?"

Anita got up and walked behind the couch where Bert and Jessica were seated. "It's not a skeleton. It's more like a skull. My daughter Cindy is in her last year at NYU. She wants to be a social worker of all things. I guess sometimes the apple doesn't just fall far from the tree but it's plucked and thrown across the orchard. Her thesis is on the developmental problems associated with poverty in children. She's been spending a lot of time studying kids on the lower east side of Manhattan. She loves to eat at Big & Juicy Burgers. That could be a problem."

Olivia spoke first. "Honey, you only have something to worry about if Cindy has a pre-existing condition."

"She's diabetic," Anita replied.

Bert said, "Then tell Gerald to take the fast food restaurants in that area off the list. It should be a simple procedure. You said their distribution system is automated."

"I thought you were good friends with the CEO," Jessica said.

"I am, but Gerald can be unpredictable and I'm afraid if I request too many adjuncts to the original plan, he'll pull the plug."

Jessica replied, "Why don't you suggest to Gerald that you pick out the target areas together. Someone has to compile a list of the districts where the restaurants will be receiving the d.o.a. meat. Or we can all do it and then you can deliver the list to Gerald. I'm sure it's the last thing he wants to do."

Anita clapped. "That's a brilliant idea! Thank you, Jessica. I feel so much better. Now, if I could only talk my daughter into changing her vocation."

"We should probably start working on that list soon. Shall we save it for the next meeting?" Jessica said.

Everyone agreed. As they got up to leave, Anita thanked them all for coming. She walked upstairs to her bedroom. Larry was already in bed reading. She went over and kissed him on the forehead. He looked up from his book. "You're certainly in a better mood. Good meeting?"

"Great meeting."

"You ever going to tell me what you four talk about?"

Anita smiled as she walked into her huge closet and said, "Never."

24

It was their second trip up to Sunshine Kennels, a small-time puppy mill operation behind the breeder's house in Solano County, a rural part of the east bay about thirty miles east of Berkeley. Through her network of activists, Perry was alerted to the sub-standard conditions at the kennel. An elderly woman named Irene Patchett raised sheltie terriers in her back yard. The long-haired black and white spotted dogs were confined to whatever Irene happened to deem suitable living arrangements. Dogs were housed in empty refrigerators, water barrels, even an abandoned stove. Some were in cages and all were without adequate shelter, food and water. The two birthing dogs never left their cages. They were impregnated as soon as their litters were weaned, the puppies sold to pet shops and private parties. Neighbors had complained about the unsanitary conditions and the sheriff's department dispatched several officers to the house a few months back. They found a number of infractions and issued Irene a warning citation, giving her thirty days to fix the problems. Irene gladly complied, but once the citation was written off, the kennel fell back into disarray.

The first time Perry and Spencer visited Irene, they posed as mother and son wanting to buy a dog. Irene made them wait on the front porch. When she returned a few minutes later, she was holding three puppies. It was hard for them to resist grabbing them and leaving, knowing that the little dogs would be returned to subpar conditions. They told her they couldn't make up their minds and would come back at a later date. Irene mentioned that she'd be gone the last two weeks of the month. Otherwise, she was available. Perry thanked her for her time and silently thanked her for that vital piece of information.

Spencer was visibly nervous as they got closer to Sunshine Kennels as the sun was setting. "Are you sure our source is reliable? I'd hate to be there and have Irene's crazy uncle Burl walk in on us while we're bagging dogs."

Perry was driving a fellow activist's van. They weren't sure how many dogs they'd be rescuing, so it was equipped with enough cages, food and water for fifty shelties. If there were more, collapsible cages were stacked in the back of the vehicle.

"The activist who set this rescue up is über efficient and ultra conservative when it comes to planning a raid. She always has a back-up plan."

Spencer's shoulders relaxed a little. "What does that mean?"

"Well, she found out that Irene has a friend, Carlene, who comes to the house to feed the dogs twice a day, once at 7:30 a.m. and then again around 6:00 p.m. Lana found out where Carlene works and made sure that one of her co-workers invited her over for dinner."

"How the hell did she do that?" Spencer was starting to believe that these women had super powers.

Perry laughed. "Honey, we are so well-connected it's scary. Anyway, the co-worker promised to keep Carlene at her place for at least three hours. That gives us enough time to bag the dogs, as you so eloquently put it, play a game of cards on Irene's deck, take a nap and head back home. Does that put your mind at ease, just a little?"

"Yes, it does. Thanks."

Perry exited the freeway, then made a left at the bottom of the ramp onto Decker Blvd. Ten miles of country roads later, Perry pulled up to Sunshine Kennels. As she backed up and parked under the faded, rusty sign, the dogs started barking. She wasn't too concerned because the nearest neighbor was a good 400 yards away and couldn't see Irene's house unless they drove around the street corner. It was dark with only Irene's porch light providing just enough light to see where they were going.

Perry opened the back doors of the van, exposing the interior filled with cages. She grabbed her gloves, camcorder, headlight and bolt cutters. Spencer did the same.

"Ready?" Perry looked at Spencer who was fumbling with his head light. She took it from him and untangled the elastic band, then placed it on his head. He was calmer than before, but she could tell he was still nervous.

"Ready. Let's do this." They walked up to the chained backyard gate. He took his bolt cutters and deftly cut the link. The lock fell to the ground. He pushed the gate wide open. They turned on their camcorders. As they approached the kennel, the smell of feces and urine mixed with unwashed dogs was overwhelming. They both raised their neck scarves over their noses and continued, walking by rows of wooden and mesh boxes balanced on cinder blocks. The dogs, many puppies, peered out from their enclosures, clawing at their cages, fear and desperation in their eyes. Some of the dogs were stuffed into refrigerators, the doors replaced with the same cheap wire mesh. By now, the dogs were furiously barking, especially the puppies. Spencer heard moaning to his right. He looked over and his head light shone into a small cage where a dog lay on her side. She was too weak to lift her head. Her teats were enlarged, indicating that she had given birth to a litter not too long ago. Her eyes were encrusted and her coat was matted. Spencer guessed she had mange.

Perry tapped Spencer on the shoulder and pointed forward. He complied.

They walked to the end of the kennel, assessing the situation. On their way back, they turned off their cameras and counted the number of dogs.

"I counted thirteen," said Spencer.

"Seventeen on my side. Thirty dogs. We have plenty of room. Let's get to work."

As rehearsed, Spencer took the right side of the path and Perry the left, taking two to four dogs at a time and placing them in the van's cages. The food bowls were filled with kibble. The water bowls would be filled right before they took off.

The puppies were easy to handle and the breeders were as well, due to their weak conditions, but some of the adult males were feisty. Instead of carrying them, Spencer and Perry fit them with collars and leashes.

With all the dogs securely placed in the van, they returned to the kennel, checking for dogs they may have missed. As they reached the back of the property, Spencer watched as Perry stared at a spot about ten feet from the last open cage. She walked toward it and Spencer followed. It was a shallow grave. So shallow that the tail of the sheltie was visible. She had Spencer shine his light on the small mound, then took out her camcorder and recorded it. Stopping the recording, she knelt down and clawed at the dirt until she uncovered a dog. It was obvious from the belly that it was a female. There was a bullet hole in her head. Perry started to cry then quickly stopped herself. She needed to be strong for herself, Spencer and the dogs. She took a video of the tragic scene, then said, "Let's gut this hellhole."

"With pleasure."

They used all their strength to kick, push and knock down the prison cells. Every time Spencer kicked in a cage, he felt a surge of energy. One by one, Perry picked up the 12-pound cinder blocks and threw them as far as she could. Spencer followed her lead. When they were done, nothing but a pile of splintered wood and twisted wire mesh remained. The cinder blocks were erratically strewn outside the main kennel area. The refrigerators were pushed over on their sides and buckets that contained dog food were opened, the contents scattered. The wildlife was going to have a feast.

As they were leaving, they heard a dog barking inside the house. They tentatively walked up the rotted wooden steps to the back porch. Through a window, they saw a sheltie scratching furiously at the door and barking. Spencer turned the door knob, but it was locked. He tried the windows. They didn't budge.

"What should we do? We can't leave this dog behind. It's not right."

Perry looked around the yard. Trash was strewn everywhere. She walked over to a broken chaise lounge. A faded, torn bath towel lay across it. She wrapped the towel around her right fist and punched through the window next to the door.

Spencer laughed. "You're crazy and I love it!"

Unlocking the window latch, she pushed it up and climbed inside. The sheltie had retreated to the corner of the kitchen, shaking. When Perry approached the cowering pooch, she held out a dog biscuit. Reluctantly, the dog took it. She scooped the small canine into her arms, unlocked the door and walked to the van.

After securing the cages and filling the water bowls, Perry drove off with a van full of hope and promise. The dogs were quiet, except for an occasional bark or whine. Despite the smell, Spencer insisted on riding in the back with the dogs. He spoke softly to each one, assuring them that everything was going to be okay. He stayed a little longer at the two breeders' cages. One of the females put her face up to the cage door and licked Spencer's fingers. She closed her eyes and an ochre-colored liquid dripped out. With gloved fingers, Spencer wiped it away.

"Don't you worry, okay? We'll clean you up and you're going to feel so much better."

Spencer went to the front of the van and knocked on the window, then slid it open.

Perry said, "Yes?"

"Can I keep one of the dogs?"

"Sure. Those puppies are so cute."

"I want one of the breeders."

"They're in pretty bad shape, Spencer."

"I know."

"It's up to you."

Spencer smiled. "Thanks." He went back to the cage where the mama dog was sitting up, waiting for him. He took off his glove and put his fingers through the wire and touched her muzzle.

"What would you like your name to be, huh pretty girl?" Spencer closed his eyes, hoping a name would pop into his head. The van took a corner and Spencer almost lost his footing. He steadied himself and again closed his eyes. The name Gilda appeared in his mind. He grimaced, pushed it away and waited for a better name, but Gilda reappeared. Opening his eyes, he looked at the sickly dog.

"So that's the name you like? Fine. Just know that I may call you Gilley, too. It's a nickname." Spencer looked at the other dogs, many puppies, in the clean cages. "I bet a lot of these pups are yours. You poor thing." Gilda continued to lick her new friend's fingers, the taste of human skin mixed with the cage's metal bars. "You're safe now, Gilley. You'll never be mistreated again."

Perry was thrilled that Spencer was interacting with the dogs. She knew he desperately needed to bond with someone. She felt like they had become friends, even though she was clearly more of a mother figure than a friend. Still, Spencer reminded her of a younger version of herself. Perry didn't fit in as a teenager and had trouble relating to her peers. It was the opposite with animals. All they asked for in return was affection and love and she was glad to comply.

Fifteen minutes later, Perry pulled into the Solano Veterinary Clinic parking lot. The clinic was housed in a 1950s-style building: utilitarian, no-frills and little style. It reminded Perry of a very large Foster's Freeze. The architecture was almost identical with a bright blue roof which sat on a white, rectangular building. A blue stripe edged the base of the clinic. She drove around to the back of the building and backed up to the double doors. Spencer opened the van's back door and hopped out. He brushed the hair off his shirt.

"Geez, Spence, you smell like a dog."

"I guess that's what happens when you're in an enclosed space with thirty dogs." As he prepared for the dogs' departure, three people in white lab coats came out to greet the new arrivals. A woman with shoulder-length, light brown hair and a toothy smile walked up to Perry, extending her hand. Perry shook it.

"So nice to meet you," said Perry. "I can't thank you enough for helping us."

"I'm Dr. Shelby Nolan and you are very welcome. You don't know how long we've wanted to legally shut down Sunshine Kennels. Every damn time we got officers to go out there, Irene would either have the place just decent enough to pass the inspection or she'd temporarily correct any infractions. She's been circumventing the law for years." Dr. Nolan motioned the two other people over. "I'd like you to meet Shannon and Doug. They're my vet techs."

After introductions, Spencer and Perry began handing the cages to the techs. The dogs became more animated, their barking almost deafening. It took over three hours to unload the dogs and get them all situated in the clinic's kennel. At first, Dr. Nolan refused their assistance, claiming that they had done enough, but Spencer and Perry insisted on helping with the required examination, shots and bathing.

With the exception of Irene's house dog, the terriers had little if any human contact up to the rescue. Food and water was dispensed through the cage door and its floor was designed for elimination of urine and feces. Irene removed the puppies from their enclosures only when she had a prospective customer or was transporting them to a pet shop. As a result, the amount of human contact at the veterinary clinic was sensory overload. Despite being handled with love and care, the dogs squirmed and twisted as they were examined, given shots and bathed. As soon as they were placed in the kennel cages, they fell asleep.

Spencer showered and changed in the clinic's bathroom. While waiting for Perry to do the same, he went over to Gilley. She had been washed and combed, but the mange made her look like a she-wolf. Tufts of black and white hair were surrounded by scabbed, raw skin. Her trimmed nails were a welcome contrast to the rest of her neglected body. "I'm coming back for you, Gilley so you be a good girl." Spencer gave her a kiss on the head and she returned his affection with a lick on the nose.

"Don't worry. She'll be fine." Dr. Nolan gently pet Gilley's back. "We'll take good care of her and I'll give you a call when she's ready to be picked up."

"Thanks. Do you know about how old she is?" Spencer said.

Shelby gently opened the dog's mouth. She checked her teeth, then felt her rib cage and spine. "I'm going to guess that she's around two to three years old."

"That's all? I thought she was much older."

"Breeders start these mothers young. They use them as soon as they go into heat. It's pathetic. I bet this dog never touched the ground. She was stuck in that cage and constantly impregnated."

Perry walked out of the employee's bathroom. Her hair was wet and she looked freshly scrubbed. She walked up to the vet and hugged her hard. "Thank you so much."

Shelby said, "No, thank you. This is why I became a veterinarian. I'm available any time you need help. I know discretion is key, but I do have a couple of associates in the Bay Area that I think would love to donate their time and services. Would you like me to talk to them?"

Perry's eyes lit up. "That would be super!" She handed Shelby her business card. "Here's my contact info." She turned to Doug and Shannon. "And thank you both, too. You were incredible."

One more good-bye to Gilley and they were off. Spencer looked over at Perry. "Are you okay to drive? If you're too tired, I can take over."

"Thanks, but we only have another fifteen minutes before we're home, so I can handle it. Speaking of handling it, you were amazing. I was really impressed."

"I learned from the master, especially how to break into a house. By the way, do you want me to transfer the film footage onto a USB drive? You could send it to the newspaper."

"That would be great." Perry was exhausted. After the surge of energy she acquired from rescuing and cleaning the dogs, her body slipped back into normal mode. She was sore from head to toe, especially her arms. Flinging the cinder blocks seemed like a good idea at the time. The first thing she was going to do when she returned home was take a long bubble bath. Spencer, on the other hand, had completely different plans.

"I'm still pretty psyched from the rescue. Do you feel like watching a movie when we get back to the house?"

Perry shook her head. "I'm whipped. I wish I still had the energy of a twenty-four-year-old. Instead, my middle-aged body is screaming for relief. Savor and appreciate that energy source while you've got it."

"Why, because it's gone in the blink of an eye? That's what my mom always says."

"Not really. It feels like another lifetime when I was your age. When my daughter, Callie, was born, my mother said that she'd grow up so fast. Not true. It felt like an eternity."

"Why do you think?"

"Callie was a tough kid to raise. She was stubborn and argumentative and ridiculously active. When she came back from Trick or Treating years ago; I think she was five or six; some jamoke was giving out mammoth size Hershey chocolate bars. Callie wanted to eat the whole thing in one sitting. Her dad and I told her she could have some of it, but not the entire bar at once. She crossed her arms and told us that if she couldn't eat the whole thing, she didn't want it at all. Her dad and I ended up devouring the humongous bar that night. I still remember the movie we were watching: *Jurassic Park*."

"That's stubborn. Is she still like that?"

"I don't know. We haven't spoken in a couple of years." Perry took the Ashby exit off the freeway.

"Can I ask what happened?"

"She doesn't approve of my vegan lifestyle and to prove it, she married a butcher. I used to go to her place in Taos, but she would make a point of serving meat. And not just any meat. Large slabs of steak and other cuts of flesh that were cooked rare. She always had a couple of side dishes that I could eat, but the point was made. After a few visits, I asked her if she could forgo the animal flesh until I left. I only stayed a weekend at a time. She refused and her meathead husband agreed. They told me if I didn't like it, tough. I think that was two years ago. We haven't spoken since."

Spencer shook his head. "That's harsh. What did you do that was so horrible? Force collard greens and Brussels sprouts down her throat while watching *Forks over Knives*?"

"Worse. I made her go to protests with me. We would picket the circus, protest animal research at UC Berkeley. I thought her presence would make an impact on people because she was young. It did help the causes. Unfortunately, Callie would get teased at school for participating in the demonstrations. She turned on me big time. She started eating meat, going with her friends to fast food restaurants and throwing the empty wrappers in our trash so I could see them. By this time, her dad and I were divorced. They became thick as thieves, their minds were one and their goal was clear: piss me off. Ah, here we are. Home sweet home."

Perry pulled into the driveway. She looked at the clock. It was past midnight. Once Spencer's feet hit the ground, he felt incredibly tired. As they walked through the backyard gate, he said, "Whoa, I feel like I've been hit with a two-by-four. No movie for me tonight."

Perry patted him on the back. "Get some sleep, kiddo. We can check out the videos tomorrow, okay?"

Spencer nodded and waved good-bye as he headed to the cottage. Perry watched him go. He was really a great person and she felt that once his demons were exorcised, he'd be an unstoppable force for the animals. Sooner or later, she'd find out what happened between him and his sister.

25

Bonnie didn't mind wearing long-sleeved shirts during warm days to cover up the bruises Gerald inflicted after a particularly rough night of sex. She was happy to come into his office whenever he called, indulging his desire for blow jobs. If she began to feel any animosity toward her boss or started to think about calling Kanen, she would simply take out her new business card and read it: *Bonnie Rydover, Marketing Director*. Admittedly, her new position at the company brought new positions in bed, but the CEO's appetite for kinky sex was becoming commonplace. Bonnie was learning how to keep the pain to a minimum without depriving him of pleasure.

Her new office was twice the size of the old one. Instead of a glass door, it had a solid one for privacy, which she relished. She was a full-fledged executive and it was only a matter of time before she took over the company, becoming Hinton's first female CEO.

She was about to make a call when her assistant, Tammy, brought in the mail. She dropped it into Bonnie's 'in' box. "When you're done reading *San Francisco* magazine, do you mind if I look at it? The guy on the cover is hot."

"Not at all," Bonnie replied. "I'll put it on your desk when I'm finished reading it."

"Thanks."

Her curiosity piqued, Bonnie sifted through the pile of mail until she found the magazine. Staring back at her in glorious color was Kanen Weston. He was standing in front of Weston Foods looking every bit as handsome as when she first set eyes on him. Memories of their time together at the marketing convention played in her head.

She quickly flipped through the magazine until she came to the article. A smiling Kanen stared back at her, his pale blue eyes inviting and warm. She read about his childhood. How he and his two brothers were raised vegan and to date, not one of them had tasted animal flesh, eggs or dairy. Kanen's prominence in the company began before he was in high school. His predilection toward marketing and advertising came so naturally to him that he worked in the marketing department throughout high school and college.

Bonnie realized that she should stop reading. The more she knew about Kanen, the more tempting it would be to call him, but she was losing the battle of internal jousting. One more page and the article was finished.

She should have been prepared, but she wasn't. The interviewer's last question and Kanen's answer threw her. 'Our female readers would love to know if you're available and, if so, if you only date vegans.'

Kanen replied that when he marries, his wife will be vegan. He wants to be with a woman who has compassion and empathy for all beings.

Bonnie closed the magazine and sat back in her chair. Not comfortable, she got up and sat down on her new, brown leather sofa, kicking off her shoes. She chided herself for getting upset. After all, Kanen had no place in her future either, but the prospect of having to shut him completely out of her life left a hole in her heart. And Gerald certainly didn't fulfill her sexual needs. If anything, his antics in bed made her long for romantic and loving sex.

She closed her eyes and relived her first night with Kanen, his lean and toned body against hers, touching her tenderly, with desire. Her breath started to slow, then her hand went down to her crotch. When her cell phone rang, Bonnie jumped off the couch, adjusted her skirt and answered the phone. It was her mother.

"Hi dear. I'm not interrupting something important, am I?"

"Not at all, Mom. Is everything okay?"

"Yes, I just wanted to invite you over for dinner next Wednesday, around 7:00."

Bonnie checked her calendar. "Sounds good. I'll see you then."

"You're more than welcome to bring a guest, if you like."

"What do you mean a guest? Like a friend?"

"Like, you know, someone you're seeing."

"Sorry. No one on my dance card, Mom. I'll be flying solo for dinner."

She could hear her mother sigh and felt a twinge of regret for not having someone special in her life. Her mom said, "That's fine, Bonnie. We'll see you then."

She hung up the phone and stared at it, willing herself to put it down and forget about Mr. Weston. Calling him would only complicate her life.

A knock at the door brought her back to work. "Come in."

Tammy walked in carrying three 11" x 14" storyboards. "These were just delivered by courier from Ames & Leeson."

She handed the advertising agencies' mock-ups of the latest marketing campaign to Bonnie.

"Thanks, Tammy. Can you please ask Monica to come in?"

Monica Givens was the new assistant marketing director. She was older than Bonnie by a good fifteen years. Her conservative clothing and shoulder-length mousy brown hair worn in a flip gave her the appearance of an extra on the television show, *Mad Men*. Bonnie loved the fact that she wasn't the slightest bit sexy or appealing to the men in the office, especially Gerald.

Five minutes later, Monica knocked on the open office door and walked in with her day planner. Bonnie motioned for her to sit down at the small, round table graced with a vase of purple and white irises. For the next hour, she pushed aside all thoughts of Kanen and concentrated on her work.

It was almost 9:00 p.m. when Bonnie walked to the underground parking lot and got into her car. The late model Volvo S80 hummed to life. Leaving the lot, she made a right on Sutter Street. At a red light, she glanced at the passenger seat. Sitting next to her purse was *San Francisco* magazine. Bonnie was going to put it on Tammy's desk, but kept it instead. She was confused. Her feelings conflicted. The dialogue in her head between 'practical Bonnie' and 'horny Bonnie' became so distracting that she forgot to turn right on Grant Street. When she realized her error, she was already approaching Leavenworth, the heart of the Tenderloin. She always stayed away from this part of town and for good reason. It was unsavory during the day, but when the sun set over the city by the bay, the Loin became a freak show and every possible combination of human lowlife slinked out onto the sidewalks and streets. Even surrounded by steel, Bonnie felt uneasy. She sat at the red light and planned to turn right at the next street.

She was about to turn on the radio when something struck her car. She looked up and found a skinny, hollow-eyed man standing in front of her hood, baseball bat in hand. He smiled and displayed a crooked set of teeth, front tooth missing.

"How about a ride, sweetie?" the man shouted. Bonnie put the car in reverse but when she turned around, a man was standing behind the vehicle. He also looked homeless, his clothes worn and dirty. He pounded on the trunk of the silver Volvo. The light turned green, but she was unable to go. Heart pounding, Bonnie laid on the horn, hoping to scare them off and attract attention, but they stood there, stone-faced. The few people who were in the area ignored the scene. Either it was all too familiar or they didn't want to get involved.

Bonnie picked up her phone and dialed 911. Before the dispatcher answered, she jumped as a third man knocked on the driver's side window. He had greasy hair, a full beard and small, red-rimmed watery eyes.

He screamed, "Put the phone down now and open the door!" He pointed a gun at Bonnie's head. Obediently, she dropped the phone without hanging up. She slowly put her hand on the door handle, but before she could release the latch, a tall figure with long dreadlocks descended on the bearded man. He knocked the gun out of his hands and put him in a headlock. Frightened, the other two intruders fled. Without thanking him, Bonnie stepped hard on the gas and sped away. As he watched her go, Cody picked up the gun and put it in his pocket. He looked down at the bearded man. "What the hell's the matter with you? Don't we have enough trouble in the Loin without you attacking women in cars?"

The man sat up and rubbed his shoulders. "I need money."

"Get it the accepted way. Earn it." Cody walked away and continued to his destination.

Bonnie tried to calm down. She thought she was going to hyperventilate. She took deep breaths as she turned right on Larkin. Her first inclination was to call Gerald. She picked up the phone and heard the 911 dispatcher.

"Are you there? Are you okay?"

"Hi. Sorry. I'm fine now. I'm out of danger."

"Are you sure?"

Bonnie replied, "Yes, thank you. I'm fine." She hung up and dialed Gerald's cell phone. It immediately went to voicemail. She decided not to leave a message.

By the time Bonnie got home, she felt emotionally spent and terribly alone. She wanted to talk to someone and tell them what happened. Her parents would only make her feel worse, admonishing her for driving in such a dangerous neighborhood. She wasn't speaking to her only sibling. She destroyed her relationship with Kanen and she was too busy working to sustain friendships.

Her appetite destroyed and suddenly feeling very tired, Bonnie brushed her teeth, washed her face and slipped into bed, crying herself to sleep. As she drifted off, her last vision was of the tall, dreadlocked man who saved her life.

26

Days away from the second Feeding the Hungry event, Team America met for the purpose of getting an update on the progress of d.o.a.'s infiltration into the meat supply at Hinton Industries. After a meeting with Gerald on Skype, Anita received reassurance that the tainted meat would be sent only to the designated restaurants. He asked her for a list of the cities by the end of the week. He needed time to set up the channels of delivery. She was stunned at Hinton's control over the quality, cost and distribution of chicken and beef in the country. One thing was certain: she was glad to be on Gerald's good side and she would never set foot in another fast food restaurant as long as she lived, regardless of how hungry she was.

Even though Team America's members had little in common, their political leanings were very much aligned. All were Republican senators and shared the same disdain for poverty-level Americans. They couldn't be convinced that this stratum of society had fulfilling lives. In addition, if these people suffered from life-threatening illnesses, the expediency of their demise was essential. Attempts by well-meaning citizens to help the downtrodden were pointless. Of course, the senators didn't rule out the exceptions, the individuals who were able to leave their dismal lives behind and climb up into the second tier of society. But it was so rare. The cost and energy expended to help a few couldn't be justified in their eyes.

Anita walked into her study a few minutes after her guests had arrived. In her hand, she held notes from her Skype meeting with Gerald.

"I'm sorry to keep you all waiting. I wanted to print my notes." She waved them in the air, then sat down next to Jessica, who was helping herself to another cookie.

Bert said, "So what does our partner in crime want from us?"

"He's requesting a list of every restaurant and its address that will receive the tainted meat. Before you protest, I found a fairly easy way of compiling the list."

Olivia said, "I'm glad you added that, because I was about to holler. I don't know about you all, but my computer skills are less than admirable."

Looking through her notes, Anita scanned the first page, then the second until she found what she was looking for. "If it's okay with everyone, we'll break down the country into four sections with each of us taking approximately twelve states. I found a website that lists all the fast food restaurants by location, but we need to concentrate on the three that Hinton distributes to: Big & Juicy Burgers, Delaney's Fried Chicken and Victory's. City-data.com lists the top twenty-five most dangerous cities and…"

Bert broke in. "Wait a minute. This sounds more complicated and time-consuming than I imagined. Can't we use our aides to compile the information?"

Jessica shook her head. "Bert, even if your aide had no idea why they were putting together the data, we can't have anyone outside our core group knowing a single aspect about this project. Can you imagine if they put two and two together? Pardon my French, but we'd be fucked. My aides are smarter than the average bear and once the drug is disseminated and people start dying from *natural causes*, they may, just may, believe we had something to do with it. Hell, we don't even know how the drug is going to play out. This is all very experimental. Testing a drug on male prisoners tells us how the drug is going to react with male prisoners."

Anita said, "Sorry Bert. I agree with Jessica. We have a week to deliver the list to Gerald. It shouldn't take us that long. Olivia, what do you think?"

"I don't mind rolling up my silk sleeves and putting in some hours over the computer. The end result is worth the effort."

Bert sighed. "You're all right. I shall grin and bear it."

"I did some digging last night and came up with a few nuggets of info. I made copies for everyone." Anita read from her notes. "Here are some interesting facts. You'll love this Bert. According to the DEA, Baltimore and San Francisco have the highest numbers of heroin addicts and heroin-related crime of any cities in the nation, plus Oakland was ranked number nine in the top one hundred most dangerous cities. Rocky Mount, North Carolina, was ranked number forty-one in case you were interested, Olivia. Virginia and Montana did make the top one hundred." Anita turned the page and continued. "Chicago, New York and Boston have the highest heroin-related hospital admissions in the country and New Orleans has one of the highest crack problems which has also led to their leading the nation in murders -- 95 per 100,000 people -- that are known to be directly related to drugs. Don't we live in a messed up world?"

Jessica nodded. "Now we have a chance to lighten the crime rate, so to speak." She grabbed another cookie. "In case anyone was wondering, our researcher has invited me to join her for dinner next Thursday night. Anyone else interested in meeting the woman who has made this project possible?"

All three shook their heads.

"She's all yours," said Olivia. She turned to Anita. "Are we done or do you have more fun facts?"

"I've got tons of facts. You can check them out here." She handed each senator a copy. "Happy reading."

27

efore work, Kanen decided to have breakfast in downtown Mill Valley. He wanted a change of scenery and felt like being in a social environment. He found a parking spot easily and walked to Coffee Talk, a favorite hangout of the young, upwardly mobile crowd. Kanen didn't care about the ambience as much as the fact that they carried a line of vegan pastries. As he waited in the queue, he grabbed a copy of the *San Francisco Examiner* and perused the front page. A teaser photo to the right of the masthead showed a picture of a sheltie terrier and the caption read, *'Sunshine Kennels' dogs stolen. Property destroyed. See page 3 in Towns Section.'* Intrigued, he turned to the story and smiled as he read about the puppy mill raid.

Kanen ordered a tall almond latté and a blueberry scone, then found a seat and continued reading the article. One photo showed the rows of cages, some of the dogs huddled in the corners of their tiny enclosures. Others were standing, barking at the photographer. Another photo was the aftermath of the raid. Splintered wood mixed with wire mesh in a jumbled mess. Dog food was strewn on the dirt ground, mixed with garbage. To Kanen, it was a glorious site. He chided himself for not having the courage to participate in a raid on a puppy mill or engage in an activity that would free animals from cruelty. His position at Weston Foods was a big reason he resisted breaking the law. If he was caught, it wouldn't bode well for the reputation of the company and he never wanted to jeopardize his parents' business. They worked too hard to have it compromised because of their son. His father and mother were both active in civil disobedience when they were in their early 20s, but now they were responsible owners of a very large and profitable company. They preferred to contribute to animal rights' groups rather than take part in protests and rallies.

After reading the article, he thought of Bonnie. He wasn't sure why. Perhaps because she would disagree with the modus operandi of the liberators. Working in the corporate world gave her a biased opinion of flagrant law-breakers. Animal cruelty laws existed in every state, but the article made it clear that government inspectors didn't enforce the laws to the best of their ability, most likely due to a lack of resources and personnel. Animal welfare wasn't a top priority with any government institution, whether it be on the federal, state, county or city level. Until non-human animals were able to voice their opposition to abuse, they had to rely on the small number of people willing to speak up for them. Kanen knew all too well that those voices were still too few. Too easily dismissed.

The marketing meeting ended a little after 10:00 a.m. The Weston employees decided which quotes would be used for their new energy bar packaging. Michelle suggested Jeremy Bentham's famous quote, *'The question is not, Can they reason? nor, Can they talk? but Can they suffer?'* It was unanimously accepted. Maureen added, *'All beings tremble before violence. All fear death. All love life.'* Buddha. Jeremy would add graphics to some of the quotes and they would meet mid-week for review.

Back in his office, Kanen surveyed the magazines on his desk. A lot of ideas came from ads, articles, whatever caught his eye. It was one of the aspects of his job that he loved. He refrained from reading the articles, preferring to do that at home. He picked up the latest copy of *Sports Illustrated*. Serena Williams was on the cover in a post-serve pose. Kanen marveled at the amazing shape she was in. He wondered if she was still a vegan. A few years ago, Weston Foods sent a package of assorted energy bars to the Williams' sisters. Serena's assistant sent a thank you note, waxing poetic about how much Serena and Venus loved the bars.

Restless, Kanen wandered into Jeremy's office. The young graphic designer was staring at the computer screen, his light green eyes hidden behind glasses. His long hair was pulled back in a braid that fell just past his shoulders.

"Knock knock," Kanen said as he walked up to the desk. Jeremy looked up and motioned for Kanen to come over.

"Dude, tell me what you think of this." Kanen looked over Jeremy's shoulder. "I know we talked about animals next to the quotes, but I think this looks better, don't you?" Jeremy had placed an illustration of Buddha next to the words.

Kanen said, "Yeah, I do. After all, Buddha said it, right?"

"Definitely." Jeremy moved the small Buddha figure to the lower right hand corner of the quote. "Did you want to talk to me about something?"

"Nope. Just checking out the wrapper designs. I think it's a great idea and I can't wait until we're using them." Kanen's cell phone rang. He looked at the number. It was Spencer. He felt a pang of guilt. "Got to take this. Later, Jeremy."

Kanen walked outside into the courtyard. "Hey Spencer. How are you?" He didn't do anything wrong, technically, but Kanen feared Spencer would have a breakdown if he knew that he had been with his sister.

"I'm great. I wanted to see if you could come over for dinner this Friday. My parents will be there and so will Perry, my landlady."

Kanen definitely noticed a difference in Spencer's voice. He sounded upbeat. It was a welcome change.

"That sounds great. Why don't you email me your address and time. My email is 'kweston@westonfoods.com."

"Will do. I'm glad you can make it."

"Me, too." Kanen was about to hang up when he was struck with a thought. "Your sister's not going to be there, is she?"

Spencer laughed. "Not unless she crashes the dinner. Why?"

Kanen tried to sound nonchalant. "Just curious. Well, I'll see you Friday. Would you like me to bring a bottle of wine or a 6-pack?"

"Wine. Your choice of flavor."

"You must be a wine expert, using a fancy word like flavor."

"That's me, a sommier or somel..."

"Sommelier."

"Yeah, that's it. A customer's coming over. I have to go. See you Friday."

As he put his cell back in his pocket, Kanen smiled. He was looking forward to the dinner party, to meeting the parents that raised two children who couldn't be more diametrically different in beliefs, temperament and lifestyles.

The Tesla Roadster's GPS took Kanen easily to Spencer's. He parked behind an aging dark blue Toyota Camry. Walking through the back gate, he noticed Spencer's cottage on the left. Someone called his name. He turned to the right and saw Spencer behind the BBQ on the main house's deck. "Hey Kanen. Come on up!"

Kanen climbed the stairs and was met by an attractive older woman with golden green eyes. They were beautiful. She held out her hand. "I'm Perry Seidel. You must be Kanen."

"I am. Nice to meet you. Spencer's told me nothing about you."

Perry gave Kanen a blank stare. He quickly said, "You know how people say 'I've heard so much about you?' I thought it would be funny if I said I've heard nothing about you."

Perry smiled. "Ah. I get it."

"Not funny, huh?"

She shook her head. "Keep trying."

Kanen handed Perry the wine, then they walked over to Spencer. Marinated red bell peppers, eggplant, zucchini and Portobello mushrooms were being placed on the hot grill. He put the tongs down and gave Kanen a hug.

"Great to see you again," Spencer said.

"You, too. Are your parents here?"

"Not yet."

Perry said, "What can I get you to drink?"

Kanen replied, "A glass of what I brought would be perfect, thanks."

Perry disappeared into the kitchen and returned momentarily with the wine bottle, a glass and a corkscrew. She sat down and proceeded to open the bottle. "I have to say that I love all Weston's energy bars, but my all-time favorite is the Lemon Meringue Pie bar. I don't know how you do it, but I can taste the lemon, the lightly toasted meringue and even the graham cracker crust. They're beyond amazing."

"That's my favorite, too," said Kanen. "Before my parents became vegan, my dad's favorite pie was lemon meringue. He vowed to veganize it. His next step was turning it into a convenient energy bar. The man's a genius."

Spencer said, "I haven't tried that flavor. My favorite is the almond cacao. It's out of this world."

"I remember you telling me when we first met. You two are in luck. I happened to have some in the car and you can each have a box of your favorite. I'll go get them so I don't forget."

"Thanks!" said Perry.

"Yeah, that's cool," Spencer added.

While Kanen searched for the boxes of bars in his trunk, Heddy and Roger Rydover pulled up behind him. He looked up as they were getting out of the car.

Even though they were close in age, Heddy looked nothing like Perry. The former was wearing a long-sleeved orange polyester shirt that sported a large bowtie. Her pants were black polyester. Her shoes, sensible tan-colored flats with tassels. Shoulder-length light brown hair with austere, curled under-bangs, resembled Buster Brown.

Roger Rydover gave off the same conservative air. The tan polo shirt hugged his pot belly and barely tucked into his 501 Levi's.

Kanen walked over to them. "You must be Spencer's parents. I'm Kanen Weston."

They exchanged pleasantries, then walked up the stairs to the deck. While Kanen placed the boxes of energy bars on the table, Spencer came over and gave his mom a big hug, then gave his dad a slightly smaller one.

"I love this area." Heddy pointed to the cottage. "Is that where you live?"

"Yes, it is, and he's been an ideal tenant," said Perry as she approached the group. "Hi, I'm Perry Seidel. So nice to meet you both."

Heddy smiled. "Nice to meet you, too." The contrast between the two women wasn't lost on her. She suddenly felt dated, as if her look expired in 1955, even though Heddy was born in '68. She self-consciously looked down at her tan, bland loafers, and glanced over at Perry's bright aquamarine sandals. Her toenails were painted fuchsia.

"Dear, are you okay?" Roger said, as his wife stared at the ground.

Her head snapped up and she looked stunned. "What? Oh yes, I'm fine. Just fine." She said to Spencer, "What are you cooking, dear?"

"Grilling veggies. I marinated them," he said proudly.

"They look delicious," said Heddy. She eyed the bottle of wine on the patio table. "Could I trouble you for a glass of wine, Perry?"

"Not at all. Roger?"

"Yes, thanks."

As the sun set, the five of them sat at the patio table enjoying their dinner al fresco. Roger kept waiting for something or someone to set his son off on a tirade, but Spencer was a delight. He laughed more and seemed genuinely at ease.

Kanen said, "I read an article today in the paper about a raid at Sunshine Kennels, a puppy mill in Fairfield. I almost started applauding."

Roger said, "What's a puppy mill?"

Kanen replied, "It's where dogs are mass-produced. The bottom line is profit for these cretins, so the animals are treated like commodities. This place looked particularly bad. The photo of the cages was haunting, but the picture the liberators took after they totally thrashed the place was fantastic." Kanen looked over at Spencer just as he gave Perry a slight nod and smile.

"Wasn't it against the law, stealing the dogs and destroying property?" Roger asked.

"Technically yes," Kanen replied, "but…"

"But nothing," Roger interrupted. "Let the authorities do their job."

"That's a joke," said Spencer. "The kennel was fined a few times but they fixed the problems. As soon as the citations were lifted, the owner went right back to the way it was. You know they found one of the breeding dogs shot to death and buried in the yard?"

Heddy said, "That's horrible. I'm glad they stole them. I wonder what they did with all the dogs."

Spencer replied, "They found someone to take them and adopt them out."

"That's funny. It wasn't in the article I read," said Kanen. He looked over at Perry and Spencer.

Spencer said, "I read it online."

Perry stood up. "Would anyone like dessert? I made strawberry shortcake."

Everyone nodded. "Sounds great. Let me help you." Heddy got up and walked into the kitchen behind Perry.

Roger stood, his belly grazing the table. "Do you know where the restroom is?"

"Yeah," said Spencer. "Go through the kitchen and make a left. It's the first door on the right."

Kanen gave Spencer a knowing smile. "What?"

"You did it, didn't you? With Perry."

"Are you kidding? She's old enough to be my mother. As a matter of fact, she's older than my mom. You're sick."

"Not that, but she is attractive. You and Perry raided the puppy mill."

Spencer was silent.

"Come on. Tell me. What was it like to liberate those poor animals from such abuse?"

Spencer looked over at the door to the house. They were still inside. He looked back at Kanen with such intensity, Kanen wasn't sure what he was going to say. He brushed a lock of wavy dark brown hair out of his face and said, "It was fantastic. A total rush."

"I'm jealous!"

"Jealous of what?" Roger said as he sat back down at the table.

Without missing a beat, Kanen replied, "Your son's grilling skills. I'm a total Dilbert in front of a barbeque."

"You can thank me for that. I taught him how to grill the perfect steak. Of course, that was many years ago, before he became a vegan. The vegetables were really good, Spence."

"Thanks Dad."

Perry and Heddy returned carrying plates, forks and an exquisite strawberry shortcake.

"This is divine," said Heddy as she took a bite. "I can't believe it's vegan. Isn't this whipped cream?" She poked the fluffy white clouds of whipping with her fork.

"Nope. It's coconut milk. I refrigerated a can of organic coconut milk, then took off the thick top part, leaving the liquid. I added a little vanilla extract and stevia, then whipped it up. Pretty amazing, huh?"

"I love it. Roger, isn't this delicious."

He nodded. "Really good. You'll have to give Heddy the recipe."

It was nearly dark. The lights on the patio and candles illuminated the table, adding a tranquil ambience to the gathering. Kanen looked out at the back yard and saw a small light appear and then fade, then another and another. The entire backyard was filled with the magical lights. "Those look like fireflies, but we don't have them out on the west coast, do we?"

Perry laughed. "No. They're called firefly lights and they blink on and off when the sun goes down. They run off solar power. Cool, huh?"

"Yeah."

Heddy looked out over the back yard and her eyes widened. She could see the lights flickering on and off in the trees, in and around the bushes and close to the cottage. "They look like fairies dancing in your garden. I love it! Where did you get them?"

"Online. I don't remember the name of the website. If you'd like, I'll find it and email you."

"Fantastic. You can get my email address from Spencer. Aren't they beautiful, Roger? I can see them in our back yard by the willow tree."

Roger said, "They're very nice." He didn't sound convincing.

Perry liked Heddy. She was sweet and she loved the way she spoke to her son. Roger, on the other hand, was the kind of man Perry divorced over five years ago. She saw the same stubbornness and rigidity in his beliefs. She would have bet her house that Roger controlled the relationship.

"Would anyone like tea or coffee or an aperitif? I have sherry and a marvelous cognac," Perry said as she stood.

Heddy was about to say something when Roger broke in. "Thank you, but we should be going. I'm getting up early tomorrow for a game of golf."

Spencer saw the disappointed look on his mother's face. "I'd be happy to drive you home if you'd like to stay, Mom."

Heddy would have loved to continue chatting with everyone, but she felt bad for Roger, going home alone. "That's okay, sweetie. I'm feeling a little tired anyway. Thank you for having us. I had such a lovely time. Don't forget to look up that website for the lights."

"I won't. I'm glad you could make it. It was really nice meeting you both," Perry said.

Roger said, "You, too."

After they left Perry, Spencer and Kanen retired to the living room, each with a snifter of cognac. After taking a sip, Kanen said, "I've never had cognac this good. It's unreal."

Perry said, "It's Hennessy Cognac Paradis. Can you taste the cardamom and cinnamon?"

"Carda what?" said Spencer.

"Cardamom. It's an Indian spice, kind of citrusy," Perry replied.

Spencer took another sip and let it linger in his mouth. "I taste both. It's really good."

Perry noticed Kanen typing on his iPhone. "Are we boring you?"

He looked up. "Not at all. I was looking up the cognac online…Shit, this stuff is $1,000 a bottle?"

Perry laughed. "Yes, this stuff is expensive. I think it's worth it, don't you?"

"If you can afford it, which I'm guessing you can or you stole it…like you did the dogs." Perry looked over at Spencer who nearly choked on his drink. Kanen continued. "Don't get mad at him. I figured it out while you were in the kitchen with Heddy. I think it's fantastic, by the way. What you two did to the place was epic. I wish I could have been there."

Spencer said, "Thanks." He turned to Perry. "Are you mad?"

Perry replied, "No, but it's vital that the fewer people who know about this the better. Please don't tell anyone, Kanen. If word got out that we did this, we could go to jail."

Kanen pretended to zip his lips. "I won't say a word. How are the dogs?"

"I heard that they've all been adopted out." Spencer gave Perry an impassioned look. She said, "Fine, you can bring her out."

He practically leapt off the couch and as he ran out of the house, he said, "Be right back!"

Moments later, he returned. In his arms, he held a small female sheltie terrier. Her mange was better but she still looked like she was breaded and deep-fried, her hair matted and dull.

"This is Gilda, but I call her Gilley. She was one of the two breeders at the kennel." Spencer sat down next to Kanen and gently stroked the dog's head. She looked up at him and licked his face.

Kanen put out his hand to pet her and Gilley flinched. He stopped and then slowly tried again, touching her tentatively at first because he didn't want to hurt her. It was apparent that Gilda craved affection over her comfort level, so he stroked her with a little more confidence.

"This isn't contagious, is it?" Kanen said.

Perry got up and went over to where they were sitting. "It's called Cheyletiella mange and it's not contagious to humans. She was treated with medication when we rescued her, so it should go away in the next couple of weeks. Poor Gilda was covered with it. She still has trouble walking because she spent her whole life in a cage, impregnated or nursing. Your friend here insisted on adopting her. I'm really glad he did."

"She's my pal, aren't you Gilley?" said Spencer. He kissed the top of her head and rubbed her belly. "I can't wait until she's better. I want to take her to the beach and play ball with her and Frisbee and give her the life she deserves." He turned to Perry. "What do you think will happen to the owner of Sunshine Kennels? What was her name, Irene?"

"Irene Patchett. I heard that the Animal Legal Defense Fund wants to prosecute her. Based on our video, they feel they have enough evidence to charge her with animal cruelty. Fortunately, they don't need us as witnesses."

"I hope she's banned from ever having another animal again." He looked down at Gilley's small, fragile body. He doubted she could have lasted through another litter.

Kanen said, "I don't understand how this woman was allowed to get away with keeping animals in substandard conditions without being fined or prosecuted."

Perry sighed. "I know. You would think it would be so easy to shut these puppy mills down. Animals are very low priority for law enforcement and the humane societies are overworked, underfunded and understaffed. If violations are found, the breeder is cited, and then they're given a chance to fix the infractions. Many times there's no follow-up visit or it's a cursory one. It's a huge problem, just not important enough to garner the attention it deserves."

Gilley had fallen asleep in Spencer's arms. "I'm going to put her back in the cottage."

"Can I come with you? I haven't seen your place yet."

"Sure."

Perry watched them walk across the yard to Spencer's place. She was struck with a sense of pride. These two young men, so compassionate and willing to help animals in need. They were the future of the animal rights movement, and she felt confident that they would take it to the next level. There was already an increased awareness in the general public about veganism and the raw food diet. When she became vegan over twenty years ago, few people knew what it was. They looked at her as if she had three eyes. She was tough enough to brave the ridicule and taunting, but it still bothered her. Many restaurants now offered vegan meals on the menu. Perry marveled at the variety of vegan products at mainstream grocery stores, like Safeway and Lucky's. Target even carried its own line of vegan meats.

"I love your property, Perry," Kanen said as he walked over to the couch, Spencer in tow. "And Spencer's cottage is sweet."

"Thanks."

Kanen looked at his watch. "It's only 9:00. Do you feel like going dancing? There's a great club about a mile from here called Jauncy's. They have a big dance floor and a deejay who plays R&B and funk, none of that disco or techno crap."

Perry looked at the two young men, one tall, blonde and striking and the other lanky with a tousle of dark brown wavy hair and light brown eyes. "That sounds like a blast. I'm in. Spencer?"

Spencer would have loved to go dancing. The problem was he didn't know how to dance. A loner in high school, he wasn't invited to parties and didn't attend the school dances. Under normal circumstances, he would have outright declined, but the cognac loosened him up and he felt a little less inhibited than normal.

"I don't know." He held up his snifter. "This has made me kind of tired, plus I don't want to leave Gilley alone for that long."

Kanen said, "Don't be a wimp. It'll be fun and we don't have to stay long. Gilley will be fine. She's reveling in being cozy and snug, something she's never had."

"Do you remember if they played Average White Band or The Commodores?" Perry asked.

He thought about it. "Uh-uh. I did dance to *Fire* by the Ohio Players. What a great song!"

"I grew up listening to them. Come on, Spencer. I haven't been dancing in a while. I'll even drive. Say yes."

"Only if we leave when I'm ready to go."

Perry said, "I promise."

28

Twenty minutes later, they entered Jauncy's, one of Berkeley's more popular clubs on Shattuck Boulevard, walking distance from the UC Berkeley campus. The place was packed, mostly with twenty-somethings. Michael Jackson's *Billie Jean* blared over the speakers and the dance floor was filled to capacity. Perry suddenly felt very old. She gave Kanen a look, then shouted over the noise, "I feel like I'm in a travelogue, *Granny goes to the Disco*. I don't see one person over twenty-five."

Kanen laughed. "Don't worry about it. Once you're on the dance floor, who cares? Right Spence?"

"Whatever you say."

Kanen made a beeline for the dance floor and they followed, Perry grabbing Spencer's hand.

Kanen was a natural. Spencer, on the other hand, looked stiff and self-conscious. As Perry danced, she made eye contact with Spencer and mouthed, 'follow my lead.' She pumped her fists in the air and moved her head back and forth to the beat. Spencer smiled and did the same. Once he loosened up, Perry moved her body right and left, slightly raising her feet.

Billy Jean segued into *Play That Funky Music* by Wild Cherry and it looked like a fire was lit under lead-footed Spencer. He totally got into it and, remarkably, looked like he'd been dancing his whole life. He let the music in and, for a rare moment, he wasn't thinking about animal suffering. He was released from his self-imposed torment. Kanen and Perry looked at each other and started laughing. She danced over to him and said, "I believe we just popped his dancing cherry!"

Oblivious, Spencer continued to dance, sweat forming on his forehead and upper lip. A scantily dressed young girl decided to dance with him. He didn't object one bit.

Kanen continued to dance with Perry, despite getting more than a few nods and smiles from attractive girls. He was satisfied hanging out with the older woman and wasn't in the mood for any other female interaction.

It was nearly 1:30 in the morning when the deejay announced last call. Perry had to practically drag Spencer to the car, he was so reluctant to leave. He talked her into dancing to one more song. She was glad he did. *Give Up the Funk (Tear the Roof off the Sucker)* by Parliament, embodied seventies funk. Perry couldn't remember the last time she had so much fun.

As they piled into the car, Kanen turned to Spencer. "If I had known that dancing would remove the stick up your ass, I would have suggested this a lot earlier. You're a natural, you know that?"

Spencer sat back in the seat and wiped his brow. "Thanks. If I had known that it would loosen me up, believe me, I would have started a lot earlier."

Perry said, "Thank you both for making me feel so special."

"You were hotter than most of those girls, right Kanen?"

"Definitely. I'm thinking we have to do this more often."

"Perry, you should invite those women you had over the other night. I bet they'd have a good time, too."

Perry replied, "Are you kidding? I'm not sharing you two with those broads!"

"Fine, but if you change your mind, I think it would be fun."

Kanen chimed in. "I agree. You'll still be our favorite."

Perry said, "I'll think about it." She knew that her vegan friends would absolutely flip if they went dancing with two young, very hot vegan men. Still, a slice of jealousy cut into her psyche that bothered her. She wasn't sexually attracted to Kanen or Spencer. They were younger than her daughter, but she loved the attention. Maybe she'd want to share them later, but one more jet to the club with her 'men' alone was definitely in store.

29

The cab pulled up in front of the YMCA on Turk Street and Senator Bertram Kathala paid the fare. As he got out of the taxi, Sabrina swiftly walked out of the Y to greet him. Her full-length caftan billowed around her ample body exposing her Birkenstock sandals. As before, she was delighted by his involvement in the Feeding the Hungry program. Bert extended his hand. Sabrina ignored it and gave him a hearty hug.

"So nice to see you again, Senator! You decided to dress more for the occasion. Casual in the Loin is definitely the way to go."

Bert flashed back to the incident at the social welfare office. He shuddered remembering being thrown up on, his shoe taking the brunt of the assault. He now wore jeans, running shoes and a dark green button down shirt.

"So I learned. Do we have a big crowd for the giveaway or is that a silly question?"

"Very silly question. We're packed to the rafters. So many families and individuals are not making ends meet. One meal isn't a lot, but it helps."

Bert put his hand deep into his satchel and pulled out a stack of papers. "I received these 'buy one, get two free' coupons from three of the fast food restaurants in the area. I have enough to give each person two. That should help."

"Wonderful! Thanks Senator. Why don't we go inside?"

Together, they walked through the YMCA's worn and graffitied double doors. As they approached the makeshift stage in the gymnasium, Bert couldn't help but scan the crowd, hoping to see Cody. He noticed a lot more families, many with young children. Yet, no sign of the tall man with the beautiful voice.

Sabrina spoke first. "I'd like to welcome you all to our second food giveaway with Senator Bertram Kathala. I was just informed that everyone who receives a bag will also get two coupons! Isn't that great?"

A few people let out a shout of appreciation, but most were impatient and wanted their fast food. As before, the tables were lined up along the perimeter of the gym and volunteers stood by, ready to hand out the bags of food.

Sabrina continued. "If we could get everyone to form lines at the front of each bank of tables, we can begin."

As the lines formed, Bert again scanned the crowd. He was about to give up when he spotted Cody at the far end of the room, standing close to the front of one of the lines. He excused himself and walked over to Cody, who was wearing a worn and faded denim shirt, the sleeves too short for his long arms. His pants looked like first generation Dockers, their cuffs barely covering his ankles. Despite his appearance, Cody smelled like he had just showered. A faint scent of Ivory soap hung in the air.

Bert said, "Did your friends come for the giveaway this time or do you need another four bags?"

Startled by his recollection of their first meeting, Cody said, "Hey Mr. Senator, I don't want to be any trouble. I'll just take one bag like everyone else."

Bert smiled. "I wasn't being facetious, Cody. I meant it. I think it's great that you want to help others. And don't worry, I won't make you sing for your supper."

Cody relaxed. "I was going to ask for three or four more. They couldn't make it on account of their situations."

"No problem." When it was his turn, Bert grabbed four food bags and graciously handed them to Cody. "Do you mind if I go with you to deliver the food?"

Cody shook his head as he packed the bags into his backpack. He didn't want the senator to see his dog friends gulping down burgers and fries meant for people, but it would be hard to refuse his request. "I don't mean any disrespect, but two of my friends won't see anyone but me. I think Della would like to meet you, though."

Bert said, "Sounds good. Shall we go?"

166

As they walked down Turk, people waved and greeted Cody. He would return their salutation with a big smile.

"I don't mean to pry, but how did you end up in the Tenderloin?"

"I was living in Topeka when they, the court, had me committed to the Barnaby Institution. They said I was a junkie. They were probably right. I don't remember much from that life, back in Kansas. When they felt I was ready, they gave me a one-way ticket to San Francisco. That was seven years ago."

"Are you clean?"

"As I'll ever be. It's not easy living here, but I don't want to go down that rabbit hole again. It's ugly and dark. Know what I mean?"

Cody cut across Leavenworth to Ellis. Bert had to practically run to catch up to him.

"Honestly, I don't know what you mean. I'm not what you'd call a thrill-seeker. I never experimented with drugs and my drinking is minimal."

Cody replied, "Never inhaled?"

Bert laughed. "No. Never. I guess I'm a pretty boring guy."

"If I had to pick boring or broken, I'd be as boring as all get out."

Bert was just about to ask Cody how he was able to memorize every Cody Brant song when they stopped in front of a large, forest green garbage bin behind Thang Long Vietnamese restaurant. Despite the cloudless, bright blue sky, darkness seemed to envelope this piece of real estate. The sour smell of rotting food was strong The smell coming from a battered cardboard box on the right side of the bin was stronger. Cody approached Della's hovel, her home for the past seven years. Her head was barely visible, hidden by a threadbare blanket. Grey, matted hair stuck out indiscriminately like it was trying to break free from the head it was forced to live on. Bert stayed back while Cody walked up to the seemingly lifeless form, then squatted next to her. He brushed the dreads from his face.

"Della, it's me Cody. Are you up?"

An inaudible reply came from the blanket.

"What?" Cody said.

"I said go away, please."

"I brought you some food and this." Cody put down his backpack and produced a bag of fast food and a clean blanket. He waited for Della to peel the covering off her face, but she didn't respond.

"Della?"

"Not today Cody."

Ignoring her, he took the burger and fries out of the bag and placed them in front of her, hoping that the aroma would entice her. Instead, she turned over and faced the inside of the cardboard box. As she turned, Bert could see how emaciated she was, barely enough skin to cover her bones.

After waiting a few minutes, Cody looked over at Bert and shrugged. He got up, leaving his offerings in front of Della's sleeping body.

As they walked away, Cody explained Della's condition.

Bert said, "She needs to be in a hospital where she can get the medication she needs." He was emphatic. Cody just shook his head.

"She's been in and out of institutions her whole life. When I met her, she had just come out of St. Francis' over on Eddy. As soon as the pills they gave her ran out, she said she wasn't taking them anymore. She didn't like the way she felt. Hard to believe she prefers this way, huh?"

Without answering, Bert wondered if d.o.a. would kill someone who was bi-polar. Della would certainly be better off dead than living the life, if that's what it was, she was currently living.

"Have you tried talking her into getting help?"

"Lots of times. It doesn't work. I gave up a few years ago. Besides, she's pretty far gone. Most of the time, she's doesn't even remember her name."

As they approached the corner of Turk and Steiner, Cody said, "This is where I leave." He pointed up the street. "The Y is that way."

Bert held out his hand and Cody shook it. "Thanks for letting me walk with you. I wish you the best."

Cody nodded and continued to walk up the street. As Bert watched him leave, he noticed Cody favoring his right leg, then he stopped and leaned against a wall, head back and clearly in pain.

Bert's first inclination was to help, but as he started to walk toward him, Cody straightened up and began walking again.

Less than a mile away, Bonnie was preparing for her first marketing presentation as director. It was a chance to prove to Gerald and her peers that she was worthy of the title. Her assistant was forced to check the conference room multiple times to make sure the easel holding the advertising boards was in the proper position, folders were directly in front of each chair and the beverage table was fully stocked.

Bonnie walked over to Monica's office. The small room used to be hers. Certificates, awards and slogans were replaced with framed vintage photographs of Hinton's famous clients. An eight-foot chicken sat on top of the first Delaney's Fried Chicken in Mobile, Alabama. Once the restaurant expanded into a national chain, they ditched the large, expensive hen sculpture and replaced it with a chicken-shaped sign. Another grainy black and white photo displayed the founder of Victory's flashing the victory sign with one hand and holding a burger in the other.

"Where did you get these photos? They're classic."

Monica said, "Believe it or not, I found them on eBay."

"I believe it. You can find anything there." Bonnie glanced over at the pile of papers in Monica's In Box. "Is the work load too much?"

Monica followed her boss' gaze. She would have loved to tell Bonnie the truth. She felt that too much of the mindless, useless work was thrown on her desk. Work that could have been done by Tammy, but she held her tongue. If the rumors were true about Bonnie and Gerald, Monica wanted to stay on her good side. "Not at all. I was planning on staying late and getting caught up."

"Good. We'll be starting the meeting in five minutes."

Monica watched Bonnie leave. She had to admit, the woman was beautiful. Statuesque at 5' 8" with long legs, her light grey and pink suit hugged her slender body. Monica felt dumpy compared to her young boss. She absently played with the ruffles on her shirt, then raked her fingers through her hair, getting her pinkie stuck on a bobby pin.

At five minutes past three, only one person had yet to arrive. Bonnie stood at the front of the long conference table next to the easel waiting for Gerald. He knew very well that this presentation meant a lot to her. She kept her anger and disgust hidden well. Instead, she imagined the adulation and appreciation he would give her once he was introduced to the latest marketing campaign.

Lloyd Winter, CFO, glanced at his watch. It was 3:15. One minute later, Gerald strode in and sat down without so much as an apology. As he opened the folder in front of him, he said, "So, what have you got to show us?"

With a big smile, Bonnie welcomed everyone to the meeting. As practiced, she began by reciting current marketing figures, pleased to report that Hinton was still the leading supplier of ground beef and chicken patties and chicken nuggets in the United States. Then, she turned the floor over to Jake Leeson of Ames & Leeson Advertising.

Jake and Bonnie had been working on the new campaign for weeks and they couldn't have been more pleased with the results. With the exception of Jake, Bonnie and Sid Welfry, Hinton's account executive at the agency, the average age in the room was fifty-five. Undeterred, he proceeded to sell the business-to-business ad campaign, walking the executives through the oversized magazine ads on foam core boards. When he finished, he asked if there were any questions. A few hands were raised and Jake delivered the answers with precision.

"I have a question," Gerald said. His right hand was perched on the folder, his left, hidden from view. Bonnie knew exactly where it was.

"Yes?" Bonnie waited for his praise.

"For Jake," Gerald said and turned his full attention to the agency co-founder. "While I found the ads compelling, I also felt they were a bit too feminine."

Jake clearly looked confused. He glanced at Sid but, he too, was at a loss. "Can you be more specific?"

"No, I can't, but since you and our director of marketing worked on these together, I suggest you ask her. I would like to see revised versions in a week. Can you do that?" He looked at Bonnie who was holding it together like a pro. Inside, she was crumbling at warp speed.

"Consider it done," she said.

"Good." Gerald brushed aside the folder, then left the room without another word. Sid began the process of dismantling the easel and gathering up the ad slicks as the rest of the employees went back to their offices.

"I'm really sorry, Jake and Sid. I thought you put together an excellent presentation."

"Thanks. I feel the same about your input. Your predecessor, Dell, was too old school. I thought his ideas sucked," Jake said.

Sid added, "I second the motion."

Bonnie smiled. "I appreciate the support." She gathered up her papers. When they were the only two left in the room, Jake lowered his voice and said, "I don't mean to be disrespectful, but do you know what Gerald's talking about? I didn't detect an ounce of femininity in those ads."

Before she completely lost her cool, she took a deep breath and said, "Why don't we meet on Monday and recalibrate our strategy. I'm sure we can come up with a more masculine, balls-in-your-face campaign."

Jake laughed. "I'll have Ramona call Tammy and set up an appointment. Until then, chin up."

It took her all of two minutes to grab her purse and take the elevator down to the garage. As she got in her car, Bonnie did her best to stifle the anger and embarrassment she felt. By the time she drove past the black and white striped garage arm in the air, the tears flowed freely.

Back in the office, Gerald slammed down the phone after Tammy informed him that Bonnie had left for the day.

It wasn't difficult finding Weston Foods. The building took up half the block on Folsom and Seventh Streets. It was an unremarkable brick and glass structure. Bonnie guessed it was at least fifty years old. She pulled into the lot and found a visitor parking spot. She grabbed her purse, pulled down the visor and checked herself in the mirror. Her eye make-up was all but gone, mixed with the dried tears on her cheeks. She rubbed them clean, re-applied the mascara, added eyeliner and a brush of shadow.

Bonnie knew that if she spent too much time in the car, she would no longer have the courage to talk to Kanen, so she quickly brushed her hair, applied a light gloss to her lips and walked through Weston's glass double doors.

She was immediately struck by the casual atmosphere. Immense close-up photographs of exotic fruit hung on every wall. Bonnie could identify the star fruit, lychee nuts and pineapple, but one completely eluded her. She looked at the green prickly oblong-shaped fruit.

"It's jackfruit," said Connie, the receptionist. "Isn't it a trip?"

"Definitely. How does it taste?"

"Like heaven on earth. Can I help you?"

Bonnie self-consciously adjusted her skirt. "Is Kanen available?"

"Is he expecting you?"

"No, he's not."

"Your name?"

"Bonnie Rydover."

Connie picked up the phone and punched in some numbers. "There's a Bonnie Rydover here to see you…okay, I'll tell her."

She hung up the phone. "He'll be out in a few minutes. Why don't you have a seat and please help yourself to the energy bars on the table."

Too nervous to sit and lacking an appetite, Bonnie just smiled and continued to stand and admire the photographs on the wall. A few minutes later, Kanen appeared in the doorway. She couldn't tell if he was happy or angry to see her. She walked over to him and held out her hand. "Nice to see you again."

Kanen shook it a little harder than normal, then walked her back to his office and closed the door.

"What the hell are you doing here?"

"I missed you."

"Please Bonnie. Cut the crap. Did you get dumped by the meathead I saw you with or are you planning on using me again behind his back?"

"I'm sorry. I had no idea he would show up. I had such a wonderful time with you that I didn't want to ruin it. I was going to tell you about Ger…him."

"Bullshit." Kanen walked over to the windows and stared outside. He put his hands in his pockets then took them out. She rattled him, even when he was angry with her. "Tell me why you're here and please don't lie."

"Can I sit down?"

Kanen nodded and Bonnie went over to the couch, then patted the spot next to her. "Please sit down."

He ignored her. "Talk."

"I'm confused right now. My career path was as clear as a landing strip and now…now someone turned the lights off and I don't…I have no direction. I'm…so…lost." Bonnie broke down sobbing. She put her hands up to her face, clearly embarrassed by her outburst. Kanen hadn't known her for long, but he was convinced that she was a woman who didn't like to show weakness. He sat down next to her and lightly touched her shoulder.

After her tears subsided, she grabbed a tissue from her purse and blew her nose. "I'm sorry. You must think I'm such a wimp."

"The opposite, actually. Whatever happened must have been pretty bad for you to be this upset." Kanen glanced at the clock. It was almost 5:00. "Why don't we go somewhere and talk. I'm not comfortable doing it here."

"Are you afraid people will find out that you're fraternizing with the enemy?"

"Yeah, I am. C'mon. We can walk to Shelby's Hangout. It's only a couple of blocks."

They easily found a corner booth and both ordered dirty martinis.

"I really do miss you. That wasn't a lie," Bonnie said as she took a sip of her drink.

Kanen sat back in the seat and stared at this woman that he never thought he would see again. Even with tear-stained make-up, he found her irresistible. The marketing director of the one of the largest meat suppliers was stealing his heart and he was too weak to stop it. As if she knew what he was thinking, she said, "We're kind of like Romeo and Juliet, huh?"

He grinned. "Instead of the Montagues and Capulets, it's the Meat Eaters and Compassionates." For the first time, Bonnie smiled. Kanen took her hands in his. "Tell me, Ms. Rydover, what hath the house of Meat Eaters wrought upon you?"

"If I start from the beginning, we'll be here all night, so I'll give you the Reader's Digest version." She took another sip of the martini and could feel her nerves smoothing out. Kanen was intently looking at her, his interest in her story apparent. It's one of the attributes that she loved about him and one that was completely absent from Gerald's dark soul.

"When I started working at Hinton four years ago, I was a lowly marketing research tech. My goal was to be CEO. I know it sounds crazy, but I'm very driven and determined. I figured if I played the game to win, I would. I did everything right."

"That included sleeping with the boss."

"Yes and also graduating with a masters in integrated marketing communications. I couldn't get to the top with sex alone." Suddenly embarrassed by her admission, she looked down in her lap. "You must think I have no morals and I don't blame you. Saying it out loud for the first time repulses me, too."

Kanen's silence deepened Bonnie's shame. She suddenly wanted to leave. Without looking up, she grabbed her purse, but Kanen gently took hold of her arm.

"I'm not going to condone what you did, but I'm also not going to judge you. What happened today?"

Bonnie kissed Kanen on the cheek. "Thank you," she said. He smiled and brushed strands of golden blonde hair away from her face. "Go on," he said.

"The last day of the marketing conference, I was ready to quit. I was so disgusted by Gerald. He was treating me harsher and with more disdain. I never got the chance because he made me the director of marketing. Dell Turner was fired and I was a step closer to the top. I can't tell you what a thrill it was for me. I knew I could do a better job than Dell. Today was my first marketing presentation as director. I rehearsed it so many times, I could have run the meeting backwards." Bonnie finished her martini and ate the olive. As she thought about it, her emotions began to surface again and it took all her will power to sublimate them. Crying once in front of Kanen was bad enough. Twice and he'd probably run for the door. She composed herself and continued. "When the presentation was over, I could tell it was well-received by everyone, then Gerald says, 'I found the ads were a bit too feminine.' He told us he wanted to see new ads in a week." She shook her head. "There wasn't an ounce of femininity in the ads. That asshole was demeaning me in front of everyone. I don't want to spend another minute in that office. I'm done catering to his sadistic streak."

"So you quit?"

"Not yet." Bonnie glanced over at the other patrons. It was still too early for the after-work crowd and, as a result, the bar had only a smattering of customers. Still, Bonnie lowered her voice. "I know something that could potentially send Mr. Hinton away for a very long time."

"Insider trading?"

"A lot worse. I'm not comfortable talking about it in public. Can you come over to my place?"

"Bonnie, aren't you being overly dramatic?" Kanen scanned the room. The closest people were at least eight feet away. They looked like college seniors and they were drinking beers and talking way too loud. "I think it's safe."

But she shook her head. "What I'm going to tell you makes insider trading look like stealing a candy bar from a vending machine. Trust me. We need to be alone."

Kanen got up to pay the tab and Bonnie went to the restroom. The martini made her a little high and she liked it. On a work day she rarely, if ever, had a drink before six, but this wasn't an ordinary day. It was the day Bonnie began to feel the self-imposed chains loosening. A feeling of exhilaration began to emanate from her heart, then she looked in the mirror and nearly gasped. Her mascara had pooled underneath her eyes, making her look like she was knocked out in a boxing ring. Her hair was tousled and a few blemishes that she covered with concealer were exposed. The normally well-coifed woman was a mess.

Five minutes later, Bonnie walked out of the restroom with the same face she wore that morning. Her purse weighed a ton because it carried precious cargo. She'd rather suffer the heavy weight of cosmetics than look askew.

As they approached the Weston Foods' parking lot, Bonnie said, "You can follow me, if you'd like."

"Let's carry the intrigue further. Give me your address and I'll meet you there, lest you're being followed."

"Very funny," Bonnie said. Still, she surreptitiously scanned the parking lot. Finding nothing suspicious, she continued. "I live at 664 Chestnut Street, apartment 9."

"I never did like chestnuts."

"You'll like this one." Bonnie got in her car, but not before she gave Kanen a hug. "Thanks for being there for me today."

"You're welcome. I have a few things to finish up in the office, but they won't take long. Fifteen minutes tops."

He waved as Bonnie sped out of the parking lot, then he turned and opened the office door. Michelle was standing at the receptionist's desk, arms crossed, looking disappointed. She walked up to Kanen. "Please tell me that wasn't the Hinton woman."

"It was," Kanen replied as he walked past her and into his office. Michelle followed him and closed his door.

"Do not get wrapped up with her."

Kanen went around to his desk and clicked on his e-mail. "Don't worry about it, Mom."

"Too late."

He looked up from the computer screen. "I'm an adult, Mother. I can handle it."

Michelle walked up to his desk. "Kanen, I understand why you're attracted to her. She's a beautiful woman but, honey, she works for the largest..."

"I know! Please don't get involved. I know what I'm doing."

She threw her hands up in the air. "Fine! I'll shut my mouth." Michelle left the office, slamming the door. A few seconds later, she came back. "That was childish. I'm sorry. I just don't want you to get hurt. If you need to talk, I'm here, sweetie."

Kanen walked over to his mom and gave her a big hug. "I love you, Mom."

"I love you, too."

Bill walked in carrying a bowl of strawberries. "Did I miss something?"

Michelle shook her head. "It's all good." She grabbed a strawberry from the bowl and popped it in her mouth. Kanen took one, too, then went back to his computer and shut it down. He grabbed his jacket and walked past his parents. "See you later."

After he left, Bill turned to Michelle. "Okay, what happened?"

She took his hand and led him into her office. "You're not going to believe this one."

30

The limousine pulled up in front of the Armory building in downtown Norfolk. The limo driver parked and quickly went around to the passenger door and opened it. Senator Anita Minefeld and her aide, Cal Drexler, stepped out and were immediately taken aback by the line snaking around the block. Apparently, the Feeding the Hungry campaign reached beyond the initial invitees less than a month ago. From the length of the line, half the city was there for a free meal. Families increased the line's girth, mothers and fathers stood side-by-side with two, three and sometimes four children. Most were under seven years old.

Anita muttered, "Shorter lines are just around the corner." Then she laughed at her pun.

"What did you say?" Cal said.

"Nothing. Just talking to myself." She turned to the limo driver. "Please wait here. We won't be longer than an hour."

The driver nodded. He was clearly uncomfortable. The gas for the limo ride from the airport cost more than most of these people had in their bank accounts, if they even had accounts. He got back in the car, locked his doors, cracked the windows and slunk down in the seat.

Anita and Cal walked into the foyer and were greeted by Gretchen Furst, a tall, wiry woman with short grey hair and gold-rimmed glasses. Her thin nose barely held the glasses in place. She pushed them up to the bridge of her nose and then held out her hand.

"So good to see you again, Senator Minefeld. And this must be Cal."

Anita shook her hand. "It's a pleasure, Ms. Furst."

"Please, call me Gretchen."

She nodded. "Thank you for putting this together for the second time. We really appreciate the effort. Why don't you start letting people in?"

Anita and Cal proceeded to walk into the large auditorium. Oversized boxes containing 3,000 bags of meals sat ready for distribution. Volunteers were preparing for the event while eating their own free meal. One of them waved to Anita from the other side of the room. As the volunteer approached, holding a hamburger in hand, the senator's smile turned to a look of shock.

"Surprise!" She hugged Anita hard.

"Cindy, what the hell are you doing here?"

She pulled away from her mother's embrace, dejected. "I thought you'd be happy to see me. I found out about Feeding the Hungry from my history professor. I wanted to surprise you. I guess that backfired."

Anita recalibrated her emotions. It wasn't difficult considering they had decided not to taint the meat until the third giveaway. Still, she would have to figure out how to keep Cindy away from the next one.

"I am happy, dear. That was my 'shocked and so glad to see you' face. People confuse it with my disappointed face all the time. I'll have to work on that. How long are you in Norfolk?"

Anita watched as Cindy put the last bite of hamburger in her mouth. "Just for the weekend. I drove down with Rashad. He goes to NYU, too, and wanted to help out." She turned around and waved to a young, African American boy who was stacking the meal bags on the tables. "I should get back to helping. No preferential treatment for the senator's daughter, right?"

"That's right. If you're not busy, join us for dinner."

"Can Rashad come, too?"

"Of course, dear."

"Thanks, Mom. See you later." Cindy turned on her heels and practically skipped back to her place behind the table. She gave Rashad a hug and pointed in Anita's direction. With a heavy sigh, the senator turned to Cal. "Let's get this over with."

Senator Minefeld stood at the podium and waited as the recipients began streaming in. Orderly lines were formed at the five tables and once they started handing out the food, she began her speech. It was nearly identical to the last one. She knew no one was listening. They came for the food, not to hear a senator prattle on about how she was doing everything in her power to help get Americans back on their feet, employed and prosperous.

Cal noticed a reporter making his way toward the senator. He alerted Anita to the impending exchange and suggested that she talk to her constituents. At the very least, it would cast her in a positive light. Agreeing, Anita walked up to a couple, the mother holding a toddler in her arms. Husband and wife were modestly dressed. Their daughter wore a pink dress with ruffles at the hem.

"Hi. I'm Senator Minefeld. And you are?"

The woman smiled, her teeth crooked and tobacco stained. "Nice to meet you. I'm Kathy Groves and this here is our daughter, Ella." She picked up her daughter's arm and waved it at the senator. The little girl pulled away from her mother.

"I'm Kent. Thank you for the food. We appreciate it. It's been a really tough year."

"We're glad to help. Hopefully, we can keep the program running for at least another couple of months." Before they could respond, Anita said, "Take care and God bless," and she moved on to the next person in line. In sharp contrast to the couple, an elderly man was stooped over and dressed in rags. A tattered baseball cap covered greasy hair. He mumbled incoherently and picked at the loose threads on the blanket draped over his shoulders, covering half his body. Anita was getting ready to say something benign to the crazy man when the reporter strolled over.

"May I ask you a couple of questions, Senator Minefeld?"

Relieved, she turned to the reporter. "Of course."

"Do you think that these people would be better served by providing jobs and shelter as opposed to the quick fix of a few free meals?"

"Most definitely and I assure you that I will do all I can to change the lives of my fellow Virginians in the months to come. I would like to permanently relieve their suffering."

"And how do you plan on doing that, Senator? Wave your magic wand?"

Anita chuckled. "If only it were that easy. I will be introducing a bill in the Senate addressing this issue."

All eyes were on the senator and reporter. No one noticed that the crazy man left his place in line and was standing directly behind Anita. She heard a few grunts and felt something lightly touch her behind. She turned around just in time to see the man close up his filthy blanket and return to the line, head down and mumbling. She tried unsuccessfully to see what happened. The horrified look on Cal's face confirmed her fears. Before she could say anything, Cal said, "Don't move! I'll be right back."

He grabbed two of the meal bags from the nearest table, rifled through them until he found the napkins and delicately wiped the offensive substance from his boss' skirt. All were too stunned to speak. Even the reporter stood there, mouth open, at a loss for words. Finally, Senator Minefeld said to the reporter, "And that concludes the interview. I'll be going now."

With Cal in tow, Anita walked to the exit like a woman on fire. She practically sprinted to the limo, opened the door, unzipped her skirt and threw it in the street, oblivious to a very stunned aide.

"Cal, my suitcase is in the trunk. Get it, please."

"Yes, Senator."

The limo driver heard the exchange and popped open the trunk. Cal grabbed the suitcase and brought it inside the limo. Anita had removed all her clothing below the waist. Her suit jacket was in her lap. She took the suitcase from Cal. "Please wait outside." He complied.

Cindy knocked on the limo window. "Mom, are you okay?" News of the incident had spread throughout the hall in record time. "I came out as soon as I heard what happened."

"I'll be out in a sec. Wait there."

Five minutes later, composed and in control, Senator Minefeld emerged from the limo wearing a new outfit. She had the offending garments in a plastic bag and handed them to her aide. Cindy went over and hugged her mother.

"You poor thing. That must have been horrible. Did you call Dad?"

"No, I didn't call your father. He'll read about it soon enough. What am I saying? It's probably already up on YouTube. I've had some bizarre encounters as a senator, but this one really takes the cake." She looked over at Cal. He was still holding the plastic bag. She gave him an exasperated look. "Get rid of the bag. I don't want to see it."

"Right away. Sorry, Senator." Cal looked around until he spotted a trash can. It was already full of empty cans, bottles and wadded up bags from the giveaway. Cal placed the plastic bag on top of the trash, then pushed it down as far as it would go. He took a Purell sanitizing hand wipe out of his coat pocket, opened it and vigorously rubbed his hands.

Cindy said, "I got to get back. Sure you're okay?"

"Fine. Why don't you and your friend come by the Four Seasons Hotel at 7:00 p.m. and we can all go to the restaurant together?"

"Sounds great, Mom. See you then."

It wasn't until Anita was in her hotel room that the enormity of the incident hit her. If it wasn't mortifying enough to be the recipient of a homeless man's ejaculate, she would be the butt of countless jokes. Every late night host would give it their own original spin. She even imagined *Saturday Night Live* doing a skit about it.

Ignoring the constant ringing of her cell phone, she stepped into the shower and turned on the water as hot as she could stand it. She scrubbed every part of her body until it was red, then stood under the running water, listening to it beating down on her skin.

Much to her delight, the wet bar was stocked with Jamieson Scotch. She filled the tumbler with the amber liquid and watched as it jumped and slid over the ice cubes. The aroma of the single malt scotch tickled her olfactory nerve and erased the last remnants of tension. The phone continued to ring, but not as often. She still wasn't in the mood to answer it. Lifting her glass in the air, she made a toast. "To d.o.a. You've arrived not a moment too soon."

31

I t took Kanen a few minutes to comprehend what he had just heard. He was aware of all the conspiracy theories that popped up faster than they could be verified. The internet gave them a wider audience, but many were too difficult and outrageous to confirm. If what Bonnie overheard was true, the potential to mass poison hundreds of thousands of Americans would soon become a reality.

In addition to overhearing Gerald's phone conversation with Anita, Bonnie photographed the subsequent text strings between the two. Kanen was overwhelmed.

"This is unbelievable."

"If you knew Gerald, you wouldn't think so. It's the senator's attitude that blew me away. I looked her up online and she impressed me as a decent person. So, what do you think we should do?"

"First of all, don't use your computer at work to communicate with me. Gerald could be monitoring it. We don't know when they're planning on distributing the drugged food. Until we do, it's going to be almost impossible convincing the authorities to act."

"I have the text messages. Wouldn't that be enough to have them launch an investigation? At the very least, it would stop the project from moving forward."

Kanen stood up and walked to the kitchen to refill his water glass. "You know it's illegal to copy someone else's text messages without their approval? You could be arrested or fined and I'm not sure if the texts would be admissible as evidence." He sat down next to Bonnie and took her hands in his. "I don't like telling you this, but if we're going to stop these demons from killing off God knows how many people, you're going to have to get more information."

Bonnie looked down at their hands intertwined. "The thought sickens me."

"Me, too."

"Why don't I make dinner and afterwards, we can work out a plan. On top of the list is figuring out what to say to Gerald when I walk into the office on Monday. He's probably fuming because I left early." She got up and went to the kitchen. "I know! I'll tell him that I went home and started to work on a new, more masculine ad campaign. I wanted to surprise him."

"Great lie. You do it well. A little too well."

"It's been part of my life for so long, I can't remember not lying or stretching the truth to get what I wanted. Look where it got me."

"You're being facetious, right?"

She laughed. "Yes, you dope." Bonnie opened up the refrigerator, scanned its contents and then did the same with the freezer. "You're not going to believe this, well maybe you are. I don't have anything that you can eat."

Kanen got up and walked over to where Bonnie was standing. "I find that hard to believe." He opened the fridge's crisper bins and pulled out a head of cauliflower and three zucchinis. "What do you call these, T-bones?"

"I meant as a main dish."

"Do you have any potatoes?"

Bonnie went over to her pantry and grabbed two russet potatoes and a large yam. She proudly held them up. "Ta da!"

"Rice? Quinoa? Pasta?" Kanen said as he grabbed the tubers from her outstretched arms.

"I know I have rice." She reached into the pantry again and placed a box of Uncle Ben's white rice on the counter. "Not even opened."

"Good. Let it stay that way. White rice? Really? Do you know how innutritious it is?"

"I do now."

Kanen smiled. "Get me the cutting board, a knife and your steamer. You have a steamer, don't you?"

"Yes sir!"

184

"Good. I'll fix dinner."

For the next forty-five minutes, Kanen deftly wielded the chef's knife. He chopped and sliced the veggies, steamed them, then lightly bathed them in olive oil. A squeeze of fresh lemon juice, salt, pepper and garlic powder finished off the dish. He brought the bowl over to the table where Bonnie had set out plates and silverware. She included wine glasses and took the liberty of filling them with a pinot noir.

"I still don't see a main dish," she said, then quickly added, "Just kidding. It looks yummy and smells good, too. Thanks for cooking."

"You're very welcome."

Bonnie helped herself to a plate of veggies, then handed the bowl to Kanen.

She stacked slices of yam, potato and cauliflower on her fork and took a bite. "Wow. This is really good and I can't believe how easy it was to prepare, but I got to tell you, I don't think this is going to fill me up and I find it really hard to believe that you can be satisfied."

"I wouldn't mind walking to Whole Foods after dinner and picking up dessert."

"Uh oh, does that mean I have to partake in a non-dairy, no egg treat as well?"

"You bet your ass it does and I promise you'll love it."

Bonnie stopped smiling and looked at Kanen seriously. "I read your interview in *San Francisco* magazine. You really wouldn't marry a non-vegan?"

She caught Kanen mid-bite, ready to devour a chunk of zucchini. He put the fork down. "No, I wouldn't. I was born and raised vegan. I've never eaten animal flesh, eggs or dairy. I don't expect you to understand, but veganism is a lifestyle. It's stronger than most people's religious convictions. I wouldn't even conceive of eating a cow or a pig any more than you would consider eating a kitten or a puppy. You wouldn't, right?"

Bonnie got up from the table, clearly upset. Kanen followed her.

"Sorry, that was out of line. Seeing you at the convention was fantastic, but we haven't officially gone out on a date yet. Why don't we start there and see where it leads? I realize the onus is on you. I'm not changing my eating habits."

"Yeah, I know. That sucks. The last thing I want to be is like my brother."

"Spencer's a good guy."

"He's a freak." Bonnie sat back down at the table and continued eating.

"No, he's just overly sensitive and has a hard time controlling his feelings of helplessness. Why are you two so angry at each other?"

Immediately, her body tensed and her mind ached. "We're not going there now. Maybe I'll tell you some day when we're munching on tofu pups and drinking almond milk."

"Bonnie, I really like you but if my lifestyle is too extreme for you, I understand."

"I was just kidding."

"Maybe. Maybe not. It would be a huge adjustment for you. I'll help you expose the fast food scheme. After that, if you don't want to see me, I understand, okay? The last thing you need is pressure."

As badly as she wanted to be with Kanen, Bonnie also realized that their worlds were very different. The internal conflict was anything but quiet. "I'll think about it. Now, let's finish up dinner so we can gorge on dessert."

Bonnie was amazed at the selection of non-dairy frozen desserts. She never bothered to look at the section before, always opting for the dairy versions. Even Double Rainbow made soy cream in a variety of flavors, like Cinnamon Caramel and Very Cherry Chip. They finally decided on a pint each of caramel fudge chip and espresso cream made with coconut milk by a new vegan company out of Emeryville, a small town in the East Bay. Back at the apartment, they spooned out the frozen dessert into bowls shaped like bunnies.

"This is delicious. Are you sure it doesn't have any milk in it?"

Kanen cocked his head. "I'm introducing you to a whole new world, aren't I? May you continue to be in awe and wonder."

"Yes, may I," she said with a sly grin.

"Let's figure out how to stop your maniac boss from killing off tons of people, then we can play."

Bonnie mixed the two flavors together, swirling them around the bowl and taking a spoonful. "Don't you think our world would be a better place if the scum of the earth were killed off? They want to eliminate people in America's hellholes, not the good guys, you know?"

"I'm not going to play devil's advocate with you. There are a lot of undesirable human beings that live in what you call America's hellholes. But how about the humans who run corporations that wreak havoc on the environment, third world countries, us? And they live in gated communities and mansions. They use more natural resources than most small towns. Should we annihilate them, too, or just give them the power to kill off who they want, deeming themselves better than what they consider the dregs of society? No one has the right to play God. Instead of poisoning the people we think are worthless and not deserving to live, why don't we help them? Can you imagine how much more productive they could be if they were healthy and happy?"

Bonnie got up and put her dish in the sink. She sat back down opposite Kanen on the couch and sighed. "You're right. It's not the solution." She eyed a bottle of Tylenol on the coffee table and picked it up. "I read that some people are allergic to Acetaminophen and get skin reactions that can be fatal. My dad goes into anaphylactic shock if he's stung by a bee. I get a bee sting and it swells slightly. Who knows what this drug will do to people who don't display any signs of illness, like kids. Little kids."

"Exactly. All we have to do is figure out how to expose your boss and Senator Minefeld without putting you in harm's way."

They sat there for a few minutes, both lost in thought. Finally, Bonnie said, "I have a plan."

32

Spencer was cleaning the dishes when he heard something outside, like someone or something was hopping in the back yard. He went to his front window and saw Perry doing cartwheels on the lawn. He dried his hands and opened up the front door. Gilley rushed past him and ran straight to Perry. She was mid-cartwheel when the dog ran between her legs, surprising her. Perry stopped and greeted Gilley, whose mange was almost gone. She was more animated, too.

"Wow, she looks like a totally different dog and what a sweetheart."

Spencer walked over to where they were sitting, a tennis ball in his right hand. "I know. She still doesn't bark. In a way, it's nice."

They sat on the lawn, enjoying the last remnants of the day. Gilley was lapping up the attention, getting her belly rubbed and head scratched. Spencer threw the ball and she ran for it. Perry watched her sprint across the yard. "Isn't it amazing? Here's a dog that was caged her entire life and still runs for a ball when it's thrown. I guess some actions are hardwired."

Gilley returned with the ball and dropped it in Spencer's lap. He picked it up and threw it farther than before and she ran even faster to retrieve it. The firefly lights started to appear as the sun set. The trees and shrubs came alive with the intermittent lights. Their soft glow adding to the evening's charm.

"Besides doing cartwheels, what are you up to tonight?" said Spencer. He lay back on the grass.

"Nothing else. Cartwheels was the only thing on the list. Mission accomplished. Have you ever done them?"

"As a kid. It's been a long time." Without prompting, Spencer got up and, tentatively at first, performed a cartwheel. "I forgot how much fun they are."

"I know!" Perry rose and joined her tenant. From afar, they could have been mistaken for children, completely carefree and engaged in exuberance. Gilley dropped the ball and stared at her friends as they laughed and seemed to dance across the grass. When they stopped they dropped to the ground, sprawled out, breathing heavily.

Spencer said, "I'm so winded. I have got to start exercising." He rolled over onto his back and Gilley came to him and put her head on his chest. He stroked her side, completely taken by the sheltie terrier. "So boss, what's our next gig?"

"I was wondering when you were going to ask me that. Actually, it's still in the planning stages, so I'm not allowed to talk about it."

Spencer sat up, prompting Gilley to jump into his lap. "I'm part of the rescue. Doesn't that count for something?"

"It should, I know, but those are the rules. They want to make sure that every piece is in place, every scenario is examined, before the rescue is revealed. A few years ago, a plan was prematurely announced. One of the rescuers took incomplete information and tried to perform the rescue herself and failed. The consequences were deadly. Since then, they decreed that the rescuers involved wouldn't be told of the operation until every detail was completed."

"Can you give me a hint?"

Perry looked at him sideways. "Come on Spencer, you know I can't. By next week, I'll have something to tell you, okay?"

"Fine." He got up and threw the ball. Gilley chased it and Spencer ran after her. "Go on, girl. Get that ball!"

Perry watched her tenant, the temperamental and sometimes moody young man, running after the rescue dog. He had changed immeasurably since she first met him. She knew he needed to focus his anger and anxiety into doing something productive and rewarding. Her assumption paid off. He was not as focused and a little rattled when they stole the two beagles, but when they liberated the puppy mill dogs, Spencer was cool and calm. Regardless of the horrific conditions and the mass suffering he witnessed, he was completely in control. Perry thought about her daughter, Callie. She longed to see her again. To speak to her again. Perry's closeness to Spencer magnified their estrangement. Whenever she thought about calling her, she hesitated. The anticipation of an argument stopped her cold. Even with all of Spencer's emotional problems, she wished her daughter was more like him.

While she was deep in thought, Spencer practically sat down on top of her. He was irritated. "I really think you should make an exception and tell me what our next heist is going to be. I deserve to know. I'm putting myself on the line."

Perry was pissed. "Listen kiddo and I do mean kiddo. You need to let this go. I'll tell you when I'm given the go-ahead. If you don't like it, you're out of the mission. Period."

"Ouch."

"Well, you won't leave it alone." Spencer looked dejected and then she felt bad. "Have you thought about meditating?"

"Why does everyone ask me that?"

Perry laughed. "Because you desperately need to incorporate it into your life. Every day. You want a quick lesson?"

The sun was setting and the sky was a mixture of thin, denim blue clouds stretched across the darkening sky. Light pink clouds filtered through them, emulating a Maxfield Parrish painting.

"Right here?"

"Sure. It won't take long. First of all, lie on your back, close your eyes and take a deep breath through your nose and exhale through your mouth."

Spencer complied. He lay down on the soft grass with Gilley by his right side, Perry on his left. He inhaled deeply and let it out, then opened his eyes and looked to Perry for further direction.

This is going to be fun, she thought with a sigh. "Dear, keep your eyes closed the whole time. Let your body relax and continue to breath deep. As you inhale, imagine that you're pulling energy in from the earth and as you exhale, let all the negative energy leave your body."

Perry watched as Spencer's feet began to turn outward, a sign that he was letting go of the tension. His inhale was long as was his exhale. It was one of the few times she witnessed a relaxed Spencer.

She was about to continue her narrative when he put his hand on her leg. His nails were bitten down to the skin. With his eyes closed, he looked angelic. His dark, wavy hair swept across his forehead, barely covering his ears. His cheeks displayed a touch of color. Perry hadn't been with a man in years and the warmth of Spencer's hand felt good. Almost inviting. She was about to put her hand on his when she glanced at her veiny, liver-spotted skin. Ashamed at herself for even contemplating romance, she reluctantly took his hand and put it next to his leg. Spencer opened his eyes and looked up at Perry. "Was that out of line?"

She nodded. "I'm twice your age. My daughter is older than you."

"So? It's just a number. Twenty-four, forty-eight. Who cares? I don't."

"I do."

Spencer sat up. "Look at you."

"I would but my stomach is in the way."

"It's not funny. You're beautiful and kind and thoughtful and…" He started to lean toward her but Perry stood up. "You want to go to Jauncy's?"

"Dancing? Sure. Let me feed Gilley and change into my dancing clothes."

Spencer jogged to the cottage with Gilley in tow. Perry felt like she had just dodged a very dangerous bullet. She was attracted to this twenty-four-year-old kid. She knew it was wrong and was determined not to let her libido trump logic. The last man she dated was James Landon and that was over three years ago. He was five years older than her and in good shape for his age. A jogger, he ran three miles a day, had a great job as a landscape architect and was even leaning toward a vegan diet when they met. The problem, and it was a big one in Perry's eyes, was that James' interest in her life was negligible. Whenever they were together, he would talk about his day at work, the chats he had with his children and whatever else he felt like espousing. When the conversation eventually landed in Perry's lap, James' attention span was absent. His eyelids would flutter as he tried to stay awake. Eventually, his head would fall onto his chest and then bob up as he momentarily opened his eyes. Three minutes into Perry's recitation of her day, she felt compelled to sit next to him so he didn't fall out of his chair in a dead sleep. When she called off the relationship he was flabbergasted, which reinforced her decision.

Spencer and Perry were on their third round of Bloody Marys when they worked their way through the crowd and ended up in the middle of the dance floor. It was a Wednesday night and but Jauncy's was packed. The speakers blasted Bruce Springsteen's *Dancing in the Dark*. Perry's mind flashed on the 1984 video of a fresh-faced Bruce wearing tight jeans and a short-sleeved shirt; the sleeves rolled up even shorter. His dancing was stilted, but he still looked sexy. She closed her eyes and imagined she was a younger Courtney Cox, the girl Bruce chose to dance with him on stage. She was really getting into it when she lost her balance. Spencer grabbed her arm, preventing her from falling. He then pulled her to him and, before Perry realized what was happening, kissed her. It was sensuous and exhilarating. His lips were soft, slightly parted. He had his arms around her and her body was pressed against his. Her head was screaming that this was so wrong, but her alcohol-fueled emotions were at the helm. At the moment, Perry let it be. She decided to deal with the fallout later. Her decision gave her carte blanche to revel in the pleasure. She felt like an enamored teenager with the carnal knowledge of an adult.

If not for the Bloody Marys, Spencer never would have had the chutzpah to grab his landlady around the waist and kiss her. His meager attempt while they were on the grass paled in comparison to this bold move. He had been trying to figure out how to kiss her when he noticed that she was starting to fall. The timing was perfect. As he let himself enjoy the music and Perry's body, he once again was able to abandon the internal turmoil and chatter.

Springsteen's voice stoked her fire and when the song was over and Spencer released her, she felt dizzy and aroused. It was a rush she had felt when she was younger, maybe when she was Spencer's age. She looked into Spencer's eyes and knew exactly where he wanted to go and what he wanted to do. It was up to Perry to keep the fire burning or extinguish it before it gained any more fuel. As Spencer took her hand and led her off the dance floor, she cursed herself for having three drinks.

Back at their table, Spencer said, "Shall we go?" Before she could answer, he pulled her sweater off the back of the chair and draped it over his arm, then drained his drink.

Perry sat down and leaned back. When she did, the room moved unnaturally. Or was it her? "I am not okay to drive. Are you?"

Always a lightweight when it came to alcohol, Spencer knew that he wouldn't pass the drunk driving test. Sadly, he shook his head. Perry put her hand on his back. "I'll go get us some waters."

Spontaneously, Perry let out a sigh of relief. She and Spencer had a great working relationship and a wonderful tenant/landlord relationship. Adding sex and lust to the equation could potentially obliterate both. She knew how precarious it was from experience. Explaining it to the young neophyte wouldn't be easy.

She sat back down at their table wedged between a booth and the window. She watched a couple around her age walk by, hand in hand, and felt a tinge of sadness. When she looked back at Spencer, he had a melancholy smile on his face.

"What?" Perry said.

He placed her hand in his. "Honestly, I don't give a shit what other people think." His eyes became cloudy. "But I know you'll be judged more harshly than me. You're the one who will get the stares and the glares and I don't want you to have to deal with that, even though you look amazing. You know that, right?"

"I underestimated you, Spencer. At your age, I wasn't even close to your maturity level. Ironically, it makes me want you more, but we have to put a kibosh on our attraction to each other for a number of reasons, least of which is my concern over what people think. Thank you for being so understanding."

Spencer said, "This is killing me."

"You'll be just fine. Better than fine, now let's dance. I love INXS."

Perry grabbed his hand and led him to the dance floor. From behind, they looked the same age. Her skinny jeans and long-sleeved tee hugged her toned body. Void of inhibition and the confines of anxiety, Perry was free to completely let go. And she did. It wasn't her intention to ignore Spencer, but she danced alone to the pulsing beat of *Suicide Blonde*, her long braid moving in the direction of her fluid body. Spencer danced beside her. He enjoyed watching her, clearly lost in the music. Neither of them noticed a young couple staring at them, thoroughly jealous of the bond they so obviously shared.

33

"She was kickin' up dust and swirlin' it around. She thought she was lost, but that cowgirl got found." Cody's voice was pitch perfect, singing loud and clear as he strolled down O'Farrell. As he approached the corner, he could hear San and Fran barking. "I'm coming. Don't get impatient, now.

"Sometimes I pretend I don't see her at all, when she's dancin' to the music in her head by the stalls. That cowgirl's got grit as hard as the ground. She thought she was lost, but that cowgirl got found."

It was an unusually warm afternoon in San Francisco, yet Cody was wearing his signature dreads underneath a black Stetson. The Duster Coat was newly cleaned, its brass buttons reflecting the sun and his dark brown cowboy boots polished. To a stranger, Cody looked like he was an extra in a Rastafarian cowboy flick, but most in the Loin knew the friendly man who was always ready to lend a hand to someone who needed it.

When he reached his destination, he took off his backpack, squatted and dug into it.

"What the hell do you think you're doing?"

Cody looked up. Standing on the other side of the fence at Jake's Auto Repair and Salvage was Jake himself. His gnarled hand held the dogs' chains tight. He dared them to bark. Bow-legged and slightly bent over from years of working on cars, the man looked a lot older than forty-five. He growled at Cody, "I told you I don't want you feedin' my guard dogs."

Cody put the food back in his pack and stood up. "They're skinny. Too skinny. Starving skinny."

"I ain't blind. It keeps them alert. I can't have lazy guard dogs now, can I?"

Cody looked over at their empty water bowl. "They're out of water, too. They need water, man."

Jake released the chains and walked to the fence, about one foot away from Cody. "These ain't your dogs, cowboy. Now go and rustle up some black cows and water 'em and feed 'em, but leave my fuckin' dogs alone." He walked over to Fran and kicked him, causing the dog to yelp. Cody felt helpless. He wanted to pick Jake up and drop him on the razor wire and watch him wriggle and squirm, but he held his anger in check. Reluctantly, he walked away and vowed to return in the middle of the night when he was sure San and Fran would be alone.

Relieved that the Social Services Department was open, Cody strode in expecting a long wait. It must have been an unpopular hour because he was fourth in line. He towered over the elderly woman in front of him. Cody looked down on her thinning, dishwater blonde hair. She was bundled in filthy blankets from below her chin to her ankles. She looked up at Cody and glared. "Stop breathing on me!"

"I'm sorry. I didn't mean to."

"Bullshit. All men mean to. Knock it off."

Cody backed up a few inches. He looked around, hoping to catch a sympathetic eye. No one even glanced his way. They were all used to the outbursts and degradation. A young boy of about eighteen sat against the wall biting his nails as if it was his last meal. He bit and chewed nonstop. The man sitting next to him didn't notice. He was too busy snoring.

Sondra Levy gave Cody a big smile, her straight white teeth positively glowed in contrast to the unsightly choppers in the room.

"Cody! What a surprise. I haven't seen you here since you came to the Loin. What can I help you with?"

He leaned his large hands on the counter and smiled back. "What's the name of the senator who was giving out the food?"

"Bertram Kathala."

"Do you have his number?"

Sondra looked confused. "I do. You want to call him?"

Cody nodded. "Now."

"This minute?"

"Please. It's very important."

"Hold on." Sondra went into the adjoining room, grabbed the phone book and placed it on the counter. She turned to the government listings, the green pages, spotted Senator Kathala's San Francisco office number and wrote it down on a piece of scrap paper.

"Here you go."

Cody accepted the piece of paper then stared at the phone on the wall behind the desk. Sondra followed his eyes. She should have known that he wouldn't have access to a phone. She reached from under the desk and produced a cordless phone, then handed it to Cody. "You can use it in that room over there for privacy, okay?"

"Thanks."

As he waited for the senator's office to answer, he noticed the room's dull white walls, battered furniture and worn linoleum floor. Instead of framed pictures, the Social Services '10 Rules for a Better Life' graced one wall. The three-foot by four-foot poster was torn at the edges and discolored. Cody wondered if anyone took the time to read it.

On the third ring, the phone was answered. "Senator Kathala's office. Can I help you?"

"This is Walter Cattlin. Can I speak to Senator Kathala, please?"

"I'm sorry Mr. Cattlin, but the senator is in Washington, D.C. Is there something I can help you with?"

"Can I have the number?"

"Of course, but it's after 5:00 there. You can leave a message."

"I really need to speak to him now." Cody's voice was laced with anxiety. The senator's aide picked up on it. She softened her voice.

"Mr..."

"Cattlin."

"Sorry. Mr. Cattlin, if you tell me what it's regarding, perhaps I can help."

"If I do, will you promise to tell the senator?"

"I will."

Cody began to tell the aide about San and Fran. How they're starved, denied water and mistreated.

"There's got to be laws against that, right?"

"Yes. Animal cruelty laws are enforced by San Francisco Animal Care and Control, not the federal government. Would you like their number?"

"Only if you promise to tell Senator Kathala to call me back. Tell him Cody Brant from the Tenderloin wants to talk to him."

"Is this a joke?"

"No! He just knows me by that name."

Reluctantly, she said, "What's your number?"

"Hold on."

Cody opened the door. "What's the number here?"

Sondra turned to Cody. "Are you kidding me? We're not your answering service!"

"Come on. Senator Kathala's calling me back."

"Just this once, Cody. That's it. 415-334-0566."

He shut the door and recited the number to the aide. In turn, he was given the humane society's number.

Ten minutes later, Cody handed the phone back to Sondra. He thanked her and was leaving when she asked him to step back into the room he just vacated. She followed him in and shut the door.

"What was that all about?"

Cody explained everything to her, from the encounter with Jake to the promise from Animal Care and Control that a humane officer would check out the claims of abuse. When he finished, Sondra went over and gave him a big hug.

"You're a wonderful man, Cody. I hope the dogs are taken away from that creep. Why did you want the senator to call you back and how am I going to find you when and if he does?"

"I figure that he represents everyone in the Loin. The people and the animals. He should know what's going on. I'll come by at 1:00 in the afternoon every day. If he calls, tell him to call back then."

Sondra laughed. "Cody, he's a senator! If he calls the first time, it'll be a miracle and you're asking him to call again?"

"Yup."

And he did. Three days later, Cody walked through the door of social services at 1:00 on the dot and Sondra waved the portable phone above her head. "It's him! Senator Kathala!"

With his long legs, it took five steps for Cody to grab the phone from Sondra. He walked into the empty office and closed the door.

"Hello Senator Kathala."

"Cody, or is it Walter?"

"Your choice."

"What can I do for you, Cody?"

Cody proceeded to tell the senator about the dogs. He also told him about his conversation with the humane officer. When he was finished, Bert said, "I think it's great that you're looking out for these creatures who don't have a voice, but you know I don't have jurisdiction over city and county laws. Only the federal level."

"I know that. I have an idea. We all appreciate the free food you've been handing out and I know it's going to end soon, right? A lot of us are on food stamps and welfare. How about giving some of us in the Loin and in other cities the job of helping dogs and cats that aren't treated right? You could pay us a little more than we get from welfare, give us cell phones and we'll report abuse. We can take pictures and send them to the humane officers. We'd be helping them out. I think it's a great idea, don't you?"

Bert was a dog lover. He couldn't care less about cats, but ever since he was a child, his family had dogs. Pit bulls. When he retired, he planned on adopting a couple of pits from the shelter. He hated hearing about dogs being mistreated, especially pits like San and Fran. He knew that Cody's plan was out of the question. Giving that kind of responsibility to welfare recipients wasn't going to fly in Congress. He'd be the laughingstock of the entire Hill, but he also liked Cody and didn't want to make light of his proposal. In addition, he didn't want Cody at the third food giveaway where the d.o.a. tainted meat would be introduced.

"I'll tell you what. Our next food giveaway is only a week away. Why don't we meet at the social services office when I'm done at the Y? I'll bring you four meals and you can show me San and Fran, okay?"

"I can do that. Why can't we talk at the Y?"

"It'll be easier for me to talk to you at the office. More privacy there."

"Okay. Thanks."

"My pleasure. It is going to cost you. I want to hear you sing *We Shall Dance* again."

"My pleasure."

Kanen arrived early at his parents' house. It was 5:45 and he was expected at 6:00. He tried getting out of it, knowing that his mom and dad were going to grill him on his relationship with 'that Hinton woman.' Bonnie swore him to secrecy, though he would have loved to get advice from his parents on how to handle the poisoned meat.

He grabbed the six-pack of Crazy Cat Lager, slowly got out of his car and walked up the fifty-seven steps to his parents' turn-of-the- century Victorian. Kanen appreciated the architecture, but much preferred an open, modern floor plan. Exposed wood beams and tempered steel were more to his liking than dark paneling and wainscoting. His home was bathed in sunlight. One of the living room walls was glass and looked across a valley. He wouldn't have it any other way. He also knew how fortunate he was to be living in Mill Valley, one of the wealthiest Marin County enclaves. Not bad for a twenty-four year old.

Kanen knocked on the door and walked in. He was hit with the aroma of grilled onions and peppers, fresh garlic, too.

"You making your famous fajitas, Senõr Weston?"

"Si."

Bill flipped the onion concoction over with the spatula, sprinkled it with pepper, and then wiped his hands in his apron. He went over and gave his son a hearty hug. It was generously returned.

"I haven't seen you in, what's it been, forty-eight hours? My, how you've grown!"

"I have a feeling I'll be growing even more after this meal. It smells great. I bet you could make the fajitas blindfolded."

"I tried, but your mother made me stop after I nearly minced the oven mitt."

"She's such a killjoy."

"You must be talking about me again." Michelle strode up to her son and gave him a hug and kiss. She lowered her voice. "Did you bring that dreadful girl with you?"

"She's not dreadful and I did not bring her."

"Kanen…"

"Mommie Dearest…Let's not talk about her, please. It's one part of my life that I'd rather not discuss, okay?"

Bill said, "Fine with me."

Michelle stared at her son and shook her head. "Fine. Just be careful. Promise me."

"Promise." Kanen crossed his heart. "Let's eat."

After dinner, the three Westons retired to the living room. A pot full of green tea sat on the table with three mugs. As Bill poured tea into each mug, he said, "I talked to Grant today. He and Jenny will be coming to visit next week. We're going to have a barbeque on Saturday. Can you make it?"

"Sure. I haven't seen my baby brother in ages. Will Dillon be here, too?"

"Uh-huh. Family reunion."

"Nice," said Michelle.

Kanen said, "I don't mean to switch gears, but something's been on my mind."

"I thought you didn't want to talk about Meat Girl."

"I don't Mom and please don't call her that."

"Fine. You're not going to get all esoteric on us, are you?" Michelle said.

"Afraid so. Here's the thing. I totally believe in reincarnation. I used to believe that our spirits inhabit human bodies in order to grow and become enlightened. But what state is a spirit in when it's created? Is it so deficient that it has to reincarnate over and over and over again until it's ready to…what? Never come back to earth? Where does it go? And if a spirit is so 'perfect' before it's reincarnated, why would it want to be in a human body? The suffering on this planet is so immense and off the charts horrific, what kind of crazy spirit would want to be in the body of a starving child in Chad or a girl in Saudi Arabia whose every movement is restricted? It doesn't make sense to me."

Bill looked at Michelle and, without saying a word, she nodded.

"Son, I'd like to introduce you to Dimethyltryptamine, DMT for short, otherwise known as the spirit molecule. It might answer some of your questions. I have a couple of hits left from when your mom and I took it a few months ago."

Kanen shook his head. "Can't you just answer my questions?"

Bill said, "Just because we're your parents and possess highly evolved minds," he smiled and looked at his wife, then continued, "doesn't mean we know everything. And if we did know the answer to those extremely heavy questions you seem to ask us every few months, we'd prefer you find the answers yourself."

Kanen laughed. "You're the only parents I know that give their kids drugs."

Michelle said, "That's not true. You know Nick and Rose Dirkee. They smoked pot with little Davey when he was a teenager."

"I stand corrected." He turned to his father. "I realize that I asked you some heavy questions, but a drug is your answer?"

Bill looked at Michelle. "Is this our kid? Your mom and I aren't druggies, but we experimented with different drugs when we were your age. Do you even smoke pot?"

"Occasionally. I prefer alcohol when I need to unwind. Kind of square, huh?"

Michelle took a sip of her tea and smiled. "To each his own, son. The difference between DMT and other drugs is that the molecule is found in all living beings and scientists don't know what its function is, especially in the human body. After taking the drug, some researchers believe that it connects us with our spirit, our soul. That's why your dad and I thought it might answer your questions. I could answer based on my beliefs and experiences, but I think you should find out for yourself. Why don't you take it with your friend that works for Hinton? Maybe it will knock some sense into her."

Kanen re-adjusted himself on the chair. Growing up with progressive parents, he was used to unconventional conversations. The love and respect he felt for them was monumental and he knew it was reciprocal, except when it came to his love life. They didn't approve of Bonnie and he didn't blame them. He also knew she wasn't as bad as they thought. At least not anymore.

"Tell me more about DMT. How long does the experience last?"

Bill said, "That's the great part. You feel like you're on a two-hour journey but from beginning to end, it's only ten to twenty minutes. Everyone's experience is different, but there are some elements that are similar, like seeing geometric shapes. The ones I saw were spinning and colorful, almost florescent. You know the screen savers with the shapes that wiggle and dive through space? Well, the ones you see on DMT are mind-blowing. Maybe it's because they've been organically created."

Kanen interrupted. "So this drug is a hallucinogenic?"

Michelle said, "Duh."

Kanen gave her a dirty look.

"Sorry. I thought it was evident. I saw geometric shapes, too, but more like the ones you see in crop circles and sacred geometry, like the flower of life. After that, I shot out of my body and…"

Bill cut in. "Hold it Michelle." He turned to Kanen. "We don't want to influence your experience. If you want to take it with a friend, I'll give you two doses. Before smoking it, think about the questions you asked us. See where it takes you."

Kanen said, "Fair enough. I'm definitely intrigued." He glanced at his watch. It was close to 9:00 p.m. "I should go. Thanks again for dinner."

"Any time. Let me get you the DMT." Bill got up and walked toward the hallway.

"Jim and Nita Yarkulsky," Michelle blurted out.

"Huh?"

"They smoked pot with their kids. Of course, Robyn and Jill were over twenty-one."

"Good to know, Mom. Really good to know."

34

It was Monday morning and Bonnie was anything but calm. She tried everything to even out her nerves, yet nothing seemed to be working. A few weeks ago, she would have had no problem faking her way through the day at Hinton, satisfying Gerald's enormous ego and larger sexual appetite. But after spending time with Kanen and mentally reliving the humiliation at the marketing meeting, Bonnie's inner demon was shriveling up and dying. Subconsciously, she was no longer feeding it the fuel it needed to survive.

For the sake of their plan, she had to put on the show of a lifetime. She called Kanen on her way to work.

"I don't know if I can do this. Facing that asshole is going to be so difficult."

Kanen was sitting at his desk. He had arrived at work early. "You've been faking it with him for years. Just remember what we talked about and you'll do great. When you hang up, erase my number from your phone and no texting. We can't have a communications trail. When you get home, call me on your land line. Good luck."

"Thanks. I can't wait for this day to be over."

Bonnie made sure she arrived at the office before Gerald. She wanted to settle in, listen to her messages and orient herself before the fireworks display. As she walked down the hallway she was relieved to discover that, so far, she was the only one there. Quickly, Bonnie turned on her computer and while it was booting up, she listened to her voice messages. A few were sales calls. One was from Jake at Ames & Leeson Advertising asking her to call him back so they could set up a time to review the ads. The last two were from Gerald's secretary, asking her to call as soon as she got the message.

Bonnie was perusing her e-mails when her secretary knocked on the door. "Come in."

"Hi. Gerald wants to see you right now."

"Okay. Thanks."

After composing herself, she brushed her hair, put on a fresh coat of lipstick; his favorite shade; and walked down the hall.

It was unusual for Kanen to have more than one mugful of coffee in the morning, but he was exceptionally nervous. He was not only afraid of what might happen to Bonnie when Gerald confronted her, he was disgusted by what she may have to continue doing for the sake of implementing their plan. Imagining that man's hands on her body and vice versa almost made him physically ill. Instead of having tea or a smoothie to settle his nerves, he opted to jolt them into super drive.

While waiting for a new pot to finish brewing, Kanen struck up a conversation with Manny Olivos, Weston's distribution manager. Manny began working for Weston as a truck driver. His outstanding work ethic paid off and, eight years later, he was promoted to his current position from warehouse manager. Kanen didn't know much about his personal life, but he and Manny could easily talk about the usual guy things like sports, women and night clubs.

Manny reminded Kanen of a Mexican Matt Damon. He was around the same age, tall and slender with a stub of a nose and light brown hair. His skin tone was the color of a mocha latté.

"Kanen. Just the person I wanted to talk to."

"Nice to see you, too. Did you have a good weekend?"

"I did. We had a big family picnic over at Golden Gate Park. I think our family took up half the park!"

"Are you still the only vegan?"

"Funny you should ask. A few family members have given up meat and dairy after watching me shrink from over two hundred and fifty pounds to one seventy. One of my cousins, Mike Flores, works for Hinton Industries. You know who they are, right?"

Kanen's eyes lit up. "Hell yeah."

"After working with all that raw meat and witnessing how it's handled by the other employees, he went vegan. Now, it's harder than ever for him to be there. He works in the trafficking department. It's the final phase in distribution where the meat is sent out to the restaurants."

"You're kidding, right?" Kanen's emotions were somewhere between exaltation and heightened fear. He couldn't help but think that he was being set up by Hinton, a man whose moral compass was non-existent.

Manny looked confused. "Why would I be kidding? He wanted me to ask you if there were any openings here."

Kanen's tension eased. It was replaced with a euphoria he could barely contain. "You know that better than me, Manny. It's your department."

He chuckled. "I know, but you're the boss and I wouldn't want to be accused of playing favorites."

Behind him, the coffee machine gurgled, indicating the carafe was full. As Kanen filled his cup, he noticed his hand slightly shaking. It wasn't the caffeine. He knew he should discuss this latest turn of events with Bonnie, but timing forced him to make an executive decision. He hoped it was the right one. "It's called nepotism and I appreciate your concern. Do you have a minute? I'd like to talk to you about it in my office."

"Sure."

As soon as she shut the door, Gerald turned into Lucifer. He was apoplectic, his face getting redder by every insult he hurled at her. She stood stick still, breathing deep to keep her composure, but she could feel the tension in her body and the sweat starting to seep into her armpits. She prayed he'd have a heart attack.

"Where the fuck did you go after the meeting? How dare you leave the office without a word! You didn't return any of my calls. I give you the career of a lifetime and you throw it in my face! Get out of my office. Get out of this building. NOW!"

Bonnie steadied herself and walked up to the front of Gerald's oversized desk. She put her hands on the desk and leaned over, treating him to a prime view of her cleavage. Her red ruby heart necklace hung an inch above her breasts.

"Let me explain. If you're still mad at me, then I'll leave."

As he stared at her breasts, his jugular returned to normal size and his face began to lose its bright red shade. "Talk."

"After the marketing meeting, I felt like a failure. The last thing I wanted to do was disappoint you and I did. From the sound of it, I did big time. Instead of staying in the office and dealing with my daily responsibilities, I went home and began working on the ad campaign. I didn't tell you I was leaving and I didn't answer my phone because I wanted to surprise you. Jake and I will have some great stuff to show you by next week. Please don't be mad at me." She licked her lips. "I'll make it up to you."

"Come here." Gerald patted his leg. As she walked around the desk, she almost hoped he'd fire her, but then she would have failed Kanen and he was the one person she didn't want to disappoint. She glanced at his beefy thigh before sitting down on his lap. He stood up, almost knocking her to the floor and took off his pants.

"How can I fire a bitch who's so fucking hot?"

He sat back down and lifted Bonnie's dress. Roughly, he grabbed her lace thong and pushed it to the side, then moved her back onto his lap. She took one look at Gerald's fat, hairy legs and wanted to run for the door. But she had come this far and wasn't about to quit now. While he gyrated and made short grunting and moaning sounds, Bonnie did her best to convince him that this was exactly what she wanted. She closed her eyes and smiled as Kanen's beautiful face filled her mind's eye. The vision didn't last long. Thankfully, Gerald had the sexual stamina of a tick with a sex organ to match. She stood up and immediately grabbed some tissues from his desk drawer.

"Use the bathroom, for God's sake." He pointed to a door at the far side of the room. Up until then, Bonnie had no idea he had a private bathroom. He'd never offered it for her use before. One more thing to despise him for, as if she needed another reason.

When Bonnie returned, Gerald was on the phone. He waved her away and she gladly obeyed. Back in her office, she busied herself with work, but couldn't take her mind off what had just happened. She desperately wanted to shower. She could smell Gerald on her skin, a mixture of expensive cologne, sweat and animal fat. She surmised that the man must eat meat at every meal because the cloying scent of animal cartilage, flesh and muscle wouldn't leave her nose. She wondered if he always smelled like that or if Kanen's influence was rubbing off on her.

35

Jessica wasn't sure why she accepted Lenore's dinner offer. Yeah, she was. She loved the attention. When Lenore wasn't explaining her latest research study with d.o.a. in excruciating detail and in a language Jessica swore wasn't English, she was asking Jessica a million questions about herself. Someone was sincerely interested in her life. Even her parents didn't show her that kind of attention. Of course, as a senator, she received all kinds of false praise, fawning from lobbyists – the same devotion one would receive from a mosquito before and while it sucked your blood.

But Lenore already had funding. She didn't need Jessica's influence in Washington. She enjoyed her company. Jessica's non-existent dating life and few friends in D.C. gave Lenore front and center consideration.

When Lenore answered the door, Jessica handed her a bottle of wine and a bouquet of yellow tulips.

"These are gorgeous! I love tulips. Please come in."

Lenore gave Jessica a hug. It lasted longer than most platonic hugs. She didn't mind at all.

The house smelled like garlic bread and marinara sauce. "Don't tell me. You're making spaghetti with red sauce and garlic bread."

"Wrong. Penne with red sauce and garlic bread. You politicians think you're always right."

"Not me, but I'm usually damn close."

While Lenore put the flowers in a vase, Jessica checked out the apartment. It was small and very tidy. She was expecting a lack of design skills, but Lenore had everything down to a science. Go figure. The theme was faux country and the Gingham Goose store would be proud. From the gingham couch with embroidered daisy pillows to the blue and white checkered rug, the only thing missing was a grain silo and wagon full of hay bales. Farm animal figurines were aplenty. Two shiny porcelain sheep frolicked on a shelf next to a cow pitcher. Below them sat three small bowls, their shapes ranging from a head of lettuce to an eggplant to an ear of corn.

In a cabinet all to itself, Lenore proudly displayed her salt and pepper shaker collection. In addition to the country theme, she had salt and pepper shakers from different states. From the size of the collection, she may have had all fifty represented.

"My parents gave me the state shakers. Before I was born, they traveled all over the country." Lenore pointed to a bisected Golden Gate Bridge, one half salt and the other pepper. "That one's over thirty years old. I bet they don't even make it anymore."

I hope not, thought Jessica. "It's certainly unique."

"I know!" Lenore ducked into the kitchen. "Would you like a glass of wine? Your wine, actually. The one you brought."

"That would be nice. Thanks." Jessica could hear her fumbling in the cabinet for wine glasses. It reminded her of herself, except by this time, Jessica would have dropped or broken something. Not a second later, she heard the breaking of glass and an expletive. Two klutzes having dinner.

"Are you okay, Lenore?" Jessica walked into the kitchen. Lenore was squatting down, brushing glass fragments into a dust pan.

"I'm fine. It's a good thing I bought a case of wine glasses at Costco. I should have bought two. You know what my mom calls me? The nutty professor, except I'm actually the nutty researcher, but that's not a movie. The nutty professor is. Have you seen it?"

"Both versions."

"Me, too. Which one is your favorite? I like the Eddie Murphy version better."

"I have to go with the original. I love Jerry Lewis." Switching gears, she said, "How is your research going? Any progress with d.o.a.?"

"Sadly, no." Lenore dumped the broken glass into the trash and gently grabbed another one from the cabinet. She filled the two goblets and handed one to Jessica.

"Cheers," she said.

"Cheers."

Jessica followed Lenore into the living room, where they sat on the couch.

"I'm isolating the components of the drug, trying to determine what caused the acceleration of illness and death in the prisoners. I can't replicate the results in rodents, so I've been forced to use human tissue and blood from the two test subjects that survived. Truth be told, I'd much prefer the inmates. I don't know why the authorities at Fillmore stopped my research. Every subject was on death row and they all suffered from a debilitating, if not fatal, illness. Would it be so tragic if they died before living out their sentence in a postage stamp-sized cell at taxpayer's expense?"

A woman after my own heart, thought Jessica. "I'd be happy to look into it and see if there's anything I can do to help."

Lenore nearly jumped off the sofa. "That would be awesome! Thank you!"

"No promises, mind you. With a Democrat-controlled senate, rights of prisoners sit alongside rights of veterans. If Republicans can't take back the Hill, you'll be seeing abortion clinics on every corner and the homeless getting free housing."

"Isn't that a frightening thought?" Lenore refilled her glass. "This wine is delicious." She rose. "I'm going to check on the pasta."

Jessica leaned back on the sofa. She hated the pattern but it was comfortable. She felt like she was on a cloud. The wine softened her thoughts and lightened the events of the day. Her father stopped by unannounced, once again. She hated how he came into her office and made himself at home, as if he was subletting his old stomping grounds. 'This is where historic bills were created by yours truly' he would declare as he rolled his cigar around in his fingers before sticking it into his mouth. He knew she hated the smell. Once a senator, always a senator. The only thing larger than his ego was his belly. After enduring forty-five minutes of the great ex-senator pontificating, her aide reminded her of an important meeting. Begrudgingly, her father left. Not once did he ask Jessica about herself. She was used to being talked at, so it didn't bother her. Feeling just the slightest bit guilty, she imagined slipping some d.o.a. into her father's scotch. The old man suffered from high blood pressure and already had one heart attack. It wouldn't take much to overload his system.

"Ta-da!" Lenore placed the bowl of pasta on the kitchen table. "Dinner is served." She went to the oven to retrieve the garlic bread. Reluctantly, Jessica lifted herself off the couch and sat down at the kitchen table. Steam was rising from the freshly tossed pasta and the aroma from the garlic bread sent her senses soaring.

"This looks delicious."

Lenore beamed. "I never cook for anyone but myself, so this is a treat for me, too." She placed a large helping on her guest's plate, then clumsily plopped a serving on her own. A few tubes of penne slipped through the tongs, one dropping into her wine glass. She sighed. "It's never ending, is it?"

Jessica gave her a sympathetic smile. Their eyes met and for a few seconds the women felt a tiny jolt between them, like a lost, buried desire that never had a chance to surface until now.

36

Spencer lay on the couch, reading a book. Gilley was by his side, quietly snoring. Her left paw rested on his chest. Every once in a while, he would look over at the sweet dog next to him. It was hard to imagine her not being in his life. Saving her was one of Spencer's proudest moments. The knock on the door startled them both. Gilley jumped up and ran to the door. Instead of barking, she looked at the door and then to Spencer.

"Who is it?" Spencer said as he walked to the door. He was wearing sweats and a t-shirt.

"Perry."

He opened the door and resisted the urge to give her a kiss. After their talk at Jauncy's, he was determined to keep his hands to himself.

"Do you have minute?" she said.

"Sure. Come on in."

Perry sat down on the couch and Spencer joined her. She placed a folder adorned with various sized butterflies on the table and patted it. "This is our third assignment. The one I've been waiting for. The one you tried to pry out of me not too long ago. Well, Mr. Rydover, the wait is over." She paused just long enough to irritate Spencer. He was about to say something when she continued.

"Are you familiar with Dr. Nicholas Crowden?"

He shook his head. "Should I be?"

"If you belonged to Truth for Animals, you'd know who he is. The group has been trying to shut down his lab at UC Berkeley for years."

Perry pulled a photograph out of the folder. "This is the evil doctor." Except for the lab coat, Crowden looked like he worked for Domino's, delivering pizzas. He had unkempt black curly hair, almond shaped deep brown eyes and a roman nose. He had an olive complexion, marred by a smattering of acne scars. Other than a slightly protruding belly, he was in decent shape for a thirty-eight-year-old.

"Nicolas Crowden is trying to prove that smoking causes ulcers. He uses cats. Last count, he had ten in his lab. He affixes a mask to their mouth and places a cigarette at the tip, forcing them to smoke an unfiltered cigarette until it's gone. No butt. These animals endure this five days a week at two packs of cigarettes a day. At the end of three months, he kills the cats and opens up their stomachs, hoping to find ulcers. To date, not one goddamn ulcer has been discovered. Cost to taxpayers: $80,000 a year. Cost to the pain and suffering of over 300 cats: incalculable. Before cats, he used dogs. And before that, he was addicting rats to nicotine."

Perry pulled out two photographs. One showed the cats, their bodies restrained in boxes. Only their heads were visible. Strapped to their mouths were devices that held lit cigarettes. The cats' eyes were closed, their heads enshrouded in smoke. The second photo revealed the cats' living conditions. Cages were stacked on top of each other. Their cell afforded each cat approximately one foot of stretching room. They had a bed and bowls for food and water.

She continued. "As Axel Munthe said, 'The cruel, wild beast is not behind the bars of the cage. He is in front of it.' We have a rare opportunity to save these cats and destroy this sadist's equipment."

She saw the fear on Spencer's face before he said a thing. "I know this sounds scary, but we have been planning this rescue for a while. We had to make sure that every piece of the puzzle fit and room for error was less than two percent."

As if she detected his trepidation, Gilley jumped into his lap and began licking his face. He smiled. "Before you give me the specifics, would you like a beer?"

"Only if it's ice cold."

"I think I can manage that." Spencer got up and went to his fridge, extracting a large bottle of Sapporo. Then he took two frosted glass mugs out of the freezer. He poured equal amounts of beer into the mugs and handed one to Perry. "Is that cold enough for you?"

He watched Perry put the mug up to her lips and take a long swallow.

"Perfect. Thanks." She kicked off her shoes and sat back down on the couch with her legs crossed, then she took peach-tinted lip balm out of her right pants pocket and deftly applied it. "Crowden has two assistants. One of them has only worked there for a couple of months. The other one for over three years. He's neighbors with one of our team members. We'll call him Hal for security purposes. Hal had no idea that Jeff even worked in a lab, let alone one that tortured cats. It wasn't until there was a block party and Jeff had a tad too much to drink. He started complaining about Crowden and couldn't seem to stop. When he was done, a plan began to hatch to rescue the cats. Our group met in stages and fleshed out the operation. Hal is the only one who has contact with Jeff. He has no idea who we are or how many people are involved."

"Still, what if it's a set-up?"

"We thought of that. We go to great lengths to hide our involvement in animal rescues. No one is allowed to donate to or belong to any animal rights or animal protection groups. That includes sanctuaries and even wildlife services. We never meet at each other's homes and we never ever meet all together. After combing through every possible scenario of how he might have known, we've come to the conclusion that it was dumb luck Jeff decided to bend Hal's ear."

Spencer was still not convinced. "So Jeff works for this animal tormentor for three years, helps him fuck up these cats and all of a sudden decides he can't take it? Why now and isn't he afraid of losing his job once the lab is destroyed?"

"At this point, he doesn't care. He wants out. Haven't you put up with a job long past hating it? Jeff is married and has two children. He's the sole supporter. As much as he wanted to leave, he stuck with it. It's a good thing he didn't look for another job because he'd be a suspect once they discover the cats gone and the lab ruined." Perry took another gulp of cold beer. She patted her lap. "Come here, girl." Gilley jumped into her lap and curled up into a small, furry ball. "Any other questions before I continue?"

"Not right now, but I'm sure I'll come up with some later."

"Yes, I'm sure you will and that's why I think you're perfect for rescues. You don't take things at face value. You're curious and that's what makes for a successful operation."

"Thank you. By the way, you look really nice."

"Spencer, focus." She self-consciously pushed her hair out of her face, then reached into her pants pocket and reapplied the lip balm. Spencer raised his hand. "Yes?"

"Just curious. Do you always have lip balm and ponytail bands on you?"

"As a matter of fact, I do. In my left pocket, always in my left pocket, is a tissue." She pulled a slightly used tissue out of her pocket and dangled it in the air, then put it back. "In my right pocket, always in my right pocket, are a band and a balm." Again, she reached into her pocket and pulled out the evidence. "I'm a wreck without them."

"Good to know."

"Because…?"

"If you reach into your pocket and come out empty-handed, you might come unglued and I want to be prepared. Okay, you can continue."

"Two weeks from now, another lab in the building is relocating to a smaller facility. They'll be moving equipment and animals at 1:00 a.m. That's when we move the cats out. Jeff will provide us with an access card and lab coats. He estimates that there will be around ten movers plus the lab assistants, so we'll barely be noticed. Fortunately, the researcher who's moving will be out of the country. The move coincides with an international conference in Geneva and he's a speaker, so he couldn't get out of it. Since Jeff won't be there, he's given Hal a diagram of the lab and the building. We'll take all the cats in one trip. We'll only need four cages, two to three cats to a cage. They'll be sedated. Before we leave the lab, we destroy the equipment. The movers will be parked on one side of the building and we'll be on the other side. There are cameras everywhere, but the SUV we're using will have fake plates and peel-off paint. We'll drop the cats off at a safe house."

"Disguises?"

"But of course. We'll both be wearing wigs and elevated shoes. You get a goatee and diamond stud earring and I get to be a blonde with glasses. If I have to speak, it will be with a British accent, lovey."

"I want an accent, too."

"Won't that be a little odd? Two lab assistants from different countries?"

"Yeah, I guess. Say something else with your accent."

With flawless ease, Perry said, "I find you American men so serious. Could it be that you toil at work for hours or is it all the beef you consume?"

Spencer clapped. "Excellent, Ms. Seidel. I do have one more question. Why did you pick me? I belong to animal rights groups. I picket. I'm very vocal about my beliefs. Geez, I'm probably being watched by the feds as we speak."

"Sometimes, a person's character is ideally suited for this type of work. I just knew you'd be perfect under the stress. I took the chance of asking you after I ran it by the group. You may be involved in an animal rights organization or two, but I don't think you're on the government's radar. At least I hope not."

"I'm glad you took that chance. This is the most fulfilling work I've ever done. Instead of making me more anxious and depressed, I feel liberated. I'm making a difference and it feels great. It doesn't hurt that my partner is thoroughly enjoyable."

"Thanks, Spencer." Perry gently picked up Gilley who was still sleeping on her lap and moved her to the cushion. She got up and stretched, then finished her beer. "You're a gracious host and now I must bid you a good night or as they say in jolly ole' England, 'later guvnor. Ta Ta. Bye lovey." She tipped her imaginary hat and walked out the door.

Spencer tipped his 'hat,' then said to the closed door, "Bye love."

Kanen glanced at the clock on the wall. It was 6:45 p.m. Bonnie said she'd be there at 6:15. He wanted to call her, then thought better of it. In case she was with Gerald, he didn't want his number appearing on her cell. He was bursting at the seams, wanting to tell her about his conversation with Manny.

The table was set, complete with candles and the casserole was in the oven. The salad was made. All it needed was dressing. He tried reading *New Yorker* magazine, but he couldn't concentrate. Kanen got up and went to the living room window. He thought about the events of the past few weeks. Meeting Spencer, then Bonnie was enough to give him a headache. Throw in his affair with Bonnie then the discovery of a plot to poison the poor and it was no wonder Kanen was having problems sleeping. He was looking forward to Bonnie spending the night. Maybe she'd cure his insomnia.

He wondered if she got lost. The streets in Mill Valley's hills could be confusing. They wound around the mountains, changed names and many led to dead ends. She had never been to his place and she wouldn't let him give her directions, claiming her GPS was sufficient. Finally, there was a knock on the front door. He looked through the peephole and there she was, looking lovely with her blonde hair tied back, face slightly flushed. He smiled and opened the door.

"Nice place, but what a bitch it was to find." She walked into his arms and gave him a kiss.

"I was getting worried."

"I'm sorry. I was going to call, but I kept thinking that I was on the right street and I'd see you soon. Then I'd hit a cul-de-sac and realize I was on the wrong road. I think my GPS had a nervous breakdown."

She walked into the foyer and looked around. The dècor was definitely masculine, but also soft. She liked it. It wasn't the typical Plexiglas frames, steel and glass furniture and recessed lighting. When she saw the glass wall in the living room, she walked straight to it. It was so clean, that if the early evening light wasn't bouncing off it, Bonnie would have sworn it wasn't there.

"So this is what vegan energy bars buy you. The whole vegan thing is looking a lot more appealing."

Before Kanen could protest, she said, "Just kidding." From where she stood, the koi pond and reflecting pool were in clear view. Ferns surrounded the pond and an ancient-looking wooden bench sat at the edge of the pool. At the far right side of the yard was a built-in barbeque with a brick oven. "Your back yard is so tranquil. I can so easily see you meditating out there. Am I right?"

Kanen walked up behind her and wrapped his arms around her waist. She dropped her head and he kissed the back of her neck. For a split second, Gerald's big blotchy face appeared. Her head jerked up and she almost gave Kanen a fat lip.

"Hey!"

"I'm sorry. Work popped into my head and totally ruined the mood. Are you okay?"

"Fine. Let's eat. I've got some exciting news to tell you. First, tell me what happened with Gerald."

Bonnie decided right after it happened that Kanen wasn't going to know about her latest sexual encounter with her boss. She wanted to be honest with him, but knew that he wouldn't be able to stomach the truth. He'd look at her differently. He might not even want to be with her anymore. Sure, he knew about her history with Gerald, but now that they've become involved, his feelings for her were stronger and the last thing he would want to hear is Bonnie being forced to copulate with the CEO. She couldn't bear it. She knew Kanen would have a fit. She chose her words carefully.

"As I suspected, the big G called me into his office, yelled and screamed at me for leaving early and being incommunicado, then told me that I was fired. I convinced him that I was working on a new ad campaign over the weekend and told him to give me a chance to present it next week. He agreed. Before I left work, he told me that he reserved a cottage for us in St. Helena this weekend. I thought it would be a perfect opportunity to get more information from his cell."

Kanen placed the steaming casserole on the table next to the salad and dressing. As he spooned a generous helping onto each plate, he said as nonchalantly as he could, "You're not going to sleep with him, are you?"

"Hell no! I'm planning on getting sick. Very sick. At least that's what he'll think. Gastrointestinal flu comes to mind. I'll have to check his phone when he's in the shower." She took a bite of the casserole. "This is delicious. What's in it?"

"It's a layered veggie casserole. There are mushrooms, onions, yams, broccoli, and peas in my special sauce. Or should I say, secret sauce."

Bonnie took another bite. "It can stay a secret as far as I'm concerned because I'm not making it. You know I don't like to cook, right?"

"Ooh, that's a deal breaker. I guess this is our last meal together."

Bonnie looked like she was about to cry, so Kanen quickly said, "I'm kidding. It's actually a good thing. If you don't cook, you can't accidentally slip in any meat or dairy. I like being in control of the kitchen, which leads me to my great news. I was in the office kitchen this morning when our distribution manager, Manny, walks in. He asks me if there are any openings in distribution because his cousin works for…wait for it…Hinton Industries."

"I can tell where this is going. Continue, vegan chef."

"What does his cousin do? Manny tells me he works in the factory, packaging and shipping the burgers and chicken patties and nuggets to the fast food restaurants."

"This isn't a set-up, is it?"

"That's what I thought, but how on earth would anyone know that you found out about the plot, let alone tell me about it? It's kismet."

"Kiss what?"

"Kismet. Fate."

"Kind of like us, huh?"

"Yeah."

"So have you talked to the cousin?"

"Only on the phone. I wanted to run this by you, in case you want to be there."

"I think it would be too risky. I've told you everything I know. You can represent us both."

Kanen poured the dressing on the salad and doled it out. "I suppose you're right. The fewer people involved, the better. You realize that this guy could get us the evidence we need to put away your sick ass boss for a long time?"

"Not to mention the senator. I wonder if anyone else is involved."

"I can't believe only two people planned this. Where did they get the drug from? That person would have to know what's going on, right?"

She nodded. "Let's talk about something else. I don't want to think about it right now." Bonnie took a bite of the salad. "Yummy dressing. Did you make it from scratch?"

"Yes, I did. Extra virgin olive oil, lemon juice, paprika, garlic, salt, pepper and a touch of mustard."

"You're definitely doing all the cooking. I'm really good at clean up."

After the dishes were put in the dishwasher, Kanen and Bonnie retired to the living room. She lay on the couch and put her feet in his lap. While giving her a foot rub, he shared memories of growing up with entrepreneurial parents. They were creative and experimental and never refused a stray animal he or his two brothers would bring home. It was as close to idyllic as one could get.

Bonnie told Kanen about her life in the Rydover family, living in a fairly conservative household, skipping the part about why she and Spencer were estranged. The omission wasn't lost on Kanen.

"What happened between you and Spencer?"

Bonnie grabbed the remote and turned on the 60-inch flat screen television. The room was engulfed in surround sound. The roar of hooves was in front of and behind the couple. Twenty or more horses were running across a prairie.

"Not much to tell." She looked back at the screen. "Have you ever seen a more magnificent sight? I always wanted a horse when I was a little girl, but we couldn't afford it."

Kanen stopped massaging her feet, then he muted the television. "First of all, I believe there's a lot to tell about your strained relationship with your brother, but obviously you don't want to share that with me right now and that's okay. I respect your privacy."

"Thank you. What's the second thing?"

"I was going to tell you that those free-spirited wild horses you see on TV are being rounded by our government to appease ranchers, but I thought it would put a damper on the evening."

"Bingo. How perceptive you are. Do animal rights people always see death and destruction when they see animals? If so, what a burden that must be."

He unmuted the sound and watched the horses running across a stream. They ran as one: chestnut-colored mares with their spotted foals, tan stallions alongside other stallions. A lump formed in Kanen's throat and as he turned to Bonnie, she could see tears forming in his eyes.

"I know that wild horses are cruelly rounded up by helicopters and kept in holding pens. Some are sold to private parties; others are sold to kill buyers who send them to slaughterhouses. It's all done because sheep and cattle ranchers don't want to share the land. My heart hurts for these animals and all the other creatures that humans subjugate, torment and slaughter, but you're wrong. It's not a burden. It's the price I pay for having compassion for all beings, not just the ones we call pets. I'll be right back."

Kanen moved Bonnie's legs off his lap and walked out of the living room into the hallway. A few seconds later, she heard a door close. Bonnie swallowed hard. She regretted being so harsh and insensitive. Her first inclination was to follow him, but she stopped herself. In her eyes, Kanen was the embodiment of masculinity, charm, intelligence and success. When she thought of vegans and vegetarians, her brother came to mind. He was her point of reference, and they never looked like Kanen. She started having second thoughts about their relationship. With her attitude and lifestyle, she could conceivably piss him off on a daily basis.

With a heavy heart, Bonnie got up from the couch. The sun was setting on the plains and the horses had settled in for the evening. She took one last look, then grabbed her coat and purse. She was heading for the door when Kanen emerged from the bathroom. He looked surprised.

"Where are you going?"

She let out a sigh. "I'm sorry that I upset you, and I'm afraid I'll do it again, shooting off my mouth. Being insensitive. I don't mean it. It's who I am and I don't know if I can change."

Kanen walked up to her. He took her coat and purse and threw them onto the chair. "I like you, Bonnie. A lot. We're no Ozzie and Harriet. We're not even Ozzie and Sharon. I don't know if we'll work, but right now I'm willing to try. Are you?"

"Yeah, I am." They hugged. "Shit. Now I'm the one getting emotional." Bonnie wiped her eyes. "You bring out the best in me, Weston. No one's ever done that."

"We're already making progress. Did you want to continue watching TV?"

"Uh-uh." She took his hand and started walking down the hallway to the master bedroom.

37

"When did you say he was coming home?" Lana took another bite of the kale and quinoa salad. "By the way, this is delicious. Jeannine, can I hire you as my private chef?"

Jeannine laughed. "I'm very pricey. You couldn't afford me!"

Perry cut in. "To answer your question, Spencer should be walking through the gate any minute. Do we have a crush on the young lad?"

"Hell yeah," Lana said. "He's adorable and compassionate. I just want to run my hands through that gorgeous shock of chocolate brown hair." She pretended to rough up a head of hair. The sterling silver and gold bracelets on both arms rattled. "Where was he when I was his age?"

Gretchen said, "If I'm not mistaken, you were having baby number one with idiot husband number two."

Lana said, "Shit. You're right. I may have a mom crush on the kid, but I know he's got a hard-on for you." She looked straight into Perry's eyes and watched her blush.

Lana gasped. "Have you done anything with the cutie-patootie?"

"Please. Do I look like I'd sleep with someone younger than Callie?"

All three women said, "Yes!"

"I am shocked. He's only twenty-four," Perry said.

"I'll be twenty-five in a month."

The women all turned and, to their horror, saw Spencer standing at the top of the stairs with a huge grin on his face. "If I had known you ladies would make me feel this good, I would have hung out with you a long time ago."

"A long time ago you would have been seven!" Lana said. "Get over here you peeping Tom. Since when do you go sneaking around your landlady's house?"

Spencer sat down next to Lana. "Perry said that she'd be hosting the monthly dinner again because Alica wasn't able to. She went out of town, right?"

Lana nodded.

"So she invited me to your potluck and told me to bring dessert." Out of his jacket pocket, Spencer presented five chocolate bars. He laid them on the table. Gretchen picked one up and read the label.

"Rescue Chocolate. Peanut Butter Pit Bull. Where did you get these?"

"Republic of V. It's that great vegan store on University Avenue, right next to Out of the Closet. The owner was telling me about the chocolates. She said an ex-ballerina in Brooklyn adopted a rescue pit bull and decided to make vegan chocolate bars and donate the profits to animal rescue organizations."

Jeanine said, "What a great idea." She checked out the bars. "Peanut Butter Pit Bull, Pick Me! Pepper. That sounds good. Let's see, there's also Forever Mocha, Mission Feral Fig and Fakin' Bacon. Wow, I can't wait to try them. Thanks for bringing dessert, Spencer."

"You're welcome." He turned to Lana. "If you wash your hands, you can run your fingers through my hair any time."

The women laughed. Gretchen returned from the house. "What did I miss?"

"Only the fact that Spencer was standing over there longer than we thought."

"You little scamp. It's a good thing I didn't say anything incriminating," said Gretchen. She turned to Perry. "Can I borrow your book, *Change Your Thoughts, Change Your World*? I saw it on your bookshelf and I've been wanting to read it."

"You can't borrow it. You can have it."

"You didn't like it?"

"I did. I just don't think I retained any of the information. That goes for all the self-help books. When I'm reading them, I can't get enough of their insights and adages. I'm wowed by their words, but when I finish, my retention is minimal. I might as well have someone throw the book at my head. At least I'd get a lump that would last longer."

Gretchen nodded. "I totally agree. I read Ekhart Tolle's bestseller, *Be Here Now.* It was mind blowing, just don't ask me what it was about." She put her fists up to her head and fanned the fingers out and said, "Poof."

"Poof is right, you ding-a-ling. The name of the book is *The Power of Now*," said Lana. "*Be Here Now* was by Krishna Das."

Jeannine said, "Can you see us losing brain cells? Ram Dass wrote *Be Here Now*. Krishna Das sings kirtan, Hindu devotional music. I hope you're taking notes, Spencer. This is what your brain will look like twenty years from now." She made a small circle with her fingers and thumb.

Lana added, "It ain't pretty, sweetie."

Spencer said, "I'd settle for being as funny as all of you. You guys are great. So what if you can't remember the name of a book or what the book was about. You're all healthy and vegan. That's good enough for me."

Perry said, "Unless you want a gaggle of older women stalking you, stop talking now! The men our age pale in comparison to you, my dear."

When dinner was finished, Perry made tea. Coffee for Spencer. After bringing out the beverages, she sat back and said, "Spencer, can you hand me the Fakin' Bacon chocolate bar?"

Spencer complied. As he swept his hair away from his eyes, he said, "What do you think if I shaved my head?"

All the women yelled at once, "NO!"

Spencer looked shocked. "It's the trend, especially with older men."

"That's because male pattern baldness looks a helluva lot better without hair. I don't know what these guys are thinking when they sport a weenie little ponytail slithering down their neck, while it looks like Siberia on the top of their head. You shave off one hair and you're banned from our group." Gretchen looked over at Perry. "Right?"

"Definitely. Spencer, you have beautiful hair. Samson hair."

"Who?" said Spencer.

Perry replied, "It's a bible story. Samson's hair defined his strength. When it was cut off, he was a weakling. The point is, please don't shave your head. You'll make four women very sad."

Spencer fluffed up his dark brown locks with his hands making him look sweet and sexy at the same time. "Okay. The hair stays."

Gretchen ran her fingers through her hair. It was short but thick. "I wonder what it would be like to be bald. Hair is such a big part of my identity. Always has been. It's been long and blonde, now it's short and whitish gray. I could dye it purple, if I wanted to."

Jeannine cut in. "Remember when you had those pink streaks? That was pretty wild."

"I won't be doing that again, but I could if I felt like it. Hair is so versatile. I love it!" Gretchen took another bite of chocolate. "And I love this, too."

Lana said, "Even though I don't have the balls to do it, I think shaving my head would be so liberating." She touched the ends of her shoulder-length, salon-colored ash brown hair. "Think of the money we would save on haircuts, coloring, hair care products. Maybe I should re-think this bald thing."

"Get a grip, Lana. First of all, you have an odd-shaped head. You'd probably look like Larry David and get a lot of sideways looks from strangers. Secondly, you love your hair and you should. You have great hair. Spending hundreds of dollars every few months is totally worth it." Perry threw her head forward and then back, her hair falling lightly around her face. "I'll never go bald. I love my hair too much. What about you, Jeannine?"

"Perish the thought! I'd look like a worm. My features are too large to be pretty without being surrounded by hair." She touched her rather large nose to prove her point.

"Our group sure has some heavy conversations. Hair and chocolate. Next month, let's talk about scissors and dirt," Lana said.

There was a loud knock on the front door. While Perry went to answer it, the group continued sampling the chocolate. Gretchen broke off a piece of the Fakin' Bacon bar and ate it.

"This is delicious. It really tastes like bacon. Who would have thought these two flavors complemented each other?"

"I love the Peanut Butter Pit Bull. Amazing!" said Lana.

"Well if it isn't the old gang. Where's Alica and who are you?" Callie said looking at the only man in the group.

Perry said, "You all remember Callie? Spencer, my renter, meet Callie, my daughter."

She was every bit as lovely as in the painting. And more. In person, Callie DeMitri had a deep tan and straight auburn hair that fell four inches past her shoulders. Her eyes were a deep gold. Spencer couldn't help but stare at her eyes.

"In the painting your eyes are blue but they're so much prettier in person." After he said it, he was shocked. Never was he this bold with a woman. It must have been the work of Perry et al.

"Thanks. Nice to meet you, too."

Gretchen came over to Callie and gave her a hug. The other women followed suit.

Jeannine said, "Your mom didn't tell us you were visiting. How long are you staying?"

"Mom didn't know I was coming. Surprise! I'm not sure how long I'll be here. It's up to her." She looked over at Perry.

"You can stay as long as you want to, sweetie. Me casa es su casa."

Callie smiled at her mother. "It was great seeing you all. I'm going to unpack and then sack out. I've been driving for over fifteen hours."

After she left, Perry looked at the group and raised her eyebrows, then said in a low voice, "She left the butcher. I wish I could sing and shout, but that wouldn't be respectful, would it?"

A lot of head shaking.

Spencer said, "We should all go to Jauncy's."

"Isn't that the dance joint on Shattuck?" said Lana.

"Yeah and they play great music, like R&B and funk. Who's up for it?" Spencer was practically dancing.

Jeannine said, "I'm out."

"Sorry, Spencer, I'm beat. Maybe another time." Lana got up and stretched. "Plus, you got to give us old gals more of a notice. I don't have my dancing shoes on." She lifted up her leg and showed the group a turquoise and gold tennis shoe. "When I dance, I wear sexy heels." She looked at Spencer. "Rain check?"

"Sure." Spencer looked dejected. He turned to Perry.

She said, "I have to get Callie settled in, so I'm going to pass as well."

From inside the house, Callie yelled, "Mom, where are the sheets? I can't remember where you keep them."

"I'm coming!" Perry replied. She turned to her guests. "Stay as long as you want. Finish up the chocolate. Continue your riveting conversations."

"It'll be tough without your input, but we'll try," said Lana. Jeannine and Gretchen nodded.

Back in the house, Perry grabbed the sheets for the guest room bed. As she and Callie put them on, she said, "So, tell me what happened."

"Can't it wait until tomorrow? I'm so tired."

"Of course, sweetie." Curbing her desire to find out why her daughter left her life in New Mexico behind was beyond difficult, but Perry gave her daughter a big hug and kiss instead of pressing her for details. "Sleep well, Callie. I love you."

"I love you, too, Mom." She squeezed her eyes tight to stop the tears from coming and turned away so her mother couldn't see. "Good night."

Kanen was thrilled when Mike Flores agreed to meet him. Then his excitement turned to fear. What if someone from Hinton Industries followed Mike? What if Mike was part of the plan and he wanted to work at Weston Foods to sabotage the company? 'I'd make a lousy spy' he thought to himself. He sat in a darkened corner of Tacqueria Mexicano. The restaurant and bar was located in the south west quadrant of the Mission District in San Francisco. His blonde hair was covered with a baseball cap and he bought some fake prescription glasses from a costume shop. His light skin and refined features were in sharp contrast to the clientele, so he felt that some facial altering was necessary. As he drank his beer, his eyes darted back and forth between the two entrances. He took out his cell and looked again at the photo Manny sent him of his cousin. As soon as he put his phone down, Mike appeared in the doorway. He was short and stocky. His long black hair tied back in a ponytail. His features resembled more American Indian than Mexican. He caught Kanen's nod and walked over to the booth, introduced himself and sat down.

"I've never had a job interview like this before. Is this normal for Weston?"

"No. I wanted to keep it away from the office. You'll know why soon." Kanen took a large swig of beer. "So, Manny tells me that you're a really hard worker. One of the most conscientious people he knows, regardless of being related. Why do you want to leave Hinton?"

The waitress appeared and Mike ordered a beer. Kanen ordered a second one.

"The place sucks. It's dirty. I've seen rats where the meat is packaged and it smells like rotting flesh. About three months ago, I became vegan and now it's harder than ever working there. Can I tell you this in private?"

"Of course."

"Big shot, Gerald Hinton, brags about how his meat is high quality and his standards are better than O'Neill Meats. That's bullshit. I don't know what O'Neill's does, but any beef patties or chicken that's expired or smells funny is repackaged and moved to a different area of the plant. We call it 'junkie food' because it gets shipped to the fast food restaurants in the poorest neighborhoods. Is that shitty or what?"

"It doesn't surprise me. I've also heard rumors about some shoddy practices at Hinton. Have you noticed anything different lately? New policies or additives to the meat?"

Mike eyed him suspiciously. "You know about the changes? Everyone at the plant had to sign a confidentiality agreement. We were told that if there was a leak, we'd be fired on the spot. No severance, no nothing. Gone."

Kanen moved a little closer to Mike. "I'm going to tell you something that will blow you away. You have to promise that you won't tell a soul."

Mike crossed his heart. "I've kept secrets a lot worse than you'll probably tell me."

"I doubt it." Kanen made a quick sweep of the restaurant. No one was paying attention to them and if they were, it wasn't obvious at all. A couple sitting closest to their booth was out of earshot.

"Hinton Industries is planning on placing a drug into the junkie meat. It supposedly speeds up whatever illness a human has, like cancer, heart disease, diabetes, and the person dies a lot sooner than normal. They want to cull the crowd, so to speak. Clean up the dregs of society by killing them off sooner than their disease would."

Mike felt like someone punched him in the gut. He didn't like working for the meat supplier. Hinton paid minimum wage and the benefits were meager, but he never imagined that they would willingly kill people.

"We were told that the company developed proprietary flavor enhancers and they were going to test the market on the older meat, the 'junkie' meat. They said it was revolutionary and would change the fast food market, giving our clients an edge. Shit. It's poison. I can't believe it."

Kanen agreed. "It's vile, but I believe that only the CEO knows about it. I think your superiors were told that it is a flavor enhancer. Very few people know about the plan."

Mike looked hard at Kanen. "How do you know about it? Is it an animal rights thing?"

"Hell no. Someone from inside Hinton found out by accident. I can't tell you much more. Manny spoke highly of you and I'd be happy to hire you at Weston, but I need you to do me a big favor. As it stands, we don't have enough proof to go to the FBI and stop this from happening. What's the lag time from when the meat arrives at the distribution center to when it leaves for the restaurants?"

"A couple of days."

"Do you know when Hinton is planning on contaminating the meat?"

"A week from today, which means the meat will ship to Big & Juicy Burgers, Delaney's Fried Chicken and Victory's on Wednesday or Thursday."

Kanen said, "What I need from you is a copy of the confidentiality contract you signed and a sample of the meat. Are you comfortable with that?"

Mike downed his beer, his hand slightly shaking, and ordered another one. "I'd be happy to shut that place down. I'll ask them for a copy of the agreement. By law, they have to give it to me. As for the meat, I'll pocket a burger or a piece of chicken and put it in my lunch box."

"Do they know you're a vegan?"

Mike snickered. "If they did, I'd be laughed out of that place. You'd think more of my co-workers wouldn't be able to stomach meat after being around it all day. Who knows? I may not be the only vegan, but I doubt it."

Kanen took a deep breath and let it out. It felt like he'd been holding it in the entire time and could finally exhale. He liked Mike's confidence. It reassured him that their strategy for stopping the poisoning could work.

38

"Tell me something, Mr. Senator. Do you think my friend, Della, matters less than any other human being?"

Bert had just come from the Y where the third Food Giveaway had taken place. The implementation of the d.o.a.-laced meat was postponed again, much to the disappointment of Jessica and Olivia. Bert was relieved when Anita held an emergency meeting, letting them know that the process of turning the drug into powdered form was taking longer than anticipated. She reassured them that the fourth giveaway would be the one. Instead of changing plans, Bert met Cody at the Social Services office. They sat across from each other in the same empty room Cody used the first time he contacted the senator.

The glare from the big man's eyes caused Bert to look away. His discomfort was clearly due to guilt.

"All I said, Cody, was that I'd like to implement the animal watch program with you first because I know you and I trust you. I'm not familiar with the other people you mentioned."

"You didn't answer my question."

Bert sighed. "No, I don't think she matters any less than another human being, but look at her life, if you can call it that. She's miserable. Her life consists of lying on the ground in her own filth, eating what she can find or what you bring her. You even said that she does nothing to help herself. You know what? I do think she matters less than, say a person who has an illness and does something about it."

Cody looked down at his large hands and shook his head. Bert felt a tinge of fear. "You think Della is worth less than you?"

"Yeah, I do."

"How about me?"

Bert nodded.

"A terrorist?"

"Wait, a terrorist? Really?"

"Yeah. Which one is worth more?"

"Della."

"What about that guy who lost millions of dollars of people's money investing in his Ponzi scheme? What was his name again?" Cody tapped his head. "Madhoff. Bernie Madhoff."

"Can we please get back to the point, which is that I'd rather start the program…"

"Answer the question, Mr. Senator. You look at Della and she's all smelly and dirty and you see worthless. She didn't hurt anybody but herself, but this Bernie Madhoff. He ruined lots of people's lives. His son committed suicide, didn't he? Yeah, I'd say Della is worth a million Madhoffs." Cody stood up and looked outside the window. He watched a man walk by pushing a shopping cart filled with plastic bags. The man moved erratically, as if he was being controlled by a sadistic puppeteer. "You look at Della and the other homeless people and see worthless. It doesn't have to be that way. I can't force Della to get help. If you cared enough, I know you could."

"How could I do that? You told me that she refused to take her medication."

"She may kick and scream and she's been known to bite, but Della's got to be taken to a hospital and cleaned up and put on meds again. Her head's all gummed with the disease. She needs to see through different eyes. She may end up on the street again. Maybe she won't. Show her compassion, Senator. Give her another chance. Give them all another chance. Except for Madhoff. Keep him in jail forever, because he's the dangerous one. His kind. They're greedy and have huge egos and destroy people."

He sat back down, but before Bert could reply, a shooting pain surged through Cody's leg and he gasped, grabbing his thigh.

Bert went over to him. "What's the matter?"

"I'm fine. I'm fine." But the grimace on his face and shallow breathing belied his words.

Bert made a call on his cell. "Bring the car to the front of the Social Services building now." He turned to Cody. "I'm taking you to the emergency room."

"No! I'm okay." Another sharp pain wracked his leg and this time Cody cried out.

Employees and clients were wondering what was going on behind the closed door. Before long, Bert walked out with Cody's arm around him for support. He limped to the entrance and got into the senator's limousine.

St. Francis Memorial Hospital's emergency room was filled to capacity. Not unusual for a Saturday afternoon. Cody was scared. His pain hadn't subsided, which was unusual. The typical bout lasted, at the most, five minutes. It had been over twenty minutes. It was all he could do not to scream out in agony. Thanks to Senator Kathala's prominence, Cody was immediately taken into a room and made as comfortable as possible. Already feeling incredibly guilty for being given preferential treatment, he turned to the senator while being hooked up to an IV full of morphine and said, "You don't have to stay. This could take a while and you have a lot more important things to do."

"Nonsense," Bert replied. "What's more important than making sure you're okay?"

"Getting Della help."

"Maybe singing will take your mind off the pain, right Doc? This man can do a rendition of *We Shall Dance* that will bring tears to your eyes."

Dr. Allen, an intern in his mid-thirties, looked at the senator and said, "Since my stint at St. Francis, I haven't heard a patient or employee sing, so I'm not sure it's allowed." He looked at Walter, who was starting to feel the effects of the painkiller. "Is he talking about the Cody Brant song?"

Walter nodded.

"I'm sure it will be fine if you sing low."

Walter looked sideways at Bert. "At a time like this, you want me to sing? What about Della?"

Bert said, "When I was around eight years old, I was playing softball. I hit a grounder into right field and knew I better run like hell to get to base. I was almost there when the outfielder threw the ball to first. He missed and hit me in the leg. I heard a crack and knew I had broken a bone. On my way to the hospital, my mom started singing. She had a beautiful voice and she loved to sing country. I even remember what she sang. *For the Good Times*. One of the best Ray Price songs, hands down. She coaxed me into singing with her and it took my mind off my leg."

Bert stood up and patted Walter on the shoulder. "Give it a try. I'll talk to the good doctor here about Della."

Walter complied. He began to sing low, his voice steady and sweet. The tension melted from his face and he closed his eyes while he continued to serenade the small patch of hospital he occupied along with two to three other patients.

Bert motioned for the doctor in the corner of the privacy curtain. "I know you're busy, but who can I talk to about bringing in a homeless woman who's suffering from bi-polar disorder? She refuses to take her meds and lives behind a restaurant next to a dumpster. We'd have to forcibly remove her from the street."

"All medical facilities follow the same policy, which is you can't force someone into receiving medical care. Even relatives are not at liberty to coerce someone into treatment. We do have a health care program for the homeless. Go to the information desk on the second floor. They'll be able to direct you to the person in charge."

Following through on his promise to Cody, Bert took the elevator and walked straight ahead to the information desk, where two very bored-looking women sat. When they saw the senator walking toward them, they made a meager effort to smile.

"Can I help you?" said information woman number one.

Bert extended his hand and she reluctantly shook it. "Senator Bertram Kathala. And you are?"

Both women immediately stood up, their ennui evaporating in the presence of a government official.

"I'm Sara Monroe. Very nice to meet you, Sir. How can I help you?"

Bert told them about Della and her condition. Sara said, "You'll want to speak to the director of the hospital's Health Care for the Homeless Program. Her name is Courtney Hoppe. I can give you her direct line. She's here Monday through Friday, from 7:30 a.m. to 5:30 p.m."

Sara grabbed a piece of paper and, after looking up Courtney's number, wrote it down and gave it to the senator. He thanked them and went back to the ER only to find Cody fast asleep. The results from the lab and x-ray were not yet available, so Bert sat in the waiting room. He thought about the current circumstances and almost laughed out loud. He was attempting to help the very people he wanted, for lack of a better word, to murder. He never would have looked twice at Cody if it weren't for his amazing voice and open compassion for others less fortunate than himself. And Della. A crazy woman who he thought chose her destiny. Now he realized that her illness prevented her from making logical decisions. These were two people out of so many throw-aways, ignored by society for being too crazy, too uncomfortable to face. Of course, programs were in place to assist these lost people, but they couldn't help them all. Besides Cody, did anyone else know Della? And if they walked by her, did they look? Did they care?

The senator looked around the waiting room and didn't like what he saw. Many of the people were downtrodden, beat up by life. A young girl, probably in her late teens, was cradling her right arm, the hand heavily bandaged in a towel. Spots of blood seeped through the worn terry cloth. Her eyes looked like black orbs. Clearly, she was high on something. She stared off into space, barely moving. Waiting for her turn to get help. Behind her, an elderly man sat hunched over, arms around his waist, quietly moaning. Bert still believed that there was little hope of rehabilitating many of the Loin's residents: the prostitutes and their pimps, heroin addicts and hardcore alcoholics. He knew that less than five percent in the above categories recovered and stayed that way. In the back of his mind, he even knew that getting help for Della would be short-lived. She'd most likely back slide into her disease and take up residence next to the dented dumpster, unless someone claimed the space in her absence.

"Senator Kathala?" Dr. Allen broke the internal chatter.

"Yes?"

"The results are back from the lab for Walter Cattlin." Dr. Allen sat down next to him. "Walter suffers from sciatica as a result of a pinched nerve in his groin. It's not uncommon and it can be treated with pain medication, but I encourage exercising. There are movements designed to reduce the occurrences of flare-ups. There's an easy-to-follow workout regimen in this pamphlet." He showed it to Bert. "Do you know if Mr. Cattlin has a history of drug or alcohol abuse?"

"Yes. He was a junkie up until five years ago. He told me he's been clean ever since."

Dr. Allen stood. "That rules out giving him prescription painkillers. Shall we see if he's awake?"

Bert nodded and followed the doctor. Walter slowly opened his eyes upon hearing their footsteps. He looked serene. Gone was the clenched jaw and pained expression.

"How are you feeling?" Bert asked.

"Good. No pain." He looked at the doctor. "So, do I have a tumor, cancer, diabetes?"

Dr. Allen shook his head. "No, Walter. You have sciatica due to a pinched nerve in your groin. It's still debilitating. This pamphlet has some easy exercises in it and I highly recommend that you do them. They'll greatly reduce the pain and if you're consistent, you could get rid of the condition for good."

Walter was handed the small booklet. He leafed through it and then put it on the side table. "Thanks, doc. What if the pain comes back?"

"I can give you some over the counter medication. Extra strength Tylenol, but that's it."

Cody looked at Bert. "You told him about my past?"

"I did." He thought Cody was going to be mad. Instead, he smiled and said, "Thanks for looking out for me, Mr. Senator."

"My pleasure."

"Did you get help for Della?"

Bert took a deep breath. "Cody, Dr. Allen informed me that under law, we're not allowed to force someone to get treatment. Before you say anything, I have an idea and I'm going to run it by the director of the homeless program on Monday."

Cody sat up in bed. "Can you tell me about this plan?"

Dr. Allen said, "I'd like to hear too, if you don't mind."

"Not at all," Bert said. "I'd like to see if the hospital would be willing to dispatch one to two health professionals twice a week to walk the streets and talk people like Della into getting treatment. Perhaps they could perform cursory exams and even dispense a minimal amount of drugs."

"I think that's a fantastic idea," said Dr. Allen. "God knows we need to help the forgotten homeless. It's worth a try."

Bert looked expectantly at Cody. "I agree. I would love to see Della off the streets."

On Monday morning, Cody and Senator Kathala met with Humane Officer Mark Kelley at the San Francisco Animal Services building on 43rd Street. They hammered out a preliminary plan to help neglected and abused animals in the Loin. This time, without prompting, Bert agreed to include other residents who wanted to be part of the operation. Cody vouched for their strength of character and integrity. He agreed to instruct them on the use of the office-issued cell phones, the rules of conduct and the importance of filling out the paperwork when they worked a case. The pay was nominal, but the rewards of their work were priceless. Cody could barely contain his excitement when he was given a box filled with everything he needed to get started. The Social Services office even agreed to let his animal 'task force' use one of their few vacant rooms.

As Bert sat in first class on United flight 45 to D.C., he felt immensely pleased with himself and that was rare. So little progress was made in Congress due to the countless special interest groups and lobbyists. Because he was personally funding both programs, Bert eliminated months of committee meetings, guaranteed dissention and a possible veto. It was simple and easy and it made a small dent in his savings account.

Bert accepted a glass of chardonnay from the flight attendant, along with an appetizer. She gave him a big smile. An inviting smile. It reminded him how nice it was to be single. Being a politician did have its perks.

He thought about d.o.a. The plan was going to be implemented at the end of next week. The restaurants would be receiving the tainted meat at the same time the senators executed their fourth and final food giveaway. He also thought about Cody, a man he'd grown quite fond of over the last few weeks. He allowed his mind to preview what Della might become if she were given proper medication and care. Then Bert relived his first visit to the Social Services office. The crowded waiting room, the fetid air. The young woman with track marks on her arms and dead eyes. The hopped up teen who couldn't sit still. And that bitch who lost the contents of her stomach on his shoe. He could still smell the vomit. Bert picked up his cell and made a call.

"Did you have fun in the Loin?" Anita was fixing dinner in her expansive kitchen. The steaks were under the broiler and the salad was almost done. She was slathering butter on the garlic bread.

"Always do. And how was your lovely food romp in Arlington? Did you avoid any further embarrassment, short of wearing a tarp?" said Bert.

"Indeed, I did. Very uneventful. So, are you ready for next week's giveaway?"

Bert looked down at his shoes. "Most definitely."

39

With the exception of going to work, Kanen and Bonnie were inseparable. The day before she left for her wine country weekend with Gerald, Kanen talked her into meeting him at Sun Lei Ha, a vegan restaurant at the edge of the Tenderloin. She had told him about her altercation when she was driving through the Loin, but he convinced her that during the day, the likelihood of it happening again was remote. Plus, he promised to be at the restaurant early and wait for her out front.

True to his word, Kanen walked up to the corner to meet Bonnie as she quickly crossed the street. Their embrace was followed by a kiss. He looked her up and down and then circled her.

"What are you doing?" she said.

"Checking for abrasions, run-ins with thugs. You know, the usual stuff that happens in the Tenderloin."

"Very funny. This place better be good. I'm starving."

"If you like Vietnamese food, it's the best."

As they headed to the entrance, Bonnie looked across the street. On the corner, ready to step off the sidewalk, she saw the man who saved her life that night. "Oh my God, that's the man I was telling you about. The one who chased those guys away from my car."

They watched the tall, black man with dreadlocks cross the street. At first, he seemed to be talking to himself, but then they realized he was singing.

"Now's your chance to thank him," said Kanen. He saw the fear in Bonnie's eyes.

"That's okay. He probably doesn't even remember, being a druggie or alcoholic."

"Are you kidding me? The man came to your aid. The least you can do is thank him. Plus, he looks lucid to me. Come on. I'll go with you."

Reluctantly, she followed Kanen to the corner and approached Cody as he stepped onto the curb.

"Excuse me. I don't know if you remember, but a few weeks ago I was driving on Sutter and…"

"Of course I do. Those idiots surrounded your car like roaches. You must have been really scared."

Bonnie's stance softened and she smiled. "I was terrified, but you came to my rescue and I never had a chance to thank you, so…thank you very much."

"I did what anyone should have done, but you're welcome." He took a small bow.

Kanen put out his hand. "Not everyone would have helped, so I thank you, too. I'm Kanen."

Cody shook Kanen's hand. He had a strong grip. "Walter, but everyone around here calls me Cody on account of I like to sing Cody Brant's songs." He saw the surprised look on their faces. "I know. What's a black man doing singing country? What do they call that, an enigma?"

Kanen laughed. "Yup. That's what they call it."

"You two have a good evening."

Cody started to walk away when Kanen said, "Would you like to join us for dinner? We were going to Sun Lei Ha and dinner is on me."

"Thank you, but no. I have a lot to do before the sun goes down."

"Thanks again," said Bonnie.

A final wave and Cody walked up the street.

Inside the restaurant, Bonnie and Kanen were shown to their table. The decor was simple. Framed photos of Vietnam hung loosely on the light green walls. They looked like they were cut out of a calendar. Many were faded from the intrusion of sunlight bathing the interior of the little restaurant. The metal chairs were just comfortable enough to sit through a meal.

Bonnie took in the scene. "Is this how you impress the ladies, taking them to the finest restaurants in the ritzy part of town?"

"Once you try the food, you're going to eat those words."

"I hope you're right."

Only a few other customers were there. It was still early for the dinner crowd. Kanen ordered a beer to start and Bonnie did the same. As they read the menu, she said, "I'm so glad I was able to thank that man."

"Me, too. I thought you were exaggerating about how big he was. You were pretty accurate. I wouldn't want to cross him."

The waiter placed the beers on the table. "Are you ready to order?"

Kanen began, "We'll start with the Treasure Dumplings and then we'll have the Phnom Penh Transparent Rice Noodle Soup, Sun and Moon Patties, and the Enlightened Tofu."

Normally, Bonnie would have protested a man ordering for her, but this was Kanen's domain and navigating a vegan menu was definitely not her forte. She actually enjoyed not having the responsibility. She sat back and studied her boyfriend. His profile displayed a strong jawline, aquiline nose and small, but perfectly shaped ears. His lashes were long and his lips full. She couldn't have conjured up a better looking man if she tried. But Kanen exuded more than sex appeal. Perhaps it was his compassion, his lifestyle that separated him from the other men that tried and failed to win her heart.

She brought the bottle of beer to her lips and took a long swallow. It was light with a lemony floral flavor. The carbonation tickled her tongue. She looked at the label. "Tiger Beer. Never heard of it. Isn't Singha the popular Vietnamese beer?"

Kanen said, "It is, but it's not vegan, so they import Tiger Beer. Do you like it?"

"Very much. I thought beer was made with hops and barley. Crap like that. How could it not be vegan?"

"Oh grasshopper, you have so much to learn. In its purest form, beer has four ingredients: water, malt, hops and yeast. A lot of breweries will add animal products or animal parts for head retention, coloring and flavor. For example, gelatin is used as a clarifier, you know, to remove the cloudiness. They may also use insects for coloring and serum albumin, a protein taken from animal blood, for a foamier head. Aren't you glad you asked?"

"No. It's gross and I eat meat."

"Not tonight."

"No, my love. Not tonight. Didn't you say you wanted to talk to me about something?"

"Yeah, I did." Kanen took a drink and set the bottle down, purposefully, as if he was trying to delay the question. He was about to speak when the waiter brought over their appetizer. He placed the dumplings in the middle of the table and gave them each a plate with dipping sauce. Kanen eagerly grabbed a dumpling, dunked it in the sauce and popped it into his mouth. Bonnie followed suit.

"Wow. This is delicious," she said and grabbed another one. "Okay, talk to me."

"I was at my parents the other night and, since they are supposedly older and wiser, I asked them some very heavy questions concerning the human condition and reincarnation. Instead of answering, my mom told me that I should try this drug called DMT."

"Is it a prescription drug?"

Kanen laughed. "That's so cute. With the exception of few drugs, my parents consider the pharmaceutical industry the devil's workshop. I'm not too fond of them either. DMT is actually an illegal drug because it's a hallucinogenic. I'm sure my parents got it from the same guy they get their pot from."

"Vegan hippies. What an anomaly."

"Come on. Don't stereotype them. Veganism isn't mainstream, but it's certainly not confined to hippies. Samuel L. Jackson and James Cameron are vegans. They don't look like patchouli-scented, commune residents to me." Kanen popped another dumpling in his mouth. "Getting back to the reason I brought this up, I was going to try it and was wondering if you'd be interested in joining me."

"Why does your mom think that taking DMT will answer your questions?"

"Some scientists call it the spirit molecule because, after conducting studies of people taking it, they found that many of the subjects reported being shot out of their bodies and into space, connecting with aliens or godlike beings. My mom…"

Bonnie put up her hand. "Hold it right there. Are you kidding me? I have no desire to meet aliens or God or…God knows who. I can't believe your parents would take this drug. If I told my mom and dad that I'd smoked marijuana once, they'd have a fit."

"Once?"

"Yeah. I never wanted anything to interfere with my goal, you know, muddle my brain so I wouldn't have the edge over my competition. I needed to be at my peak performance level through high school and college. So many of my friends smoked pot and got lazy and stupid. LSD was out of the question and so was ecstasy."

"So you hung out with the nerds?"

"No. They weren't my species, either. I was a loner."

Kanen gave her a sympathetic look.

"Don't feel sorry for me. It was my choice."

The waiter returned with their entrees. He placed the banquet before them, Bonnie's eyes getting larger with every dish. As they filled their plates, she continued. "So tell me, were you a stoner in high school or a druggie or…what?"

"I don't fit quite nicely into any category. Growing up with progressive parents, my brothers and I didn't really rebel. Mom and Dad made it clear that if we wanted to experiment with drugs they wouldn't condone it, but they made us promise to be careful and to never drive under the influence. I smoked my share of pot and tried other drugs, like mushrooms and ecstasy, nothing major. The only thing I do now is occasionally smoke pot. I have to disagree with you about the possibility of meeting aliens, though. I think it would be really exciting."

"I don't understand how meeting an alien would answer your question about reincarnation."

"Me, neither, but I'm going to find out. Are you sure you don't want to do it with me?"

Kanen took a bite of the Sun and Moon Patty. "So delicious!" He fed her a bite and she agreed.

"Right now, my answer is no. When we get back to my place, let's Google it. I'd like to get more clarity."

"Sounds fair. I didn't realize you were so pragmatic."

She laughed. "That's just the tip of the iceberg, buddy."

The restaurant had filled up since they arrived. Most of the clientele were vegan or vegetarian. If there were omnivores, they were brought to the restaurant by a 'veghead.' One would be hard pressed to find an out-of-towner in their midst. Nearly every travel guide warned tourists to stay clear of the Tenderloin. Muggings, stabbings and a groping or two could put a damper on any trip.

40

Perry's normally quiet home was upended with Callie's presence. It wasn't that she was loud or even intrusive. She was another body inhabiting the same space and that made Perry uncomfortable. She loved the solitude and if she wanted to sleep in or stay up late, she didn't have to be concerned with another person's privacy or feelings. After two years of not speaking to her daughter, she was alternately thrilled with their reconciliation and discomforted by her living in the same house. After all, Callie was her mother's daughter: opinionated, determined and stubborn.

It was the morning before the cat rescue at the lab. Usually, Perry was calm before a liberation. She would close herself off from the rest of the world and wrap her mind around the task. It wasn't possible with Callie there. Perry's confidence began to wane and she knew she had to rectify it before her nerves took over and doubt had a chance to seep in. She followed the delightful aromas of bread and coffee into the kitchen. Callie was slathering almond butter on her toast. The coffee was brewed.

"I could get used to this," Perry said as she gave her daughter a kiss on the cheek.

"Morning, Mom. You want me to pop a couple of slices of bread into the toaster?"

Perry nodded. She went over to the cupboard and grabbed a mug in the shape of a penguin. Years ago, when Callie was a baby, Perry decided to collect animal mugs with the intention of handing them over to her daughter when she moved out and had a place of her own. Instead, Perry became attached to each and every one of them: the kangaroo whose pouch was the cup, a frog, a flamingo whose long pink neck curved into a handle, and her favorite, a komodo dragon. Its green and gold body wrapped around the center of the mug twice. It had blue rhinestones for eyes. Callie's dating and subsequent marriage to the butcher made Perry's decision to keep the collection easy. She never regretted it.

After she poured herself a mugful of black coffee and added a touch of soymilk, Perry walked outside on the deck. Spencer was playing ball with Gilley on the lawn. She waved.

"Good morning."

He waved back.

"Would you like a nice hot cup of Joe?" She lifted up her mug.

"How can I resist? I've got to feed Gilley and then I'll be up."

She nodded and went back inside, just in time to dress up her toast.

Callie looked up from the paper. "You two are pretty close. Is he the son you never had or…?"

"Or what?"

"Come on, Mom. You look fantastic for your age. All that healthy eating."

Perry did her best to look stunned. "Please. Spencer is younger than you. Give me more credit than that. I don't even treat him as a son. He's more like a peer."

"Well, I think he's cute, even if he is a hardcore vegan."

Spencer appeared at the kitchen entrance, holding a PETA mug. Gilley was by his side.

"Good morning, Callie."

"Spence. Can I call you that?"

"Sure."

"I tend to shorten everyone's name. I don't know why. I like nicknames. You can call me Cal if you want."

"Actually, I like the name Callie." Spencer filled his mug with coffee and took a sip.

Perry said, "Would you like some toast?"

He shook his head. "I already ate." He was about to ask Callie what her plans were for the day when he noticed she'd gone back to reading the paper. Perry started walking outside and he joined her. The air was cool and brisk and invigorating. They were comfortable, both wearing jeans and sweatshirts. They settled in at the patio table. Perry said in a low voice, "Are you ready for tonight?"

"As I'll ever be," he answered matching her volume.

"Nervous?"

"Yup. Are you?"

"I wasn't until Callie showed up. Having someone in the house is unnerving, especially since I can't tell her what we're doing. Instead, I told her that a friend invited me over for dinner and since we'll be drinking, I'm going to spend the night."

"Good plan. How do I calm my nerves? I tried meditating this morning, but I couldn't concentrate."

"Being nervous isn't especially a bad thing. It keeps you on your toes. We could go over the plan if you'd like and then, before we head out, go over it again."

"What if we get caught?"

"We won't."

"Humor me. What would happen to us?"

Perry sighed. She was surprised it took Spencer this long to ask the dreaded question. "Worst case scenario, we're convicted of breaking and entering a research facility. It's considered a felony and we could be fined $5,000 and spend up to five years in jail."

Spencer leaned over, picked Gilley up and placed her on his lap. She looked up at him with such adoration that it brought tears to Perry's eyes. "She really loves you."

"I love her, too." Spencer pet her as she settled in. "Cats being forced to smoke cigarettes, then killed and dissected. I'm willing to take the chance to save them from that fate. They're worth the risk just like Gilley and her family were."

"I agree."

"Do you think someday people will look at other species with kindness and treat them with respect?"

Perry just smiled. "I'm going to get more coffee."

"I don't think so, either."

When Perry returned, Callie was behind her. "Mind if I join you two?"

Spencer replied, "Not at all. By the way, how are you doing?"

"Except for the fact that my husband left me for his butcher-in-training, I'm just dandy."

"He left you for a guy?" said Spencer.

"No, Spence. You don't think a woman could be a butcher? The tramp loved hacking up dead animals." She saw the look of disgust on his face. "Sorry. That was uncalled for. Bottom line, Gregg was having an affair with this woman and he moved out. Taos isn't a very big town. I think there's a little over 5,500 residents. I knew that if I ran into them enough I'd feel a compulsion to run into them with my car, so I hightailed it out of there. And here I am."

"Things will get better."

"And you know this how?" said Callie, amused by this young man.

"I can tell you're a strong person."

Perry cut in. "He's right. You have a great sense of self and determination. And you know you can stay here as long as you need to."

"Thanks, Mom. I appreciate that. My friend, Marcy, will be shipping the rest of my possessions here this week. Don't worry. I don't have a lot. I'm giving Gregg all the furniture and the kitchen stuff, except for my animal mug collection."

Perry said, "When did you start collecting animal mugs?"

"About two years ago."

Perry and Spencer sat in the back seat of the van. Both were wearing their disguises and, after checking each other out, decided that they were authentic-looking. Fake IDs were clipped onto their lab coats and Perry replaced the lip balm and ponytail band in her right pocket with a syringe and ten vials of diazepam.

She looked over at Spencer and said in a British accent, "How are you doing, champ?" A small trickle of sweat seeped from the base of his light brown, short-cropped hairpiece and rolled down the side of his face. He wiped it away.

"I'm fine. You?"

She gave him a thumbs up. "Is the wig too hot?" She lightly touched her blonde, pixie-cut hairpiece, adjusting it slightly.

"A little."

"Try not to think about it and don't touch the goatee. If you're sweating, the moisture could move it if you try to manipulate it. You'll only be wearing them for an hour or so." Perry looked at her watch. It was 12:55 a.m.

The driver, also wearing a disguise, said, "We're here." He pulled up to the research facility. It resembled a large shoe box. There were no adornments whatsoever. The color of the building could be described as dirt brown. The foliage was sparse and very pedestrian. Juniper bushes, star jasmine and Manzanita shrubs encircled the laboratory. He parked a couple of spaces to the right of the moving van. Perry noticed that the movers were standing in front of the main entrance.

Perry said, "Do you have the memory stick?"

"Yup," replied Spencer.

"Camcorder?"

"Check."

"From this point on, we say nothing about the operation, especially in the elevator and the lab. Let's do this, Spencer-roo."

Spencer rolled his eyes. He got a kick out of Perry, this vibrant woman who dedicated her life to helping animals. Most women her age were comfortably employed or married or raising a family. But here she was, at one in the morning, ready to risk her freedom for the lives of ten lab cats. He wished his mother had that kind of passion for something instead of subsisting to please her husband.

With all the confidence they could muster, Perry and Spencer walked over to the group of movers. Both noticed the camera pointed at the doors. In a flawless British accent, Perry said, "Hello gentlemen. You must be moving Richard Allbright's lab."

A tall, stocky man who resembled a Cro-Magnon said, "Are you the assistants that are supposed to let us in?"

"We are not. I'm sure they'll be here soon. For security reasons, I'm not authorized to allow you entrance. Sorry."

Perry swiped the card key and the green light went on. She pulled the door open and she and Spencer walked across the entry and into the elevator. Perry pushed the button for the third floor.

As they ascended, Spencer went over the plan in his mind. His nerves had smoothed out, somewhat. His goatee was itchy and he almost scratched it, then he remembered what Perry said and endured the discomfort. He looked up nonchalantly and made note of the security camera in the upper right-hand corner.

The elevator doors opened to a brightly lit hallway. The beige linoleum floor was polished and clean. The walls were a light green as were the doors to the labs. Except for the faint whooshing sound of the heating system overhead, it was surprisingly quiet, especially considering that caged animals were behind almost every door. They swiftly walked down the corridor, barely making a sound, until they came to room 314. Perry took out the second key card and swiped it. She turned on one bank of overhead lights and scanned the room. Spencer took out the camcorder and began filming the white walls, white floor, white everything. Jeff's sketch of the room was highly accurate. Facing the left wall was Dr. Crowden's brown metal desk. It was exceptionally neat. A thick stack of papers sat to the left. On the right were a stapler, tape dispenser and a framed photograph of the researcher and his wife sitting at the beach. His computer screen displayed a screen saver from years ago. Flying toasters slowly flew across the monitor. A photo taped to the side of the screen showed an anesthetized cat with an unlit cigarette dangling from its mouth. The caption read, "Got a light?" On the opposite side of the room, five metal boxes sat side by side, a hole in the front of each box. Six inches from the opening was a mask attached to a tube. Spencer walked over to the boxes and slowly filmed each one. When he reached the last box, he turned off the camera but continued to stare at it. He closed his eyes and transported himself into the box. He felt claustrophobic as he tried to move his arms and legs. Then the mask was placed over his nose and mouth. Perry softly called to him. He didn't answer. As she walked toward him, she could hear his labored breathing. She grabbed his arm, jerking him back into reality. She brought him over to the cats.

"Sorry."

Perry replied, "Please don't let it happen again. Turn the camera back on."

Spencer obeyed and began filming the cats. As he slowly swept passed the cages, he noticed the distrust in their eyes. Humans were the enemy. They followed the camera until it left their cage and moved on to the next prison cell. All ten cats were different. There was a long-haired and short-haired calico, a short-haired tuxedo, an orange and white male and three gray and white tabbies, a Burmese, a Russian Blue and a Persian. They had room to stand up and turn around. A worn towel served as their bed. The food and water trays were attached to the cage bars.

The cats were quiet until Perry opened up their cage doors. Some of them howled, others hissed as they crouched in a corner, trying their best to disappear, anticipating their daily ritual. A few tried to scratch her. Her gloves protected her as she gently held them, then injected each cat with a syringe full of diazepam.

Five minutes later, all ten cats were asleep in the transport cages. They were stacked on the wheeled cart by the door and covered with a sheet. Spencer entered the password to the computer, found the files and videos of the experiments that Jeff identified and copied them onto the memory stick. Once he logged off, he joined Perry who had begun trashing the equipment. She was cutting the smoking tubes into little pieces. They looked like elbow macaroni. She found a small torch in one of the cabinets and partially melted the metal boxes, careful not set off the smoke alarms. The masks, used to hold the cigarettes in place, were burned to crisps the size of potato chips. Spencer cut up Crowden's research papers and ripped up the photo of the smoking cat. Using wire cutters, he reduced the cat cages to a pile of metal pieces. They looked like silver pick-up sticks.

They admired their handiwork for a few seconds before they closed the door to the once sterile environment. At the very least, it would take a while to replace the equipment and the data. By that time, every animal rights group and major newspaper in the country would have the video and research papers on Crowden's fallacious experiments.

Together, they pushed the cart with their precious cargo toward the elevator, thankful that the movers were four floors above them. Hopefully, they wouldn't cross paths. Instead of exiting on the first floor, they would be getting off on the second and take the exit to the upper parking lot.

The elevator door opened and Spencer nearly froze. Three of the movers with a lab assistant stared back at them, along with cages filled with rats. Unlike the cats, they were very much awake and highly anxious. They clung to the metal sides, noses twitching, eyes searching. The group moved aside and Perry, with Spencer's help, pushed the cart between the rats and the movers, barely squeezing in. Perry pushed the button for the second floor. She felt the lab assistant's eyes on her.

"Do you work in this building?" said the twenty-something assistant. She was short and skinny. Her round glasses were too big for her long face.

Her accent flawless, she said, "Actually, we work with Dr. Langley in Justice Hall."

Spencer's nerves went into overdrive and he began to sweat. A small bead formed on his forehead. He wanted to wipe it but didn't want to bring attention to himself, so he let it slide down the side of his cheek. It landed on the edge of his goatee.

"What are you doing here?" the assistant asked, sounding unconvinced.

"The same thing you're doing. Moving some animals and equipment over to Dr. Langley's lab. He insisted we do it at this hour to avoid noise and traffic."

The elevator came to a stop and the doors opened to the second floor.

"Enjoy your evening," Perry said as she and Spencer wheeled the cats out of the elevator. Once the doors closed, they moved quickly in case the assistant wasn't buying the story. As they approached the exit, Spencer noticed a camera above the door. The light was blinking and the lens seemed to grow as they got closer.

"Ahem…"

"I see it," said Perry. "Let's get the hell out of here."

Jeff had told her that she'd need the key card to exit, but in her haste, she forgot. When she opened the door, the alarm went off. The van was parked a few feet to the right. The driver jumped out, opened the back doors and the three of them practically threw the cages into the back. Spencer climbed up to secure the cages while

Perry and the driver ran to the front of the van and took off. Hearts pounding, they prayed that security wasn't fast enough to follow them.

"Son of a bitch! I forgot about using the card key. I'm sorry guys. That was stupid." Perry shook her head.

Except for the sound of the cages being locked into the van's side brackets, it was quiet. All three strained their ears, listening for the sound of sirens.

"How long will the cats remain sedated?" Spencer said.

"They'll be waking up in an hour. It gives us plenty of time to get them to the safe house."

The driver turned left on Fulton Street from Bancroft Way and that's when they heard it. The distinctive sound of a police siren. Perry turned to the driver and said, "Plan B."

Without a word, he turned left on Durant Street. After three blocks, he pulled into a parking garage, drove the van down to the bottom floor and killed the engine.

They got out and Perry said, "We need you Spencer."

By the time he opened the back doors, the driver and Perry were peeling off the red rubber exterior, revealing the vehicle's original silver paint. Using a screwdriver, Perry replaced the license plates with new ones. In less than ten minutes, their ride was transformed. The siren had since disappeared and Spencer's heartbeat had returned to normal.

Spencer walked through the front door to his home after 2:30 in the morning. He was beyond exhausted. Gilley met him at the door, wagging her tail so hard, he thought it would fly off her body. He picked her up and let her lick every inch of his face. Before adopting her, he couldn't conceive of letting a dog slobber on him.

"I was going to ask you if you missed me, but I think I know the answer. I missed you, too, little girl."

After he kicked off his shoes and got a glass of water, he sat on the couch in the dark. It was a full moon. The light coming through the windows illuminated the cottage, the ideal ambience for Spencer's mood. He held Gilley tight as the images of the laboratory cats, huddled in their cramped, steel cages crowded his brain. The terror in their eyes would never leave him. The row of smoking machines, where the cats were forced to smoke cigarettes for hours, would never leave him. The rats crowded together in their cages, looking at a world they'd never escape into, would never leave him. The vision morphed into pictures of female rhesus monkeys, their babies taken away to be used in isolation experiments. Babies locked away for months at a time, eventually developing psychoses so their brains could be studied and then dissected. Spencer trembled, lightly at first, then it escalated. Gilley jumped off his lap. She looked up at her rescuer with a concerned look on her face, but Spencer didn't notice. His eyes were shut as he hugged his body, willing it to stop. It wouldn't. His body wanted to purge the pain. Spencer knew that, even if he succeeded in alleviating the images from his body, others would fill the void. There was too much evil in the world. There was too much apathy. And Spencer was still too sensitive.

The key was under the planter on the front porch, just as she said it would be. Perry put it in the door knob and quietly turned it. It was late and she didn't want to wake her friend who so graciously allowed her to spend the night. Taking off her shoes, Perry walked past the living room and into the guest room. The bed had been turned down. A fern green washcloth, face and bath towel were stacked at the edge of the bed.

After washing her face and brushing her teeth, Perry shed her clothes and relished the way the fresh sheets felt against her skin. She shimmied a couple of times, enjoying the moment. She thought of Spencer and hoped he was okay. This rescue was by far the most dangerous and carried the highest risk factor. In addition to being on edge, she worried about his state of mind. As they sat in the parking lot, waiting for the siren to pass, she watched as he methodically removed his goatee and wig. He lowered his head and massaged his scalp. Then he told them that he wanted to sit in the back with the cats and comfort any that woke up prematurely. As a mother, she wanted to wrap her arms around this sweet, caring boy.

As a woman, she wished he was beside her in bed. Her exhaustion turned to anxiety and she sat up, rubbing her face in her hands. "Stop it," she said out loud. "You're almost fifty for Christ's sake."

She lay back down on the soft pillow and seriously thought about re-entering the online dating scene. Her last foray into the dating pool yielded very few prospects and those were eventually eliminated, but if it took her mind off Spencer, then it would be worth the plunge. As she closed her eyes, she relived the cats being taken out of the rescue cages and placed in small rooms equipped with beds, two and three-story cat perches and toys. Disoriented, the cats weren't quite sure what to make of their new surroundings. They were used to either being confined to a small cage or stuffed into a metal box. Their freedom was baffling. The veterinarian who provided the safe house saw the worried look on Spencer's face. She assured him that they would adjust in a few weeks, then they would be available for adoption.

Relieved that the rescue, in the planning stages for over a month, was finally over, Perry fell into a deep sleep.

41

She was having difficulty keeping her eyes closed. She looked over at the man by her side, lightly snoring, his arm draped across her chest. She stroked the blonde hairs on his forearm and felt aroused. Instead of waking him, Bonnie gently moved his arm and got out of bed. She put on her bathrobe, walked into the kitchen and grabbed a bottle of beer from the fridge. She took a deep swallow as she thought about tomorrow night and her impending weekend. She never wanted to look at Gerald's grotesque body again. She didn't want to take orders from him or have to deflect his advances, but she knew that it was necessary. The drug was entering the fast food meat next week and she was determined to help uncover the scheme and put Hinton's CEO away for life.

Bonnie opened her laptop. She went to the Google page and typed in DMT. Over 30,000 results appeared. She clicked on a YouTube video titled, 'My crazy DMT trip.' With the volume low, she watched as this conservative-looking young woman described meeting beings of light and communicating with them through thought. They filled her with love and healing light. She watched as her spirit body glowed. Then she was back to earth, in her body. The next video she clicked on was of a middle-aged pharmacologist. He had crazy white hair and black-rimmed glasses with thick lenses. He reminded her of Albert Einstein. He had taken DMT in a study with a number of other participants, conducted by psychologist Sydney Faris. His journey was vastly different. After watching geometric patterns in various shapes, sizes and colors float around the room, he glanced over at Dr. Faris. Instead of a man in a white lab coat, he saw a giant Lego person. It freaked him out, so he closed his eyes and waited for the drug to wear off.

It was close to 3:00 a.m. when Bonnie shuffled off to the bedroom. She was still feeling ambivalent about taking DMT, but too tired to give it any more thought. At the moment, she craved the human touch. She lifted Kanen's arm and placed it around her, holding it close to her body. His warmth cradled and soothed her. She felt whole.

The eager, young nurse followed Cody as he deftly navigated the bowels of the neighborhood. His cell phone was safely tucked away in the inside pocket of his backpack, along with dog food and water. Twice, RN Ellen Adderly, had to ask Cody to slow down. Her short, chubby legs and endurance level were no match for the tall, muscular man who was used to walking swiftly and with purpose.

Fifteen minutes later, they arrived at the back of Thang Long restaurant. Taking a burger out of his backpack, Cody walked up to the battered cardboard box, which was even more ragged than the last time he visited his friend. Despite the large garbage receptacle next to Della's encampment, empty food wrappers and scraps of uneaten food littered the area. Ellen adjusted quickly to the stench of the garbage and Della's filthy hovel. She was used to dealing with noxious odors and bodily fluids at the hospital. But when she saw a rat the size of a puppy run along the side of the dumpster, she almost screamed. She held it in, lest Cody think she was a wimp. She hoped he didn't see her shudder.

"Della. It's me, Cody." He squatted next to her immobile body and touched her head. It was warm. He looked down at her feet. They were exposed and the big toe on her left foot looked like it had dried blood on it. Cody motioned for the nurse to come over.

"It looks like something gnawed on her toe and I think I know what it was," Ellen said as she turned to where the rat had disappeared. "We've got to get her out of here."

"Whether she wants to or not, right?"

"Stop talking about me like I'm not here." Della opened her eyes. They were hollow with deep bags. She looked at Cody, then glared at Ellen. "Who the hell are you?"

Ellen said, "I'm here to help you, Della."

"The hell you are."

Cody stepped in. "Ellen here wants to see that you get better and nice and clean. You'll have a bed to sleep in and food when you're hungry. I'll come visit you."

"I'm not interested." Della turned her back to them. The blanket slipped off of her, revealing a bony shoulder.

Ellen was about to touch Della when she thought better of it. She was afraid the woman could come unhinged and, emaciated or not, do some damage if she wanted to. Ellen decided to take a different approach.

"Della, the city is tearing this building down later today. They were going to move you, but Cody and I insisted that we take care of you instead. All you have to do is say the word and we'll have a vehicle come and take you to the hospital where…"

Della whipped around so fast, Ellen was hit by her blanket. "Where you'll tie me down and pump me full of drugs. You look like a woman, but you're the devil and I'm not going anywhere with the devil, so fuck you." She looked at Cody. "Stay away from her, Cody. She'll take your soul."

"No she won't, Della. She's a nurse and she wants to help you, like I do." He put his large hand on her tiny shoulder. "I promise on my mother's grave that I will not let anything bad happen to you. Please trust us. Please." Cody looked like he was going to cry. It certainly softened Ellen's heart. They waited for a response.

Della sat up and surveyed her home. Her body ached inside and out. She looked down at her bloody toe. She touched her matted hair and examined her dirty hands, the nails long and curved. Then she looked at Cody and said, "Don't let them hurt me."

Tears fell from his eyes. "I swear to you that I won't let anyone hurt you." He nodded to Ellen. She took out her cell phone and made the call.

Fifteen minutes later, an ambulance arrived. While waiting, Cody had gathered up all of Della's possessions that she deemed valuable. He placed them in a plastic bag.

As the EMTs brought the stretcher over, Cody saw the fear return to Della's eyes. He held her hand and began to sing.

"I'm leaving West Virginia with the good book in my pack and I'll listen for your voice when I'm hungry and feel lack..."

As they laid her on the gurney, Della held tightly onto Cody's hand. He continued to sing in his smooth, melodic voice as they drove to the hospital. Ellen sat beside him, taking Della's vitals, grateful that the intervention went well. It was her first and she hoped that there would be many more. Since last year, she had been working in the emergency room at St. Francis. Every month, she would implore her supervisor to implement a program to proactively help the homeless. And every time, she would be told that they didn't have the funds. It took Senator Kathala to bring the intervention project to life. Ellen was a Democrat, but the Republican senator was her hero.

42

She looked at her cell phone. It was Gerald. She took a deep breath and put the phone to her ear. "Are you on your way?"

"I'll be there in five minutes. Wait downstairs."

"See you soon."

She hung up and took another deep breath then blew it out. "Come on, Bonnie. You can do this. Just once more."

She picked up her overnight bag and purse and headed out the door. Bonnie knew this would be the last time she'd have a chance to learn more about the operation before the plan was implemented next week. She was determined to see this through.

She walked out of the apartment building and was hit with a gust of biting cold wind. It was a perfect day to leave the city and enjoy the warmth of Napa County, company excluded.

The black stretch limousine pulled up to the curb and Bonnie inwardly groaned. She assumed Gerald would be driving, leaving his hands occupied. All bets were off in the back of a limo. She mentally slapped herself. *'Deal with it Bonnie and quit bitching.'*

The driver got out and took Bonnie's bag, then opened the back door. She slid in beside Gerald and, to her relief, he was on the phone. He put a finger to his lips and she gladly complied. From the sound of the conversation, Gerald was not happy. He pulled a folder out of his briefcase and opened it in such a way that she was unable to see the contents.

Bonnie had no idea who he was talking to or what it was about, but the call lasted a glorious forty-five minutes. While waiting, she helped herself to a chilled bottle of Veuve Clicquot champagne. The first glass calmed her nerves. The second gave her a pleasant high. When he finally removed the phone from his ear, the limousine was pulling up to the front of Chateau Bon Amie, a vintage bed and breakfast in the hills of Saint Helena, and Bonnie was relishing the last sip from her third glass of $165 champagne. So far, the excursion was great.

Instead of apologizing for being an absent companion, Gerald looked at the empty champagne flute and scowled.

"I hope you left a sip for me."

Bonnie picked up the bottle, looked at it carefully and said, "The bottle is half full and you can have the rest." She placed it back in the ice-filled bucket and left the limo. When her feet touched the ground, she almost toppled over. She righted herself and continued to walk to the B&B, giving little thought to whether or not Gerald was behind her.

Fashioned after a French villa, their room for the weekend was exquisite. Hardwood floors were partially covered with a light pink floral area rug. The walls were painted mint green. The overstuffed bedspread boasted a pink and mint green toiles design. The paintings on the walls were original oils, depicting the French countryside. Bonnie loved it all: the lace pillows, pedestal sink in the bathroom and especially the French doors opening up to a spacious balcony, complete with hanging baskets of fuchsias and petunias. The only thing missing was Kanen.

Gerald came up behind her and put his arms around her waist, squeezing a bit too hard. It brought Bonnie back to reality and the task at hand. He was about to whisper in her ear when she said, "I'm starving. Can we get something to eat?"

"Let's do it first," he replied.

Determined to stay chaste for the weekend, she dug in her heels.

"I'm so hungry I could pass out. Can we go out for a bite, please?"

He abruptly removed his hands from her waist. "Fine." Clearly agitated, he headed for the door. "Let's walk. I don't want to get in the limo again."

"Sounds good to me," she said as she smiled at the empty bed, then closed the door behind her.

Two cocktails, an appetizer, main dish and dessert later, they came back to the room. Both were clearly stuffed.

She walked out onto the balcony, enjoying the view of the vineyards. The setting sun turned the sky a soft orange and the grape leaves a golden yellow. Bonnie watched a cat as it walked slowly, deliberately between the vines. She heard the bathroom door close and then load groaning.

"Are you okay?" she called to Gerald. He didn't answer.

"This may be easier than I thought," she said in a whisper and went back to observing the vineyard cat.

Gerald flushed the toilet and joined Bonnie on the balcony.

"Are you okay?" she said.

"My stomach's a little upset. It might have been the Carpaccio. I usually don't eat raw beef. I think I'll be fine."

Bonnie internally counted to five, then put her hand to her stomach. "I might not be so lucky." She went to the bathroom and turned on the fan, but made sure that Gerald heard her soft cries of anguish. Sound effects in full swing, Bonnie hoped she didn't overdo it. Hunched over, clutching her stomach, she emerged from the bathroom, then tore off the bed covers and got into bed, curling up in a fetal position.

"Jesus, Bonnie."

"Horrible cramps. In my stomach. Could you get me some Pepto Bismol or Alka Seltzer…anything? Please!"

She waited a few minutes after Gerald left, then jumped out of bed and went straight for his briefcase. She quickly scanned the contents. All she found were documents relating to a business deal that Gerald had been working on in the limo. Disappointed, she closed the leather case. Next, she grabbed his cell phone sitting on the dresser. Bonnie typed in the password and went directly to his texts. A few were from his daughter. One from his wife, wishing him a productive weekend with Hinton's CFO, and then there was a text string from Anita. She was about to open it when she heard Gerald asking someone down the hall for more toilet paper. Returning the phone to its original screen, she jumped back into bed and was rocking back and forth when he opened the door. She didn't bother turning to look at him.

"I got you some Pepto Bismol and Alka-Seltzer."

"Thanks," she said quietly. Slowly, she got up and picked up the bottle filled with electric pink liquid. She looked up at him. "Spoon?"

Without a word, he left and returned a few minutes later with a teaspoon and a tablespoon. She took the tablespoon, walked into the bathroom and closed the door.

After making more noise and flushing the toilet, she emerged and got back into bed. Gerald was out on the balcony with a flute of champagne, his stomach clearly feeling better. He didn't bother to ask Bonnie about her discomfort. She didn't expect any sympathy from her boss. After all, he invited her up to Napa for a weekend of sex. She knew he was more irritated than concerned for her well-being.

As she lay in bed, perfecting the fetal position, her thoughts drifted back to the day she started working for Hinton Industries. She was younger, but not so innocent. Bonnie knew exactly how to endear herself to Gerald and she waited less than a month after being hired to garner his attention. She found out where he ate lunch, when and where he golfed, even wheedled out of his secretary where he got his hair cut. Almost a year later, rumors were circulating through the hallways and offices that Bonnie Rydover was having an affair with the CEO. Before meeting Kanen, she would have considered her ascent a major accomplishment. Lying in bed, she felt more like a prostitute.

Three hours later, Bonnie was fast asleep. Gerald was sitting up in bed watching television. The volume was up and, despite his partner's state of unconsciousness, he continued to make comments aloud. In the middle of the *Expendables 2*, he fell asleep. His loud snoring woke Bonnie. She sat up and looked at Gerald's heaving chest, his mouth agape.

"Gerald?" She gently shook him. "Gerald, are you awake?" He let out another snore, louder than the last. Satisfied that he was out, she quietly left the bed, grabbed her cell out of her purse, then his cell from the dresser and went into the bathroom. When she opened up the text thread between him and Anita, she couldn't believe her eyes. Their communication was anything but discreet. She knew he was brazen, yet couldn't understand why he wouldn't delete his communication with Anita. She snapped a photo of the text string.

"Bonnie, are you going be a while?" Gerald's voice boomed.

"Not really. I'll be out in a minute."

"Hurry. I need to use the toilet."

She looked down at her nightgown: no pockets. She thought of putting the phones in the vanity drawer, then realized one of them could ring. In an act of sheer faith, Bonnie placed both phones in her left hand, opened the door with her right and walked past Gerald. He was standing outside the door and barely glanced at her as he took a step inside the bathroom and closed the door. She placed his phone back on the dresser and put hers in her purse.

When he returned to bed, he nudged her. "You feeling better?"

She put her hands to her stomach. "Actually, the cramps are worse."

"This has turned into a shitty vacation." He rolled over and went back to sleep. Fully awake, Bonnie ruminated over her relationship with this insensitive, selfish lout. Her goal of becoming CEO of Hinton Industries seemed laughable, but when she first took the job as assistant marketing director, it was anything but a joke. The ferocity and determination she displayed was almost manic. As a result, she had no friends, save Kanen. No one at Hinton liked her and now she knew why. She was so driven by a desire to succeed, it never occurred to her that her co-workers were anything but an impediment to her goal. Now she had a new objective. One of the first things she was going to do when she returned to San Francisco was call her brother. Their estrangement had gone on long enough. Spencer was her only sibling and her guilt for what she had done was overwhelming. Lying in the four poster bed, as close to the edge as possible, she started to cry. As the emotional outpouring escalated, she used her willpower to cap her sorrow. She didn't want to wake the sleeping ogre and this was not the place to unleash years of pent-up anguish and remorse. She held her breath until the tears subsided, then got up and went outside on the balcony. She hugged her body and drank in the cool, crisp night air. Her thoughts went to Kanen. She missed him and wished his arms were around her, comforting and warming her. She knew he cared for her. Would he insist that she become vegan? It was hard for her to imagine adopting a lifestyle where no animal products were used or consumed. She must have owned at least three leather jackets, two or three wool coats, silk shirts, and dozens of leather shoes, including a variety of boots. Steaks, fried chicken, scallops, even lobster. No more. Never to eat again. And cheese! No more Swiss or Havarti, cream cheese, yogurt. Bonnie's stomach was starting to hurt for real. It was hard for her to fathom giving up everything she loved for a man she met a mere few months ago.

Back in bed, she resolved to talk to Kanen as soon as the fast food debacle was over. She tossed and turned for a while, then fatigue overtook her and within minutes, Bonnie was asleep.

The limousine pulled up to the entrance of her San Francisco apartment at 10:30 Saturday morning. A very anxious, but relieved Bonnie sat opposite from a very disgruntled and sexually frustrated Gerald. He was on the phone the entire trip, intentionally avoiding conversation with the woman who ruined his weekend. Every once in a while, she would grab her stomach in a mock cramp and groan.

Before she left the car, she wanted to tell Gerald she was sorry, but he held up his hand to silence her and continued his phone conversation.

After putting away her clothes and toiletries, Bonnie called Kanen. He answered on the first ring.

"Did the jerk give us what we needed?" Kanen wanted to ask her if he forced her to have sex, but held off.

"Did he ever. Wait until you see what I got. When can you be over?"

"I have a better idea. Come over to my place. I have a surprise of my own."

"I'll see you in less than an hour." Bonnie was beaming.

"I can't wait."

43

Jessica sat at her desk and stared at the reams of paper before her. A group of constituents was arriving in an hour and she still had a lot of paperwork to shuffle through before they invaded her office. She was positive they all had a laundry list of complaints about how poorly Congress was running the country. She had just returned from the Senate floor after a two hour debate on S.45, the bill to dismantle the Endangered Species Act. The opposition from the Democrats was fierce. They rabidly defended the ESA, much to her disappointment. Too many businesses in Montana wanted to expand, yet were paralyzed by the law enacted in 1966 by Congress under the Johnson administration. Jessica couldn't understand how her fellow senators would rather see an endangered species like the yellow-striped lizard survive than a human endeavor succeed. According to the Center for Biological Diversity, the planet loses dozens of species to extinction every day. What's one more? And do we really need another lizard? In Jessica's order of importance, humans came first. Well, most humans.

As she began the tedious process of whittling down her inbox, Talbert knocked on her door then opened it. Jessica looked up. "Yes?"

"Your 3:00 appointment is here."

Jessica glanced at her calendar. "I don't have a 3:00. I have the group from Montana coming at 4:00."

"She said that you know her by the name d.o.a."

At first, Jessica was horrified. She thought Anita or Olivia was playing a cruel, dangerous joke on her, but then she realized that they would never risk divulging the plot, even to an aide. Her shock turned to joy. "Tell her I'll be there in a minute."

She grabbed her purse and frantically searched for her lipstick. After she applied it, she brushed her hair, then checked herself in the mirror. Satisfied, she pushed the intercom and told Talbert to let d.o.a. in.

As she stepped into the office, Lenore's eyes widened. "Your office is awesome! It's everything I expected and more. The dark wood is so exquisite and the curtains are perfect and look at that desk. Awesome!"

Jessica shook her head. The woman definitely wasn't what you would call the stereotypical researcher. She gave her a hug. It was enthusiastically returned.

"So, you just happened to be in the neighborhood?"

Lenore blushed. "I know I should have called, but I really wanted to see where you worked. I'm so impressed, Jessica. Oh, should I call you Senator Olshansky when I'm in the senate building?"

Jessica laughed. "Not at all. I have some time before a horde of angry Montanans descends on my office. Would you like something to drink?"

"Tea sounds nice."

"Tea it is. Please, have a seat. I'll be right back."

Lenore was too nervous to sit. Instead, she went over to the large window and looked out at the expansive view of Jefferson Park. Normally, she would have called first, following the proper protocol. Her fear of being rejected gave her the courage to stop by unannounced.

Talbert walked in first, carrying a tray with two mugs, a basket full of tea bags and a plate of ginger cookies. He placed the tray on the coffee table. Jessica sat down on the couch and Lenore followed suit. The women talked about the latest research findings and Jessica filled Lenore in on her conversation with her friend from the National Institute of Biomedical Imaging and Bioengineering concerning the use of prisoners as research participants.

At 3:50, the women stood. "Thanks so much for seeing me, Jessica."

"It was my pleasure. Next time you decide to stop by, and do so by all means, please call first. It's rare that my schedule allows me respite."

"Definitely."

As she turned to go, she stopped. "I was wondering if, you know, maybe we could go to dinner tonight. As long as I'm in town, it would be awesome to see where congress dines."

Jessica said, "Dear Lenore, I would love to go to dinner with you and I'll take you to my favorite steak house, but you have to do me one little favor. Please stop saying 'awesome.' The word is so overused by everyone and, don't take offense, but it's driving me batty."

For the second time in less than an hour, Lenore blushed. "I'm so sorry. I didn't realize I said it that much."

She lightly touched her arm. "You do."

"If anyone else told me that, I'd be offended. Coming from you, I take it as a way of bettering myself."

"I'm glad you feel that way and I am sorry if I crossed the line. I'm just so tired of hearing that word describe everything from a piece of toast to a cataclysmic event. I actually overheard a mother tell her husband that their child had taken an awesome poop. You can say it all you want when I'm not around."

Lenore replied, "Well in that case, I'll have to strike it completely from my vocabulary."

This time it was Jessica who blushed. "Why don't you come back around 5:30? We can go to T-Bone Tony's from here."

"Aweso…Great. I'll see you then."

Jessica had a few minutes before her constituents arrived. She needed the time to compose herself. Her body was trying to convince her mind to accept the premise that she was attracted to Lenore Fitzwater. Yes, she was a bit of a goof ball and her decorating acumen was on the level of a 1950s Iowa housewife, but she liked her. In her distinctive scientific versus salt and pepper collection personality, her quirkiness made her very attractive. Physically, she wasn't much to look at, but Jessica wasn't either.

There was a knock on the door, then Talbert opened it and announced the arrival of her 4:00 appointment.

"Be prepared, Senator. They're all wearing t-shirts that say, 'We've got a bone to pick with Congress.' They don't look too happy."

"That's just awesome. Show them in."

44

Spencer poked his head out of the covers and squinted at the clock. It was 7:30 a.m. He would have liked to disappear under his blanket, but the person knocking on the door was unrelenting.

"Hold on! I'm coming!" He slipped on his sweats and a t-shirt. Gilley was already at the door when he opened it. Staring back at him was Callie. She looked like she'd been up for hours: her auburn hair was pulled back in a high ponytail. She wore a tank top with cut-off jeans. She wasn't wearing any make-up, but once again, Spencer was mesmerized by her dark gold eyes. He swore there were flecks of light gold suspended in her irises.

"Is this going to happen every time we meet?"

"What?"

"Staring at me like that. It's unnerving. Cut it out."

Spencer ran his fingers through his hair. "It's a compliment, you know."

Callie's voice softened. "I realize that. It's just that it makes me uncomfortable. How would you like it if I did that to you?"

"I'd love it." They laughed and then there was an awkward silence. "So…can I help you?"

"Mom made pancakes and soy sausage and wanted to know if you'd like to join us."

"Sounds great. I'll be there in five."

Callie craned her neck to get a better look at Spencer's home. He noticed and said, "I'm afraid you'll be disappointed. I'm not much of a decorator. Feel free to look around while I get ready."

He opened the door wider, then went into the bathroom with Gilley in tow and closed the door. Callie was surprised at how neat it was. She expected the typical mess and acrid, stale smell that young men tend to create and delight in living in. At least that was the case with her husband. Callie made sure dirty clothes and misplaced food didn't sit out for long. Except for a dinner plate and fork on the coffee table, the cottage was tidy. Even the kitchen semi-sparkled.

"Did my mom tell you that this used to be where I lived when I was a teenager?"

"She did. She also said you had parties and trashed the place."

"Guilty as charged, but boy did we have fun."

Spencer emerged from the bathroom looking more alert. He had brushed his hair and his teeth. His face was washed. "Did you want to see the bathroom, too?"

She walked over and peeked in. Except for the shower curtain and towels, it looked the same. "Just as I remembered it. Ready to go?"

He nodded and they walked out. Perry was standing on the deck.

"Good morning!" she yelled and waved. "Hey Gilley! Come here, girl." She held up a chew toy and squeezed it. It let out a loud squeak that sent the small sheltie terrier running toward the house and up the stairs. Perry threw it across the deck and Gilley ran after it, grabbed the toy banana and started chewing on it. The high-pitched sound only made her chew it harder and faster.

When Spencer and Callie stepped onto the deck, Perry said, "I hope this isn't too early for you."

"It's fine. I like being awakened by someone making me pancakes and vegan sausage. There's coffee too, right?"

"Are you kidding? The day doesn't begin until I've had my cuppa joe." Perry directed them both to the kitchen where they filled their mugs with fresh brewed coffee.

Spencer took a bite of the buckwheat pancakes smothered in coconut butter and maple syrup. "Delicious."

"Thanks. I love making breakfast. It's my favorite meal of the day."

Callie said, "The only way Mom could get me out of bed in the morning was to make me breakfast. The smell lifted the sheets right off of me."

Spencer said, "Are you a vegan again?"

"Nope. Does that bother you?"

"Yeah, it does. It's hard to believe that someone who knows all about factory farming could still eat flesh."

Perry could see the tension growing and she didn't want to be a part of it. After two years of estrangement, she was happy to be talking to her daughter again and she didn't want to mess it up. "I'm going to get the paper."

Barefoot, she walked through the house and opened the front door. Normally, the newspaper was on the porch. She looked around, then saw it in her camellia bush. She shook her head as she reached over the porch railing and grabbed it. A few of the white flowers had been knocked off. She made a mental note to call the Berkeley Times and complain. For the fourth time.

Once inside, she unfolded the paper and perused the front page. She could hear her daughter and tenant raising their voices, so she decided to delay her return to the deck. She turned the page and the article's headline made her heart pound. At the bottom of page two, she read, 'Berkeley Lab Broken Into, Animals Stolen, Equipment Destroyed.' The article said that a man and woman posing as lab assistants had stolen ten cats around 1:15 a.m. from the lab of senior researcher, Nicolas Crowden. It went on to laud the work of Crowden, calling his contribution to science invaluable. It described the perpetrators as a tall male in his early twenties with short, light brown hair, a goatee and diamond stud earring. The woman was medium height, British, and in her early forties with short, blonde hair. The lab equipment was completely destroyed, costing the university tens of thousands of dollars. The vehicle they were driving was a cherry red Ford van with Arizona plates. It had yet to be found.

That was it. There was no mention of Crowden's smoking study or that he'd been receiving research grants from the National Institutes of Health for over ten years and, to date, had not yielded any conclusive findings on the relationship between smoking and ulcers. Perry knew that sending the actual research documents to the paper would be pointless. The Berkeley Times rarely, if ever, reported anything negative when it came to the largest and one of wealthiest universities on the West Coast. The activist group insisted on sending them the research papers, hoping the newspaper would expose Crowden as the freeloader he was, exploiting federal funds at the expense of animal suffering.

"Mother, get out here and save me from this vegan piranha!"

Leaving the paper in the living room, Perry went out on the deck.

"At least you're both alive."

"Barely," said Callie. "You told me he was a vegan. I didn't realize he had the conviction of a mercenary."

"All I'm saying is that…"

"I know what you're saying, okay? I grew up with a female version of you and I don't need to be preached at or bonked over the head with your beliefs. We'll get along just fine if we leave veganism off the table. Please."

Perry looked over at Spencer. He had a pained look on his face, a look that she wore many times when she and her daughter argued over her decision to stop being vegan.

Spencer's first inclination was to get up and leave, but he relented. He didn't want to isolate Callie and certainly didn't want to upset his landlady. "Okay. It's off the table."

Perry turned to Callie. "What are you up to today?"

"Job hunting. I have to find work."

"Does that mean you're going to stay in Berkeley? You know you can live here as long as you like."

Perry replied, "Thanks, Mom. I'm done with Taos and really done with my marriage, but I also want my own place. I want a fresh start in my old stomping grounds."

Spencer said, "What kind of job are you looking for?"

"Something in the art field. I was a curator in Taos for an art gallery and loved it."

"They're looking for a salesperson at the bookstore I work for. Maybe you could do that while looking for the job you really want."

Callie laughed. "Working with you? That would be interesting."

When Callie got up to refill her coffee mug, Perry said to Spencer, "The paper reported the lab break in. No mention of Crowden squandering funds, but we were described to a tee in our disguises. The paper's in the living room, if you're interested. Page two."

Before Spencer could respond, Callie came back. Without a word, he grabbed his plate and mug and went in the house to read the article.

In a low voice, Callie said, "He's more of a fanatic than you."

"Gee, thanks sweet daughter of mine."

"You know what I mean. He's totally into the whole animal rights movement, trying to turn everyone into vegans by blasting it into our faces. I saw all the horror movies, including *Earthlings*, *Peaceable Kingdom* and the one about animal experimentation. What was it called?"

"*Monkey Business.*"

"Yeah. Heartbreaking. I know what's going on. I just don't want someone telling me what to do and making me feel guilty for not doing it."

"You think he's bad now? It is nothing compared to when he first moved here. He was downright…"

"Rabid?" Spencer said.

"Jesus Christ! Are you half dingo with that crazy super hearing and stealth of yours?" Perry said.

Spencer crouched down on the ground, narrowed his eyes and growled. Gilley ran over to him and licked his face, causing him to fall backward. He laughed and gently wrestled with her. "It's the vegan diet."

Callie rolled her eyes. "That's my cue to scoot." She got up to leave and looked at Spencer playing with Gilley. His dark, wavy hair was tousled and, even though he'd been up for over a half hour, his eyelids still had a hint of sleep. He was definitely adorable and even a little sexy, but Callie couldn't get past his fervent beliefs. As she used to tell her high school friends who would come to the house for dinner, 'People who don't think veganism is a religion don't know vegans very well.'

"How horrible was it?" Kanen said as they embraced.

"Not as bad as I thought." They walked out onto the deck, taking in the afternoon sun. "I wish I could have taken a video of the evening. The look on Gerald's face when I came out of the bathroom looking like hell was priceless. Without being able to use me, I was completely disposable to that turd. He even scoffed at going to the store for some Pepto Bismol and Alka Seltzer. I can't believe that I used to look up to him. It makes me shudder."

She quickly changed the subject. "You will not believe what I got on my trusty little cell phone." As she went to retrieve her cell from her purse, she said, "Do they still have dungeons for convicted felons? I'd love to see Gerald hanging by his toes, his head being gnawed at by rats."

"Why would you want to put rats into the same room as that crazed maniac?"

"I keep forgetting that I'm in the presence of an animal rights warrior. You like rats, too?" Kanen was about to respond when Bonnie put up her hand. "You can tell me later. Right now, you have to see this."

She gave her phone to Kanen, highlighting the screen shot of the text string.

Anita: Still set for Monday?

Gerald: Yes. Shipment leaves Thursday

Anita: Can't wait

Gerald: Enthusiasm shared. Have you calculated how many will be affected?

Anita: Rough estimate over one million in 3-5 mos. That's just a start

Gerald: Bonzai!

Anita: ☺ Still doing food giveaway

Kanen was euphoric. "Their text totally aligns with what Mike told me. They sprinkle the d.o.a. on the meat Monday and it goes out to the restaurants on Thursday. Do you know what the food giveaway is?"

"No. I never heard Gerald talking about it. I can check it out next week."

"Okay. The ship date gives us plenty of time to get a sample of the tainted meat and take it to the FBI. Great job, Bonnie. I'm relieved that you didn't have to literally 'take it' for the cause."

"You're relieved? If that asshole even tried to touch me with his thick, meaty fingers, I would have gotten sick. No faking." She put her arms around his waist. "So, what did you want to show me?"

"Ah yes, the surprise." He took her hand and they walked downstairs to the garden. They passed the koi pond, then made a left through a break in the hedge into a wooded area. Surrounding them on all sides were redwood trees, ferns and azalea, rhododendron and camellia bushes. The faint, soft scent of the flowers lifted into the air and circled around the couple. They followed the stepping stones to a large gazebo. In the front was a stone Buddha. He wasn't in the typical pose: large-bellied, bald, laughing. This one was the historical sage known as Gotama Siddhartha Gautama. He wore a headdress of beads, sat with legs crossed, hands resting in his lap. His eyes were closed as if in deep meditation. To his right was a small rock fountain. Water bubbled out through a hole in the top rock.

"This is beautiful. I thought your yard ended at the hedge."

"That's what I like people to believe. The tea room was finished this morning."

They approached the four hundred square foot wood and glass structure. It resembled a sanctuary more than a traditional Japanese tea room with its unfinished oak walls and round windows. Stone steps led up to the entrance. As Bonnie walked through, she touched the smooth frame and inhaled deeply. "Do I smell incense?"

"It's the frame. It's made of cedar." Kanen looked up at the ceiling. She followed his eyes and saw a majestic monarch butterfly kite. From wing to wing, it was close to eight-feet and hovered over the room. A slight breeze from outside made the kite flutter, giving the illusion that it was in flight.

Large pillows lined the floor's baseboards. In the middle of the room was a small fire pit. A decorative grid sat on top and a rustic-looking tea kettle rested atop. Four round pillows surrounded the pit. In the corner of the room, a table was set with tea cups and a box of organic green matcha tea.

Bonnie said, "I had no idea you were a tea man."

"Actually, I'm not. But when you go through the traditional Japanese ritual of making tea in this environment, it tastes wonderful. Almost magical."

"Hmm, I haven't seen this soft, sensitive side to you. It's intriguing."

Kanen came up behind her, put his arms around her and kissed the back of her neck. "Not sexy, just intriguing?"

Bonnie closed her eyes, "Now it's sexy."

"There's one other thing I want to show you," Kanen said as he took her hand and led her to a door in the back of the room.

"It better not be another tea kettle."

He just smiled.

It had been almost a week since Della was admitted to St. Francis Hospital. Everyone there knew her because of her daily rant. They also knew Cody. He never missed a day visiting his friend, providing emotional support and a seemingly endless supply of chocolate. Della's favorite was Hershey's dark chocolate bar.

Della's physical transformation was astounding. When Cody first visited, he didn't recognize her. Bathed, shampooed and wearing a nightgown, she looked and smelled like apple pie. Della had smelled the apple and cinnamon-scented lotion on one of the nurses and asked for a bottle. As she applied the lotion to her body in long, slow strokes, she was transported back to a time her mother prepared Della's favorite pie, letting her press the doughy crust against the pie pan. It was before the signs of bi-polar took up residence in her psyche, before she wondered what the disease had in store for her. Would she be grocery shopping like a normal person or driving for hours, ending up in a strange town, deflecting unwanted stares, cursing herself and this unwelcome affliction?

The sores that covered her face, arms and legs were beginning to heal. Her nails were clipped and one of the nurses bought her knee-high socks with a chocolate bar pattern. She was medicated, yet her feisty, fiercely independent personality managed to pierce the drug's veil of normalcy. Della kept the staff on edge with her intermittent complaining and repeated requests to leave.

Cody got off the elevator on the fourth floor, greeted the nurses by name, then knocked on the door to Della's room before he entered. It was small and neat. A single bed was against the right wall. Next to it sat a plain, brown night stand with a lamp and a pitcher of water. Opposite the bed was a desk and chair. A dresser was provided, its drawers nearly empty, save the clothes donated from Goodwill. The organization had an agreement with the hospital. Volunteers would visit the patients and give them a chance to pick out clothes at no cost to them or the hospital. It was Della's third day at St. Francis when Goodwill showed up with two boxes full of women's clothes. Overwhelmed by the choices, Della jumped into bed and pulled the covers over her head. She refused to come out, so the nurse on duty did her best to pick out clothes that would fit her patient. When Goodwill left, Della's new wardrobe consisted of two pairs of jeans, a pair of dark green cotton shorts, three t-shirts in various colors, a long-sleeved light blue silk shirt, a pair of tennis shoes and light gold flats, and a leather belt. It was only after everyone left her room that she checked out her new wardrobe and tried everything on.

Della was sitting at her desk when Cody approached. He looked over her shoulder.

"What are you writing?"

"A letter to my daughter."

He was dumbfounded. "You have a daughter?"

She looked up from her letter with tears in her eyes. "Alexandra. I called her Alex for short. She was taken away from me when they had me committed. My ex-husband and his family. She was only ten. The nurses told me that if I write to her, they'll try to find her. Maybe then they'll let me leave."

Cody knelt down and put his arm around Della's shoulders. "That's wonderful. How old do you think she is?"

"Twenty."

Cody looked into Della's eyes. They were the clearest since he met her. "If you want to see Alex again, you're going to have to stay on your medication. You know that, right?"

She started crying. "It makes me feel funny, Cody. My mouth is dry and my skin is itchy. Sometimes, I feel like I'm going to throw up."

Cody took out his phone, pushed some buttons, and then showed Della the screen. Staring back at her was a photo he took of her not more than two weeks ago. Bundled in filthy blankets, only her face was visible. Chapped lips, swollen eyes and sores covered her face. The image made her cry harder. Cody consoled her then said, "I was in this room when the doctor told you that there could be side effects. He also said that they could go away after time and if they don't, they'll adjust the dosage. Work with them, Della. Help yourself and then, when you see Alex, she'll see how far you've come."

Della grabbed a tissue and blew her nose. "Did I tell you that the hospital is going to get me new teeth?"

"That's wonderful!"

"Yeah." She blew her nose again and wiped her eyes. "I might look pretty again."

Cody kissed her forehead. "You look pretty now, Della." Cody took a Hershey bar out of his pocket. "Almost forgot to give you this."

Her eyes lit up and she took it from him. "I'll save it for after dinner. Can you stay?"

"I wish. I have some business to do, but I'll see you tomorrow, okay?"

She nodded and walked him to the door. "See you later."

From her window, Della watched as Cody walked down the street, his dreadlocks swaying with each stride. Growing up, her parents warned her not to tangle with black people. 'Sooner or later, they'll rob you or con you. They hate white people because of what we did to them.' It wasn't until she was living on the street that she met Cody. He helped her find shelter and brought her food and blankets. It was Cody that wanted her to get well, get her life back, even though she hated living within the confines of a small hospital room. If she wanted to go outside or in the rec room, she was accompanied by a nurse. She felt like a prisoner. She also knew that, despite the drug's side effects, she was feeling better. Her mind was clearer, not shrouded in a gauzy fog.

"I love you," Della said as the figure disappeared around the corner.

Cody hoped that his friend would make a full recovery. Della was so fragile yet strong enough to survive living on the street for as long as she had. He knew the torment she suffered. He was in a state mental hospital for almost two months before the doctors felt he was healthy enough to live on his own. His recovery was hastened by memorizing every Cody Brant song. When he felt like he was going to die if he didn't get a fix, he would tuck himself away in the corner of his room, grab his iPod and listen over and over again to his idol sing a song until he memorized it. It didn't hurt that Walter was born with a gifted voice. Day after day, song after song, from *The River of Love* to *Friends in Whiskey Bar*, he added the tunes to his repertoire. One day, as he was singing *Papa Broke the Floor*, a crowd began to gather around the door to his room. Totally unaware, eyes closed, Cody belted out the song. When he finished, the sound of applause scared him half to death. After much persuasion, he began to perform for his fellow patients in the recreation room. The adulation from the patients and most of the employees gave Cody the drive to memorize every song.

When he was discharged, Cody was told that he would be given a Greyhound bus ticket to one of three places: Houston, Boston or San Francisco. They never explained to him why they picked those cities, but he didn't care. Cody had wanted to live in San Francisco ever since he was a little boy. Every Friday night, he and his dad would watch *The Streets of San Francisco*. He wanted to be a detective just like Michael Douglas and Karl Malden, driving up and down the hills of the city, siren screaming, lights flashing, with the Golden Bridge in the background, rising like a bright orange monument to the city.

Cody made it to the city, but all he could afford on his disability allowance was an apartment on Taylor Street in the bowels of the Tenderloin. He couldn't see the Golden Gate Bridge from his window, just the building next door with its faded and chipped gray façade. The only resemblance to the television show was the near constant whine of sirens. On more than one occasion, the flashing lights from the police cars would bounce off the buildings and shine into his room, waking him. His desire to leave the Loin began to fade after he met Della and other street people who needed his help. He made it his life's work to tend to the homeless and abused, mistreated animals. He made a promise to himself to get out of the Loin at least once a week and enjoy the city outside the confines of his odious neighborhood. He lost count of the number of times he'd walked over the Golden Gate Bridge. He would also take the bus to Ocean Beach and visit the bison in Golden Gate Park. He even rode the cable cars when he wanted to tool around the city like a tourist.

Cody touched his cell phone inside his coat pocket. He slowed down as he turned the corner. At the end of the block, on the opposite side of the street, he checked out Jake's Auto Repair and Salvage. Jake wasn't in sight, so Cody slowly approached the shop, careful not to let San and Fran see him. Their barking would reveal his location and render his plan useless.

Cody was thirty feet away when Jake appeared. Quickly, he crouched down behind a tree trunk, took out his cell phone and put it on video mode. He simultaneously hoped to catch Jake mistreating the dogs and prayed Jake didn't harm them.

When the skinny pit bulls saw Jake approach with a bag of dog food, they stood up and walked toward him, as far their chain leads would allow. San was moving too fast and the lead jerked him back. Jake laughed. "Stupid mutt. Don't you know by now that's going to happen?"

He went over to their food bowls and poured a little over half a cup of kibble into each bowl. San and Fran greedily began to eat it.

"Slow down!" Jake yelled and kicked the dogs, causing them to yelp.

Cody flinched but kept the phone steady. Slowly, the dogs returned to their food. Within thirty seconds, the kibble was gone. They both looked up at Jake, their eyes full of hunger. He ignored them and walked back to the office. Once they realized that they weren't getting more, the emaciated dogs slowly walked back to their house, an empty oil barrel with unwashed towels for bedding.

After he turned off the camera, Cody sat with his back against the tree trunk and closed his eyes. He quietly sang to himself. *"When it feels like nothing's working, nothing's going your way. When the storm is at your door and you simply want to fade away, think of me. I'll be there to help you…*" It comforted him and helped him pass the time. About forty-five minutes later, Cody watched as Jake drove away in his pick-up truck. He jumped up and ran across the street.

"Hey San and Fran. Come here!"

The dogs sprang from their bed barking, and went to greet their only friend. Cody pulled a bag of dry dog food from his backpack. He pushed two collapsible bowls through the fence, then squeezed the bag through and poured healthy servings into each. While they ate, he took a video of their 'dog house' and of the empty water bowl. When the dogs were done, he filled the empty bowls with water from his bottle.

As the sun began to cast dark shadows on the auto repair shop, Cody said good-bye to his canine friends. They were a little fatter, quenched and a lot happier. He had two more dogs to videotape before he went home for the evening.

45

Tuesday morning, Mike Flores walked into work. Normally, he loathed entering the processing facility. It reeked of decaying animal flesh and ammonia. For nine hours, he was surrounded by steel and metal equipment, and sweaty bodies. The sound of steam emitted from the hoses, constantly in use in order to clean blood and pieces of flesh off the packing tables. But today was different. If all went well, he was about blow the lid off Hinton Industries. Mike had met yesterday evening with Kanen to solidify the plan. After work, they would meet at Tacqueria Mexicano and Mike would hand over the damning evidence.

Lunch box in hand, Mike clocked into work at 8:00 a.m. and put his valuables in locker 17. He glanced down at the front pockets of his cargo pants. He had put some small rocks in each pocket so they had some heft. Once he slipped one or two burger patties into each pocket, they hopefully wouldn't stand out.

His high top sneakers squeaked across the newly scoured floor as he made his way past the packaging area into the trafficking department. He nodded to Jim and Luis, two of his work friends. They would sometimes have lunch together but outside of work, they were strangers. Mike didn't even know where they lived and he liked it that way.

As Mike worked, he would occasionally glance over to where the junkie meat was being processed. He could see the employees sprinkling the powder, the 'flavor enhancer,' on the chicken nuggets, chicken patties and beef patties. He was astounded at how cavalier the company was in its handling of the powder. Then again, he understood that no one knew but the CEO and if a few of his employees inhaled the drug and died, Hinton could easily fill their positions. After all, assembly line workers were dispensable to a man who had no problem killing off hundreds of thousands of Americans.

At 11:55 a.m., Mike left his station and walked over to Luis who sprinkled the junkie meat with d.o.a. as the conveyer belt brought it past his station. His first inclination was to hold his breath, the smell was so offensive, but he reminded himself that today was his last in the building.

"Que pasa?" Luis said without looking up.

Mike stood to his left. "Bien. Estás listo para comer? (Good. Ready to eat?)"

"Si." Luis signaled to the floor manager. As he did, Mike nonchalantly grabbed two patties off the conveyer belt. He dropped one into his open pocket, then bent down and stuffed the other into the gap between his ankle and high top.

The alarm sounded and the conveyers came to a halt. Mike tried to stay calm as Gene, the foreman, quickly walked over. Luis put his hands up in the air, thinking he was the one targeted. He only put them down when Gene told Mike to stay where he was.

"What the hell, Miguel?"

"Sorry. I forgot to bring lunch and I'm hungry. We only get a half hour and I didn't want to starve." Mike took the beef patty out of his pocket. He was about to grab the one in his shoe when Gene took the meat from him and said, "You know I should write you up for this."

"You have my word, Mr. Lynn, I will never do it again. I swear in the name of Jesus Christ."

Gene said, "Coming from a religious person that should mean a lot, but you Mexicans wear big ass crosses then shoot and knife each other to death, so why should I believe you?"

Mike kept his temper in check. He was so close to accomplishing his goal, he didn't want to blow it. "Go ahead then. Write me up before I call my homies and carve you to pieces. We Mexicans are all in gangs, too, you know."

"Get into my office. Now!"

"Let me save you the trouble of filling out the paperwork. I quit."

As his co-workers watched in shock, Mike grabbed his belongings from the locker and slammed it shut. As soon as he got into his car, he took the beef patty out of his sneaker top and dropped it into his lunch box. He nervously wiped his hands on his jeans, removing any remnants of the drug from his fingers. To his knowledge, he didn't have any life threatening illnesses, but he didn't want to take any chances.

On his way home, he called Kanen. After years of oppressive work, he finally had luck on his side with a new job and hopefully a new career at Weston. He always envied Manny and now he'd be working alongside him.

Perry was tired. It was only 9:00 p.m. and she just finished reading chapter fourteen in *A Love Too Soon*, the latest bestseller by Toni Zohrn. She picked up her bookmark and admired it. It was purchased at the Museum of Modern Art when the Van Gogh exhibit was on display. As Van Gogh was by far her favorite artist, she revisited the exhibit two more times, thrilled that she was in the presence of *Starry Night Over the Rhone*, *Irises*, and *Vase with Twelve Sunflowers*.

The bookmark was a slightly faded reproduction of *Starry Night Over the Rhone*. It was small, only one inch wide by four inches high, but the more she stared at the famous painting, the deep blue sky above a dark ocean exploding with bursts of yellow and white stars, the more she felt the energy of Van Gogh's passionate strokes pierce her heart. It emanated from there and spread throughout her body. The faces on the couple standing by the shore were too small to detect any detail, yet it felt like they were staring up at her. Perry was overwhelmed with sadness. It was as if Van Gogh's tormented life seeped into the canvas and oils, even in a tiny reproduction. She forced herself to bury the replica in the pages of the novel, amazed at how it affected her so deeply.

She got up from the living room couch and stretched. She smiled as she remembered that Callie was spending the night at a friend's place. She had the house to herself again, if only for one night. A joint sat in an ashtray on the coffee table. She grabbed it and put it in her mouth. As she lit it, there was a knock on the back door.

"Hello Spence."

"You busy?"

"Aside from almost lighting my nose on fire, I'm free. What's up?"

From behind his back, he produced a DVD, *The Great Beauty*. "Do you and Callie feel like watching a movie?"

"Didn't it win an Academy Award for Best Foreign Film?"

"I believe it did."

"Callie's spending the night at Rina's, but I'll watch it with you." She lit the joint and inhaled, then handed it to Spencer. He took a hit.

"Just you and me, huh?"

"Don't get any ideas, young'un."

"Too late."

Perry put the movie in the DVD player and turned on the television. "If you like older women, why don't you go out with Callie? She's smart and beautiful and not your mother's age."

"Actually, you're a year older than my mom."

"Not only are you a dingo, you have the charm of an executioner."

He sat down on the couch next to Perry. Gilley lay at his feet. "Sorry. I've never been known to have a way with words. They tend to have a way with me. Perry, Callie is a nice person, but she's not you. You don't look or act anything like your age. You're beautiful and sexy as hell, funny and talented and the best partner in crime I could ever ask for. Can't you give us a chance?"

Perry realized that she shouldn't have gotten stoned. The timing was horrible. The pot made her way too vulnerable and Spencer's eyes were turning her into a horny landlady. The last time she had sex was…she couldn't remember, but it was crystal clear in her memory when she last kissed a man. It was Spencer on the dance floor at Jauncy's. And it was wonderful. After being with men her age and older, he was like a root beer popsicle on a hot, humid day. He had tasted delicious and sweet and pure. She loved it. Perry's thoughts were interrupted by the television. A preview of an action movie came blaring onto the screen. She looked over at the young man sitting next to her and she wanted to reenact that kiss. Instead, she said, "Can we talk about this after the movie?"

Spencer took another hit off the joint. He held it in for a good five seconds and exhaled a huge cloud of smoke, blowing it forcefully up into the air. When he looked back down at Perry, his eyes were red and very affected.

"I knew you were going to say that."

"Am I that predictable?"

"Uh huh. But I'm not."

"I beg to…"

Before Perry could finish her sentence, Spencer leaned over and kissed her. He puts his arms around her and she all but melted into his body. His passion entered her like a soft, smooth lightning bolt.

"Let's go in the bedroom," he said, his voice thick and heavy.

"Okay…wait, no. Not now."

"When?"

Perry stood up. She was clearly conflicted. Another preview was on the screen. A high speed train was barreling through the Alps. She looked back at Spencer. "I don't know and don't give me any shit. I'm not in the mood. I'm not sure what I'm doing, but I do know that we need to watch the movie. Okay?"

"Yes, ma'am."

"And don't ever call me ma'am again!"

"Fine. I thought pot was supposed to mellow you out."

Perry laughed a little louder and longer than usual. "Under normal circumstances it does. These are anything but normal circumstances."

Spencer took her hand and pulled her back on the couch, then sat a good two feet away. Perry gathered her hair in a ponytail, then fished around in her right pocket for a hair band. When it was apparent that there wasn't one, she started to get up. "I'll be right back."

Spencer pulled a hair band out of his back pocket. "Is this what you need?" He tossed it to her.

"Is your hair long enough to use this?" Perry said as she tied her hair back.

"It's not for me. I bought some for you, in case that right pocket of yours was empty."

"Thank you, Spencer. I'm touched."

"You're very welcome, Perry."

For the next two hours and twenty minutes, they were transfixed by the sounds and sights of the movie. One amazing scene after another grabbed them by their senses and took them to another place, not just Rome, Italy, but outside of the Berkeley city limits, somewhere up in the stratosphere, away from their doubts and anxieties. Away from the real world with its cruelty and strife.

Spencer was the first to speak. "That wasn't a real giraffe, was it?"

"No, a very realistic CGI. So, did you like the film?"

"I loved it. And I want to buy the soundtrack now."

"I know! The music was unreal. It went from chamber to disco to classical to, I don't know what. And the movie was fantastic. I felt like I experienced Jep's life. Every scene was like a work of art. You want to watch it again?"

"Now?"

"Sure."

"Let's do it."

It was almost two in the morning when the movie ended. Perry got up and stretched and said, "I'm going to bed." She walked down the hallway, stopped and turned around. "Are you coming or not?"

46

She was positive that Spencer was the best lover she ever had, hands down. Feet, too. And that scared her. How could she sustain a normal relationship with such a young man? She knew their age difference would turn heads and set criticism flying. Even the fantastic sex couldn't assuage her fear that people would talk. She wasn't sure that she could bear the criticism. She was affected by what others thought, especially those close to her. Callie would look at her sideways and what would Spencer's parents think? They would find out eventually and she was certain they would have a fit. Their twenty-four year old son with a forty-eight year old hussy.

"Good morning." Spencer turned on his side and smiled.

Perry marveled at how beautiful he looked, even with sleepy sticks in the corners of his eyes.

"Good morning," she replied and ran her hand through his hair. It got stuck on a knot. They laughed. She leaned over and kissed him, not caring if her morning breath would offend him.

Aroused, he started to kiss her neck as he moved on top of her. She stopped him.

"What's the matter?" Spencer said as he lay back down next to her.

Perry put on her pale pink satin robe. "Callie could be home any minute. I'm not ready to have her find out about us."

"Find out that we slept together or that we're seeing each other."

"Both."

Spencer got out of bed, gave Gilley a hug, and started to dress. Perry continued. "I never gave a second thought to what people thought about my veganism. I believed in it so fiercely that I isolated friends, family and even my daughter. I could have been less adamant but I don't regret it. I really like you, Spencer. You're handsome and smart, but what I find undeniably sexy about you is your conviction for helping the animals. You're not apologetic and you don't dilute your beliefs to please others. And you literally stuck your neck out for ten laboratory cats. Not many people would do that."

Perry stood beside Spencer as he slipped into his shoes. "I'm willing to give us a chance but I have to take it slow, so don't rush me and please don't tell your parents yet."

"You've made me very happy." Spencer kissed Perry long and slow. She was tempted to jump back into bed, but the opening of the front door changed her mind. Spencer jetted out the back door with Gilley in tow. He was halfway across the lawn when Callie walked into her mother's room.

Perry did her best to look nonchalant. "How was your sleepover at Linda's?"

"Fun. How was yours?"

Perry's heart jumped to her throat. "What do you mean?"

She followed Callie's gaze to the bed. Both pillows had perfect head imprints.

"Please. It so smells like sex. So, where's Romeo or should I say Vegansaurus?"

"Callie, please don't judge me."

"I'm not. You've been celibate long enough and who to better end your dry spell than a stud muffin. You two are like peas in a pod. Who cares about age? I don't. You've been breaking the mold for so long, why stop now? You are going to be the envy of every middle-aged woman this side of the western hemisphere."

Perry went over and hugged her daughter hard. "Thanks, sweetie."

"Let me make you breakfast for a change." And with that, Callie went into the kitchen. Perry glanced in the mirror on her way to the shower and was delighted by the image staring back at her. She looked radiant.

As the credits rolled, Bonnie sat and stared at the screen. She almost refused Kanen's request to watch *Earthlings*, the documentary about humanity's use of animals as pets, food, clothing, entertainment, and for scientific research, but relented out of her love and growing respect for him. However, she wasn't prepared for what she witnessed.

She started to speak, then broke down. Kanen held her while she sobbed on his shoulder. She flashed on the incident that drove a wedge between her and her only sibling so long ago. She finally understood why Spencer hated her so much. She represented the insensitivity and apathy of humans. All their greed and unspeakable cruelty he piled onto his sister.

"I feel so guilty. I was...I still am one of the Nazis. I'm going to hell for sure." She started crying again. Kanen could have said many things to comfort her. Instead, he remained silent. He wanted to leave her with the images. He wanted them seared into her memory. Bonnie was the fifth person he introduced *Earthlings* to and every time he watched it, his heart ached. It was unbearable to sit through every time, but it was worth it. Left to watch it on their own, he knew they wouldn't. As soon as images of baby male chicks being ground alive at an egg factory or piglets having their teeth pulled and tails cut off without anesthesia came on the screen, they'd grab the remote faster than they could take another breath. Kanen also knew that his friends wouldn't seek out information on animal exploitation, choosing to remain ignorant so they could continue to eat animals, wear their skins and coats, and be entertained by them without guilt. Granted, the media continued to do an excellent job of hiding the blood and gore and guts. After all, their businesses thrived on advertising dollars from pharmaceutical companies, fast food restaurants, zoos, and water parks. It wasn't the first time he held someone while grief and guilt overcame them. One of his best friends, Jeff Arlington, was almost inconsolable. It didn't help that he was a sales rep for GlaxoSmithKline Pharmaceuticals.

"I must look horrible," Bonnie said as she wiped a pool of tears mixed with mascara from under her eyes.

"Not at all," Kanen said as he brushed hair away from her face. She was now aware. She couldn't use the ignorance card when it came to animal exploitation. It was a pivotal moment for Kanen. If Bonnie continued to eat meat and dairy, it would be the end of their relationship. He gave her a kiss.

"Why don't you freshen up and I'll take you to my favorite restaurant in the city. We need to celebrate Mike's success. I have a call in to the FBI. Believe it or not, I had to leave a message on their hot line. Everything's automated nowadays. Speaking to a live person will be non-existent in the near future."

"It's crazy." Bonnie walked toward the hall to the bathroom. "I'll be ready in five minutes."

"I can't believe it's been almost a year since I've been in the city." Perry glanced over at Spencer who had been smiling ever since they left Berkeley. She let him drive the '58 Corvette Roadster, even though driving a pristine vintage car in San Francisco always made her nervous. He swore that the restaurant he was taking her to had valet parking and that it was in a good part of town, so she relented and even let him drive.

"How come?"

"I don't know. I love Berkeley and hanging out in the east bay. It never occurred to me to come to the city, even though San Francisco has some great museums and restaurants and night clubs."

Spencer pulled up to the curb in front of Three Pears Restaurant & Bar. The valet was around his age. He opened the driver's door and said, "Sick car!"

"Thanks." Spencer looked over at Perry. She just smiled, letting him regale in the glory.

Seated toward the front of the restaurant, they ordered cocktails to start. Perry looked around, thoroughly charmed by the Arts & Crafts decor. She admired the Craftsman furniture and the equinox patterns above the doorways and stenciled on the walls. Someone at a table on the other side of the restaurant looked familiar.

"Spencer, isn't that your friend, Kanen?"

He looked up from the menu. "It sure is. Can I ask him to join us? It looks like he's alone."

"Of course."

As he walked across the restaurant, his face dropped. Sitting down next to Kanen was his sister, Bonnie. She leaned over and kissed him, then picked up her menu.

"Is this a joke?" Spencer said.

Kanen looked like he got caught with his pants down. Bonnie remained strangely calm. She felt as if it was meant to be, running into her brother after years of estrangement in a vegan restaurant.

"Do you want to sit down?" Bonnie said.

"Fuck no, I don't want to sit down. What's going on? Kanen?"

Spencer clearly looked betrayed and Kanen felt horrible.

From the other side of the room, Perry watched a fairly animated Spencer talking to Kanen and a woman. She was tempted to go over, then decided that it would be too intrusive, so she patiently waited for his return.

Bonnie said, "Spencer, I beg you not to make a scene. Will you please sit down so we can talk?"

"There's nothing to say." Spencer turned to Kanen. "Nothing."

He went back to his table. "We're leaving."

"Why?"

"I don't want to talk about it."

Perry took his hand. "Listen to me, Spence. If there's a problem, leaving is not going to solve it. You…"

"I can't be in the same room with my sister."

Perry took a second look at the woman with Kanen. The resemblance between the siblings was strong. At the moment, they both had an intensity that was quickly filling up the restaurant.

"Spencer Rydover. This has got to stop. You want to be with me? Then act like an adult. Whatever happened between you two is coming out tonight or you're going home with someone else because that Vette's being driven by me."

The waiter arrived with their cocktails. As he left, Kanen and Bonnie walked up to the table. Bonnie said, "Can we sit down?"

At the same time, Perry said yes and Spencer said no. Perry extended her hand to Bonnie. "I'm Perry."

"Bonnie. Nice to meet you." She turned to Spencer, who was staring at the wall. "I want to tell you something Spencer and I need you to look at me."

Spencer continued to stare at the wall. It was difficult for him to think straight. He felt open and exposed. No one understood how the sight of his sister brought back the incident in excruciating detail. He was perceived as being stubborn and overly dramatic, but what happened on that day in Robbie Turner's back yard shaped Spencer's identity.

Finally, he turned to face his sister. His eyes were moist. His hands shook. Bonnie sat down next to her brother. She wanted to touch him, hug him, but she knew it was too soon.

"You need to hear this too, Kanen. When I was eleven years old, I was hanging out with the boys in our neighborhood. They were tough and I wanted to be like them, but they kept telling me to get lost. My best friend moved away a few weeks earlier and I was determined to be part of the boys club.

"Finally, the guys relented but Robbie said in order to be part of their group, I had to prove that I was worthy. As we walked to his back yard, I was nervous. I knew his dad had an extensive gun collection because Robbie bragged about going with him to the range and shooting. I had visions of this kid doing a William Tell number on me.

"Once we got to the yard, Robbie went into the garage. I knew that's where the guns were kept, but instead of hauling back a rifle, he walked toward us holding a newborn kitten. His cat was nursing four kittens and this one was the runt. Robbie said that it probably wouldn't make it, so I had to kill it if I wanted in. All eyes were on me. John Mercer pushed me and said I was too weak. After all, I was just a girl. Kevin Trainor laughed and said I didn't have the guts to do it. I wanted to fit in so badly that it didn't occur to me to refuse. I convinced myself that I was doing the runt of the litter a favor. Robbie placed the kitten on the ground, its tiny legs barely moving. Then, he went over to the flower bed and pulled out one of the border's bricks. He handed it to me and smiled." Bonnie looked down at her hands, took a deep breath, then continued.

"I closed my eyes and..." Tears ran down Bonnie's face. Everyone at the table was silent.

"I heard someone gasp. When I looked up, I saw Spencer standing by the fence. He took off and I went after him. I grabbed him by the arm and told him that if he ever told anybody what I did, especially our parents, I'd kill another kitten." Bonnie wiped the tears from her face. "I'm so ashamed. Will you forgive me?"

Spencer was doing everything in his power to keep it together. He wanted the image of that small orange and white kitten to vanish from his mind. Hearing the incident out loud for the first time made it so much more vivid and grotesque.

"Give me time, Bonnie."

She nodded. "I understand." Bonnie looked up at Kanen. "Do you think I'm a monster?"

"No."

The tension had all but dissipated. Silence filled the space. Finally, Perry said, "Why don't you both join us for dinner? Is that okay, Spencer?"

"Sure."

Bonnie said to Spencer, "I watched the movie *Earthlings* tonight. I really had no idea how horrible it is for animals and I understand now why you're so passionate about helping them."

Spencer shook his head. "I'm not used to this Bonnie. How long has it been? Sixteen years with the other Bonnie? I never thought we'd be in agreement, but I'm really glad we are."

Bonnie took Spencer's hand. "Me, too."

For over three hours, the two couples shared food, wine and stories. Bonnie was delighted with her brother's new relationship. She had a strong feeling that Perry's influence had a lot to do with the way Spencer handled her apology. When the bill came, Kanen insisted on treating.

It wasn't until Spencer pulled the car into the driveway that he realized how emotionally fried he was. He also felt like the coiled spring living inside his chest loosened up. No one would ever accuse him of being mellow, but it was certainly an improvement.

He and Perry walked hand in hand to the back yard. They could hear Gilley softly yipping, anxious to see her cottage mate. The lights were on in the main house and they could see Callie by the kitchen window.

Perry snuggled up to her new beau. "Would you like company later?"

"Very much. I'm tired, but not that tired."

"Great. I'll see you in a half hour."

47

Anita was furious. The video, known on the internet as "Senator Jizm" was still being widely circulated and watched, even though the incident happened weeks ago. It had been viewed over 26,000,000 times on YouTube. The snickers behind her back from fellow senators were unnerving, not to mention the Democrats' delight at having a Republican humiliated. Her husband reassured her that it would soon be forgotten, but even he and his cronies would watch the video and howl with laughter. Friends told Anita to ignore it. Like every other viral video, they reassured her that it would fade into the internet cloud, not forgotten but certainly replaced by some other absurd video, like a dancing baby, piano-playing cat or talking dog.

Team America agreed to adjourn for at least two months. The gravity of their latest scheme was too great to risk being seen together.

In her last conversation with Gerald, he assured her that the meat would be dusted with d.o.a. early in the week with a distribution date of Thursday. Once the tainted meat was sold at the fast food restaurants, Anita prayed that the creep who ejaculated on her back would be the first to eat it and die. She was sure he had more than a few illnesses that d.o.a. could home in on. He was less than an inadequate human being. He was detritus, littering America's landscape, using precious resources that he had no business using. She anticipated the number of fatalities and smiled. She started to forget about the humiliating video. Anita wanted to keep track of the deaths, but she knew that it would be unwise and she wasn't one to flirt with disaster. She left her home office and happily got into bed. She lay back on her Tempur-Pedic pillow and pulled the Ralph Lauren paisley sheets up to her neck. Little did she know, it would be one of the last nights she'd be spending in her own bed.

It was past two in the morning. Cody couldn't sleep. He was too excited from the events of the day. As quickly as he showed the Humane Society the video of Jake abusing his dogs, a Humane Officer was dispatched to the garage. San and Fran were taken from Jake and he was charged with animal cruelty. From Jake's they went to Carmen's, the little mutt with mange. This time, Cody had proof that the dog was not given the proper necessities. Her mange had gotten worse, causing her to furiously scratch her cracked and bleeding skin. Carmen was taken from her back yard prison and the owners were slapped with cruelty and neglect charges. Some of the other humane officers trained by Cody were achieving success as well. He sat up in bed and looked around his apartment. It wasn't much, a small, poorly lit bathroom, a bedroom and living room. The kitchen was tiny and outdated, but all the appliances worked. It was free will that made his worn living quarters so beautiful. And it was the animals' loss of free will that made Cody work harder at giving them a better life. One that wasn't filled with pain and suffering. No being deserved that.

Cody lay back down on his faded sheets and thought about his chores for tomorrow. He was going to visit two more animals in crisis, then check in on Della. Her progress was encouraging. She was talking less about leaving the hospital and more about her teeth getting fixed and seeing her daughter. The human resources department had begun its search for Alex. They reassured Della that finding her wouldn't take more than a week or two. She had wanted Alex to see her with a beautiful smile, but the dental work wouldn't begin for another three to five weeks.

Nurse Adderly only had a few minutes to visit Della before she met Cody for their 'greet and grab,' as she liked to call it, convincing the homeless to accept medical care and shelter. She enjoyed being a nurse, yet she felt that her true calling was outside the hospital, on the streets, in the alleys and crevices where the throwaways were stashed, ignored by the so-called respectable members of society. She would listen patiently as some would ramble on about everything and nothing. Ornate hand gestures and erratic movement would accompany the one-sided conversations. When it was her turn to speak, she would address them as if they were the most important person she knew. And in her eyes, they were. Even as a little girl, her heart ached when she walked past a homeless person curled up in a doorway with nothing to comfort them but a dirty blanket or a pillow made of newspapers. She was taught by her parents not to make eye contact. She didn't agree. It didn't feel right to pretend they weren't there. That they didn't exist. She knew that they were people who lost their way. Ellen grew up with loving parents and siblings. She never doubted that she would be taken care of, so it didn't make sense to her why someone's child was living on the street. 'They're crazy,' her parents would tell her. It wasn't until she became inquisitive outside her parents' teachings that she learned how a person's life can bring them to their knees and the only place they felt at home was outside four walls and without any responsibilities or obligations. During her second year at San Francisco Community College, Ellen decided she wanted to be a nurse. She could help the sick and injured and also extend her compassion to the city's homeless population. What better place than the Tenderloin?

"Can you stay and play Hearts?" Della said as she went to her desk to grab the playing cards.

"I wish I could, but I'm running late. Cody and I are meeting up in a few minutes," Ellen replied.

"Greet and grab?"

"That's it. Wish us luck."

"Good luck."

"Thanks, Della. How about if I come by later this evening and we can play cards?"

"I'd love it. See you then."

Medical bag slung over her shoulder, Ellen hustled up the street to Anytime Liquors at the corner of Hyde and O'Farrell. Cody was already there, talking to a very animated and agitated man. The heavily bearded ex-Marine was in his late thirties, dressed in worn, faded army fatigues. He was clearly drunk, his eyes watery and stance unsteady. As Ellen approached, she noticed the man's left hand touching his pants pocket. Cody didn't seem to notice. He was too busy talking.

"Danny, all I'm saying is give the program a chance." He turned to Ellen. "Nurse Adderly and I just want to help you."

"I don't need help from you or her." Danny shot Ellen a look that practically stopped her breath. Many of the homeless refused her assistance and some were belligerent, but few elicited the fear she was now experiencing. She watched again as Danny's hand touched his pocket. She lightly squeezed Cody's arm.

"You're right, Danny. You don't need us. Let's go, Cody."

Cody ignored her and persisted. "Just try it, this once. You'll have your own room. They'll feed you and…"

"Get out of my face! I don't want your help!" Danny reached into his pocket and Ellen screamed.

Clearly confused, Danny pulled the small flask out of his pants, unscrewed it and took a swig, then held it out to Ellen.

"I think you need this more than me."

Ellen shook her head. "I'm fine." She handed Danny her card. "If you change your mind, call me or come by the hospital. There's no judgment. No blame. We really do want to help you."

Danny took the card and put it in his pocket, along with the flask, then he walked up the street, tripping a few times over his feet.

Cody faced Ellen, resting his hands on her shoulders. "You okay?"

"Yeah. I thought he had a knife or gun. Are you ready to sweet talk another lost soul?"

"I am if you are."

"Let's do it."

With the addition of the fourth Feeding the Hungry event, at which Cody was hoping he'd be able to nab some extra bags with Bert's blessing, this was turning into a very busy week. Up until lately, spare time was something he always had plenty of. Now his days were eaten up by visits with Della, helping Ellen and monitoring the living conditions of the Loin's dogs and cats. He didn't mind. He enjoyed his newfound purpose, but all the work was keeping his mind up at night and he didn't like it. He never had trouble sleeping, except when his leg seized up. Since his emergency room visit, the pain was gone, managed by the exercises he faithfully executed. Before another attempt at getting to sleep, Cody sat up and surveyed his small bedroom and smiled. He was a lucky man. He was a free man.

Kanen was sitting at his desk when his cell phone rang.

"This is Kanen Weston."

"Mr. Weston, this is Special Agent William Serra of the FBI. You called us yesterday?"

"Yes, I did. I need to talk to you as soon as possible."

"I can meet you right now."

"Great. How about in ten minutes at Koffee Katz over on Folsom near Brannan?"

"See you soon."

Kanen hung up and texted Bonnie *Meeting with FBI. Will let you know when it's over.*

Suddenly, the thought of speaking to the FBI made him very nervous. He rubbed his hands against his jeans, wiping off the sweat, then he unlocked the bottom drawer of his desk and took out the manila envelope. He grabbed the cooler and, with as much composure as he could muster, he told his secretary he would be back in about an hour.

Kanen sat at a corner table in the back of the coffee shop. The longer he waited, the more paranoia started to creep in, making him doubt the validity of William Serra. What if Bonnie was working with Gerald the whole time and set Kanen up? That didn't make sense, unless the whole thing was made up, a ruse to discredit Weston Foods, a vegan company, accusing a meat supplier of mass murder.

Kanen shook his head, trying to dislodge the doubt.

"Are you okay?" Special Agent Serra stood in front of the table. He was a tall man in a dark blue suit with a red and white paisley tie. He took off his sunglasses revealing dark brown, bloodshot eyes. Kanen guessed he was in his mid-forties.

"I'm fine. Are you Special Agent Serra?"

He extended his hand. "I am. May I sit down?"

"Sure. Can you show me your badge, please?"

Serra dug into his pocket and produced an authentic-looking FBI badge. "You want to tell me what this is all about?"

Kanen laid out the whole plan, producing copies of the text messages and Bonnie's recollection of the initial conversation to Mike's consent form and finally the tainted meat. William stared at the beef patty wrapped in aluminum foil.

"You know this sounds crazy. A senator and the CEO of one of the largest meat processing companies in the country conspiring to kill off hundreds of thousands of citizens because they're poor?"

"I know. It sounds ludicrous, but here's the proof. You have two days to test that meat for a drug. I couldn't obtain it any sooner, so you guys have your work cut out for you, but I'll tell you something: If you doubt me and think this whole thing is a joke, you're going to allow millions of pounds of beef and chicken to enter the food system and there's no telling how this drug is going to affect people."

"Would you be willing to come to the office and tell my superiors what you just told me?"

"Of course. I need to call my office and tell them I'll be gone for a while."

Kanen made the call, then followed William Serra to FBI headquarters.

As they approached the offices on Golden Gate Avenue, Serra motioned for Kanen to follow him into the underground parking lot. After descending three floors, he parked next to Serra's government issued vehicle, a late model Dodge Charger.

The elevator opened to an office that every movie and television show recreated down to the pale green walls and standard issue metal desks and chairs. Kanen was ushered into a windowless conference room. Six FBI employees were already seated, laptops opened, waiting in earnest for the fair-haired vegan to re-tell his story. As soon as the door was closed, Serra introduced Kanen to the four men and two women. Again, he told of the plot to poison the inner city fast food restaurants. His evidence had been taken from him upon arrival. Serra explained that the FBI's main research lab was in Virginia. Due to the time constraints, the meat was being overnighted to the lab where they could analyze it before Thursday.

When Kanen was finished the Deputy Director, Jenna McMillon, said, "Does your friend at Hinton realize that we need to interview her as well? She couldn't have thought that she would be immune from speaking."

"Actually, we figured if I gave you all the information, she wouldn't have to get involved."

"Wrong," said Agent Jim Bricks. "She needs to verify everything you just told us. Otherwise, you could be a vengeful vegan, wanting to wreak havoc on a mega-million dollar meat company. Right?"

Kanen looked the agent in the eye. "I'm the marketing director of a multi-million dollar energy bar company. No doubt, you've thoroughly investigated my past, present and, so it seems, decided on my future as an angry vegan bent on destroying a company with a huge lie. Why would I take the time and energy to call you guys with a make-believe story, implicate a senator who I'd never heard of until recently, and piss off the CEO of Hinton Industries?"

Bricks replied, "Because you're dating the ex-girlfriend and she wants revenge."

"Wrong. She found out about the plot and did the right thing by letting me know. Besides, the last thing I want to do is get on the FBI's shit list. Why don't you call Bonnie? Ask her." Kanen was mad. He didn't think it would be a cakewalk meeting with government officials, but he certainly wasn't prepared for being perceived as a sociopath.

Serra said, "Calm down, Mr. Weston. We already contacted her. She's on her way to the office."

Twenty minutes later, Bonnie was shown to the conference room. The woman who felt invincible up until a few short months ago, was feeling vulnerable and exposed. She knew that employees at Hinton were aware of her affair with Gerald, but to have outsiders know was humiliating. She had never doubted her intentions until she met Kanen. Sitting in the midst of FBI personnel, he looked like an orchid among the thistles. Their suits were drab next to his Tommy Bahama Hawaiian shirt and jeans. Her first inclination was to sit next to Kanen, yet all she could do was offer him a weak smile. As soon as she was seated and poured a glass of water, the questioning began. To the best of her ability, she recounted the first time she heard Gerald speaking to Anita on his cell phone. She explained where she was at the time and avoided looking at Kanen when she told them she was checking out Gerald's wife's fur coat collection.

Jenna McMillon said, "Why did you wait so long to tell anyone?"

"I didn't want to jump the gun. What if they called it off? I would have lost my job, my credibility."

Serra said, "So, you would have continued to work for a man, sleep with a man who was willing to poison and potentially murder thousands if not hundreds of thousands of people?"

All eyes were on Bonnie. She didn't know how to answer. How could she tell them that the idea of wiping out the poor and indigent didn't bother her back then, back when all she wanted was to be CEO of the company?

"I wanted to obtain as much evidence as possible before saying anything, otherwise I may not have had enough information to convince anyone of the conspiracy, especially the FBI. Besides, the timing was perfect. Kanen was introduced to Mike days before the drug was applied to the meat."

Jenna smirked. "Yes, it worked out well, didn't it?" She stood and stretched. "You're both free to go. Please be available if we need to contact you. Like you're on call."

A knock on the door was followed by a young man handing Jenna a piece of paper. She read it and smiled, then looked up at Bonnie and Kanen. They got the hint and left.

Jenna said, "Lab Services tracked down the NIH researcher who developed the drug. Are you ready? It's called d.o.a."

Jessica called an emergency meeting of Team America. Anita was livid. She had made it clear that they were not to meet for a couple of months, but Jessica was adamant and she could hear a fair amount of fear in the junior senator's voice.

Once the group was assembled, Jessica began. "Lenore got a call this afternoon from the FBI." She waited, anticipating reactions from her peers. Instead, they all stared at her, straight-faced. They couldn't even imagine that it would have anything to do with their scheme. She continued. "They asked her about d.o.a. Its interactions with humans, when she began testing the drug and where, and did she know anyone who might have gotten the drug from her."

The group sat up straighter. Bert stood up and started pacing. "What the hell? Who could have…"

Anita interrupted. "Let her finish, Bert."

"Finish what? Putting a nail in my coffin?"

"Sit down, Bert." Anita pointed to the couch. "Continue, Jessica."

"Lenore was clueless. She said the only way the drug could have left her lab was if another researcher took it or someone came in and stole it, but no break-ins were reported. She added that security in the building was air-tight. That didn't convince the agents, especially since the lab break-in last week over at UC Berkeley. She's meeting an agent at the FBI's Laboratory Services in Virginia tomorrow morning. So here's my question: Have any of you told anybody else about d.o.a.?"

Everyone shook their heads.

"Not a soul," said Olivia with conviction.

"The only other person who knows is Gerald Hinton," Anita said. She went straight for the bar and grabbed the Glen Fiddich. Her hand shook as she poured herself a generous amount. "If someone overheard my conversations with Gerald or saw our texts…"

She took a big gulp of scotch.

Jessica said, "We don't know anything yet, so let's not jump to conclusions. I told Lenore to let me know what happens tomorrow. Should we meet tomorrow night?"

"I don't think we should be seen together. Even now is risky," said Bert. He avoided Anita's glare.

Olivia agreed. "This is serious. This is damn serious. If the FBI knows about d.o.a., they most certainly know about the plan. Hell, the FBI could be listening to this conversation. Ever since Dick Tremblay became director, I haven't trusted those bastards. I say we discontinue all communication. I would love to know what you hear from Lenore, Jessica, but not at the cost of revealing my involvement. As a matter of fact, if I were you, I wouldn't talk to her again."

It was Jessica's turn to be defensive. "How the hell am I supposed to do that? She's clearly rattled and I'm her only friend."

They all looked at Jessica in surprise.

Bert said, "When did you two get all cozy?"

"We're not cozy. We're just friends. We've gotten together for dinner a few times. No big deal." Her muddy brown eyes blinked a few times and she pushed an imaginary strand of hair out of her face. "So, that's it then? No more meetings?"

Anita took the last sip of her scotch and immediately poured herself another. She finished it in two gulps. As she filled the Waterford crystal glass for the third time, she said, "Hold on now. Everybody, just sit down." Reluctantly, they took their seats. Anita continued. "All we know is that Lenore, Jessica's pal, was questioned by the FBI. It could be about her research at the prison. Maybe a prisoner is suing the government. Or, someone could have stolen the drug from her lab." She turned to Jessica and mouthed, 'Not you.' She continued. "The point is, it may have nothing to do with us or Hinton. We could be getting paranoid for no reason. Our plan could still go off perfectly. Did I tell you that the shipment is going out on Thursday?"

"Thanks for the slurred speech. We all want this to work and it'll be a damn shame if it doesn't, but I still say we stop seeing each other for a while. No contact at all." Olivia stood up. "I'm leaving. I hope to see y'all sometime, not soon."

Bert said, "I second the motion. We have the food giveaway this Saturday. Unless I hear otherwise, I plan on being in California, handing out fast food bags of d.o.a.-laced burgers. Ladies?"

"I'm in," said Jessica.

"Me, too," said Olivia.

Anita held up her hand and nodded.

An hour after her guests left, Anita sat in her study. The lights were off. She was still drunk. It was the only way she could cope with the situation at hand. In her gut she knew that Gerald somehow leaked the scheme and her 'fingerprints' were all over his cell phone. It was a matter of time before she received a call from Gerald or the FBI. Or both. She was thankful that Larry was out of town. She desperately wanted to be consoled, but she didn't want him implicated, so she stayed in the dark room, wondering what it would be like to be in jail for the rest of her life.

Her cell phone rang, the light casting an eerie glow throughout the room. She glanced at the number. It was Larry. She got up, ambled over to the bar and poured herself another tall glass of scotch. By the time she got back to the couch, the phone stopped ringing. He left a message. She didn't bother listening to it.

48

Gerald asked his secretary, Tina, to call Bonnie and have her come to his office to discuss the upcoming marketing meeting. He rubbed his crotch. It had been way too long since he and Bonnie had any sexual contact. At first, he believed her reasons for being unavailable. She had been sick the weekend in St. Helena and was now working hard on the new advertising campaign. Still, he was beginning to feel neglected.

Five minutes later, Bonnie walked into his office. Instead of her usual sexy attire, she wore a conservative buttoned up, long-sleeved floral shirt with a knee-length skirt. Her shoes were flats, not the spike heels he favored. She wore her hair back in a braid.

"You wanted to see me?" Bonnie walked up to the front of his desk. She knew what was coming and, as determined as she was to refuse any sexual request, she felt uneasy. As much as she wanted to quit, she knew that if she stuck it out for another month, she could leave with a full pension. Money still trumped desire.

"I dropped a pen under my desk and was wondering if you could pick it up." Gerald began undoing his belt.

"I don't believe I can help you with that, Mr. Hinton."

Stunned, Gerald glared at her. "I believe if you don't help me find the pen under my desk, Miss Rydover, you'll be cleaning yours out. I'm not going to ask again." He unzipped his pants and was pulling them down when his phone buzzed and Tina's voice came over the speaker.

"Mr. Hinton, there are some gentlemen here to speak with you. They said it's urgent."

"Do they have an appointment?" Gerald replied, irritated that he was being disturbed.

"No, sir, but they claim they don't need one. They're with the FBI."

Gerald quickly pulled up his pants and fumbled with his zipper.

"I take it that you can find the goddamn pen on your own, sir?"

Bonnie opened the office door. As she walked past the government agents, she said, "He's all yours."

While he was being questioned by the agents, Bonnie practically skipped back to her office. She texted Kanen. *FBI in office with dickhead. Hope he's led away in cuffs.*

Ten minutes later, Gerald walked with the FBI agents down the hallway to the elevator, but he wasn't in handcuffs. However, his complexion was a shade lighter than pale. The office was in a heightened sense of anticipation and anxiety. Tina burst into Bonnie's office. "What's going on? Where are they taking Mr. Hinton?"

As nonchalantly as possible, she replied, "Why are you asking me?"

"You seem to be the closest to him. Do you know?"

"I don't know. I'm not close to Mr. Hinton at all. Excuse me, but I have to go to the ladies' room."

It took all her strength not to smile. All eyes were on her as she walked to the restroom. Bonnie knew her reputation at the company was tainted by her affair with Gerald. She never cared until recently.

In the bathroom stall, she texted Kanen with the great news. *Gerald at FBI. Hope they're nailing his ass.*

Kanen wrote back. *I believe a celebration is in order. Tonight. My place.*

Bonnie's phone was ringing when she got back to her office. She picked it up.

"This is Bonnie."

"This is Miriam Hinton."

This was one call she wasn't expecting. She steeled herself. "How can I help you?"

"You can start by telling me what the hell is going on. Tina called and told me that Gerald was being questioned by the FBI." Bonnie had never spoken to Miriam before, but from the sound of her voice, she didn't seem that upset.

"I'm in the dark, too. If I find anything out, I'll let you know."

"I guess this puts an end to your affair with my husband. It's a shame. You've kept that sex hungry jerk from pawing me. I've had a nice reprieve. I can always hope that the feds arrest him and throw him in jail. Then I won't have to deal with him at all." Miriam hung up so abruptly, Bonnie stayed on the phone, believing she was pausing between statements. When she realized that Miriam wasn't there, she put the phone down and had to laugh. It seemed the women in Gerald's life got more out of using him than enjoying his companionship. She imagined Miriam dancing through her expansive mansion, thrilled that she didn't have to share it with her misogynist husband.

Bonnie returned to the office after a long, enjoyable lunch with the assistant marketing director, Monica Givens. It was the first time Bonnie lunched with anyone from work. She wished that she had done it sooner.

She got off the elevator and half-expected to walk into a swarm of federal agents combing through the offices. Instead, she was hit with a palpable tension. It hung heavily in the air, turning the normally calm offices into DEFCON 4. No doubt every employee was wondering if they'd have a job by the end of the day or week.

Bonnie's heart skipped a beat when she saw the note on her desk: *executive meeting in the conference room at 2:00.* She hoped that she'd be told Gerald was in custody. A girl could dream.

Three thousand miles away, an NIH researcher was in the nation's capital being comforted by the senator from Montana. Lenore was beside herself and Jessica was doing her best to assuage her fears. She grew up with parents who offered their own daughter minimal affection, so her efforts at consoling amounted to saying 'it'll be okay' along with measured back patting.

"I don't understand how someone could have taken d.o.a., my creation, and tried to use it to kill people. How sick is that?"

It's not sick at all. It's sheer genius, Jessica thought. She said, "Pretty twisted. What else did the agents ask you?"

Lenore sighed. "When did I create d.o.a.? Did I give it to anyone? Could someone at the prison have gotten a vial of it? They're talking to all the employees at Fillmore. It's a mess. The worst part is that I've been ordered to stop testing and hand over all my d.o.a. to the feds. Is there anyone you can call at the FBI to help me get my research back on track?"

"I'll see what I can do. I have a friend in the state department. I'll give him a call tomorrow."

Lenore smiled. "Thanks so much. I really appreciate it."

"Of course. Whatever I can do to help." Jessica gave Lenore another cursory pat on the back. She had no intention of calling anyone. The last thing she wanted to do was get anywhere near the investigation.

The sun was setting behind the mountains in Mill Valley. Kanen's living room and deck were filled with filtered light and three important people in his life. Three months ago he didn't know any of them, yet today one was the love of his life and two were becoming good friends. While he and Bonnie prepared dinner, Spencer and Perry sat on barstools at the kitchen counter.

"I forgot to tell you. Mom and Dad are deliriously happy. I told them about our reconciliation and they wanted to know if we could come over for dinner this Friday. Are you free?"

Spencer replied, "I have to work at Warden's. I get off at seven. Would that be too late?"

"Not for me. Call Mom and ask her."

Perry was overjoyed with the recent events. Spencer was calmer, more in control of his emotions. She knew he continued to feel for the animals, but he used his pain more productively. In her last meeting with the animal rights group, they discussed the possibility of another lab break-in. They had an excellent connection with the building maintenance manager at a research lab at UC Davis. Dr. David Fielding was conducting research on baby rhesus monkeys, ripping them away from their mothers shortly after birth and subjecting them to various experiments. Despite the mountains of research on this subject dating back to the 1950s by primate torturer Dr. Harry Harlowe, the government continued funding the studies to the tune of millions of taxpayer dollars. She badly wanted to say something, but couldn't tell Spencer of the plan until it was finalized. She looked over at him and smiled. She had never been with a man twenty-four years her junior. She also had never met a man so kind and sensitive and loving. Soon, their age difference would start to show. When she thought about it, Perry would question the relationship, question her stamina. But just as quickly, she would set those visions aside and say to herself, 'play it as it lays.' It tempered her insecurities and fears for the time being. The future was nebulous and projecting only made her worry needlessly.

"This wine is wonderful. What did you say it was?" Perry held up the glass of deep red liquid.

Bonnie stopped sauteing the zucchini cakes and went over to where the bottle sat. "Black Bee Merlot. It's in Healdsburg off Eastside Road. Kanen and I went there a few weeks ago. We loved the merlot so much, we split a case."

Kanen added, "It's an organic winery and they paired the red wines with raw chocolate. We bought a few bars of the chocolate, too. That's for dessert."

There was a scratching at the sliding doors. Spencer went over and let Gilley in. She ran to the kitchen and lay down at Perry's feet. "Hey there, sweetie. Are you having fun?" She leaned over and scratched the dog behind her ears. "You wouldn't believe what this little dog looked like when Spencer got her from the shelter. She had been a puppy mill breeder. They never let her out of the cage and she was always pregnant. Poor thing. I hope the bastards were prosecuted."

She looked over at Spencer who, at first, was confused. Then he realized that their identity always had to be secret. Kanen had figured out their involvement, but Bonnie didn't know and they had to keep it that way.

Bonnie said, "I think I read about that puppy mill in the paper. It was about a month ago. The breeder, a woman in the east bay, came home and all the dogs were stolen. They also trashed the cages. It was great. She wasn't given a big jail sentence, but she did have to pay a fine and was prohibited from having animals. I didn't realize that Gilley was from a puppy mill."

Spencer went over and picked up the little terrier. He cradled her in his arms as she licked his face. "When I adopted her, she could barely walk and was getting over mange. If I were the judge, I would have thrown that woman in jail for a year. Give her a taste of her own medicine."

"You did a good deed adopting her, Spence," said Bonnie. It still felt so new, so foreign to be speaking kindly to her brother. Before, when they had seen each other, harsh words were exchanged and the air was thick with animosity.

Kanen was taking the salad out of the refrigerator when his cell phone rang. He looked at the caller. It was Mike Flores. He quickly answered it.

"We did it, Kanen. Hinton is toast."

"Where did you see it?"

"The story is everywhere. Turn on the TV."

"This is fantastic. Thanks for calling, Mike."

Kanen hung up his phone and turned on the television. He flipped through the channels until Gerald Hinton's face filled the screen. By this time, the others gathered around him and watched with curiosity.

Gerald was being led to the county jail, surrounded by police. Reporters were on the periphery. Kanen turned up the volume.

"This is Mary Kind, reporting live from the San Francisco County Jail where Hinton Industries CEO, Gerald Hinton, was arrested. We are unable to find out what charges Hinton is being detained on. The police department and FBI will not disclose it to us at this time. Hinton Industries is one of the largest meat manufacturing and distributing companies in the country, supplying a majority of the fast food restaurants with beef and chicken. The Hinton family founded the company over thirty years ago, Gerald Hinton becoming CEO in 2004."

A picture of Anita replaced Hinton. She was being escorted by two police officers into their patrol car. The reporter continued. "As we reported earlier today, Senator Anita Minefeld of Virginia was arrested. Again, charges are not being disclosed. The FBI has revealed that the two arrests are related. Senator Minefeld has been a representative of her state for four terms. The news has come as a shock to her fellow senators, particularly Senator Ralph Gold from Virginia."

The camera cut away to Senator Gold at a news conference. "I am deeply saddened by my fellow senator's arrest. I don't know the allegations, but I can say from the bottom of my heart that Anita Minefeld is innocent." Mary's face once again filled the screen. "Reporting from the San Francisco County Jail, I'm Mary Kind for Channel 5 News."

Spencer turned to his sister. "Did you know about this?"

Bonnie looked at Kanen and he nodded.

She replied, "You might say that I'm responsible for Gerald's arrest with the help of this guy here."

Spencer gave his sister an extra-long and hard hug and then Perry followed with the same. During dinner, Bonnie told the whole sordid story, leaving out details that she felt would upset her brother.

"Are you still working at Hinton?" Perry asked.

"If I want to get my full benefits, I have close to a month before my sixth anniversary. I'm quitting the day after." She took a long sip of wine. "A few months ago, all I wanted was to be the CEO of Hinton Industries. Now I can't wait to get out that place."

"Do you know *what* you want to do?" said Spencer.

"I'd like to stay in marketing, but before I plunge head first into job hunting, I want to take some time off, get to know myself better."

"Ahem." Kanen gave her an inquisitive look. "Are you forgetting something or someone?"

"Am I?" she said with a mischievous grin. She grabbed Kanen's hand. "Of course I want to spend more time with you."

After dinner, the two couples retired to the deck. The evening air was cool with the scent of pine trees and wild sage. Kanen had been debating whether or not he should bring up the subject. A long pause in the conversation gave him the opportunity, so he decided to risk it.

"Have you guys heard of DMT?"

Spencer had a blank look on his face but Perry's eyes lit up. "Sure. I've done it a few times. It is a trip. Do you have some?"

Kanen smiled. "I like this woman."

"Thank you."

"Will someone tell me what DMT is, please?" Spencer said.

"Believe it or not, my parents told me about it and gave me some to try. It stands for dimethyl…"

Perry cut in. "Dimethyltryptamine. DMT. It's a molecule."

Kanen continued. "Yeah, they call it the spirit molecule because scientists couldn't figure out its purpose in the human body and all living things. When you smoke it, it's supposed to take you out of your body, sending your spirit on a journey."

"What I like about it is that the whole experience lasts less than twenty minutes, so you're not stuck in a hallucinogenic trance for hours," said Perry.

"Sounds cool. Can I try it?" Spencer was ready to go.

Bonnie said, "You can tell who the experimental one is in the family. That doesn't sound like fun to me. I'm out."

Not wanting to leave Bonnie alone, even for a short time, Perry said, "You two go ahead. I'll keep Bonnie company."

"You don't have to do that. I'll be fine."

"No, really. I couldn't care less. Let the men bond."

Kanen left the room and came back a few minutes later carrying a small baggie and a water pipe. He then went into the kitchen and grabbed a canister of loose leaf green tea.

"If you'll excuse us, ladies, we're going to hang out in the tea room and take a little journey out of our bodies."

"Have fun and remember to come back," Perry said.

When they were alone, Bonnie said, "I don't get it. Why take a drug that gives you no control over your mind? Or soul? That's frightening to me."

"Let's see if I can explain it. People have always been curious about an afterlife. Do we have a soul? If so, what happens when we die? They call DMT a hallucinogenic, but what if it actually separates our soul from our body? The first thing our spirit does is soar into space. When I first tried it, I heard a whooshing sound. The next thing I knew, I felt like I was shot out of a cannon. I was scared until I looked around me and I felt this warmth and love like I've never experienced before. My body was bathed in a white/golden light. You know how movies represent angels singing? It's like a chorus, right? Well, it's not like that at all and I can't even describe the sound I heard. It was definitely ethereal and couldn't be duplicated by a human voice or instrument. It was amazing. I felt like I was out there for two to three hours. When I came out of it, I looked at the clock. Fifteen minutes had passed!"

"You weren't scared?" Bonnie asked.

"No. When I was a teenager, I was into all kinds of drugs. I never thought it would result in brain damage or that I would do something stupid. Well, I didn't get brain damage but boy did I do some idiotic things. I'm glad DMT wasn't around when I was growing up. I could see myself doing too much and it really should be used sparingly."

"I wasn't into drugs at all when I was a kid. I barely drank."

"Were your friends the same way?"

"I didn't have many friends. Let me rephrase that. I didn't have any friends. I was too busy studying. My parents couldn't afford to send me to UC Berkeley, so I worked my ass off to get in on a scholarship. My social life suffered a lot. You know how people say they have no regrets? I have plenty."

Perry refilled their wine glasses. She was definitely feeling a buzz. "Sweetie, we all have regrets, whether we admit it or not. For example, marrying my husband was a huge mistake. When I tell people that I regret being wed to a misogynistic, control freak they say, 'But you never would have had Callie.' True, but I believe if I married a man who was compassionate and respectful and really loved me for who I was, our child would have had Callie's spirit, just in a different body."

"Ah, you're one of those people who believe in reincarnation."

Perry laughed. "Guilty as charged. You don't?"

"Nope. We're born. We die. End of story."

"You need to try DMT."

Bonnie said, "I don't think so."

"I'm guessing the only person who could talk you into it would be Kanen. And may I just say that you are one lucky woman. I think he's an amazing person."

Bonnie was about to reply when Spencer and Kanen walked into the living room. They both looked shell-shocked. Spencer plopped down on the couch next to Perry and gave her a big kiss. Kanen went into the kitchen and came back with a glass of water.

Spencer pointed to the ceiling. "I went out there. Way out there! Unbelievable."

"Tell me about it. Little points of light everywhere. Surrounding me. *I* was a point of light, flying in space. It was beautiful. I felt a pure love. I know it sounds hokey, but it's true. Spencer, you were huddled in the corner on one of the pillows. At first I was concerned, then I remembered reading that a lot of people on DMT go into the fetal position. So tell us what happened."

Spencer took Perry's hand and caressed it while he spoke. "At first, I felt like I was shot out of a cannon."

Perry interrupted. "That's what happened to me!"

"Yeah. Straight up into the atmosphere. It was fun. I felt like I was flying. When I stopped, these beings were in front of me. They had really long arms and legs. I don't remember exactly what their faces looked like because they were lit up inside and everything was blurry. They formed a circle around me and touched me with their hands, like they were healing me. It felt like I was back in the womb. What time is it?"

Bonnie said, "It's 8:30. You were gone for only twenty minutes."

"It felt like two hours."

"I know!" said Kanen. He sat next to Bonnie. "And I also know why my parents wanted me to try it. I was questioning reincarnation and even incarnation. What's the point when the world is in such a shitty state? My mom told me to think about that question before I smoked it."

Bonnie said, "Tell us the meaning of life, o' wise one."

"Very funny. I think every human is a point of light. Some of us are very, very young souls and some are old and elevated, enlightened souls. Because the human population is growing so fast, there are more young souls than old ones. That's why the world is so messed up. My point? We all do the best we can. For some, it's not that good, but for the more enlightened, it's trying to raise the consciousness of the planet. So, I don't know if we can save our species, but while we're here, we have to try and it starts with seeing every being, human and non-human, as connected."

Perry said, "I'm impressed. After I took it, I didn't talk to anyone and finished off a box of Keebler Vienna Fingers. So much for my evolvement."

Bonnie gave Perry a sideways glance. Before she could say anything, Perry said, "Yes, the Vienna Fingers are vegan. Not healthy, but vegan."

Bonnie turned to Kanen. "So you're saying that I'm connected to you and Perry and Gerald and the Muslim extremists and rapists and murderers and all the other dregs on this planet?"

"As well as Oprah and Gandhi and Martin Luther King and the Dali Lama and even Gilley. Take away our corporeal bodies and we're all points of light."

Spencer said, "That's a tough concept to accept."

"I agree," said Bonnie. "This world is filled with so many evil people. People that have no respect for another's life. I wouldn't mind if they disappeared off the face of the Earth. That would be paradise."

"Gotta side with my sister."

Perry chimed in. "I'm going with Kanen on this one. If every person embodied this concept, it would completely shift human consciousness. Then we would truly live in paradise."

Bonnie said, "In concept, yes. But in execution? It's never going to happen."

Kanen replied, "And it's that concept our spirits are striving toward. I don't see it happening in our lifetime, but I sure hope it happens before the planet is destroyed. Switching to a lighter subject, why don't we all go to the tea room for dessert? I bought a new frozen coconut milk ice cream in two flavors, coffee fudge and caramel chip. I'll bring the chocolate bars, too."

They readily accepted the invitation and, after gathering up the dessert, bowls and spoons, they headed out.

The fog sat on the tops of the trees and crept down into the lower branches, giving the back yard an otherworldly effect. As they approached the tea room, small lights flickered on and off in the trees and surrounding shrubs.

"You got the firefly lights!" said Perry. "I feel like I'm in an enchanted forest. It's so beautiful."

The wall sconces emitted a soft glow in the room, creating a relaxing ambience. The pillows against the periphery of the room looked like they were floating. Kanen lit the candles as the other three sat around the stove.

Bonnie turned to Perry and said, "I just want you to know that I really like you. You and Spencer are so well-suited and I don't even think of you as being a year older than my mom."

"That was a compliment, right?" Perry said, then laughed. "I can't think about our age difference or what people think. I'm having a blast tonight and no one knows what tomorrow brings. I found it's a lot easier to live in the moment when you don't have to worry about financial security. Let's live for today, tonight."

"Aren't you the liberated, free-thinking woman of the year?" Bonnie said.

"On behalf of all the ladies out there, I accept the title with grace and humility. Thank you so much for the honor of representing feminists everywhere."

"Isn't she great?" Spencer said and gave Perry a kiss on her cheek. He turned to his sister. "So, how does it feel to be the only omnivore in the group? Rarely are you outnumbered."

Kanen prepared the tea, listening to the conversation, enjoying the repartee. The aftereffects of the DMT lingered, making the tea preparation more pronounced, special.

Bonnie said, "After watching *Earthlings,* I honestly don't know if I ever want to eat meat again. I can't get the tortured, helpless look of the animals' eyes out of my mind. All of them, from the pigs and veal calves to those circus elephants forced to perform. Why are we such a selfish species?" She looked at her brother. "I purposely pursued a career in the meat industry because you were such a militant vegan. At the time, it made perfect sense. Now I find the whole industry grotesque." She put her arms around Kanen. "If I continue to hang out with this guy and his stellar cooking, I'll be vegan before long."

"I never thought I'd hear you say that." Spencer got up and went outside. Perry's first inclination was to follow him, but she knew that when he left the room abruptly or said he wanted privacy, he truly wanted to be alone. When she was in her twenties, a man who cried or showed any 'feminine emotions' would have been unappealing to her. He was a wimp, not the archetype of the man she was meant to seek out, fall in love with and marry. As she approached her fifties, she craved nothing more than a sensitive man.

Spencer returned a few minutes later. He smiled gently, took his seat and said to Bonnie, "I forgive you."

Bonnie went over to her brother and hugged him hard. He hugged her harder.

49

The news of Anita Minefeld's arrest rocked Capitol Hill, but it put Team America's members in an absolute state of panic. They had a pact declaring that if one of them was caught during a project, they would profess to be acting alone, thereby protecting their fellow members. But they were clueless as to how much Gerald Hinton knew of their involvement and they were unable to contact Anita. If she turned State's witness, would she divulge their names? Did the FBI already know about them? Was a pounding on the door hours if not minutes away?

Jessica felt even more vulnerable because of her friendship with Lenore. They had grown close during the past few months. Jessica had started depending on Lenore for companionship. She was someone who could be trusted, unlike herself. Her thoughts were interrupted by the phone. It was her father. Jessica groaned. She wasn't in the mood. Actually, she was never in the mood to talk to Theodore Olshansky. Especially now. The man was like a demented psychic. He could tell when something wasn't right and he delighted in ferreting out the truth and making the person feel like shit.

"Hey Dad." She imagined him sitting in his wingback chair in the living room, a large cigar resting on the ashtray.

"You've heard about Anita's arrest."

"Of course."

Theodore adjusted his large frame in his seat. "Do you know the charges against her?"

"I don't."

"I do." He almost said it with gusto.

Jessica closed her eyes. "Are you going to tell me?"

"It seems she was collaborating with Gerald Hinton, the CEO of Hinton Industries, to poison fast food targeted for inner city restaurants."

"That's horrible! What were they thinking?"

"I know exactly what they were thinking. I'm coming to D.C. tomorrow and will be there by the afternoon. I'll pick you up at the Hill for dinner around 7:00."

"How do you know I'm not busy?"

"Jessica, you're my daughter. I know you very well. You're not busy, are you?"

She looked at the phone with contempt and wanted to spit into the receiver. "I'll see you at 7:00. Give Mom my love."

She put the phone down too hard and heard it crack. She didn't care. She could always get another phone. She couldn't get another life. She had a sick feeling in her stomach that her father knew Team America was involved and she was damn sure that he'd figure out some way to work it to his advantage. She may be his only child, but everyone in Theodore's world served a purpose.

Olivia threw up for the fourth time. She didn't know what to do. Visions of leaving the country pushed out more rational options, but at the moment she wasn't thinking clearly. She could empty her savings account and buy a plane ticket online in no time. She wiped her mouth and gargled with Scope.

"This is not the way I wanted to lose weight," she said to her image in the mirror. Staring back at her was a woman whose eyes were red-rimmed. Her skin was blotchy and her hair, pulled back in a small ponytail, looked dull and lifeless.

She went back to bed and placed the hot water bottle on her belly. Her stomach was empty, but still ached. After watching the news for hours, she forced herself to turn it off. From the beginning, Team America worked like a well-oiled machine. Never once did they come close to being discovered. They manipulated laws, broke laws, even created new ones without a hint of suspicion. And now this. She had known Anita since she had become a senator and trusted her implicitly. Still, she had no idea how the senator from Virginia would react to the offer of turning state's witness in lieu of a lengthy prison term. Her stomach cramped up, causing her to push down on the water bottle. She closed her eyes and chastised herself for playing such a dangerous game. Politicians dealing in illegal activities were caught all the time. The difference was the severity of their crime. Few people would understand and agree with the senators' solution to overpopulation. Killing off the bottom feeders, the leeches of society solved so many problems. They overtaxed the healthcare system, lived off food stamps, subsisted on fast food, cheap food, liquor and drugs, and lived in overcrowded conditions causing stress on the infrastructure.

Olivia's cell phone rang to the tune of *Moon River*. It was a text message from Bert: *We need to talk*. She put the phone down, threw off the hot water bottle and raced back to the bathroom.

Bert Kathala was a level-headed man by nature. Very little upset his calm demeanor. Sure, he was mad when the woman at social services puked on his shoe, but in other heightened situations, like an earthquake or a car accident, he was composed and rational. He had just gotten off the phone with Cody. They were discussing Cody's latest victory with abused dogs and Della's continued improvement. She was dutifully taking her medication. After two adjustments in the dosage, she felt better than ever. They had located her daughter and the hospital set up a visit for the two to meet next week. Cody texted Bert photos. Della was smiling and, even though her mouth needed an overhaul due to the years of neglect, she looked happy. Her hair was pulled back in a ponytail. Her eyes matched the light blue shirt she was wearing.

It was a demanding day and Bert longed for a quiet evening. He grabbed a beer from the fridge and sat down on the couch. He kicked off his shoes and put them up on the coffee table, knocking off copies of *Golf Digest* and *Fortune* magazine. Next, he turned on the television and channel surfed, trying to find the highlights of the latest football game involving the San Diego Chargers. Instead, he saw Anita being placed in a squad car, handcuffed, arms behind her back, looking ashen, and her lawyer husband by her side. He knew Jessica and Olivia were thinking the same thing he was: will Anita give them up or will she take full responsibility? He recalled an incident over five years ago when he desperately needed help getting a bill passed. He knew a lot of senators would vote against it. He called a core group of his fellow Republicans, requesting their help. Two accepted the challenge. Anita was one of them. She spent the next day and night making calls. The bill ended up squeaking by, passing by three votes.

Then Bert recalled another incident involving a congressman from Anita's home state. Davey LaVarge from the 5th District won by a landslide. He was wildly popular for the first half of his term. Then he got cocky and became involved in a Ponzi scheme with an old high school friend. LaVarge claimed he was solely responsible. When he was arrested, he was charged with financial impropriety and looking at twenty-five years in a federal penitentiary. Before the case went to trial, he turned state's witness and released the name of his friend of thirty years. His sentence was reduced to four years. Bert was always uncomfortable with Anita's assessment of the incident.

"LaVarge could have saved himself a month in prison by disclosing Renfeld's involvement at the time of his arrest. They were both fully involved. Why should LaVarge take full responsibility when he was only 50% culpable?"

Bert looked up at the ceiling and said, "We're fucked." He picked up his cell and texted Olivia.

Humane Officer Charlie David glanced at the digital clock on his car's dash as he pulled up to the curb. He was a couple of minutes early, but there was Cody, standing in front of his apartment building, wearing his black and tan cowboy boots, Levi's and long-sleeved plaid shirt. Since Charlie's first introduction, Cody had always been prompt. He respected the man's dedication and perseverance. That's why he decided to drive Cody to San and Fran's new home in South San Francisco on his day off. It also gave Officer David a chance to observe the dogs in their new surroundings.

"I can't believe I'm going to see San and Fran without chains around their necks and living in that dump of a garage. I really appreciate this Charlie."

Cody closed the car door, making sure his backpack cleared the door jamb.

"My pleasure. I'm looking forward to seeing them again, myself."

Charlie noticed that Cody's long legs were fighting for space. "You look like an accordion. Pull the lever on the side of the seat and push back."

Cody complied, giving himself the extra room. The men filled the drive time sharing animal rescue stories. About twenty minutes later, Charlie pulled up to a small, ranch-style house in a clean, middle-class neighborhood. The address was 333 Pine Cone Lane.

"My lucky number is three. I'm feeling good about this," Cody said as he followed Charlie up to the front door. Small rose bushes lined the pathway, their creamy yellow flowers welcoming them to the modest tract home. As they approached, barking could be heard inside the house. Cody smiled and yelled, "Hey Fran! Hey San!"

The barking became more emphatic as the pit bulls clearly recognized Cody's voice. Charlie opened the screen door and knocked. A tall, thin man in his late twenties opened the door, letting two very excited pups reunite with their friend.

If San and Fran had arms, they would have hugged Cody, so passionate were they in trying desperately to embrace the man who saved their lives. Their still lean bodies bumped, rubbed and leaned on their savior. Cody returned the affection. He hugged and kissed his pals as tears streamed down his face.

"Look at how healthy you are! Did you miss me? I really missed you." Cody dipped into his backpack and pulled out treats and hand fed them to the eager pups.

After a few minutes, the dogs calmed down and everyone went inside. Chew toys littered the floor and in one corner two dog beds sat side by side. Cody sat on the floor and continued to play with San and Fran while Charlie asked Len Goodman how the dogs were adjusting to their new home. Follow-up calls were part of the original Humane Society officer's protocol. Unfortunately, that luxury was abandoned a long time ago when funds were slashed and the number of humane officers was cut in half. They could only hope that the abused animals they rescued were adopted into a loving and healthy environment. Judging from the look of San and Fran, Charlie felt confident that they were being well-cared for. Len had only one concern.

"They still flinch when I go to pet them. You told me how they were treated, so I understand their fear. Will it get better? Will they eventually trust me?"

Charlie pointed to Cody playing with the dogs. "If it weren't for that guy, the chances of them trusting a human would have been iffy. Cody showed them love and attention even though he was unable to pet them. Give them time. Let them come to you and I think they'll eventually get over their fear."

Charlie glanced out back. "It looks like San and Fran took over your back yard, too." Dog toys and tennis balls could be seen strewn throughout the yard. The landscaping was sparse. Where there weren't errant trees and low bushes, weeds occupied the dirt and dying lawn. Lounge chairs and a table sat on a concrete patio.

Len laughed. "What can I say? I'm a dog person and definitely not a gardener." He turned to Cody. "You're welcome to come back any time and visit."

"Thanks. I really appreciate that."

Worn out, San and Fran lay on the floor beside Cody. Reluctantly, he got up, giving both dogs a kiss and hug. He hated leaving them, but felt so much happier knowing they had a loving home.

Back in the car, Charlie said, "Len's a good guy. The dogs couldn't have gone to a better home. Unless, of course, you adopted them. They sure love you."

Cody said, "I wish I lived in a place that allowed pets. I would have taken them in a second. Has Carmen been adopted yet?"

"No. The shelter wants to clear up her mange before she's put up for adoption."

"When do you think that will be?"

"I've heard it can take a month before they start looking normal. The shelter is on the way. Do you want to stop by?"

Cody said, "You have to ask?"

After checking in, Charlie and Cody walked to the end of the dog enclosures. There, in the second to last kennel, was Carmen. The information card identified her as a six-year-old female, mixed breed. She was curled up in bed, looking comfortable and content. Being disregarded at her previous home prepared her for life in a shelter. She enjoyed attention when she received it. Otherwise, she was resigned to being alone. A comfortable bed, temperature controlled room and scheduled feedings kept her beyond satisfied.

Charlie opened the door to her five foot by eight foot room. She looked up, acknowledged him and was about to go back to sleep when Cody walked into the room. Carmen practically bounded out of the bed and ran to Cody. As he knelt down to pet her for the first time, she began to yowl. She jumped up on his bent leg then reached up and touched his face with her front paws. As he gently stroked her little body, she continued to yip and yowl. "Little Carmen, how nice to see you!" He turned to Charlie. "Is it going to be difficult finding a home for her?"

"I'm not going to lie. At her age and condition, she won't be high on the list of adoptable dogs. Luckily, this is a no-kill shelter. It may take time, but eventually, someone will want her."

Cody sighed. "In the meantime, she'll be alone."

"Not completely." Erica, a volunteer at the shelter, stuck her head inside the room. "We spend at least once a day playing with and walking the dogs. I personally take a little more time with Carmen because she's so sweet."

Cody read her name tag. He held out his hand. "That's good to know, Erica. I'm Walter but everyone calls me Cody."

She nodded to Charlie and shook Cody's hand. "It's a pleasure to meet you. Your reputation precedes you. What you're doing for the animals in the Tenderloin is amazing."

"Thanks, but it's not just me. I'm one of three people trying to make life better for these precious animals."

"When you see the others, tell them that we all really appreciate their dedication." Erica leaned down to pet Carmen. "I'll give you a few more minutes, then Carmen's due for her medication."

As Erica was leaving, Charlie said, "I'll go with you and leave these two to reunite."

When they were alone, Cody looked Carmen in the eyes and said, "I'm giving them two months and if you haven't been adopted by then, you're coming to live with me. I don't care what my landlord says. I promise."

Carmen sighed and put her head on Cody's chest.

50

Over the next few days, information surrounding the arrests of Gerald Hinton and Senator Minefeld began to unfold. Linking a senator to a plot to blatantly kill off disadvantaged United States citizens created an uproar. Every civil rights lawyer and advocate for the poor stood on their soapbox and lambasted the government, specifically the Republicans. Colleagues of the senator were interviewed, all of them shocked and confounded by her involvement. Gerald's wife, Miriam, claimed to have known nothing about her husband's dealings and she portrayed the grieving wife beautifully. Privately, she was the happiest she'd ever been. No longer living with her philandering husband, she felt liberated. She was also the sole heir to his fortune and had begun creating a wish list the day of his arrest.

Bert, Jessica and Olivia kept low profiles during this time. They all successfully avoided being approached by reporters and their invasive questioning by getting to their offices early and leaving very late. Each had received a phone call from Anita's husband, Larry. And each one vehemently denied involvement. Their meetings were mostly social, discussing favorite bills, current projects. They had all heard of Hinton Industries, but none knew the CEO.

Of all the people being hounded by the press, Lenore had the lion's share of attention. The poor woman had to lock herself in her lab in order to get any work done. Since her research on d.o.a. was suspended, she spent her time pouring over results and computer-generated hypotheses. If she left to go to the bathroom or grab lunch in the cafeteria, she would be approached by other researchers, eager to talk to her about d.o.a. She didn't have to worry about offending anyone by using the word 'awesome.' It was one word stricken from her vocabulary.

Lenore was beyond exhausted. Between conducting research and evading fellow researchers, she had just enough energy to drive home and fall onto the couch. She desperately wanted to talk to Jessica, but was forced to leave a voice message every time she called. They were never returned. She was disappointed on so many levels. Jessica had become a friend and confidante. She was also hoping that their friendship might deepen and become more intimate. She cringed just thinking about her budding sexuality. She never questioned it because research was her first love and it left her little time to date or even have friendships. But the more time she and Jessica spent together, the more her libido began to blossom and unfold and surprise the hell out of her. She wasn't against homosexuals. She simply never imagined being one and she was pretty sure Jessica was discovering her own latent homosexuality as well, so the senator's silence was perplexing. Lenore would replay every conversation, recall every look, every touch when she and Jessica were together. Her conclusion was always the same: there was a sexual connection.

After changing into her pajamas, Lenore poured herself a glass of white zinfandel. She sat back on her sofa and closed her eyes. As her head nodded off to the right, the doorbell rang. Startled, she jerked her head up and headed to the door.

"Jessica?" she said as she looked through the peep hole.

"It's Sharon Cooper from Channel 2 News. Do you have a minute to answer some questions about Senator Minefeld's arrest?"

"Please go away or I'll call the police."

"I only have a few…"

"Leave me alone!" Lenore screamed and ran into her bedroom, slamming the door.

"When are we going to do another rescue? I'm so ready," said Spencer. He was sitting cross-legged on the grass in the back yard, stroking Perry's hair as her head lay in his lap. Gilley was on his other side, sleeping.

"Soon. The details are being worked out." Perry's eyes were closed. Her breathing was deep and restful. She recruited Spencer without any intention of becoming romantically involved. Their age difference and his volatile temperament were two huge deterrents, but over time she witnessed Spencer re-directing his anger. From the two beagles they saved to his determination and precision liberating the terriers from the puppy mill and gleefully destroying their gulag, Perry began to see him as more than a young, unruly boy whose direction wasn't clear.

"I hope it's another lab break-in. I was scared shitless, but what a rush. Did any of the media outlets run the story besides The Berkeley Times?"

"I thought I showed you the other articles. Sorry about that. The Chronicle did a story. Like the Times, it was biased. They called us terrorists in an attempt to instill fear in the public's eyes. They actually quoted the researcher saying that the stolen lab cats could possibly contaminate and infect humans. How? Of course, he didn't elaborate because it's rubbish. The only paper that painted us as heroes was PETA's newsletter. Honey, we have our work cut out for us. Do you know that the government funds vivisection to the tune of $14.5 billion every year?"

She could feel Spencer's body tighten up and he stopped stroking her hair. She sat up and saw the pain in his face. "I'm sorry. I shouldn't have said anything."

"What's the point?" Spencer said.

"To what?"

"To fighting the system. No matter how many animals we liberate from labs, there are millions, maybe billions more that will be abused. They'll never live outside a cage. We convince a million people to stop eating animals but hundreds of millions of meat-eaters will keep the industry alive. The suffering is overwhelming and even though I'm able to shut off my grief for longer periods of time, it'll never go away. I'll always be haunted by the images of what humans do to animals. I sometimes imagine being witness to an animal being hurt. I can feel my heart constrict and my breathing gets shallow. I don't want to live in a world where this kind of evil is possible."

As if she sensed his sorrow, Gilley got up and sat in Spencer's lap, licking his face. He kissed the top of her head.

Perry looked at Gilley and said, "That's the point." Perry stood up. "I'll be right back."

She sprinted to the house and disappeared through the back door. Minutes later she emerged holding a plain manila folder.

She sat next to Spencer on the cool grass and opened the folder. It was filled with newspaper articles. She picked up a handful.

"Animal Liberators Break Into Fur Farm. Free 200 Minks."

"Cockfighting Ring Broken Up By Activists. 50 People Arrested."

"Sea World Ends Entertainment with Killer Whales."

"Veganism Becoming Trend with A-List Celebrities."

She put the articles back in the folder. "Slowly but surely we're getting through to people. Not everyone. But enough that big changes can be made. You're not the only one who feels like they're drowning in the world's cruelty. I have moments where I am so intrinsically sad that I've wanted to give up. But the grief doesn't last as long as it used to and my faith is buoyed by our advances in spreading the truth about animal exploitation. Have you ever heard of the tipping point?"

Spencer shook his head.

"It's when a large group rapidly changes its behavior by adopting a previously rare practice. I see that happening with veganism. More and more people are taking their hands off their ears and removing the blinders. They're listening to what we have to say. They watch with eyes wide open."

"I hope you're right."

"Me, too."

Della looked up at the clock. It was 12:56 p.m. One minute later than the last time she checked. She glanced over to the cafeteria door. Expectant. Nervous. No longer a thin, bony frame, she filled out her shirt and pants with a curvier, softer body. Her hair was pulled back in a small braid and the nurses convinced her to let them apply makeup to her pretty face. When they were done, she glanced in the mirror and had to stop herself from crying out of joy. Her only regret was her smile. It was hideous. So many of her teeth were loose or gone. The hospital assured her that her first dentist appointment was in two weeks. Missing teeth never bothered her when she lived on the street, but then nothing affected her back then. Not even sharing space with rats and garbage.

After speaking with the doctor about the drug's side effects, her dosage was re-adjusted. A few days later, Della felt like she did before bi-polar hijacked her mind. She looked up at the clock again. 12:58. Two minutes to go before Alex walked back into her life, even for a mere afternoon, though she desperately wanted to re-build her relationship with her only child.

"How are you feeling, Della?" the nurse asked her.

"Nervous. Hella nervous. What if I don't recognize her? She's a woman now. The last time I saw her she was twelve."

"I have a feeling she'll recognize you."

Just then, a young woman walked through the door. She was of average height and weight. Her light brown hair was pulled back in a braid. She was wearing a short, hot pink dress with black heels. Her resemblance to Della was uncanny. She looked around the cafeteria. When her eyes fell on Della, she walked straight over to where her mother was sitting and held out her hand. Reluctantly, Della shook it. The nurse stood up.

"I'll leave you two alone. If you need anything, I'll be right over there." She pointed to a table at the other end of the room.

"Thanks," Della said and then patted the seat next to her. Alex sat down.

"You're so pretty, Alex."

"It's Alexandra."

"Yes. Sorry." Della fidgeted with the buttons on her shirt. "Sorry. I guess I should be saying that more, huh?"

"It is what it is, Della." Alexandra didn't look at her mother. Instead, she stared straight ahead, as if willing herself to be somewhere else. Anywhere else.

"Please call me mom. That's what I am. Your mother."

"Yeah. For the first twelve years of my life, you were. Then you disappeared and I didn't have a mother. Oh wait, my grandmother became my mom, then Dad married Gretchen and I had another mom. And now you want to be my mom again? Stand in line."

"I will. I'll stand in line. I'll do whatever it takes to be back in your life. I'll stay on my meds. I'll get a job. I just want to get to know you again. Okay?"

Alexandra sighed. As she exhaled, the pent up anger seemed to dissipate slightly. Just enough for the resentment she felt for her mother to lose its edge. She looked at Della and saw this frail woman who aged considerably since their last time together. But she was clean and looked a lot healthier and she wasn't saying crazy things.

"Okay."

Despite Della's resolve not to smile, the sides of her mouth involuntary rose, exposing uneven and missing teeth. Alexandra tried not to look shocked, but Della caught her daughter's expression and quickly closed her mouth.

"It's okay, Della. You don't have to be embarrassed."

"I...I'll be getting new teeth soon. The hospital set up an appointment for me at a dental school."

"That's wonderful. I'm really glad to see you getting your life together."

"I am. I never want to go back to the streets. So, tell me. Are you in school?

Alexandra nodded. "I'm in my third year at UC Berkeley. I'm majoring in social services."

"I'm so proud of you, Alex, I mean Alexandra." She hesitated before touching her daughter's arm. She wanted to hug, her but was afraid she'd retreat.

"Thanks." She stood. "I need to get going. I have a lot of studying to do."

"Will you come back and visit?"

"We'll see."

"Hold on. I'll be right back." Della took off in the direction of where the nurse was sitting, drinking iced tea. Alexandra watched her mother, excited and scared that they were reconnecting. Her memories of living with Della were painful. The last time she saw her mother was over eight years ago. Her father made her testify against Della, recounting to the judge about the many times she was left alone while her mother took off to destinations unknown or when depression set in and no matter how hard she begged, Della refused to get out of bed for days.

For the judge, it was an easy decision. He awarded Marvin Foster full custody of their daughter. The ruling crushed Della. Instead of trying to work with her doctor to regulate the medication's dosage, she began to self-medicate with alcohol and marijuana. She went from reckless to dangerous. When an unattended candle caught a curtain on fire, it gutted her apartment and landed her on the street.

"Here's the number where you can reach me. It's the nurse's station on the fourth floor. That's my floor." She handed her daughter the slip of paper with the information.

"Thanks." She gave her mother a hug, tentative at first, then fully embraced the woman that gave her life.

51

Jessica interrupted her father. He'd been talking for what seemed like an hour, pontificating about the good old days when Team America got things done under the radar. They never came close to getting caught.

She said, "It was a matter of time before information leaked out. I have no idea if Anita is going to incriminate the rest of us. If she does, we'll be in jail a long time. Dad, I'm really scared."

"You should be. Anita could get a significant reduction in her sentence if she reveals her co-conspirators." Theodore took a puff from his cigar, held it in and exhaled as if he had all the time in the world. He looked at his daughter. "Jessica, I don't know what's going to happen. The fact that you were planning on poisoning Americans, albeit poor Americans, on a massive scale is on par with treason. You all could get life in prison. Except Anita."

His tone was so nonchalant, Jessica wondered if he wasn't secretly happy that she failed. Failed as a senator and as a daughter.

"Isn't there anything you can do?"

He looked at her like she asked him to scale Everest. "I'll see what I can find out. You haven't spoken to the other three since Anita's arrest, have you?"

Jessica shook her head. "Of course not. Does Mom know?"

"No. She'll find out, though, if you're arrested."

That was the last straw. Jessica shot out of her chair and stood over her father. "Do you find this amusing, the prospect of your only child being incarcerated for the rest of her life? I don't get you. Why are you so cavalier about this?"

"Who do you think you're yelling at?" Theodore glared at his daughter. "Sit down!"

Jessica reluctantly returned to her chair.

Theodore continued. "This is very disturbing for me, as well. My reputation will be tarnished, too. Did you think about that or only about yourself? If you're asking for my help, I would like you to show me more respect."

It took every ounce of will power to suppress the urge to slug Theodore Olshansky, a man with an ego the size of Montana. Ever since she could remember, she had been trying to please him and very rarely did she succeed. As a consolation, he would offer to help her write better, draw better, sing better, be better. Once again, he was offering to do her a favor. If she didn't think he could save her skin from arguably her most dire situation, she would have told him to fuck off.

"I'm sorry, Dad. I should have thought about you, as well."

"Damn right." He walked over to the big picture window. It was overcast and drizzly, adding to his foul mood. After a few moments, he walked toward the door and without turning around, he said, "I'll see what I can do."

As soon as he left, her intercom buzzed. She ignored it. A few seconds later, it buzzed again. When she didn't respond, Talbert cracked the door open and stuck his head in.

"Not now."

"I'm sorry, but she's been waiting for a while. She says it's urgent."

"Who?"

"Lenore Fitzwater."

"Jesus. Could this day get any worse?"

Normally, Kanen loved Weston's marketing meetings. The ideas that flew around the room were so varied. Some were imaginative and doable and others verged on inane, but they were all taken seriously and discussed. Today, Kanen's mind was miles away. To be exact, it was about 3,000 miles to the east, in D.C., wondering what was going to happen next in the d.o.a. debacle. Senator Minefeld and Gerald Hinton remained the only two suspects in the scheme. Speculation that other senators could be involved was being discussed on every media platform. To many, it seemed unrealistic that only two people could have planned and pulled off a project on such a massive scale.

Kanen told his parents about his contribution, adding that Bonnie was solely responsible for exposing the plot. Their respect for her rose to a level where they finally approved of the relationship.

"I like that idea. What do you think, Kanen?" his father said.

"I'm sorry. Could you run it by me again?" Kanen was clearly embarrassed. He usually led the meetings. Today he was there in body, not mind.

Clive, the CFO, spoke. "I said we should send a box of our best-selling bars to famous omnivores, not vegans or vegetarians. If they like them, create a marketing campaign around them. Maybe use two or three celebs."

"It's a good idea, but I wonder if the campaign would be too expensive. I know celebrities get big bucks for commercials, even in a print campaign. I'll look into the costs. Thanks, Clive." Kanen glanced at his cell. He had a text from his secretary. *Can I see you now? Important.*

"Will you excuse me for a minute? I'll be right back." Kanen got up and went to Jean's desk. Jean motioned in the direction of his office.

Bonnie was standing at the window, watching as a panhandler stood at the corner, asking for change.

"What are you doing here? I thought you were still working for Hinton."

"I am. I told them I had a doctor's appointment. I have a great idea for a marketing campaign and I couldn't wait to tell you. Do you have a second?"

"Come with me."

She followed Kanen through the hallway and into the conference room, where the majority of Weston's employees looked at her with curiosity.

Kanen said, "I'd like to introduce you to Bonnie Rydover. She has a marketing idea that I have yet to hear about and thought it would be most appropriate at our marketing meeting to hear it together. Bonnie, the floor is yours." Kanen offered her his seat which she refused. She was too nervous to sit.

"Hi everyone. I didn't expect to be giving a presentation to such a large group, but here goes. A few weeks ago, Kanen and I went to a restaurant in the Tenderloin. As you all know, it's one of the most disadvantaged areas in the city and I would guess that it was one of the pockets that Hinton Industries planned on distributing the d.o.a. meat to. Why doesn't Weston Foods do something healthy for those people who would have been eating the tainted burgers and chicken? For every energy bar sold, give one to a homeless person or a needy family who live there. Or sell them at a fraction of the cost at inner city markets and liquor stores. Or pass them out to the homeless."

"What if we those people were incorporated into our ads?" Michelle Weston added. "I don't want to exploit them and I certainly wouldn't want people laughing at the ads, but I think if we worked on this, we could come up with a tasteful and poignant campaign."

Cynthia, Bill Weston's assistant, said, "I think it's brilliant! What a wonderful way to highlight these human beings that are more than their neighborhood. They have names and families and aspirations. Oh, I got it! What if we picked a cross-section of the 'hood' and told their story. Like a child, a homeless person, and a person who works in one of the liquor stores or restaurants. Make these people real. Three dimensional...Not society's throwaways."

Kanen cut in. "We could start with a print campaign and branch out into billboards or even television spots."

Bill said, "I love it! We could even offer scholarships." He turned to Bonnie. "This is an excellent idea. Thank you!" He stood up and started clapping. Everyone followed suit. Bonnie felt ecstatic.

Once everyone sat down Jordan said, "Where do you work, Bonnie?"

She looked at Kanen and he shrugged.

"Funny you should ask. I work at uh Hinton in the marketing department. I'll be resigning in a month."

"Hinton as in the meat distribution company?" Jordan said.

"Yup, that's the one. Long story short, I despise the place and can't wait to leave. Speaking of leaving, I have to get going. It was nice meeting you all. I look forward to seeing you again."

Once Kanen and Bonnie were in the parking lot, she said, "That was a little awkward."

"Don't worry about it. You were great and I love your idea, too. I can't wait to start working on the campaign. So, what's the atmosphere like over at the office?"

"Ever see the movie *Independence Day*?"

"Isn't that the one with Will Smith where aliens attack earth and destroy everything and everyone in their path?"

"Bingo."

"Poor baby. Why don't you come to my place after work and you can tell me all about it?"

"I have a better idea. Come over to my apartment. I honestly don't feel like sitting in traffic today, even for a little while. I'll do my best to fix a decent dinner."

"Deal." Kanen gave her a kiss. "See you tonight."

She was gone less than an hour. When Bonnie stepped off the elevator to the office, she was hit with a tidal wave of panic and fear. It was worse than when she left. She approached the receptionist's desk.

"What's going on?" she asked Carol.

"Mr. Hinton was indicted a little while ago and our stocks fell more than thirty points. The place is in survival mode."

When she reached her office, Bonnie was immersed in the dread. Her plan to stay until she was vested was crumbling. She was doubtful that Hinton Industries would survive more than a few weeks. She listened to her voice mail. One message was from a headhunter. He asked her to call him as soon as possible. Intrigued, she dialed his number.

"This is Clark."

"Hi Clark. My name is Bonnie Rydover. You left me a message about ten…"

"Yes, yes. Hi Bonnie. Thanks for calling me back. How are you today?"

"Honestly, not great. What can I do for you?"

"Actually, it's what I can do for you. I'm working with one of your competitors and they're very interested in you."

"What's the position?" Bonnie asked.

"Assistant director of marketing."

"You realize I'm the marketing director here."

"Sure do, but the current director will be resigning within a year and they want to bring someone in to eventually take over. Your wages as assistant would start at your current salary and once you become the director, it would increase by thirty-five percent. Can I set up an interview, say next week?"

Clark waited for Bonnie's response. After a good fifteen seconds, he said, "Are you still there?"

"I'm still here."

"Great. How about I call you next Wednesday at 10:30 a.m.?"

"Thank you, but I'm not interested."

52

Lenore walked up to Jessica's desk. She stared right into her murky brown eyes and said, "You took the vial of d.o.a. the day you came to my lab, didn't you?"

"I most certainly did not and I'm appalled that you have the audacity to walk into my office and accuse me of such a serious offense. Why would you say such a thing?"

"Can I sit down?"

"No."

"When I first met you, I was honored that you took such an interest in my work. It didn't occur to me that, at the time, d.o.a. was a complete failure. Why would a drug be of any interest to anyone, especially a senator when, in its trial phase, killed almost everyone who was part of the study? After you left, I could have sworn I had twenty-eight vials of the drug. I counted twenty-seven. I passed it off as having a poor memory. After Senator Minefeld and Gerald Hinton's arrests, I'm not so sure."

Jessica tried not to look upset. Her nerves were already frayed from her father's visit. She knew she could sweet talk Lenore into trusting her. At the moment, she wasn't up to the task. All she wanted to do was go home and crawl into bed, but that wasn't possible, so she put on her politician's façade and hoped Lenore bought it. She walked around her desk and over to the leather chairs. She invited Lenore to sit across from her.

"The last few days have been very trying, especially for you. I'm really sorry. While it may seem that I had a part in this whole scheme, I assure you that I barely even know Senator Minefeld. I've met her once, maybe twice. I had heard she was ruthless, so I kept my distance. And I'm glad I did. If politicians weren't in such a bad light right now, I would be happy to vindicate you from any involvement and highlight the important research you're doing."

It was hard to tell what Lenore was thinking. She was expressionless. Then, the woman broke down, covering her face in her hands.

"I can't believe what a nightmare my life has become. Reporters are in front of the institute, they're at my apartment building. Some of them even follow me. They shout out horrible questions at me like, did I want to kill the prisoners and isn't my intention to perfect the ideal death drug? I became a scientist so I could cure disease not accelerate it. What do they think I am, a monster? I take sleeping pills at night and an anti-depressant when I wake up." She looked up, her mascara pooling and nose running. "I'm sorry I accused you of stealing. I really am."

Relieved that she had averted a potential public relations disaster, Jessica said, "Is it possible for you to get away for a week or two? It should give the media a chance to redirect their energies elsewhere. Pretty soon, you'll be off their radar. Old news."

"I suppose I could stay at my parent's vacation condo in Florida for a while."

"Perfect." Jessica glanced at the clock. "So you'll be okay?"

"I guess."

Jessica walked Lenore to the office door, gave her a cursory hug and sent her on her way. She prayed that her father could work his bullying, intimidating magic and release her from any involvement. She'd rather be indebted to him for the rest of his life than a cellmate for the rest of hers.

Bert racked his brain, yet he was unable to come up with a single person he knew who could exert their influence to stop Anita from exposing him, Jessica and Olivia. He thought of calling Theodore Olshansky, but figured that the ex-senator already deduced their involvement and would do whatever was possible to exonerate his daughter. After all, he had been a member of Team America for years and was no stranger to circumventing the law.

They had been so close to pulling off the operation. The potential to eliminate so many undesirables had been within their grasp and now it was gone. All the planning and preparation for what? A fellow senator would be spending the rest of her life in prison along with one of the nation's top CEOs. Three more senators would be sharing the same fate if Anita deemed it so.

Every time his phone rang, Bert expected the worst. He poured himself another drink and went out on the balcony. His townhouse in Georgetown had a view of Clancy's Bar & Grille. He watched the young adults as they walked into the popular venue and others as they stumbled out. He envied every single one of them because he knew not one shared his troubles. Sure, they had problems, but nothing close to his. As Bert continued to eavesdrop, one of the women looked up at him. She was wearing a strapless mini-dress with high-heels. The attractive twenty-something waved and Bert raised his glass. She yelled up at him, "Come dance with me, mystery man!"

Bert smiled, grateful for the attention.

"I'm serious. Come on down and shake it like you mean it!"

Within five minutes, Senator Bert Kathaia walked across the street and approached the woman who was even more striking up close. She was standing with a crowd of people her age. He was clearly older than the group by twenty-five years. Bert didn't care. For all he knew, this could be the last time he'd be socializing and if it was, he'd much rather be doing it with an attractive group of young people than politicians who wouldn't know how to loosen up to save their lives.

The young woman said, "You look older up close."

"Don't let my age deceive you. I can dance you all under the table."

She said, "Prove it."

And he did.

Three days later, Anita Minefeld's lawyer, Larry Minefeld, called a press conference while his wife remained in custody at the District of Columbia State Penitentiary. He coordinated the conference with Gerald Hinton's lawyers, who held a west coast meeting with the press at the same time. The response from the media was overwhelming, but then, why wouldn't it be? At the moment, Larry was representing one of the most reviled people in America. Anita Minefeld managed to knock Monsanto, the Koch brothers and all the oil companies off their detested pedestals. She was without question the anti-flavor of the month.

The stress from the past week had taken its toll. Larry's face was drawn and bags hung under his eyes from lack of sleep. His daughters, Cindy and Rebecca, stood without expression beside him. He looked out over the sea of reporters, microphones in hand, cameramen off to the sides. Larry cleared his throat and began.

"I want to announce that, despite rumors to the contrary, Anita Minefeld and Gerald Hinton acted alone." Larry practically spat the words. As soon as his wife was arrested, he suspected that Team America was involved. Their closed door meetings used to pique his interest. After a number of years, the intrigue wore off and he understood that whatever was spoken between the senators was not shared with anyone else, including significant others. Anita, reticent at first, agreed to talk to the prosecutor, but before she and Larry were scheduled to meet with him, the meeting was cancelled. Without explanation, he said the senator would be charged and prosecuted to the fullest extent of the law. Larry was convinced that the ex-senator from Montana had something to do with it.

Larry continued. "Though Senator Minefeld has expressed her remorse over the plan to disseminate tainted meat to the inner city fast food chains, she has nonetheless been charged with intent to cause great bodily harm and her trial will begin August 23. There are no words to describe how our family has been impacted by this event. I called this press conference to answer any questions you may have so my daughters and I will be spared the inconvenience of being hounded in public and at our homes. We ask that you respect our privacy. Questions?" A multitude of hands flew up.

"Did you have any idea what your wife was up to?" a reporter shouted out.

"As I've said before, I did not have prior knowledge of the scheme with Mr. Hinton."

The same reporter shouted back, "With all due respect, I find that hard to believe."

"I don't give a rat's ass what you believe. It's the truth. Next question."

"They say your wife and Gerald Hinton are looking at life in prison. Is that true?"

"Unfortunately, it is."

"Is it official that no other senators were involved? The food giveaway seemed to be a thinly disguised precursor to the fast food being poisoned and at least twenty other senators participated."

Larry bit his lip and replied, "These senators were only aware that they were supplying fast food meals to the homeless and poor. Nothing more."

The question and answer period ended twenty minutes later. Larry was hoping that the reporters would heed his request for privacy as the toll it was taking on him and his daughters was extreme. The hate mail was never ending, a lot of it threatening. As a result, Larry contacted a realtor and listed the house for sale. He and Anita raised their children in the 5,000 square foot Colonial estate. He thought he'd be retiring there. Then again, he thought he'd be spending his retirement years with Anita.

Across the country, a similar press conference was taking place. Gerald Hinton's legal representation was standing in front of the media at the steps of the Hall of Justice building in San Francisco. Gerald hired the city's most prestigious law firm to defend him, though the legal pundits were perplexed as to why he would spend hundreds of thousands of dollars on high-priced lawyers when his case was pretty much a slam dunk. The evidence was indisputable. His involvement undeniable. The federal prosecutor was jubilant when he confidently announced that he was going for life in prison without the possibility of parole.

The senior attorney out of the four stepped up to the microphone. He tapped it to make sure it was on.

"Good afternoon, ladies and gentlemen of the press. I and my fellow associates called this press conference to clear up any misunderstanding that the federal prosecutor may have alluded to in his statement earlier today regarding our client. Gerald Hinton was arrested last week for allegedly being a co-conspirator involving tainted fast food beef patties and chicken. We contend that Mr. Hinton is innocent. The supposed evidence is not indisputable."

A seasoned reporter shouted out, "And Hitler wasn't guilty, either!"

The crowd erupted into laughter.

"Are the rumors true about Hinton's mistress leaking the plot to the FBI?" another reporter asked.

The lawyer responded, "Not to my knowledge."

"How did the FBI find out?"

"At this time, the Federal Bureau of Investigation is not disclosing that information."

From the back of the crowd, Perry Seidel shouted out, "If Gerald Hinton is innocent, even though he was heard telling the senator that he would love to see the underbelly of society wiped out, then who at the company collaborated with a senator to pull off a scheme like this?"

"We're not at liberty to disclose any names at this time. I thank you all for attending. That will be all."

"That's because there is no one else. He's guilty as sin!" Perry yelled.

As the group dispersed, Perry watched the four lawyers scurry off the steps of the building and into an awaiting limousine. She turned to Spencer and said, "That was a rush. My heart's still pounding."

"Woman, you have balls!" Spencer said.

"So I've been told."

Senators Kathala, Olshansky and Sundstrom could be heard exhaling within a five mile radius. Short of going back to church, they all vowed not to participate in another senatorial group, regardless of its intent.

Bert continued to meet with Cody and the other members of the humane brigade. He even visited Della at the hospital, amazed at her transformation from homeless woman to a clean and lucid human being. She told him as soon as she was given a positive evaluation by her doctors, she would be moving in with her daughter. She thanked Senator Kathala for endorsing the nurse patrol. Without it, she'd still be on the street, or worse, dead.

Olivia Sundstrom's vegan lifestyle continued to fly under the radar. Even her good friends were unaware of her dietary habits. Since her veganism was for purely health reasons and had nothing to do with the ethical treatment of animals, Olivia proudly wore her mink coat, leather jackets and shoes, and wool sweaters. She was overcome with a rare desire to clean up the inner cities. If she couldn't kill the disadvantaged at least she could make it safer for the neighboring towns. While her aides were busy compiling information on the number of homeless shelters and soup kitchens, Olivia personally called the congresspeople whose districts included North Carolina's top ten most dangerous cities and the state's other senator, and invited them to participate in a summit. For three days, they would map out a plan to address the growing gap between the wealthy and destitute.

She knew her father would come through. Jessica Olshansky, the junior senator from Montana with her mud brown eyes and obelisk-like figure, sat back in her recliner. She loved the way the thick, rich leather felt against her skin. Except for having to sever her friendship with Lenore, she was exuberant. They may have failed to implement what could have been the perfect cure for overpopulation of the underprivileged, but they came damn close. Close enough that it gave Jessica hope. Her relationship with Bert and Olivia was over. Team America was gone. She was glad. Her cohorts were older than her by a good ten years. They were from a different generation. She closed her eyes and flipped through her internal rolodex. Senator Whitney DeForrest was close to her age. She represented Florida and shared Jessica's views on immigration and welfare reform. Despite her intent to focus on Whitney's political positives, Senator Olshansky found herself mentally reviewing the senator's shapely figure and short cropped, prematurely gray hair. She made a note to call her office and set up a lunch meeting.

53

Spencer watched as Gilley ran toward him. She practically flew across the grass and into Spencer's arms. He embraced the terrier with the black freckles on her muzzle. He marveled at how dynamic and healthy she was compared to a mere month ago when she was covered with mange and barely able to walk.

After her morning meal, Gilley ran outside. When she saw Perry sitting on the deck, she made a beeline for the stairs and leapt into Perry's welcoming lap.

"Hello, little girl. You smell like you just finished breakfast. I'd recognize that kibble breath anywhere."

Perry waved to Spencer as he walked across the lawn. He waved back. "I'm already running late for work, so I'll see you when I get home."

"Sounds good. Have a great day."

"You, too."

Perry continued to rub Gilley's neck. Contented moans emanated from her little body. Eyes closed, perfectly still. It looked like she was smiling.

Spencer started up his car and Gilley sat straight up, her serene state interrupted by the sound of the car motor. She strained her neck to see him over the redwood railing and watched as he pulled his car into the street and drove away. Gilley let out a little whine.

"You and me both, girl." Perry had to laugh. Not too long ago, she was unattached. She didn't kid herself about enjoying the single life. She would have loved being in a relationship, but few dates came even close to what she was looking for; to what her spirit needed to grow and expand. When Spencer first moved into the cottage, she met an angry, tormented young man. A man whose emotions were out of sync, tangled up in his compassion for animals, his desire to help them and his frustration at not being able to do enough. Over the months, he changed considerably. Sure, there were residual demons. Demons that poked and prodded his soul with less ferocity, but they were there, nonetheless. It didn't bother her because she knew that his intentions were pure. Perry wasn't sure if she could fall in love with Spencer, but she was more than willing to play it out. Her new mantra, 'play it as it lays,' fit the situation and perfectly aligned with her state of mind.

She couldn't wait to tell Spencer about their upcoming project. They'd be driving to Southern California, specifically Westwood, home to UCLA. She had a feeling that after the rescue, Gilley would have a playmate. The operation was slated for next month. The liberation of the rhesus monkeys at the research lab at UC Davis caught a snag. The timing wasn't right and they agreed to reconsider the break-in next spring.

Callie sat down next to her mother, interrupting her musings. She placed a plate full of fruit on the table. Perry picked up a grape and popped it in her mouth.

"Did the dingo go to work?"

Perry laughed. "He left about ten minutes ago, so don't talk too loud. He might hear you."

"Really. The kid's amazing."

"Please don't call the man I'm dating a kid. It reeks of pedophilia and he's very much an adult." She continued stroking Gilley, who was now on her back, lying on Perry's lap.

"Sorry. You really like him, don't you?"

"I do. An interesting phenomenon happens as you age. The weeks seem to get shorter. It's like Sunday rolls around every four days. I'm going to wake up one day and realize decades have gone by. I don't want to regret anything anymore. I don't want to be eighty years old and think, 'I should have slept with that young whippersnapper, what's-his-name, when I had the chance.' This is my chance, while I'm still vibrant and my memory is intact."

Callie watched her mother pet Gilley. "I hear you. I think it's great and I bet he's a good lay. Most emotional guys are." She waited for an acknowledgement.

"You won't see me complaining." They both laughed.

"Where did you say Spencer got Gilley from?"

Without skipping a beat, Perry said, "Berkeley Animal Shelter."

"When?"

"About three, maybe four weeks ago. Why?"

"I saw an article on the coffee table about a puppy mill north of us that was raided and all the sheltie terriers were taken, even the owner's dog. Coincidence?"

"Totally."

"Why did you cut out the article?"

"I like keeping track of animal rights successes. You know that from when you were a kid."

"Mom."

"Yes, dear."

They stared at each other for a while, neither saying a word. Finally, Callie spoke. "Please be careful."

Perry smiled. "So, what are you up to today?"

Callie chewed on a slice of cantaloupe. "Continuing my quest for work. Now I know why they call it job hunting. I feel like I'm tracking an elusive creature. One that's challenging, exciting and well-paying. I hope it's not extinct."

"I have a good idea. Instead of looking for a job, why don't you find a store for rent? There are a few empty retail spaces off Shattuck on Adeline Street. We could go into business together. Open up a gallery. I would be your first client."

Callie almost choked on the cantaloupe. "Are you serious? You'd do that? Mom, this is amazing." Callie leaned over and hugged her mother.

Perry said, "I've been mulling it over for a while and I think we could make it work. I'll stay out of your hair and let you run the gallery, but I would like to have my paintings on display. I've been home too long. It would be nice to hang out at a gallery and converse with the public."

"I love it!" Callie said. "What if we searched for artists in Oakland and Richmond? You know, find diamonds in the rough. Give some of these poor, gifted painters a chance to show their work."

"I like that idea a lot."

"When I finish eating, you want to check out Adeline?"

"Sure. I'll go get dressed." Perry gently placed Gilley on the ground. "I'm really glad you're back, Callie. I missed you."

"I missed you, too, Mom."

Less than thirteen miles away, on the other side of the Bay Bridge, Walter Cattlin, aka Cody Brant, stood in front of a microphone on a makeshift stage in Boeddeker Park. To his left stood Sam Linden, acoustic guitar in hand. About forty people sat on the grass eager to hear Walter sing. Most of them didn't even like country music, but it was so rare to have live music in their neighborhood, they were thrilled. Della and Alex sat in lawn chairs a few feet from the stage. Walter looked down and smiled.

"I'd like to dedicate my first song to a man who has helped out our community's people and animals. I know one person whose life was saved by his efforts. Senator Bert Kathala would get my vote if he runs for re-election. He cares about all the people in this country, not just the rich. Bert, this one's for you."

Sam began to play and Walter sang, "*I can see you, standing next to him, looking like a rainbow beside a beige sky. I can hear you, talking to him, asking him shall we dance? But he can't see your beauty. He can't see your style, so when he turns away, I ask you, shall we dance? Yes, we shall dance.*"

His beautiful voice soared above the crowd and drifted through the Loin. Not far from the park, behind CVS Pharmacy, a large cardboard box shifted slightly. A calloused and nearly black foot appeared, then another. The box budged as the person inside was trying unsuccessfully to get comfortable. Softly at first, a voice could be heard, singing along with Walter's. As he sang louder, it was clear he couldn't carry a tune and he didn't know all the words. But he tried. He tried.

www.ingramcontent.com/pod-product-compliance
Lightning Source LLC
Chambersburg PA
CBHW060932120726
47910CB00002B/301